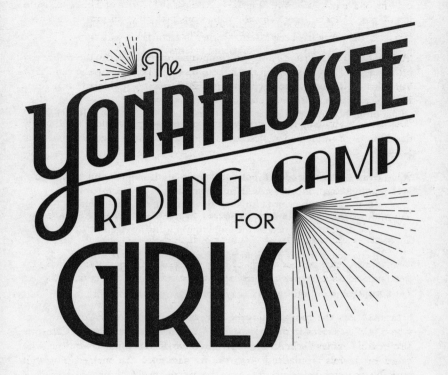

The YONAHLOSSEE RIDING CAMP FOR GIRLS

Anton DiSclafani

TINDER
PRESS

First published in Great Britain in 2013 by TINDER PRESS
An imprint of HEADLINE PUBLISHING GROUP

First published in paperback in Great Britain in 2013 by TINDER PRESS
An imprint of HEADLINE PUBLISHING GROUP

2

Cataloguing in Publication Data is available from the British Library

Paperback ISBN 978 0 7553 9519 4

Typeset in Aldine 401BT by Avon DataSet Ltd,
Bidford-on-Avon, Warwickshire

Printed and bound in Great Britain by
Clays Ltd, St Ives plc

Headline's policy is to use papers that are natural, renewable and recyclable
products and made from wood grown in sustainable forests. The logging and
manufacturing processes are expected to conform to the environmental
regulations of the country of origin.

HEADLINE PUBLISHING GROUP
A division of Hachette Livre UK Ltd
338 Euston Road
London NW1 3BH

www.headline.co.uk
www.hachette.co.uk

For Mat

CHAPTER ONE

I was fifteen years old when my parents sent me away to the Yonahlossee Riding Camp for Girls. The camp was located in Blowing Rock, North Carolina, concealed in the Blue Ridge Mountains. You could drive by the entrance and never see it, not unless you were looking, and carefully; my father missed it four times before I finally signaled that we had arrived.

My father drove me from Florida to North Carolina: my parents did not trust me enough to let me ride the train alone.

The last day we ascended into the upper reaches of the mountains, at which point our journey slowed considerably. The road looked half-made, narrow and overgrown; it twisted and turned at sharp angles.

My father spoke little when he drove; he believed one should always concentrate on the road ahead. He'd bought his first car, a Chrysler Roadster, five years earlier, in 1925, so an automobile was not a habit for him but an innovation. We stopped in Atlanta on the first night, and after we checked into our hotel, my father told me to dress nicely. I wore my lavender silk dress with the dropped waist and rosette detailing. I carried my mother's mink stole, which I had taken despite Mother's instruction not to do so. When I was a child I was allowed to wear the stole on special occasions – Christmas dinner, Easter brunch – and I had come to think of the fur as mine. But now that I wore it on my own, it felt like a burden, an accessory too elegant for me. I felt young for the dress, though it was not the dress but my body that made me feel this way. My breasts were tender and new, I still carried myself in the furtive way of an immature girl. My father, in his gray pinstripe suit, didn't look much different than usual, except that he had tucked a lime green handkerchief in his coat pocket. Not the lime green of today, fluorescent and harsh. We didn't have colors like that then. No, I mean the true color of a lime, palely bright.

At the entrance to the restaurant, I took my father's arm like my mother usually did, and he looked at me, startled. I smiled and tried not to cry. I still clung to the hope that perhaps my father would not leave me in North Carolina, that he had another plan for us. My eyes were swollen from two weeks of weeping, and I knew it pained my father to see anyone cry.

The country was in the midst of the Great Depression, but my family had not suffered. My father was a physician, and people would always pay for their health. And there was family money besides, which my parents would come to depend on. But only after my father's patients were so poor they couldn't even offer him a token from the garden in exchange for his services. I saw all this after I came back from Yonahlossee. The Depression had meant something different to me when I left.

I rarely ventured outside my home. We lived in a tiny town in central Florida, named after a dead Indian chief. It was unbearably hot in the summers – this in the days before air-conditioning – and crisp and lovely in the winters. The winters were perfect, they made up for the summers. We rarely saw our neighbors, but I had all I needed right there: we had a thousand acres to ourselves, and sometimes I would leave with a packed lunch in the morning on Sasi, my pony, and return only as the sun was setting, in time for dinner, without having seen a single person while riding.

And then I thought of my twin, Sam. I had him most of all.

My father and I ate filet mignon and roasted beets at the hotel's restaurant. Plate-glass windows almost as tall as the restaurant were the central decoration. When I tried to look outside to the quiet street, I saw a blurred reflection of myself, lavender and awkward. We were the only people there, and my father complimented my dress twice.

'You look lovely, Thea.'

My full name was Theodora, a family name. The story goes Sam shortened it to Thea when we were two. The beets tasted flat and dirty against my tongue; I tried not to think about what my brother was doing while I ate.

My father told me again that at the camp I would ride every day except Sunday. I thanked him. I was leaving Sasi behind in Florida, but it was just as well because I had outgrown him. I kicked his elbows when I posted. The thought of my pretty paint pony pained me terribly now. His coat, Mother always said, was distinctively beautiful, divided evenly between black and white patches. I thought of his eyes, one blue, one brown, which wasn't so unusual in horses: if white hair surrounded the eye, it was blue; black hair, brown.

Our meal, our last meal together for a year, was mostly silent. I had never before eaten alone with my father. My mother, yes, several times, and with Sam, of course. I didn't know what to say to my father. With all the trouble at home, I was afraid to say anything at all.

'You'll come home soon,' my father said, over coffee and crème brûlée, 'after all this mess is settled,' and it was my turn to be startled by my father's behavior. I sipped my coffee quickly and singed my lips. I was only allowed a taste of Mother's at home. My father rarely spoke of unpleasantness, any kind, personal or remote. Perhaps that's why I knew as little about the Depression as I did.

He smiled at me, his small, kind smile, and I felt my eyes warm. When my mother smiled you saw all her teeth; her face revealed itself. But my father's smile was something you had to look closely for. In this moment, his smile meant he still loved me, after all I had done. I wanted him to tell me that things would be fine. But my father was not a liar. Things would not be fine; they couldn't ever be that way again.

I have never loved a place again like I loved my first home, where I was born, where I lived until the mess commenced. One could dismiss my love of place by explaining that I was attached to the people who lived there, my mother, father, and brother. That is true, I did love these people, but I cannot remember my family without remembering the gardens where they walked, the sun porches where they read, the bedrooms where they retired. I loved the house separately from my family. I knew the house, it knew me, we found solace in each other. Absurd, but there was magic in that place.

I confess that I was as sad to leave my home as to leave my family. I had never been away from it for more than a few nights, and I knew in my bones that it would be changed when I returned.

I would be changed as well. When my parents met me again at the train station in Orlando, all that time later, they might as well have been meeting an entirely new person.

I left my home, my lovely home, and was taken to the Yonahlossee Riding Camp for Girls, an enclave for wealthy young women, staffed by graduates of the camp awaiting marriage.

I came of age, as they say, at the Yonahlossee Riding Camp for Girls.

★ ★ ★

But then, I knew nothing about the place except that it was where my parents were sending me so they wouldn't have to see me. It was dusk when we arrived, a melancholy hour I've always hated. Under the cover of enormous oak trees we drove up the long gravel road that seemed to go on forever; it occurred to me that it might be weeks before I traveled this road again.

My father clutched the wheel and squinted, completing very carefully the task at hand, which was how he had always done things. We pulled up to a square – it was indeed called the Square, I would later learn – of birch-shingled cabins and my father began to turn the automobile off; I looked around for another girl, but there was no one. I opened my own door – 'Thea,' my father called, but I ignored him. I set my feet on the loamy soil, so different from the ground in Florida now, which was parched from the summer. The air smelled wet here, but not like the ocean. The ocean was always close to you in Florida, even when you lived hours away, like we did; here you were boxed in, on all sides, by mountains.

I peered up at the building in front of me while my father fiddled with the car – he would not leave it until he was sure everything was turned off properly. Even now. And this building was something like I had never seen before, half built into the mountain. The stilts that supported it reminded me of horses' legs, tall and wobbly, not meant to sustain such weight. I always had the feeling that the building should fall, would fall. Later, so much later, our headmaster told me that this was, in fact, the safest way to build in the mountains. I never believed him.

Since it was a Sunday, the camp had already eaten dinner, but I didn't know that then and I was overcome by a terrible sensation of dread and longing. This was not my home, my family was elsewhere.

A man approached, appearing as if out of thin air, and held out his hand when he was still much too far away, ten, twelve feet, for my father to possibly accept it. I thought for an instant that he resembled my brother.

'I'm Henry Holmes,' he called out, 'the headmaster.'

The first thing I thought about Henry Holmes was that his title was odd: I didn't know summer camps had headmasters. Then he reached us and first my father shook his hand; next Mr Holmes held the tips of my fingers and bowed slightly. I inclined my head.

'Thea,' my father said. 'Theodora, but call her Thea.'

I nodded and blushed. I was not used to strangers, and Mr Holmes was handsome, with dark, glossy brown hair that looked in need of a trim. His shirtsleeves were neatly rolled up, and now that he was close I could see that he did not, in fact, resemble Sam. Sam had a happy, open face, with round hazel eyes – Mother's eyes; Sam always looked kind, calm. Mr Holmes's face was a tiny bit tense, his lips drawn together in consideration. And he was a man, with a shadow of a beard. My brother was a boy.

At that moment I would have seen Sam's face in anyone's. I had taken one of his monogrammed handkerchiefs, which was what the adults I read about in books did, gave their loved ones a memento. But of course Sam had not given me anything; I had taken it. The handkerchief lay flat against my torso, beneath my dress; no one in the world knew it was there but me. I pressed my hand to my stomach and looked Mr Holmes in the eye, as my mother had taught me to do with strangers. I couldn't ever remember meeting a man who I was not related to, though surely I must have.

'We're pleased you've decided to join us,' he said, and his voice seemed softer when he spoke to me, as if he were trying to show sympathy not with his words but with the way they sounded when they reached my ears. I told him that I was pleased to be here as well. He must have guessed that some unpleasantness had sent me to the camp so late in the season. I was enrolling in the middle of the summer; I wondered what excuse my father had made.

Mr Holmes led us up the tall staircase to the Castle, and though I would only learn later that this was what everyone called this edifice, I thought even then that it looked like a fortress, imposing and elegant. The staircase was uncovered and it must have just rained, because the wood was slick. I stepped carefully. Two gas lamps flanked the door at the top of the stairs. The twin flames burned steadily, orange and red within their glass houses. Mr Holmes opened a thick oak door, painted navy blue with yellow trim, the camp's colors, and led us through the front room, which served as the dining hall and worship site.

Mr Holmes paused by the front bay window.

'So unlike Florida,' my father said. He smiled at me, and I could see that he was pained. He had started to gray around the temples in the past year, and I saw, suddenly, that my father would become old.

Mr Holmes waved us into his office, where I sat on a brown velvet settee while my father and Mr Holmes took care of the necessary matters. I could feel Mr Holmes watching me, but I did not look up.

I coughed, and my father turned his head.

'Wait outside, Thea?' Though it was not a question. I left and wandered down the hall outside the office. From where I stood I could see the tables that were already set for the next meal, tables that tomorrow morning would surely be filled with girls. Hundreds of them. I wanted so badly to be elsewhere.

I turned back to Mr Holmes's office, and was confronted by a wall of photographs, which I had somehow missed before. Horses, and astride them, their girls. I went closer and read the tiny script engraved beneath each photo, touched the brass and felt the words. On each plaque there was the name of a horse, and beneath that the name of a girl, and then, finally, *First Place, Spring Show*, and the year. There were photos from the 1800s. The horses hadn't changed much, but the earliest girls rode sidesaddle, their legs hobbled together, hanging uselessly. You could see the march of time, both through the quality of the photographs and the girls' names and clothes and hairstyles; the last two had grown shorter as time progressed. So many people had passed through this place. The most recent photograph featured a tall girl with white-blond hair and patrician features, astride a giant horse; they dwarfed the man who stood next to them, presenting the award. *Leona Keller*, it read, *King's Dominion, First Place, Spring Show, 1930*.

I noticed a small, marble-topped table by Mr Holmes's office door, two neat stacks of brochures on top of it. *Yonahlossee Riding Camp for Girls*, the first one said, *A Summer Equestrian Respite for Young Ladies since 1876*. Beneath the cursive script was a row of smiling girls, in white blouses and white skirts, each holding a horse. The horses' ears were all flipped forward, their attention earned by something behind the camera.

At first I thought the brochures in the next stack were simply older versions. Their covers featured a photograph of what must have been the entire student body, a mass of girls straightened into rows for a picture, each one of them staring solemnly into the camera. *Yonahlossee Riding School for Girls*, the same cursive script read, *Educating Young Ladies since 1902*.

I heard a voice behind Mr Holmes's door, and slipped away and went to the window. I held a hand to the glass, my thumb blocked half of a mountain range. The view was stunning, I had never seen anything like it. Florida was flat and hot; for as far as I could see from this window there were mountain peaks, slate-gray, snaked with trees, puncturing the clouds that hung so low they must not have been ordinary clouds. The clouds I was used to floated high in the sky.

I was not so angry with my situation that I could not discern beauty.

I was assigned to Augusta House. All of the cabins were named after the founders' relatives – we had Mary House, Spivey House, Minerva House. Mr Holmes led me and my father through the Square, but I trailed a foot or two behind so I didn't have to speak. Mr Holmes's stride was enormous; he was tall and lanky and towered over my father, who had always been on the small side. Sam, who had shot up like a weed over the past few months, was taller than him now. Sam might be eating now, or maybe dinner was done. Perhaps he was still wearing his day clothes: shorts and a button-down linen shirt, an outfit chosen to make the sun bearable. We never wore sleeves in the summer, but in Atlanta every man I'd seen had worn a full suit, despite the heat. Mr Holmes wore a suit now, had emerged with Father from his office wearing a jacket.

My father walked quickly to keep up and wanted to keep his hands in his pockets, but kept removing them, instinctively, for balance.

I wondered if I would recognize the back of Father's head in a crowd. Surely I would recognize Sam's, his coarse, thick hair that Mother coaxed to lie flat every time she passed by, drawing a hand over his head by habit.

Mr Holmes opened the door to Augusta House and walked through first, but before he did he turned and gave me a little smile; I could hear him tell the girls they had a visitor, and when my father and I walked in a moment later, five girls stood by their bunk beds, hands behind their backs, motionless. It was almost dark now, and the light from a wall sconce was the only source of illumination in the room. I thought it odd that Mr Holmes, a grown man, had entered a cabin full of girls without knocking. But they had known he was coming. I wondered what else they knew.

'This is Theodora Atwell, she has come to us from Florida.'

The girls nodded in tandem, and a panic seized me. Did they do everything in tandem? How would I know?

'And this,' Mr Holmes said, starting with the girl on the left, 'is Elisabeth Gilliam, Gates Weeks, Mary Abbott McClellan, Victoria Harpen, and Eva Louise Crayton.'

'Pleased to meet you,' I said, and all of the girls inclined their heads slightly. Elisabeth, the first girl, broke her stance and broke the order, and I was so grateful. These were just girls, like me. She tucked a piece of ash brown hair behind her ear and smiled; her smile was crooked. She seemed kindhearted. I liked her blue eyes; they were wide set, like a horse's. She would be my Sissy.

I wondered, in that dimly lit cabin that smelled so strongly of wood, what had brought each girl there. Or who had brought them. We each had half of a bunk bed, a tiny closet, a washstand, a desk, a vanity. Our house mistresses roomed with each other in another cabin; we girls were to be left completely alone. I took my father's hand, which hung by his side, and hoped the other girls would not think me childish. His grip surprised me, and then I knew it was true, he meant to leave me here. I tugged my hand free of his and stepped forward.

'I'm pleased to be here.'

My father kissed my cheek and pressed me to him in a sort of clumsy half-hug; now I was embarrassed instead of sad, all these girls watching. Mr Holmes turned his head politely. Then they left, and I stood there alone in this room full of girls and felt terrified. I was accustomed to the feeling of fear – it threaded itself through my brain each time I tried a higher jump – but that fear was accompanied by a certain exhilaration.

Now I watched the unreadable faces of all these girls and they watched me and I felt frightened in a way I had never felt frightened before. There was no place to go but here, no one to take comfort in except myself. I started to cross my arms in front of my chest but then an instinct told me to stop: I didn't want any of these girls to know I was scared.

'Theodora?' the pretty girl with a full figure asked, and I remembered her name. Eva.

'Thea,' I mumbled. But I wasn't from a family that mumbled. I cleared my throat. 'Thea. A nickname.'

'Well that's better,' Eva said, and grinned. 'Theodora's a mouthful.'

I hesitated – was she making fun of my name? But then she patted the bunk beside her. 'This is you. You're my bottom.'

Sissy laughed. The sound startled, then comforted me. 'Have you ever slept on a bunk bed?' she asked. 'I have the bottom, too. It's the worst, but you're here so late.'

I pointed at my trunk, which rested at the foot of my bottom bunk; pointing was bad manners, now the girls would think I had none, but poor manners were better than explaining why I had come so late.

'My trunk's already here,' I said.

'One of the men brought it,' Mary Abbott chimed in. Her voice was fragile-sounding.

'But not the handsome one!' Eva said, and Sissy laughed.

Gates turned from her desk, where she had been writing something – a letter? I wondered to whom – and I could see she did not approve.

'Oh Gates,' Eva said. 'Don't be so serious. It's just chatter.' Eva turned to me, languidly; she moved about like she didn't have a care in the world. 'There are two men here who do chores. One is very handsome. And the other . . . you'll see.' I felt my face go hot, and quickly walked to my bunk so the other girls wouldn't see. I blushed at the drop of a hat. I busied myself with my trunk, and after a moment I noticed that everyone was changing into their nightclothes. I changed out of my clothes quickly – no other girl had ever seen me naked. Only Mother, and she was not a girl. I was careful to hide the handkerchief as I disrobed – the other girls would think me childish if they saw I'd hidden a piece of fabric from my brother beneath my clothes. Or worse than childish: odd.

Our nightgowns were all the same – mine had been laid upon the bed – soft cotton shifts with V-necklines, a mid-calf hemline, YRC embroidered over our left breasts. Over our hearts. The nightgown I had brought with me was high collared, ankle length, ruffled at the wrists. It would have given me away immediately. Mother had told me that I'd be wearing a uniform, so I didn't need to pack much; the idea had made me furious back home. I was going to be treated like everyone else! But now I was glad. I had not known my nightgown was all wrong.

The girls left in pairs – Eva and Sissy, Gates and Victoria – until only Mary Abbott and I remained. I had no choice but to follow. I didn't want to ask where we were going, but I did.

'The privies. I know what you're thinking, how can we not have a toilet in our cabins?' she asked. She dropped her voice conspiratorially: 'They think it's good for us.' Her accent was very Southern. Mr Holmes had an accent, but I couldn't place it – he spoke in clipped tones, the opposite of how everyone in Augusta House spoke. I didn't have an accent, not compared to these girls. 'But at least there's indoor plumbing. And running water for our baths.'

I nodded at Mary Abbott, unsure of how to respond. I'd always had indoor plumbing, and running water.

Eva and Sissy passed us on their way back to the cabin, along with pairs of other girls from other cabins. We looked like ghosts in our nightgowns, and I hated this place, hated these girls, my first clear, unconfused sentiment since I'd arrived. I wrapped my shawl tighter around my shoulders and hated my mother.

The privies were spotless – I was grateful for that. I didn't wait for Mary Abbott, rushed back to the cabin without once meeting anyone's eye. When we'd passed Eva and Sissy, I knew by how they smiled that Mary Abbott was not someone I wanted to align myself with. I was already in bed when Mary Abbott came in; she looked at me for a long second, wistfully, I thought, but that was unreasonable, she'd known me for an hour – and then someone entered the cabin, too old to be a woman, too young to be a girl. She barely looked at any of us. When she saw me, she nodded – 'Theodora Atwell. Glad to see you've settled in.' And then she turned off our lights.

'Good night, girls,' she called as she left the room.

'Good night, Henny,' everyone called back, in unison.

The girls said good night to each other then, in sleepy whispers; I thought they were done when Eva spoke.

'Good night, Thea,' she whispered, and all the other girls followed suit, my name whispered five times, and it seemed astonishing that I knew which voice belonged to whom; it seemed astonishing that already these girls laid claim to me.

The last girl I had known was Milly, a neighbor, and she had moved away years ago. She carried a doll with her, always. I thought she was boring, which in my family was least what you wanted to be. Other people were boring; the Atwells were interesting.

Sam liked Milly, though. She would watch him tend to his

terrariums, help him carve branches of trees into a more manageable size, listen with interest as Sam explained how his huge cane toad transmitted poison from the glands behind his eyes. Only Sam was able to pick the toad up; when I tried, it puffed to twice its normal size. Sam had a carefulness about him that animals trusted. People, too.

I did not like Milly there with Sam when I returned from a ride. And so I stole Milly's doll and buried it behind the barn. She never came back.

Sam knew what I had done. I had been cruel, and Sam hated cruelty. I think he did not understand it, the impulse to harm another living creature. It's why he couldn't ride. The thought of pressing a spur into a horse's tender side, or lifting a whip against a dumb animal – well, Sam could not imagine it.

He was ashamed of me, and I was almost ashamed of myself, but Milly was quickly forgotten, ground into the dust of a child's memory.

A girl muttered something nonsensical, talking in her sleep.

'Shh,' Gates said, 'shh,' and the muttering stopped.

In Atlanta, my father and I had slept in separate rooms. We'd never traveled alone before, so I didn't know how to interpret this, but in my great big room I'd cried, and then slapped myself for being so silly and desperate: this was nothing, I told myself, take hold of yourself. I'd fallen asleep to the noise of cars underneath my window, wondering if my father heard the same in the room across the hall, wondering if he was even awake to hear it or dead to the world.

The cars outside my window had made me feel less lonely, though that was silly – the men and women in those cars were no friends of mine.

I wondered if Sam was still awake now, listening to the Emathla crickets. I wondered what else he had heard, today, what else he had done. Mother would still be awake, reading, listening to the radio; Father would still be driving if I had to guess, twisting carefully through the mountains.

I thought of my cousin, Georgie, and wanted to weep, but I would not let myself. I had wept enough for a lifetime. Two lifetimes. Three.

The next morning a bell woke me. I sat up quickly and banged my head on Eva's bunk. Her face appeared next to mine, from her top bunk.

'You look like a bat,' I said, and she looked at me dreamily, and I admired her pretty skin, her plump cheeks.

I massaged my scalp and waited for the other girls to rise. But no one moved for a few minutes; instead they lay in their beds and yawned and stretched. I had never been alone with so many girls for so long. Mother had sent me and Sam to the Emathla school for two weeks before deciding it wasn't good enough for us; but the differences between me and those children, the sons and daughters of country people, had been so clear. Here I did not know where I stood.

All the girls looked dazed, lying in their beds. Eva was the tallest among us; Mary Abbott the shortest. Victoria was the thinnest girl, but she was too thin, with a collarbone so sharp she looked starved. My hair was neither dark nor light; I was neither short nor tall. At home I almost never saw other children. Father taught us our lessons, and when Sam and I did see another boy or girl, in town, we were always looked at closely, because we were twins and resembled each other uncannily: we both had Father's strong nose, and high, broad cheekbones. Our faces were sculpted, Mother said. And we both had Mother's hair, a rich auburn color and coarsely wavy. It felt the same, when you touched it. Our resemblance made people notice us. Here, without Sam, I was just like everyone else except a little darker, because of the Florida sun.

Someone else entered, clearly a maid – I could tell by her uniform.

'Good morning, Docey,' Eva called, and Docey smiled quickly in her direction, then poured water into each of our wash-stands. Then everyone rose and went to them – they were plain, simple walnut, but their bowls were painted prettily with delicate flowers. The rim of mine was chipped. Docey was smaller than any of us. If I had to guess, I'd say she was no more than five feet, but stronger, with mousy-brown hair pinned into a tight bun and a lazy eye. She spoke with an accent that was rough and quick, Southern, messier than everyone else's. Later I would learn her accent signaled she was from the poorest part of Appalachia.

After we washed and dressed, we walked through the Square to the same building I'd come to last night, with Father. I'd slept with Sam's handkerchief under my pillow. I'd wanted to put it under-neath my clothes again, but the risk that Eva or Sissy – I wanted to impress them most – would see was too great.

When I stepped outside, I was shocked by the sheer mass of all the girls. There were so many of them, all dressed in white skirts and blouses with Peter Pan collars, 'YRC' again embroidered over our hearts in navy. My father had told me that there would be almost two hundred girls, I suppose to prepare me, but I wasn't prepared, not for this army. The only thing that immediately distinguished them from each other was their hair – a girl with tight curls glanced at me and whispered something to her friend, and I realized I was gawking. I stepped into the crowd and tried to keep up, tried to pace my gait with theirs. I looked at all the girls' legs and realized no one wore stockings; from the waist down, we looked like a crowd of children.

Sissy caught up with me. Her brown hair was cut in a fashionable bob. I touched my own hair, which fell well over my shoulders. I'd wanted a bob, but Mother hadn't wanted me to cut it.

'You're a quick walker,' she said.

I slowed my pace. 'Yes.'

'It's hot in Florida.' Her voice was husky; it contrasted sharply with her delicate features.

'Where are you from?' I asked.

'Monroeville.'

She acted as if I must know where that was. I pretended that I did.

'What does your father do?' she asked.

'He's a doctor. And he owns orange groves.' The last part wasn't technically true – the citrus was in my mother's family – but I assumed owning land gave you currency here.

'I love oranges!' she said, smiling her crooked smile, and I smiled back at her enthusiasm. Oranges weren't a treat to me. They were a given.

'What does your father do?' I asked.

'He manages my grandfather's affairs. And rides horses. That's why he sent me here, to learn how to ride. But I'm afraid I haven't taken to it.'

'No?'

'It's too dirty,' she said. Then added quickly, 'But don't think I'm like that,' and glanced at me sideways. 'I just like other things better.'

I was surprised by the sound of my laughter. I hadn't laughed in weeks.

The other girls swarmed around us as we entered the dining hall. Clustered at tables draped with toile cloths, they spoke among themselves, and I could see they liked it here, felt at home.

Sissy pointed out my table, where Mary Abbott, Victoria, and Henny sat amid others. Mary Abbott grinned excitedly when she saw me, and I gave a small smile in return, then chose the seat farthest from her.

'Hello, Theodora,' Henny said. I started to tell her about my name, but Mary Abbott piped in.

'She goes by Thea.' Henny didn't acknowledge that Mary Abbott had spoken, went on and introduced the others at the table, a mix of younger and older girls and a teacher, Miss Metcalfe, who had very smooth skin and small, pearly teeth.

There were steaming platters of food – eggs, bacon *and* ham, raspberry muffins, grits – but I had no appetite. Mostly, everyone ignored me, and I was grateful. I thought that Sam would have loved all this food; he had started to eat like a horse the past few months. I knew exactly where he was right now: out back, tending to one of his injured animals, or feeding the insects in one of his terrariums, rearranging a branch so a lizard had a better place to sun himself. He didn't always have an injured animal to tend to, but he'd been raising a nest of baby squirrels for a few weeks. Their mother had vanished.

'Can I ask you a question?' Molly said, halfway through the meal. She had buckteeth, which made her seem younger than she was. Her thin brown hair hung loose, an inch past her waist. It needed to be cut.

'May I . . .' Henny corrected. She was chubby, with a double chin and an unfortunately placed mole on her left temple. She wasn't homely, exactly, but there was the mole. I did not like Henny but I was relieved by her presence, that there was a near-adult here along with Miss Metcalfe to keep order.

Molly continued. 'Why are you here so late?'

'Pardon?'

'Why didn't you come at the beginning like the rest of us?'

I waited for Henny to intervene, but she sat quietly, like the rest of the table, watching me. Alice Hunt Morgan, from Memphis, Tennessee, traced the rim of her glass. I'd called her Alice and she'd corrected me: Alice Hunt, she'd said, that's my full name. Now everyone waited for my answer. They were all curious, and I couldn't blame them: I was an interloper.

'It was a late birthday present,' I said, 'we were in Europe on holiday because it gets so hot in Florida during the summer.' I paused. The girls waited, heads tilted. Molly rolled a piece of her ratty hair between her fingers. 'We go every year and I didn't want to miss it, but my father wanted me to come to camp, too. So he arranged it.' I shrugged my shoulders, as if to say, it was all in the hands of generous and capable adults.

'Where in Europe?' Molly asked, but by then the other girls were tired of me, had returned to each other.

'Paris,' I said. 'I love Paris in the summer.'

Molly nodded and looked away, satisfied. I felt the back of my head for a tender spot from this morning, but there was nothing. I looked across the room and found Sissy, who smiled at me. I smiled back.

'Thea,' Henny said. So she had heard Mary Abbott; Mary Abbott was a girl one didn't have to acknowledge. 'Drink up.' She nodded at my milk. I contemplated the glass, which I had barely touched. At home we drank orange or grapefruit juice, depending on the season. Never milk. Mother had an aversion to it. We stirred milk into our tea sometimes, or Sam and I had it with dessert. For lunch at Yonahlossee, I'd soon learn, a glass pitcher of sweet iced tea, a chunk of ice floating in the amber, would rest next to Henny's plate, and she would dole it out among us carefully. This iced tea was thick and syrupy, and, I had to admit, delicious. Years later I'd crave this iced tea, its cool weight on my tongue, the bitterness of the strong tea offset by the copious amounts of sugar; I'd learn that to miss the Yonahlossee sweet tea was something of a tradition among us.

But that would be later. For now I stared at my glass of pale milk and tried not to cry.

'Thea,' Henny said again, her voice low, but I knew I would cry if I looked up. Then I could feel her gaze lift; everyone turned their seats around in the same direction and I thought this was some strange way of leaving until I heard his voice.

'Good morning, girls,' Mr Holmes said.

'Good morning, Mr Holmes,' everyone chorused but me, and Mr Holmes seemed quietly delighted at this response, even though he must hear it every morning.

After he had delivered morning announcements and led us in worship, a woman approached me, too old to be a house mistress. She was plump and short, with a pretty face.

'I'm Mrs Holmes, the headmistress. Follow me,' she said, and gestured toward the stairwell at the edge of the room. I tried to keep the surprise from my face, but she saw anyway, looked at me for a second too long so I would know I had erred. But I also knew I could not be the first person who had been surprised that she was married to Mr Holmes. When I'd seen her this morning, I'd thought she was head housekeeper, or some other staff person; even from across the room she had a matronly, interfering way about her. She struck me as impatient. I followed her obediently, slowed down so that I would not overtake her. Her waist seemed unnaturally small, as if she were cinched in, and I realized she must be wearing a corset. Even Mother didn't wear those. But Mother was so slim she didn't need one.

Her office was on the third floor, and by the time we reached it she was out of breath. As she opened the door, I stood close enough so that I could see how tightly her brown hair was bound into a bun; her hair was graying, which you could not see from a distance.

Her office was elegantly appointed, the settee upon which she gestured for me to sit upholstered in a modern plaid.

'Theodora Atwell,' she began. 'You're at Henny's table?' Before I could answer, she continued. 'I've known Henny for a very long time. She's exceptionally capable.' This seemed like a warning. She looked down at the papers in front of her. 'From Emathla, Florida. I've always thought that to live in Florida as a gardener would be sublime. You could grow anything.'

Mother said that very same thing. But I didn't want to think about Mother. 'Everyone calls me Thea.'

'Oh, I know,' she said, and smiled at me. I wondered if Mr Holmes had already told her what to call me, if they spoke often about the girls here. They must.

'Tell me, Thea,' she said, and lowered herself into her shiny wooden chair and gazed at me from across her desk, hewn from the same wood, also polished to a sheen – 'how are you liking it so far?'

'Very much,' I said, because there was nothing else I could say.

'The founders of Yonahlossee were very progressive individuals. They started this camp in 1876, eleven years after the War Between the States. Why, Thea, was this such an important time in our nation's history?'

I knew this, at least. My own great-grandfather had fled the War Between the States. 'Because the South was poor almost beyond belief. Because it was a terrible time for this part of the country. Everything was changing, rapidly, and no one was sure what would happen to the South.'

I had impressed her. 'Yes.' She nodded. Then she told me about Louisa and Hanes Bell, who had never had children of their own but who had made it their mission to provide a summer respite for females in this rapidly changing – she used my words – world. Places like this already existed in the North, for girls and boys, and in the South, for boys, but the Bells had seen a lack and filled it.

'And then the camp became a school, as demand for the place grew.' Before, she had sounded like she was rattling off a speech, one she had given before many times. Now she looked at me intently, but I didn't know why. 'So now Yonahlossee is a camp for certain girls and a school for others. But in both cases it is a place for young women to learn how to become ladies. Because, Thea, becoming a lady is not simply a thing which happens, like magic.' She snapped her fingers, then shook her head. 'No, quite the opposite: becoming a lady is a lesson you must learn.'

'In this world of uncertainty,' she finished, 'a lady is more important than she ever was.'

She was referring to the financial crisis, of course. It seemed sad that the Bells had never had children, especially since they'd devoted their lives to the young. Something must have been wrong with Louisa's organs. I had very little idea of what Mrs Holmes meant: she might as well have been speaking Greek. A lady was now more important than she ever was?

'And the name?' I asked, because Mrs Holmes was looking at me expectantly. 'Yonahlossee?'

'Oh,' Mrs Holmes said, and made a small, flinging gesture. 'An old Indian name. It has nothing to do with the camp, really. The name of Mrs Bell's horse.'

I waited for her to continue, to say something about equestrienne pursuits. I smiled to myself; Sasi was an old Indian name, too. Mother had named him after I couldn't think of anything. Sasi was an old Muskogee word, meaning 'is there.' As in, the flower is there. Mother had said that, exactly. I remembered her voice so clearly.

'I hope you'll like it here,' she said, and put her elbows on the table, and stared at me frankly, her small hands folded in front of her.

'I feel sure I will.' And I had liked it, a moment ago, liked hearing about Louisa Bell; Yonahlossee seemed like a kinder place now that I knew it was named after a horse. But remembering Mother, and Sasi, had turned me gray again.

'Your mother was sure you would.'

I was so confused for a second – had she read my mind?

'Your mother is a friend of mine. An old friend.'

This was impossible. My mother didn't have any old friends; we were all she needed. How many times had I heard her say that she and Father had stumbled into their private utopia out here in the Florida wilderness?

'You have her hair,' Mrs Holmes said, and then I knew it was true, she had known Mother.

'We went to finishing school together,' she continued, 'in Raleigh. Miss Petit's.'

My eyes blurred, and I thought for an instant that I was having an allergic reaction, like one of Father's patients; to a bee sting, a berry.

I bit my lip, and it was hard to breathe; then I started to cry.

'Oh, Thea, I didn't mean to upset you. Did your mother not tell you that we knew each other?'

I shook my head.

'Yes, I know all about you. She entrusted me, in a way. Another place might not have been suitable for you.

'Do we understand each other, Thea?' Mrs Holmes asked, after a moment.

I nodded.

'Please look at me.'

I did as she asked. Her eyes were almond-shaped. That I was

looking into the same eyes my mother had once looked into seemed impossible.

'And there's another thing: if you notice anything unusual, anything . . . bodily, please come and see me at once.'

'Bodily?' I repeated.

'Bodily. I'll expect you know what I mean if it happens.'

I told her I understood, even though I didn't.

As I walked alone to the stables for my evaluation, I thought she must mean my monthly cycle. But I already had that, and knew what to do myself.

I was glad no girl could see my red eyes; I was grateful that I had the walk to compose myself. My understanding had been that Yonahlossee was a place arrived at by accident, by circumstance.

The path past the privies narrowed into a lane wide enough for two people; trees rose on either side, blocking out most of the sunlight. I shivered, and was relieved when I emerged suddenly into a large circle of flat space, bordered by mountains.

I gasped, in spite of myself; I had told myself I would try not to be surprised by everything new at Yonahlossee. But I had never seen anything like this; I hadn't even known something like this existed. There were three stone barns, all in a row, and they were massive compared to my barn at home, as if they housed an army of horses. My barn at home was barely a barn at all, I realized, compared to this. Horses hung their heads out of their stall windows, and I saw an Appaloosa with a spotted head, a breed I'd only read about, never seen.

Grooms milled about the grounds, pushing wheelbarrows or leading horses. One man caught me staring, and I turned away, blushing; he looked like Docey's male counterpart, skinny and wiry, capable.

There were five riding rings, two with jumps. Everything

looked perfect and new, the rings freshly raked, the fences newly painted. I wondered where Yonahlossee got all its money. The few towns we had driven through on the way here had looked very poor – the buildings falling down, the people dirty – but I knew we were entering Appalachia, which was poor anyway, aside from the financial crisis. Father mentioned a terrible drought. Another reference to unpleasantness, uncharacteristic, but I was quickly learning that my life was turning into a series of surprises.

'It's unexpected, isn't it?' a voice asked, and I spun around to find a tall man standing at my left. A horse, already saddled and bridled, stood at his side.

'You startled me,' I said, my hand clapped over my heart, as was my habit when surprised. I hoped my red eyes didn't give me away.

The man laughed. He had a German accent; I'd met a German man before, Mr Buch, who used to come visit my father every year or so for business about the oranges.

'You're German?'

'Yes. I'm Mr Albrecht.'

'I'm Thea Atwell, pleased to meet you.' I curtsied slightly, to compensate for my rudeness. I recognized Mr Albrecht from the photographs hanging on the wall. He was the man who presented the awards. He was extremely thin, with a flat chin, which surprised me. I thought Germans came with square jaws. But his skin was smooth, for a man, and his teeth straight. He was, if not handsome, passable. He seemed as old as my father.

'And this,' he said, 'is Luther.' He stroked the ridge of Luther's neck, and Luther lowered his head and watched me. Luther was a homely horse, dull brown with a too-large head and small ears. But he had kind eyes.

'He's the first horse everyone here rides. Your father said you were an experienced rider?'

'Yes.'

'You shouldn't have any trouble with Luther. Tap him on over
the jumps, keep him steady through the doubles. He'll jump
anything, but sometimes he balks if you're shy.'

Mr Albrecht gave me a leg-up, and I settled into the saddle
while he adjusted my stirrups. My heart raced, from some mixture
of the shock I'd just experienced at the hand of Mrs Holmes and
the anticipation of riding in front of a stranger. Luther was huge,
over sixteen hands, maybe even seventeen, the largest horse I'd
been on. That doesn't matter, I told myself. Control is control.
Mr Albrecht mapped out the course, and I followed him to the
farthest ring. He gave me ten minutes to warm up, and I trotted
around the ring, testing Luther. I tugged on my left rein and he
tugged back; I gave him a sharp jerk. Mr Albrecht stood by the
gate and watched. He had a simultaneously formal and relaxed air
about him; he stood with his hands in his pockets, his head
cocked, his white shirt spotless, his breeches neatly ironed and
creased.

I tried to ignore the figure of Mr Albrecht watching me ride.
When he told me it was time, I halted Luther from a trot and then
asked him to canter from a walk; I wanted his reflexes sharp.
Another man had joined Mr Albrecht by the gate; I squinted – Mr
Holmes. He waved, and I bowed my head in response. I wasn't
wearing a helmet, no one in those days did, and though other
people wore gloves, they dulled the feeling in my hands. The
jumps I was to clear were over three feet tall; we weren't afraid of
anything, in those days. We didn't know there was anything to be
afraid of.

I completed the course in a blur. I could never remember my
courses after I'd finished them, someone would have to tell me if
I'd knocked down a rail, or made a wrong turn. After I jumped
the last combination, I cantered Luther around the perimeter of

the ring until the tension in both our bodies eased. I walked over to where Mr Albrecht stood; Mr Holmes was gone.

Mr Albrecht nodded, and slapped Luther's neck.

'Cool him out. You did well.'

I could still see Mr Holmes; he hadn't reached the trail yet, where the woods would swallow him. I wondered how long it would be until Sam was as tall as Mr Holmes. Right now he was still a child, or half-child, half-adult, like me.

I held on to the reins by the buckle at their end and let Luther hang his head. We walked leisurely around the ring. That Yonahlossee was not a place picked at random disturbed me, but also confirmed that my parents' plan was beyond my under-standing. Mother had chosen a place a little like paradise, as far as horses were concerned; at least there was that. That my mother could have been friends with a person like Mrs Holmes was almost unbelievable; yet I had to believe it. My mother had been cruel to me in the past few weeks in a way that I knew I deserved but was nonetheless hard to bear. My parents had not sent me into the arms of strangers; instead they had sent me into the arms of a woman who knew at least part of my terrible secret. But what part had my mother told her? Surely not everything.

Mr Albrecht had disappeared into the barn. I stopped Luther and dismounted; then I did a childish thing. I wept into his hot shoulder, salty with sweat, and for the first time in weeks I felt comfort.

CHAPTER TWO

The tunnel of woods from the stables to the Square was dark, and though I'd never been scared of being by myself, I hurried. All the other girls were in class. What kind of animals lurked in the North Carolina woods, what kind of poisonous plants? I knew all of that in Florida. Here I was an innocent.

There wouldn't be as much to be wary of here, at least concerning the natural world. Winter came every year and weeded the animals, the plants. In Florida nothing died, nothing retreated.

When it was cool enough, Sam and I liked to roam out back, past the orange grove, miles away from the house. One day, when we were eleven, I brought Sasi with us, because it was one of the last tolerable days before summer. Sasi was young then, too, could be ridden for hours and hours and still have something left. Sam was walking ahead of me, looking for blackberries; I was on horseback, following him. It was April, a few weeks too early for blackberries, but Sam thought we might get lucky.

'Is Sasi tired?' Sam called out.

'No,' I said. 'He likes it out here.'

'Do you like it out here, Sasi?' Sam asked, in an English accent, and I giggled.

We walked some more. Sam disappeared into a throng of bushes.

'Even if you find any, they'll be tart,' I said.

Sam reappeared, empty-handed.

'Because it's too early,' I explained.

Sam grinned. 'I knew what you meant the first time.'

I turned around and reached into my saddlebag for a canteen; there was a sudden dip, a feeling of weightlessness, and then buzzing. At first I didn't understand the noise, but when I felt a sting on my cheek I knew that Sasi had stepped into an underground nest of yellow jackets.

'Sam!' I screamed. I slipped off Sasi, who was stomping his hooves into the dirt, clouds of dust rising around his legs. 'Sam!'

'Thea,' he said, and his voice infuriated me: it was so calm, so slow.

'Help,' I cried, slapping at my cheeks. 'Hurry!'

'Thea,' he said, 'listen to me. Listen,' he said, as he walked toward me.

I shook my head furiously; I could feel my cheeks swell, my throat tighten. I could see red welts rise on my arm, I felt them on my neck. I tasted bile.

'Thea,' Sam said, and when he reached me he touched my forearm. 'Look at me.'

But I couldn't. I looked at Sasi, who was furiously biting his leg where he had been stung; I looked beyond Sam, at the miles and miles of scrub oak and oak trees; I looked at the sky, which was blue, not a cloud in sight. I could hear my heart beat. I could smell my sweat.

'It's not a full nest,' Sam said, but he sounded like he was speaking from a great distance. 'There aren't enough of them. But if you aren't calm you'll make it worse. All right, Thea? See,' he continued, 'they're gone.'

I looked at him. 'Sasi?' I asked.

'Sasi will be fine. He's so big,' he said, and I understood that I was not so big, that my labored breathing, my hot, scratchy face were evidence of my smallness.

'How many stings?' I asked, my voice high.

'Not that many.' But I knew he was lying. Sam had never been able to lie to me.

'Ahh,' I gasped, my throat feeling tighter and tighter, 'ahh.' We were miles from the house. I knew what happened if you were stung too many times by yellow jackets; your throat swelled, you stopped breathing, and it all happened very quickly.

I started to cry, and claw at my neck, and I could feel the welts my fingernails made, and I knew I was going to die.

'Thea!' Sam said, almost shouted. 'You'll make it worse. Look at me.' He put his hand on my cheek and it felt so cool against my inflamed skin. He held my face and made me look into his eyes, he would not let me look away, and gradually my breathing became easier. Like a snake charmer, I whispered under my breath.

'Just listen to me,' Sam said, and helped me into the saddle, and walked beside me and held my hand while Sasi trudged on, all the while keeping up a steady stream of conversation – about early blackberries, about a new jump Sasi and I should try, about Mother and Father, about Georgie, about nothing. It was the sound of his voice that was important.

When we arrived back home, late because of how slowly we had walked, Mother saw me and cried out; my face was swollen, my lips and eyelids puffy. Sam raised a hand to his forehead to sweep away his hair and I noticed that it shook, terribly, proof that he had also been scared; his fear proof that I had been in danger, that Sam had saved me with his calmness. He had always been like that, still where I was frantic.

But here I would never be miles away from camp. I would be watched, in a way I never had been.

I knocked before I opened the cabin door, a habit I'd soon forget. Our cabin was never locked, none of the buildings here were. Perhaps the headmaster's cabin, perched beyond the Square. Or maybe there was a safe somewhere in the Castle, with camp valuables. I didn't care, Docey or anyone could have anything she wanted of my things, I hadn't brought much that was good.

'Hello,' I called, as I took off my boots by the door. A flurry of dust motes slanted through the morning light. All was in perfect order, left that way by Docey. I didn't even have to make my bed here.

I pulled my boots off. The thin socks I wore while riding were damp with sweat, and the air felt cool on my feet and calves. I needed to dust the insides of my boots with talcum powder. I knew that the barn would keep a supply, but I hadn't looked. Of all the time spent with a horse, riding was such a small part of it.

I went to Sissy's closet first, found only clothes. Half her closet was occupied by party dresses, the silk soft beneath my fingertips. I thought I had a lot of clothes, but Sissy's wardrobe was triple the size of mine. And for the last year Mother hadn't bought any new clothes for herself or me. She said it would be in bad taste, with how poor everyone was becoming.

In Sissy's desk I found a few pens, a letter from her mother, *received* spelled wrong, the *i* and the *e* reversed. The letter was short, recounted a week she and Sissy's father had spent 'doing much of nothing.' A novel that looked brand-new, called *The Art of Friendship*. I traced the embossed lily on its red cover. Silly, Mother would have said. There was a hairbrush on her vanity, matted with her brown hair. Three bottles of French perfume in her drawer, full. I hadn't noticed any scent on her. In the back of the drawer I found a rolled-up velvet pouch, with little compartments for jewelry. I held a pair of ruby studs to the light, each stone identical to the other, flawless and deep pink. An oval locket, engraved with initials – not Sissy's – and a braided lock of hair behind the glass. I wondered who had died. I didn't have any jewelry this nice. Mother had said I would have her jewelry one day, but I wondered if this was still true. It was all kept in a safe. As if anyone would bother it, or us, where we lived.

The ruby earrings hurt to put in. I met resistance in both ears, especially the left, which was pierced slightly crooked. Mother and Idella had pierced them, with a hot needle and a piece of thread. I put them in less to see what they looked like and more to open the holes in my ears, but they didn't suit me anyway, were too large and surprising. Mother might have said they brought out the auburn in my hair. Despite living so far out of town, she knew what was in vogue. There was a stack of magazines in our downstairs sunroom, but Mother also read books, the same ones Father did. Still, I didn't have dresses like this, and I had never been given a piece of jewelry nearly this fine.

What had Sissy's mother said when she had given her the earrings? Maybe she had presented them to her before a party, dropped them into Sissy's hand and closed her own around her daughter's. The posts would have stung her palm, but the feeling would have been pleasurable. I'd never been to a party, only to restaurants. I could see Sissy at a dance, in the navy blue silk from her closet, the rubies exaggerating her brown hair, her smooth skin, colored by the summer sun. Passed from boy to boy, flirting in her husky voice. I was suddenly angry at my parents for sending me to Yonahlossee unprepared. They'd kept me sheltered all my life, and then sent me here, ignorant of so many things.

Eva's desk was next to Sissy's, under the window. The Square was still empty. There was a thick stack of pictures in her drawer.

Her father was very heavy, had gotten heavier as the photographs progressed. Her mother was plump. Eva would have to be careful, which I'm sure she knew. She might lose her figure entirely after children, like I assumed Mrs Holmes had. It happened to some women – Mother had told me this. The pictures were tied with a ribbon, but the rest was a mess – a tangle of paper and jewelry and pots of rouge and cream. There were sentences in French. The tins of makeup were hollowed out at the center. I wondered if she was a fast girl in a world where boys were involved. I knew about fast girls from books.

Mary Abbott's drawer was very spare. I almost didn't bother with her. Her closet was nearly empty except for a few homely dresses and Yonahlossee uniforms. Her thick letters were from her father. The postmark was Raleigh, which wasn't far from here. Mary Abbott dressed the same as the rest of us, so there was no way to know without looking in her closet that her things weren't as nice as ours. Her family must have had enough money to send her here, so perhaps the bareness of her wardrobe was due to some religious fervor. I scanned the letter; indeed, God was mentioned a few times. I liked putting the pieces together like this. I returned the letters and opened a small compact; inside, taped to the mirror, was a picture of a baby. I recognized Mary Abbott's features – her thin lips, her shocked-looking eyes. I touched the photograph, softly, and smiled. She had been pretty.

I was terrified before I knew by what; I must have seen a shadow out of the corner of my eye; then I turned and saw Mr Holmes through the window. Mr Holmes also turned, and glanced inside, straight at me. He was more handsome than any movie star I had seen: his angular jaw, his dark eyes, framed by dark eyelashes and darker eyebrows. I stared at Mr Holmes for another ten, fifteen seconds as he passed by and he looked so nice that I almost thought, let him find me. He'll understand. But he didn't stop, and I was instantly relieved the sun was too bright for him to see inside. Of course he would not have understood. I would have looked like a thief. Or worse, a lurker.

I closed Mary Abbott's drawer in a fit of relief, and as I did heard the tap of a hard sole against the floor.

'Hello?'

It was Docey, with a stack of towels. She said nothing. I didn't know where to look because of her wandering eye.

'I was looking for powder,' I said. I walked to my bed and picked up my boots. 'To sprinkle inside.' My face was hot. I held my boots to my chest, the leather still warm. She watched me for what felt like a long moment and I saw how this would go: she would tell, I would be an outsider.

'That's fine,' Docey said, and it took me a second to catch what she said, because of her accent. She turned her back to me and went to each girl's closet, removing the dirty towel and replacing it with a clean one, accumulating a mass of dirty linen in her arms. When she was done, I thought maybe she'd leave without saying anything. She looked about my age, but she had a pale, ageless face. There wasn't a trace of any sort of figure beneath her uniform. She was lean and small. I'd been stupid. I'd let myself be caught.

At my closet, she paused, as if to ask permission. I nodded, and as she got my towel, she spoke: 'I'll let you get back.' At the door she turned briefly, and in a gesture so minute I might have imagined it, she brought her hand to her ear. I felt my own ear, the earrings I had forgotten. She wouldn't tell.

Eva and I waited outside the cabin in our robes for Sissy.

'She's always late,' Eva murmured, 'her only fault.' The comment struck me as odd, because Eva didn't seem like the critical type, but then she grinned. When Sissy emerged, we left. The sun had gone down an hour ago and it was chilly, but my robe was thick and plush.

'Are you settling in?' Sissy asked.

I laughed. 'Mr Holmes asked the same question yesterday.'

'What did you tell him?'

'I told him I was. What else could I say?'

'Well, Mr Holmes could make you say anything.' She whispered into my ear. 'Henry.'

I giggled.

'Those eyes,' she said, and swooned. 'But just so you know, he doesn't flirt. He thinks he's our father.'

'Mrs Holmes would slap your hand with a ruler if she heard you,' Eva said. 'Did she already give you the founder's speech? About how grateful we should all be for women's education?'

'She said Yonahlossee was named after a horse.' I liked this, walking in a group. Other girls glanced at us curiously, admiringly.

'Oh. She doesn't like horses,' Sissy said. 'She doesn't like anything.'

She had apparently liked my mother, but never in a million years would I have said so.

'Yonahlossee is hard at first,' Eva said. 'I couldn't get out of bed. I couldn't manage to get up at the morning bell. I would miss breakfast, even my first class. At home I slept until noon every day.'

I couldn't imagine sleeping until noon. Sam woke me every morning before the sun rose. A tap on my shoulder was all it took; I was ready, eager to get started on the day. Sam was amused by my impatience. I had to ride early at home, to avoid the heat; Sasi was tacked by sunrise. 'Didn't you have things to do?'

'No. That's why they sent me here. Because there was nothing to do at home. But I was fine, actually. I liked having nothing to do.' Eva was taller than both of us, and she moved languidly. Her skin always looked slightly moist, in a pretty way, as if she'd just taken a bath. She did seem lazy.

'Didn't you get in trouble?'

She lifted her shoulders and let them drop again, lazily. 'You don't really get in trouble here, Thea. Mrs Holmes talked to me. And I got used to getting up.'

'You can get in trouble here,' Sissy said. 'I wouldn't cross Mrs Holmes.'

'Who gets in trouble?' I asked.

'Last month Gates's sister and another girl were caught smoking. Last year a girl was meeting a boy from Asheville in the woods. The smokers got a warning. The other girl got sent away the next day. No one knew what happened to her until Mrs Holmes announced it after morning prayer. It was like she disappeared.'

We were at the bathhouse now, which was nothing more than a large room full of tubs, set about five feet apart from each other, in rows. Docey wove her way through naked girls, handing out towels.

'Nobody looks,' Sissy whispered as we walked in, fiddling with a delicate diamond horseshoe that hung from her neck. Which wasn't true – I looked. Everybody looked. Bath hour was an exercise in avoiding being caught looking. Mary Abbott was the scrawniest of us, looked like you could blow her over, light as a feather. I was thin, but my limbs were defined from riding. The hot water felt good and I closed my eyes and submerged my head. I scrubbed my scalp, the greasy spot at my crown. The room was steamy with all the hot water, perfumed by the various soaps and lotions.

We were silent while we bathed, as if pretending we were alone.

Then Docey stood over me with a towel and it was over.

'Thank you.' But she had already moved on to another girl. I noted that no one else thanked her. I tried to modestly slide into my nightclothes, which proved impossible. I spotted a girl with white-blond hair in a tub near the corner, and the way her face was perched just above the water sent a chill down my spine.

Docey was attending to Mary Abbott. Gates and Victoria were shielding each other with their towels while they dressed, but you could see perfectly the shapes of their bodies. This was bizarre, I felt very keenly. The strangest thing so far in the strangest week of my life. I knew we were safe, but it seemed foolish to put us all together like this, all in one place, naked.

Victoria hurried past us on the way back to our cabins, and Sissy studied her retreating figure. Victoria had very close-set eyes, and a long, narrow face; improbably, she was pretty.

'Victoria,' Sissy said.

'She looks like a very pretty, very thin monkey.'

Sissy burst out laughing, had to stop and lean against a tree because she was laughing so hard. The only other person I could make laugh this hard was Sam. I stood nervously; what would I say when she was done laughing? We still had several minutes to fill.

'She does!' Sissy exclaimed, finally.

'You can't ever take a bath when you feel like it, can you?' I asked Sissy, after a moment had passed.

She shook her head as we walked. 'I guess you could sneak in. Like a bath bandit.' She grinned, her blue eyes crinkling, and I couldn't help but grin back. She was so lighthearted.

'Hold still,' she said, and darted behind me. I felt my hair lifted from my neck.

'What—' I started, surprised, but Sissy only wrung the water out of it, for the second time that night.

'There,' she murmured, still behind me, her hands in my hair. 'Why did you come so late, Thea?'

She dabbed water from my neck with her towel. My mother had barely hugged me when I left. It had pained Sam to look at me. This was the first time in weeks someone had touched me and not been angry, and I was surprised at how vulnerable and loved it made me feel. I wanted to offer Sissy something.

'I was sent away.' As soon as I spoke I regretted it. What had I been thinking? That this girl would offer solace, this girl who knew nothing about me.

Sissy dropped my hair, which she had twisted into a rope, onto my neck. I thought I could feel her deciding.

'Oh,' she said finally. 'Well, I was too, in a way. Sent away to learn how to be a lady.' She deepened her voice, turned everything into a joke. And I was so grateful. Sissy's cheeks were red from the steam, and her hair hung damply. She did not seem like the girl from her desk, with all that jewelry and perfume. Sissy was friends with nearly everyone here, there was always a girl waving to her, sidling up next to her to impart some bit of news. I wondered why she had chosen me, and hoped it was something besides my novelty. It seemed like it was.

'I left a girl, but returned a lady,' Sissy intoned, in the same voice, and on and on back to the cabin, where I begged her to stop I was laughing so hard. I felt a little bit like I was walking on air – to think that I had been nervous about filling the time as we walked back to the cabin. There was nothing to be nervous about around Sissy.

We entered Augusta House a pair. Our beds were already turned back by Docey, like we were at a hotel. Eva smiled at us, unconcerned, but Mary Abbott didn't like the look of us together,

I could tell. We prepared for bed: Sissy patted cream onto her cheeks, Victoria brushed her hair. Eva's leg dangled over her bunk, next to my face. Her toenails were painted. She was reading the book from Sissy's desk.

Gates was hard at work at her desk, practicing her handwriting, which was terrible, loopy and vague. Miss Lee, our matronly elocution and etiquette teacher, had shaken her head in dismay over Gates's work today. Gates paused, and shook her hand dramatically. 'It aches!' she cried. Her dirty-blond hair was cut into a bob, and two barrettes, adorned with tiny pearls, were clipped above each ear. She seemed like a girl who would not want hair in her face.

'Wait until classes begin,' Sissy said, 'then it'll really hurt.'

Gates grimaced, and everyone laughed, even Mary Abbott.

'What other classes will they have?' I asked. 'The schoolgirls,' I added, when Sissy looked at me blankly. Our mornings were devoted to classes: elocution, then etiquette, then French, then instrument (piano for me). Then lunch, then rest hour, then riding, then 'leisure' pursuits: bird-watching, botany, painting. Then free time until dinner, which we usually spent in the Hall in the Castle, short for Study Hall, though no one seemed to study there. I was bad at bird-watching: all I ever spotted were hawks and hummingbirds, which were a dime a dozen.

'The schoolgirls?' Sissy asked.

Gates put her book down, carefully, making sure to mark her place with a silver bookmark. I knew from my snooping that it was monogrammed. 'Some of the girls leave,' she began, carefully, 'but most of us stay.' Her voice was high, excited. She watched me solemnly. I felt my neck warm, the telltale sign of a blush.

'I know,' I said.

'It's just,' Sissy said, 'we're all schoolgirls. This is a year-round cabin.' She looked at me carefully for a moment, and I smiled.

She didn't understand that I was not a schoolgirl, that I was only in a year-round cabin because there had been no place else to put me.

Gates returned to her handwriting, pressing so deeply into the paper as she wrote that it tore; she cried out again in exasperation. Sissy lay back onto her pillows and picked up her needlework, a pretty embroidery of a mountain stream. I watched her patiently color in the stream, stitch by blue stitch. This place was so odd. Yesterday a dozen of us had sat outside behind easels, facing the mountains, and been directed to paint them. Henny walked behind us, murmuring approvingly at some paintings, clucking sadly at others. I had received a cluck, of course; I wasn't good at spotting birds, or stitching straight lines, or painting a leaf that looked like a leaf, pursuits I couldn't ever imagine pursuing once I left this place.

It was called the Yonahlossee Riding Camp for Girls, but it was neither a camp nor a place for girls. We were supposed to be made ladies here. I thought about where that left me. I still thought of myself as a girl, but I was not like my cabinmates. I would never be a girl like that again.

And had I ever been like them? At home I had been a girl of boys and men. There had been no one prettier, or richer, or in any way better than I was. I did wonder, of course, if such a person existed, and knew that she must, but then the thought had dropped from my head. My place in my family was so well defined I'd had no need to wonder about what could be for too long.

My mother was our standard of beauty. I knew nothing about curling my hair because Mother still wore hers up. And she had never painted her nails; the thought made me smile. I had always thought of her as timeless, like women I saw in the prints of paintings Father showed us during our lessons. But now I could see she was old-fashioned, of a different world. No less beautiful, but perhaps less becoming.

Henny bustled in and switched off all the lights, told us goodnight.

Gates lit a candle, to read. I touched the handkerchief beneath my pillow.

CHAPTER THREE

A letter from Father arrived on my seventh day at Yonahlossee. The postmark was from Atlanta. I pressed his letter to my lips. His script was slanted and flowery, like a woman's. I had never in my life received a letter. A postcard once or twice from Georgie, when he was in Missouri visiting his mother's family. But anyone could see a postcard – it was read first by Mother before she handed it to me. No one in the world knew what was inside the letter except for my father, and now me.

Dear Thea,

I was so very sorry to drive away from the camp. Although I must say that it is a beautiful place to spend some time. Before your mother knew me, she loved to be around other people; her coming out lasted nearly a year. I see so much of her in you.

We all love you very much. Take care of yourself at the camp. Think of it as an opportunity to learn more, from different (perhaps better) teachers. It bears repeating that your family is your tribe; this is but an interruption in our lives. We kept you too secluded at home. We should have sent you away sooner. You will learn how to behave around other children there, Thea. I hope that is not too much to ask. We know what's best for you, though at this moment

*you may believe, very fervently, otherwise. That is the way of parents
and their children.*

    Love,

    Father

He had called it a camp, not a school – I was here until the end of
summer, no longer. I placed the letter back into its envelope and
slid it under my pillow, next to Sam's handkerchief. I was not a
child. And it *was* a punishment, to be sent here, even though he
and Mother had said it was not; he had as good as admitted it in
his letter. Anyway, he was just parroting what Mother had said.
She was the one who had always decided what to do with us.

But mostly, I missed Father. I could hear his voice, softly
reading the words. Miss Lee would have told him to speak up.

My cabinmates were whispering about an announcement Mr
Holmes had made at lunch; Sissy told me I was lucky, here one
week and already a dance to attend. Most of the girls waited
months and months for a dance, the bright spot of a boy turning
the winter months bearable.

I closed my eyes, even though no girl used rest hour to nap.
But I was exhausted: I'd stayed up last night memorizing a Robert
Frost poem, 'The Cow in Apple Time,' for elocution. I'd read
Frost before, at home, but Miss Lee was only interested in how
we pronounced each word, how we measured our voices, not in
what the poem might have meant.

Though Yonahlossee was an odd place to me, it was quickly
turning familiar. Not missing home had at first seemed
inconceivable, but I understood how the human heart operated,
that it was fickle, capricious.

I was born in the house my parents sent me away from, built by
my father as a gift for his new bride. My mother's family was

New Florida, as those families were called, those that went there after the War Between the States when Georgia was no longer a tenable place to live. My great-grandfather, Theodore Fisk – for whom I'm named – decided on Florida because it was close, and he had heard the land there, worthless, was for the taking.

He and his wife were crackers first; wealthy landowners later. When the railroad was built – Henry Flagler was said to have been entertained and wooed in the Fisk family home – my family's fortune multiplied exponentially. Mrs Fisk served Mr Flagler a piece of key lime pie, a delicacy the Northern man had never tasted. Citrus was from then on shipped by railroad, and an industry was born.

My father's family was Old Florida, of Spanish descent. They weren't as wealthy as my mother's side: they'd herded cattle on land that no one owned until Florida began to sell this land, and then it became impossible to drive the cattle south, through newly erected fences and homesteads, toward the coast, where they would be shipped to Cuba.

Florida was a different place then. My father and his older brother, George, would require a new way of life. My father, Felix, went to Atlanta Medical School on scholarship; George, to law school in Illinois, but they both came back – each with a new wife. My mother, Elizabeth, was in her second year at Agnes Scott College and was expected to find a husband in Georgia when she met my father at a semiformal dance. She was twenty years old; he five years older. It was a perfect match.

George and his new wife, Carrie, settled in Gainesville, a stone's throw from Emathla. My father could have practiced medicine anywhere, but he wanted to help people, so he went to a place where he was the only doctor for miles and miles. This was how it was always explained to me and Sam, anyway: we could have lived anywhere, but lived here because of my father's goodness. And at first Mother, accustomed to the bustle of Miami, thought she would be lonely in such a rural place. But the magic of our home was that it destroyed loneliness. You could see other people – and Mother did, once every few weeks, tea with a neighbor, a Camellia Society meeting – but other people and places only made you love your home, your people, more.

These were my people: Sam, my mother and father; Uncle George and Aunt Carrie and their son, my cousin, Georgie.

That was our first story, how we had come to be situated in this little piece of heaven carved from the Florida wilderness. Luck, partly, but also love: Mother and Father had become engaged two weeks after meeting. George and Carrie and Georgie were part of this story, of course, not central to it but it is easy now to see how the story would have collapsed without them. We needed them in Gainesville to illuminate our own lives.

The bell rang, signaling the end of rest hour, and I woke with a start.

'Finally!' Gates said. She liked to ride as much as I did. Everyone else was already pulling on their breeches and boots. This was the first time I was going to ride with everyone else, and I was both nervous and excited, a combination I loved. I tugged my boots on with boot hooks, and saw Sissy out of the corner of my eye, watching. She smiled, I smiled back. I was eager to please her.

I tucked my shirt into my breeches. We wore white breeches here; even the suede at the knees was white. Our clothes were laundered by the maids so it didn't matter to us how dirty we got but it seemed silly to dress us exclusively in white.

When I walked outside the cabin into the smell of pine trees and sunshine, I saw Sissy had waited for me.

'A letter?'

'From my mother.' I remembered from my snooping that Eva and Sissy's fathers had not written to them, only their mothers.

'My mother writes me,' Sissy said, 'three times a week. But her letters are so boring. My sister, hardly ever, only when she's made to.'

Other girls flocked around us, all identically dressed. They waved at Sissy, and because I was with her, at me. I smiled back. I'd never smiled at so many people in my life.

'I hate writing letters,' I said, 'it takes so long to write what you could say in half the time.' There were butterflies in my stomach; I was glad Sissy provided a distraction.

Another girl walked by, so close she grazed my arm. I started to say something, then stopped. She was the girl with the white hair I'd seen bathing in the bathhouse. And, I realized with the small, pleasurable shock of recognition, the girl from the horse photograph, from the Castle. I knew even before Sissy said her name.

'That's Leona.'

We both watched Leona disappear around a bend. We had passed the privies, now we were almost at the stables. Leona was a giant, her strides covered twice the ground of my own. Her white-blond hair was pinned into a tidy bun. Her boots were navy blue, the only girl among us who didn't have black boots.

'She's from Fort Worth,' Sissy said. She said *Fort Worth* as if she were saying some other, more improbable place – Constantinople, Port-au-Prince. She was whispering now, even though Leona had disappeared. 'Her father is an oil speculator who made it big, her mother is royalty. She has her own horse, shipped by train. She's trained by masters. The shipping costs were more than her room and board.' Leona had not said hello to Sissy. I wondered if Sissy meant that Leona's mother was truly royalty, and decided she must not. I didn't know very much about the world, but I didn't think there were any princesses in Texas. 'She ignores everyone, mostly.'

Leona from Fort Worth, Thea from Emathla. Out of all the places in this world, I was at the Yonahlossee Riding Camp for Girls. It was half past one in the afternoon. I was one among dozens of girls on our way to our daily riding lesson. Sissy had threaded her arm through mine; her skin was soft, she smelled faintly of rosewater. At home, Mother would be out in the garden, a towel around her neck to soak the sweat, a worn, floppy hat on her head to protect her fair skin. My father would be working. Thursday was one of his traveling days, so he would be at someone's house, giving an injection, listening to an account of pain. And Sam.

He would be feeding his squirrels. They had to be fed often, more often than a human baby – which was what Mother always said, that Sam tended to his animals more faithfully than most human parents. And he was faithful, my brother, faithful and good. It was not the first time Sam had raised a litter of squirrels – raccoons got their mothers all the time. Their nests were always hidden in nooks that only Sam was patient enough to find.

When I had said goodbye, after everything had happened, he was out back on the porch, holding one of them.

'It has hair now,' I said, because I did not know what else to say. It was early in the morning, but still hot. It was less ugly than it had been a week ago. It looked so vulnerable; I could see why Sam loved it.

He wore his clothes from yesterday. His hair was wild, stuck out in all directions from his head. It scared me a bit. I wanted to smooth it down, but knew not to touch him. The rims of his eyes were pink. In that moment, his hazel eyes were so dark they almost looked brown. I knew in full sunlight they would look light again, translucent. Our eyes were different. Mine were plain brown, like Father's.

'Did you sleep?' I asked, though I knew the answer. I had not slept either; in fact, I had gone into Sam's room, hoping to find him. Instead, in the dim room, I could faintly see the outlines of his made bed, which looked so perfect and untouched I started to cry, though I could not say why. The sight of his perfect bed, made first by Sam, then straightened later by Mother, disturbed me. His electric fan was trained at the space where he would have slept, and it droned on and on, cooling nothing.

I switched it off and went to his window, which provided a view of our backyard. But to call it a backyard was false; it was the beginning of our thousand acres. There was no fence, no border. Mother's gardens ran into the orange grove. These oranges weren't for sale, but for my mother, who loved them, said she could not live without them.

Sam sat in the grass, next to Mother's rose garden, which was blooming. I could not smell it from here, but he could. I watched him for a long time; he didn't move, sat still as a statue. He had always been able to sit still for longer than I; I was fidgety, restless.

I could not see his face. Only his narrow back, his skinny arms. His voice was beginning to change. I knew what happened to boys' voices; Georgie was two years older and his had changed a few years ago. I could hear Sam's voice right now, a child's voice, so pretty and light. I wished I could make a recording of it before it was gone.

If Sam had turned to face me, I would have seen his bruised eye, the small cut above it. Minor injuries, healing quickly. Father called them superficial. This was the first time I could remember seeing Sam hurt. I tried very hard to remember another time but could not. I had broken my arm, twice, and bruised myself more times than I could count. That was what happened, when you rode horses. But Sam did not court danger. It was not his way.

He turned his head as if he had heard something, and he probably had: the rustle of an animal in the bushes. I saw his profile in the moonlight. We both had Father's nose, which was strong but handsome. I thought for a second that he could feel me watching him. I put my hand to the window.

'Sam,' I murmured.

He peered down at something, and I knew he held one of the infant squirrels; how unmoored he was, how badly I must have hurt him, was confirmed. Because how many times had he told me not to touch a baby wild animal, that if I did, it would become accustomed to human scent and, once released into the wild, be unafraid of humans. And wild animals needed to be afraid of us, to survive.

'Thea?' Sissy asked. 'Have I lost you?'

I looked sideways at her. She did not know the dark recesses of my heart. I knew Sam thought of me as often as I thought of him; that when he was not asleep I was on his mind. On it, threatening to displace everything else like a weight dropped in water. But he could not imagine my life here, which might be a curse or a blessing. I did not know.

Soon we arrived at the barn and parted ways. I took a deep breath: the smell in a barn was always the same, hay tinged with manure. It was a smell you either liked or did not. A groom – the handsome one Eva had mentioned my first night here – showed me to my horse: Naari, a flea-bitten gray mare with a pink muzzle.

'Thank you,' I said to the groom, 'I'll tack her up.'

I clicked my tongue and Naari looked up from her hay. There were hundreds of brown dots scattered across her white coat, hence the term, which I'd always thought was an ugly way to describe such a beautiful pattern. I was excited, though I tried not to be. I did not want to get too attached to Naari, because I would have to leave her here when I left.

After I had tacked her up, I stood in a single-file line with the other girls in my group, the horses so close Naari's muzzle almost touched the reddish tail of the chestnut in front of her. Leona stood at the front of the line, the de facto leader of my group. Her gelding was huge, like his owner. He was beautiful, a big bay with white stockings and a white blaze down his face. I also recognized him from the picture.

Sissy was in the intermediate class; I could see her in the next ring on a skinny Appaloosa, her brown bob flying in her face as she posted. I was in the advanced class, with twenty or so other girls, among them Gates, Leona, and a girl named Jettie, who sat at my dining table. The advanced class was the smallest class, and the privilege of being in it was enormous: you did not have to share your horse. All the other horses were shared except for ours.

Sissy was the weakest rider of her group. I realized it would be easier to be friends with her because I was better, much better, on a horse.

I watched Mr Albrecht shout out instructions in his quiet, firm way. I liked him. Mother had taught me less and less about riding as the years passed, and though she occasionally offered advice now, I mainly schooled myself. Mr Albrecht was a jumping master trained in Germany, he had won an individual bronze medal in the 1920 Belgium Olympics, and a team silver. He had already helped me with my seat, taught me a new way of sinking into the saddle that I found most effective. The Yonahlossee horses were all purebred; our courses designed by a jumping consultant, a friend of Mr Albrecht's from Germany; the barns were almost nicer, at least as nice, as our cabins, their corridors lined with bricks, the stalls with two windows each for ventilation and thick, sturdy shutters for the winter. Despite Mrs Holmes's best intentions, the rest of our education was secondary to horses, as I'd learned my first day when I'd skipped morning classes for my riding evaluation.

At home, Father tutored us from seven in the morning until ten, when he left to see his patients. Idella, our maid, served us breakfast while he explained ideas from books to us. The girls in my cabin thought it odd that I had never been to a real school before, but they didn't know: we were lucky to be tutored by Father, who was brilliant, who was certainly smarter than the Emathla schoolteacher. I rode all afternoon, and Sam played tennis against the garage wall, and tended to his terrariums, his rescued animals.

'Advanced!' Mr Albrecht called. 'Come!' He clapped his hands.

Leona mounted, and for an instant she and her horse looked like a centaur: part horse, part girl. Then the rest of us swung up into our saddles. Gates cut a pretty figure on a horse, slim and elegant and ramrod-straight. Jettie, short and stocky, looked powerful in the saddle.

We stood on our horses for a moment while the first group filed past us, their horses' chests flecked with white spit. It was summer, in the early afternoon. In Emathla you stayed inside during this part of the day, when the sun was high. It would have been dangerous to ride right now; you might kill your horse. During the summer I rose before anyone else and rode at dawn, before our lessons, and even then I had to carry an old handkerchief to wipe Sasi's sweat from the reins. Sam and I would go out anyway, sometimes, in the afternoons, and then we were giddy from the heat and danger of it – Mother would be furious if she knew – our brains boiled in our heads, the sun was so powerful it felt like we were lit from the inside. We would climb oak trees, me coaxing Sam higher and higher, and then lie in the embrace of a branch for hours, watching for some sign of life below – only the reptiles, impervious to the heat, presented themselves: thick black snakes, harmless, and bright green, darting lizards.

I bet it never got that hot here. These girls – they wouldn't know how to survive in such heat. Then Leona's enormous horse – he must have been over eighteen hands – began to walk, and Naari moved beneath me. We circled the ring in a single file, and then, one by one, as if orchestrated, the horses broke off and carved out their own space; I headed toward the far end of the ring, closest to the mountains. I was a Florida girl, used to hazy skies and flatness; the mountains were like clouds to me, so large and expressive they seemed like something you could reach for.

Naari was twitchy and quick; I knew immediately I would like her. She was too smart, I could already tell that by the way she tested me, twisting her barrel so she could carry her weight unevenly, tugging on the left side to see if I would notice. I did notice, I corrected her sharply, tugged back on the left rein, squeezed my calves against her side so she'd speed up and straighten out. She was intelligent but fearful, two traits that always seemed to accompany each other in horses. A squirrel climbed up onto a post and Naari skittered sideways.

I thought about the future weeks, when we would know and understand each other, and I was nearly lifted out of the saddle in anticipation. Sometimes anticipation affected me in this way, as if I could feel it coursing through my veins. I suppose it was a girlish habit.

I watched Leona lead King in a figure eight. He kept dropping his shoulder on the diagonal, and she corrected him. She stared straight ahead, which was where, Mother was always reminding me, you were supposed to look – look where you want to go, and Sasi will follow you there. Looking at my hands was a habit I couldn't quite break; neither could I pretend a broom was hooked through my arms, to keep my back arched and my arms positioned in just the right way. Leona passed through the diagonal again, and this time King trotted through smoothly. Leona turned him, abruptly, and met my gaze briefly and I squeezed Naari into a trot, embarrassed that I had been caught watching.

We filed out of the ring when our riding time was over, Leona still led, but that was fine. She was more technically expert than I, had been schooled by masters, but she wasn't better. I wasn't as physically strong a rider as Jettie, or as pretty as Gates, but I had a way with horses; I could get them to do anything I wanted. I felt strangely powerful: I was a girl of fifteen, locked away in the mountains, surrounded by strangers. But I would be all right; I would emerge from this place.

I fiddled with my books as Mr Holmes led morning prayer. I could feel Henny watching me from the corner of my eye. Sometimes I looked up and studied the ceiling when we were supposed to be praying. I had never seen anything like it before, tin stamped with an intricate pattern of flowers. Rhododendron, Sissy had told me, and later pointed out a cluster of bushes with a pretty pink flower that lined the path to the barn. I wondered, as I often did, who had done it, and if the work had taken hours or days, days or months, and let Mr Holmes's voice recede into the background. As far as I could tell, he asked for the same things every morning: health, happiness, and prosperity. I couldn't get used to all this sitting still; first at breakfast, then here, then all through classes. By the time lunch hour came, I felt like a caged animal.

And though I still missed my home, terribly, I was getting used to this new order of things. I was learning. I knew, for example, that though Yonahlossee had first seemed enormous, it was not even as large as our farm, only three hundred acres, and most of it was mountain land, uninhabitable.

Mr Holmes shuffled a stack of papers on his lectern. We all paid attention, for the most part. Mrs Holmes had caught my eye a few times when she noticed my attention wandering. She sat beside her husband, along with their three girls. When I wasn't watching the ceiling I was watching the Holmes girls, who fascinated me. Just now Sarabeth put her hand over Decca's, to stop her fidgeting. Sarabeth was the oldest, at eleven, and reminded me of her mother. Rachel was next, ten, and she was moody, a storm always passing over her face, or threatening to pass over, while her father spoke. I was jealous of them. The distinction between the Holmes girls and everyone else was very clear: they were not alone.

Decca was tall and dark like her father, and even at seven you could tell that she would continue to be tall and dark, would grow, it seemed almost certain, to be beautiful. It was unfair that nature had been so precise: each child born prettier, Sarabeth the first attempt, Decca perfect.

Decca caught my eye, and I looked away, but not before I saw her smile. I wondered what she thought of me. Did she think I was pretty? Did the other girls? I wasn't sure where I landed on this list. My mother was beautiful, this I knew, both because I could see for myself and also because it was a fact in our family. She had even modeled for a milliner, briefly, before she met Father. I looked like her, but I had always known I was not beautiful. I had my mother's hair, which was auburn and wavy, wild. I'd once seen a picture of Amelia Earhart in a magazine; the caption had called her handsome. I thought that's what I was. Handsome.

'And there's something more,' he said, and paused. He looked up, out into our midst. He stood in front of the window, which afforded the most perfect view of the mountains in the whole camp. When he looked out at us like this, it was as if the room disappeared, as if we were all on top of a mountain. Alice Hunt straightened beside me. We all felt it. 'Something very serious.' Heads snapped up. 'You all know Herbert Hoover?' A titter spread through the room. 'Oh, of course not personally.' He smiled, and I found myself smiling back. 'Though I dare say some of you *might* have met him.' Out of the corner of my eye I studied Leona, who sat next to Sissy. Maybe Leona was one of the girls who might have met the president? 'Our president has lately spoken of his belief that our country will recover from this financial crisis.' He held up a newspaper, though we were all too far away to see it. A girl in front of me yawned. 'This is a little old, of course,' he paused, as if anticipating our laughter, which of course followed. All of the magazines and newspapers were, at the very least, 'a little old.' More often they were months and months old, sent to us by our mothers and sisters.

'Here our president declares the Depression over.' He tapped the paper, lightly, with his fingertip. 'He asks for our continued effort in supporting the economy.'

Gates, who sat a row ahead, raised her hand.

'Yes, Gates?' Mr Holmes said. He folded the paper neatly while Gates spoke.

'How can we help?' she asked. I thought that she was perhaps being impertinent, but Mr Holmes didn't seem to think so.

'A good question,' he said, 'and one best answered by your fathers. To put it bluntly, money begets money.' Even Mrs Holmes smiled a little bit, behind her husband. 'Encourage your fathers to invest, to spend, to trust the banks.'

At first I didn't understand what had triggered the merry laughter that followed Mr Holmes's answer. Sissy was giggling next to me, and as I watched her pretty fingers cover her mouth I understood completely: there was nothing we could do to help. We were but daughters. The idea that we would offer our fathers financial counsel was, indeed, laughable. I smiled, too, but not because I was amused; I smiled so that I was indistinguishable from the other girls.

'Let us pray that by the time you leave Yonahlossee, you will reenter a world that will be happier,' Mr Holmes said, and stepped back so that his wife could step forward.

I hadn't heard the name Hoover since I'd left home. I thought of Uncle George, who had returned from Miami the last time and said he would not go back, that it was useless, that the bank could take it all. How President Hoover was handling the crisis was a point of contention between my father and his brother: my father thought he was handling things fine. Uncle George thought more needed to be done, and soon.

Everyone here seemed so rich and Southern, impervious to the slings and arrows of the world. And there was me, who had learned to ride from Mother, on a pony without papers. My middle name was not an important family name, my family did not have five homes stateside, or spend Christmas in Venice. We were fine, because of the citrus money, but my father was a physician, not a cotton magnate or an oil king.

Yonahlossee was where important Southern men sent their daughters. I would later learn more: an Astor, via marriage to the Langhornes of Virginia, had graduated the year before I arrived. One of the girls counted Robert E. Lee as a relative. Her family owned rubber plants in Malaysia. There were other girls' schools, but Yonahlossee was the oldest, and it must have provided a certain comfort to these men, locked away as it was in the mountains; nobody could reach their daughters here. Nobody could touch them. After World War II, these same men would begin to send their daughters to Northern schools, where they would become worldly. But in this moment, worldly wasn't what anyone was after. The South was still a land unto itself, in some ways it was a land that time had forgotten. There were girls here who refused to believe, or at least admit, that the North had claimed victory in the War Between the States.

'Thank you, Mr Holmes,' Mrs Holmes began. There was still tittering, somewhere from the back, and Mrs Holmes abruptly stopped speaking. 'Girls!' The tittering disappeared.

'On that same note, but perhaps more specifically' – here she smiled, almost imperceptibly – 'allow me to bring your attention to a way you might do more than simply keep those less fortunate than you in your prayers.' Her elocution was perfect. Miss Lee would have approved. 'In the spirit of Christian charity, please consider making a pledge for a contribution to a Fund for the Mill Girls, who live a few hours' drive from us and enjoy none of our benefits.'

Jettie and Henny stood and walked to the front of the room carrying a papered box with FUND FOR MILL GIRLS carefully lettered on its front in red. Jettie placed a stack of small papers next to it, along with a cup of pencils, and girls started to rise and scribble figures on the papers, then folding them and dropping them into the box. It resembled the kind of box Mother had brought home from the Red Cross, for which she had volunteered when we were very small.

'Thank you in advance for your generosity,' Mrs Holmes said. I didn't have any money, not a single cent. I'd never had any money, or at least any that I could touch. 'All right girls,' Mrs Holmes said. This is what she always said when she finished. It was a place maintained by routine. Mrs Holmes was nice enough, I supposed. But not too nice, which was how you had to act if anyone was going to listen to you. That's how I was when I rode.

Henny stood. We were going to class – I had elocution then

etiquette, one right after the other. They were so boring I could
have cried. My parents had never seemed interested in a daughter
who had perfect handwriting, or could spot the difference
between an olive fork and a lemon fork (an olive fork had two
tines; a lemon fork, three), but I wondered if Mother knew or any
longer cared exactly what kind of education I was getting.
Someone pinched my arm.

'Ow,' I cried. It was Eva.

'Sorry.' But she was giggling. 'You just always look so lost in
your own world. I ate so much! I love hash brown day.' She
smoothed her hands over her waist.

I smiled. 'I stuff myself like a roasted pig at every meal.' And it
was true. I did. My appetite had reappeared after the first few
days.

'Eva,' I said, as we climbed the stairs to our classroom, 'I didn't
bring any money with me.'

It felt like a dirty word, *money*, but Eva didn't seem bothered.
I'd never met someone so unconcerned.

'Oh that,' she said, 'you just ask your father.'

I nodded, and knew I would never request money from my
father. It would mean that I cared about this place.

'My father,' Eva continued, 'says he gives enough with tuition.
And Mrs Holmes comes knocking every winter, in person, for
donations to the school. My father says she's very persuasive.' She
smiled, and I noticed she had dusted her face with powder, her
cheeks with rouge, but very subtly. 'She'll probably visit your
parents, too. But maybe not, since you're from Florida.' She
paused, and bit her lip. 'I didn't mean—'

'No,' I said, 'it's fine.' We had reached our classroom; I could
see Miss Lee's broad back from behind, writing in cursive on the
board. 'I know Florida's . . .' I trailed off, and Eva looked at me
expectantly. 'A strange place,' I finished. 'Not for everyone.'

CHAPTER FOUR

The day of the dance another letter arrived, this one from Mother. It was long, over two pages of my mother's rose-scented stationery, her initials engraved at the top of the thick, cream-colored paper. EAC, the E and C flanking the ornately drawn A. Elizabeth Collins Atwell.

My mother had surprising handwriting, inconsistent and loopy. *Dear Thea*, the letter began, and went on about the vegetable and herb garden and the swarms of bees and butterflies it attracted, before concluding:

> *Sam is fine, as fine as can be expected. No one knows quite what to expect, though. It's all undecided, will stay that way for a while I predict. Sometimes I'm so angry with you. Other times I'm so sorry for you. Such a terrible thing. May God grant them and us peace.*
>
> *Everyone here misses you. Do the mountains make you feel small, Thea?*

I glanced around the room and saw that Mary Abbott was staring at me. I stared back. Her eyes unnerved me, pale, almost colorless. Mary Abbott relented, shrugged her small shoulders, and mouthed *Sorry* across the room, though of course she wasn't.

I lay back onto my thin pillow (my pillows at home were

plump and perfect, I wished I'd brought one with me) and ran my fingertips along the smooth wooden planks of our floor, marked by an infinite number of scratches. Girls wearing riding boots inside, Docey pulling the beds out to make them, dropped books. At home, no one was allowed to wear shoes in the house, only visitors, and if anything fell and my mother heard there would be a price to pay.

Sissy spun around the room, humming a waltz. When she was next to our bunk, Eva climbed down and bowed, held out her hand. Sissy accepted it, and they began to dance, Eva playing the boy's part. They both wore white skirts. Eva was taller, and more solid; her hair alone seemed to outweigh Sissy. They looked like mother and daughter dancing. Even I knew that waltzing was old news, but there was no jazz at Yonahlossee. Because it was hypnotizing, Mary Abbott had explained.

Both Sissy and Eva came from families that entertained regularly. Eva from a North Carolina cotton empire and Sissy from Monroeville, which she referred to as the center of the earth, where her father did something vague in her mother's family business, and was also the mayor. All her jewelry was from her mother's side; I assumed most of the money was from her, too.

Only Mary Abbott and I were unexcited about this evening, when boys from a boarding school in Asheville would arrive at eight o'clock, and we would all be expected to dance the evening away. I pretended to be excited, at least; Mary Abbott didn't know how to pretend.

'Another one,' Mary Abbott said when Eva had bowed and Sissy had curtsied, the waltz over. We were all startled by Mary Abbott's voice. We respected rules at Yonahlossee, and though it was likely no house mistress would pass by during rest hour, we knew they could.

Mary Abbott rose and clapped her hands like a child who wanted her way. Her squinty eyes were bright. Eva told me her father was a Methodist preacher, that her mother had died when she was an infant.

'Shh,' Victoria whispered, a finger on her lips.

Eva put a hand on her hip and studied Mary Abbott, amused.

'You'll see plenty of dancing tonight,' Sissy whispered, 'I wouldn't worry.'

Mary Abbott lay back on her bed and folded her arms. I wondered what she thought she was missing now that Eva and Sissy had stopped dancing. When I saw my friends twirling around the room, I saw two innocents.

Mother's favorite story – more beloved than the story of how she and Father met – was the story of our births, transformed into a kind of fairy tale by her, the mother who carried twins and did not know it. My brother and I were born during an early winter storm: it snowed, birds dropped from the sky, dead from the unexpected freeze, all the plants in my mother's garden shriveled and turned from green to deep russet. My parents were expecting a large boy, because my mother carried so low. So I was the surprise, not Sam. I was the child no one expected.

There was no history of twins in our family. When we were born, our family was cautious, especially of me. I had either sapped Sam's strength and was the stronger twin, or Sam had enfeebled me. I was either a selfish or useless girl. My father tried to dispel these notions, said there was no evidence. But even he was worried, a boy and a girl born together, contrary to the order of things.

We were cranky babies, both colicky. My mother lay in bed for weeks, my father tended to her and then to his other patients, who were always my father's responsibility, always, the only doctor in Emathla. A woman from town took care of the new babies, Theodora and Samuel, us. My mother had only just begun painting scenes from Grimms' fairy tales when we arrived: a swath of Rapunzel's hair circled the wall of our nursery, only partly painted gold. The mural had been painted over years ago, but I still remembered it so clearly. I had loved it.

I spoke first, at nine months; Sam waited another five, though he spoke to me earlier, in the dark, in the soft light of morning, when the rest of the house was asleep. My first word was '*orange*,' which I mangled, but my parents knew what I meant. My mother liked to attribute it to my inherited knowledge of citrus. Sam and I cut teeth late, we were both bald until age two, we hated nap time, we loved bread and orange marmalade.

But there was still the gloom of our early days: the surprise of us, then my mother's convalescence. There was always the possibility of death with childbirth, an unavoidable risk, so even before my mother went into labor there was concern she might not handle it well. The winter storm, snow on the ground for the first time in a decade, my mother in bed from the contractions. It must *mean* something, their babies born on *this* day, not any of the other, snowless days.

First me, a girl!, my father said, so my mother would know. Everyone would have preferred a boy for the first child, that went without saying, a person to inherit it all; then, as my father toweled me off and clipped my umbilical cord even closer, so it would not be agitated by clothes, another head crowned and was born quickly, much more quickly than I was, and a boy! My father did not shout this time, ashamed, confused: he'd wanted a boy and gotten a girl but now a boy? Something was wrong; the gods didn't grant wishes like that, without expecting something given in return, in gratitude.

My mother was in too much pain to hold us properly, so the woman from town cleaned us, smoothed our patchy hair, twisted bits of cotton and coaxed the mucus from our noses and mouths, the afterbirth from our ears. We were tiny. My father held each of us, one after another, to my mother's breast. We ate indifferently while my mother writhed. My mother had decided during her confinement that she would nurse her child. It was the style then to bring in a wet nurse, but who from Emathla would be suitable? Who could nourish her child as well as she could?

Dead birds littered the lawn outside. Later, by moonlight and a lantern, my father would collect them in a wheelbarrow and burn them in the rubbish heap, watch feathers float from the plume of smoke, blue feathers, scarlet, brown, white that did not hide dirt. He would watch and consider. He would feel vaguely hopeful, by the moonlight, his breath its own plume in the air, his babies small and pale but healthy, as far as the human eye could tell.

Mother would tell us that we were loved even before we were born. But that wasn't quite true: one of us was loved, the other unknown.

We would not ever leave. I had known about Miss Petit's, the school where Mother had gone, but I would never be sent there. There was no need. Soon I would go away to a finishing school in Orlando, but only for a few weeks, only long enough to interact with girls my own age, see how they behaved. Mother assured me that I wouldn't have any trouble learning the ropes. This was to prepare me for my coming out, which would happen before I graduated from college. I would go to Agnes Scott, like Mother, and Sam would go to Emory. We were to be educated. Our minds were fine, important – Atwell minds.

Sam would become either a doctor or a lawyer. It didn't matter. Something to do on the side, while he managed our farm.

We made our real money in citrus farther South – crops and land now attended to by Mother's brother on our behalf – and Sam and I would inherit that, too, but right now Mother's brother tended to it.

I would live where my husband did, but somewhere nearby. Gainesville, perhaps. Not everyone was lucky enough to live in such a secluded place; not everyone was lucky enough to make a living in the way Father did, on his own terms. And he was lucky like this because of Mother's money. He was a philanthropist – that's what Mother said. He helped people, and many of those people could not pay.

This was the story of our futures. And it was always a joint future, a combined venture.

But Mother might as well have been speaking Greek when she mentioned these things – that Sam and I would marry, and live apart. We had never been farther south than Orlando, farther north than Gainesville. I had never even seen a college. When I pictured it, I saw my own house, peppered with people. That's how I conceived of Yonahlossee, too, before I entered its world: my own beloved home, threaded with strings of girls. Of course I knew this would not be true. Of course. But I knew in my brain, not in my heart.

And Georgie? He would live somewhere nearby, it was assumed. But his future was not as well-mapped as ours. He was not Mother's child. I would say that Georgie was like a brother except that he was not; I could see him more clearly, because he was separate from me.

People can lie about their childhoods, they can make up any sort of story and you must believe them, unless you were there with them, unless you saw for yourself. It is a burden to know a person so well. Sometimes a gift, but always a burden.

★ ★ ★

It was a relief that my lavender dress, the same one I'd worn to the dinner with my father in the hotel, seemed stylish enough.

I shivered. It was almost eight o'clock in the evening but the sun still shone, a different kind of light from daylight, less severe, bluer. It had rained earlier, and the air tasted damp, the packed-dirt path springy beneath our feet. Swarms of fireflies darted through the throngs of girls. I was still enchanted by them. It was too hot for them in Florida, there we only had mosquitoes and enormous, noisy dragonflies.

I had hesitated to wear my grandmother's mink stole, afraid it might be too good for the occasion, but furs abounded. Alice Hunt brushed by me, a dead fox wrapped around her neck.

I raised my hand in a wave, but she wouldn't meet my eye. She wasn't the kind of girl who gave anyone the time of day. My cheeks burned. It was so hard to remember whom to be friendly to, whom to coolly ignore.

'Alice Hunt,' Sissy called, and Alice Hunt stopped, turned around slowly. Everyone gave Sissy the time of day.

'Sissy,' she said, her gray eyes briefly darting in my direction. 'Thea.'

Then she was on her way again, off to join the rest of the Memphis girls, who all had a soft way about them, spoke barely above a whisper, and almost never looked directly at you. They had a way of looking through you. They were widely recognized as the camp's most snobbish clique.

'The sun never sets on Memphis,' Sissy murmured under her breath, and I giggled, though the first time she'd said this I'd had to puzzle out what she'd meant. She was full of sayings like this: Mrs Holmes was wound tighter than Dick's hatband; Leona's family was in high cotton. More like she's in high oil, I'd said, and then Sissy had laughed.

Girls swarmed around Sissy and me as we walked, dressed in

their colorful silks, fur caplets and shimmering shawls upon their
shoulders, diamond barrettes in their hair. I saw Katherine Hayes,
from Atlanta, who was the biggest gossip at Camp. Her throng of
Atlanta girls surrounded her, all laughing dramatically. It seemed
to me that they were all named Katherine, but only Katherine
Hayes was allowed to use her full name. The rest were called
Kate. Katherine had wildly curly brown hair; she wore a navy
blue sleeveless dress, which was the closest anyone came to black.
I knew from the magazines that it was in vogue for the stars to
wear black. But that was in Hollywood. People in the South
didn't wear black unless someone had died.

Katherine's fingernails were painted red. The Atlanta girls
were big-city, walked around camp with their bobbed hair and
painted fingernails (Mrs Holmes would order their nails scrubbed
whenever she saw them); they were always gesturing and laughing
as if everyone was watching. And generally, everyone was
watching, like now. They *would* scrub their nails, and then give
Mrs Holmes a few days to forget before they all appeared with
freshly coated fingernails, all the same hue, like a band of exotically
clawed birds.

We all wore stockings, and so our legs gleamed. Most girls'
hemlines, including my own, were modest, but if Eva sat a certain
way you caught a glimpse of her knees.

There was so much of the world to see, and most of us had
never held a boy's hand. We wanted to do more than that, anyway,
we wanted boys to hold not just our hands but all of us, gather us
into their sturdy arms and ring our slippery curls around their
thick but tender fingers.

But none of that could happen, not to the good and correct
daughters of wealthy and powerful men, with family names and
family connections and family duties. We would be debs first,
wives second. We would all be married one day, hopefully after

we turned eighteen but before we turned twenty-one, though I doubt any of us tied marriage to passion. We'd seen our parents, our aunts and uncles, our sisters and their husbands. We weren't stupid. We understood that desire was a dangerous thing that needed to be carefully handled, like a mother's antique perfume bottle, passed down to the eldest daughter when she turned sixteen.

Yet I did not have as much to put at risk as other Yonahlossee girls. I saw this now. My family was never in society pages; my mistake could not have ruined any of my father's business deals. I had only risked my family's connections to each other.

'I can see the boys,' Sissy whispered.

I whispered, too. 'They won't bite.' We were almost at the Castle, and the boys stood in a line, their backs facing the windows. They were dressed in light-colored summer suits and bow ties, like they were playing dress-up with their fathers' clothes. I couldn't remember the last time I'd seen Sam or Georgie in a suit, even though my parents had given one to Georgie for his last birthday. They'd said he'd be applying to college soon; this was when that still seemed possible.

Sissy giggled. She was giddy tonight, and I was glad for the distraction, glad not to think of Georgie and the suit he had not yet worn, at least not in my presence.

The staircase to the Castle was narrow, only three girls could fit on it at a time. Mary Abbott, her hair pinned back in a high, old-fashioned bun, joined us on the bottom step. Sissy and I linked arms. I offered my left to Mary Abbott, who clasped my hand instead.

'Your hand is cold,' Mary Abbott said. Her voice was higher than it normally was, her eyes wide.

'Yours is damp.' It felt like a dead, wet thing in mine.

'Will you find a beau tonight, Mary Abbott?' Sissy asked,

teasing. Sissy's dress was pale green. Its square neckline was
embroidered in iridescent silver, which seemed to illuminate
Sissy's long, slender neck. Her hair had been curled that afternoon,
like mine, but unlike mine her hair wouldn't hold curls. Eva had
powdered all our faces, save Mary Abbott's, and Sissy's light
freckles had disappeared. She had painted our lips with gloss, too,
but very subtly, so Mrs Holmes wouldn't notice. Paint was
forbidden, but this was apparently one of Yonahlossee's more
bendable rules, since most of the girls I saw tonight looked a little
brighter than they usually did, their features lit. Surely Mrs
Holmes noticed. She wasn't stupid. You had to pick your battles,
I supposed.

Sissy wore a strand of pearls clasped by a bright ruby, and a
turquoise ring, the stone as big as a nickel, flanked by two round
diamonds. She wore her ruby earrings, too; they matched the
necklace. I'd never seen anyone, not even my mother, wear such
grand jewelry. She was so thin that the ornate jewels seemed to
wear her – her everyday necklace, the diamond-studded horseshoe, suited her better – but still Sissy, if not beautiful, was nearly
incandescent tonight. Her wide-set eyes – any wider, and she
would have looked odd – emphasized her otherworldly quality.
She looked like one of the fairies from *A Midsummer Night's
Dream*.

Sissy had startled Mary Abbott. 'None of us will. We're not
old enough.'

'How old do we have to be?' I asked.

'Old enough to want one,' she said, and dropped my hand,
giving it a final squeeze that was hard enough to make me wince.
Then she sped ahead, hiked her too-long dress up to her calves
and took the stairs two at a time until she was stuck behind
another threesome of girls. I looked at Sissy.

'She's odd.'

'Don't be unkind,' she said, 'it doesn't suit you.'

I was surprised, wanted to ask Sissy what she meant, but we had almost reached the top of the stairs, and we were nervous. The gas lights at the door burned, like they always did, morning and night, though during the day you could hardly see them. Then the door was opened by Mr Holmes, who smiled at us. He was opening the door for each set of girls, then letting it close again, then swinging it open – when really, he should have just propped the door open, like it was when we filed in for our meals and classes.

Though that would have ruined the effect, we would have been able to see in advance.

Our dining hall had been transformed. The Yonahlossee garden must have been robbed of all its flowers. They were everywhere, as far as a girl or boy could see. In vases, arranged by color: clusters of blood red, burnt orange, pale yellow, electric pink, pure white, flecked cream. The smaller, heirloom roses, which bloomed in dense clumps, had been woven into a thick rope that dangled from the ceiling, high enough that we could not reach it, not even our tallest girl. I'd never seen so many flowers out of a garden. My mother always thought it a shame to cut them, and when she did she never arranged her flowers according to a single color, like this. The harsh electric lighting had been switched off, for tonight; instead, huge silver candelabras held candles as thick as my forearm. The candelabras themselves were taller than I was, beautiful in the way that a weapon was beautiful: I would stay away from them, lest one of their otherworldly flames, as big as a fist, catch my dress on fire.

A group of gray-haired men was seated at the opposite end of the dining hall, partially obscured by an Oriental folding screen. Perhaps they weren't supposed to look at us. They sat at attention on their stools, each with an instrument: the band.

The boys stood in their perfect line, stretched from one end of
the dining hall to the other, while the girls messily clumped
opposite them, the random sparkle from a gem when it caught
the light. I wondered if they had flasks hidden in their pockets,
like Eva said they would. I knew from morning announcements
that Mrs Holmes was a vocal prohibitionist: drink was evil and
immoral. Miss Brooks stood near them, as if to stop an errant boy
before he made it to the other side. Miss Brooks led us on our
bird-watching and botany walks in the afternoons and taught
history during the school year, and though she seemed dull she
was nice. I liked her, at least compared to Miss Lee, who watched
everyone like a hawk.

Docey and another maid served us punch out of a giant crystal
bowl. I inclined my head to Docey, who didn't acknowledge me.
A formal serving outfit, like the kind that the maids in hotels
wore, had replaced her normal uniform: a starched black pinafore,
a crisp white blouse underneath.

'Docey's dressed up,' I whispered to Sissy when we both had
our punch.

'Look,' Sissy said, 'no, don't look, they'll see.'

This was the first time I had seen Sissy nervous. And it was the
closest I had ever been to a group of boys. I knew what they
expected of us. I also knew what we were supposed to expect
from them, which was very different – to be led in handfuls of
dances, twirled around the room underneath the watchful eyes
of adults. We wanted a certain handsome boy to take a fancy to us,
to become half of a pair for a night. And then, maybe most of all,
we wanted them to leave, so that we could pine away.

I didn't answer Sissy. I was nervous, too, but for a different
reason. Silly as this sounds, I had never been around a boy I wasn't
related to. Surely Mother and Father hadn't known that there
would be a dance, with a busload of boys in attendance.

Henny and Jettie and another senior, Martha Ladue, entered the dining hall, and something about Henny looked strange, and it was a second before I realized that her mole had been powdered over. Martha was the most beautiful girl at camp. She looked like Louise Brooks, except prettier, calmer.

Sissy nudged me. Leona was at the door, dressed in a dull gray silk, a diamond-and-pearl choker around her throat. Everyone watched her, it was impossible not to, for Leona was the type of girl who commanded a room's attention; she was tall, almost six feet, and her white hair hung down to her waist, which was a style for younger girls. I wondered if it had ever been cut.

Mr Holmes called us to attention at that moment. He stood at the head of the room then, Mrs Holmes stood next to him, a corsage of a striped cream-and-red rose on her wrist. Mr Holmes towered over his wife, as slender as she was plump. She wore the same pearl earrings, the old-fashioned skirt that fell to the floor, that she did every day.

'Let the dance commence,' Mr Holmes said, gesturing to the band, which struck up a song. We fanned out so that a boy could approach us definitively, without us having to wonder if he was really after our cabinmate, our best friend. The boys rushed toward us; I took a step back, impulsively, bumping Leona.

'Pardon me.'

'Pardon accepted,' she said; I forgot to worry about the boys and instead peered up at Leona, who stared ahead, probably hoping that a tall boy would ask her to dance. She was even taller when you were close to her. I looked down and saw that her shoes were flat, and dyed silver to match her dress. The rest of us wore heels when we dressed up. I supposed she was rich enough to have any type of shoe made, in any color she wanted.

'Thea.' I looked up, surprised by the sound of my name. I hadn't thought Leona knew who I was. 'Someone wants you,' Leona said impatiently, and I turned to face a skinny, pale boy.

'May I have the pleasure of this dance?' he asked, and I accepted his arm, realizing as we walked that a slow song was playing, which meant I would have to get close to this boy. His voice was unsteady. I looked back to Leona as I was escorted to the dance floor. She was watching, which satisfied me for some reason.

'Thea, pleased to meet you,' I said, nodding my head since I couldn't curtsy, not while we were walking. I hoped I was remembering all my manners.

'Harry, pleased to meet you,' he said.

Before I knew it we were dancing, caught up in the flock. I recognized the song – 'Carolina Moon' – even absent the words. It was one of Mother's favorite songs, and it seemed foolish, now, that I had just thought the melody was pretty, had never connected it to a place. Here I was, in Carolina, dancing to its slow, sad anthem.

'Where's your home?' I asked.

'Mainly here,' he answered, after a pause. He did not dance particularly well. He led, but barely. And yet he smelled like Sam, and Georgie; I had forgotten the smell of boys, which was so different – sharper, more pungent – than the smell of girls.

'And when you're not here?'

'Louisiana. My family's in the lumber business.' He was eager to please, Harry. His answers were questions – mainly here? Louisiana? The lumber business?

There were boys I would have swooned over here – there was a tall, black-haired boy, in a pale blue jacket, and Sissy had snagged a handsome redhead – but Harry was not one of them. Molly, the first year from my table, twirled by, her knotty hair combed. Even the youngest of us danced. Sissy had told me these dances were progressive; before the Holmeses, each girl was assigned a boy whom she danced with the entire night. He would escort her to the Castle, her white satin dancing shoes carefully tucked under his arm. There had been members of the board – Sissy's grandfather, for one – who had fought hard against the change, who thought that Yonahlossee dances should model themselves on the old, pre-war debutante balls.

When the waltz ended, I curtsied, Harry bowed, and I excused myself to the refreshment table. I accepted another cup of punch from Docey, who met my eyes briefly.

I felt a hand cup my elbow; for an instant I thought it was a boy, and I blushed, but then I turned and saw Sissy.

'Done already?' she asked.

'A little parched.' I lifted my half-empty punch cup. 'You're not dancing?'

'Did you see the boy I was dancing with?' I nodded. 'Boone. I like him.' She lowered her voice. 'I *really* like him.'

I felt a strange pang of jealousy. We stood for a second, lulled into a trance by the music. I studied my punch, which was blue, strangely – almost black. Swollen blackberries bobbed on the surface, which the younger girls had picked yesterday with Mrs Holmes during elocution class. My mother's citrus sherbet punch, an old family recipe, was light pink, tasted cold and sweet and creamy, only slightly tangy.

Sissy broke the silence. 'I saw you talking to Leona.'

'Not really. For a second. She knew my name.'

'I'm surprised. I thought she only knew her horse's name.'

'You don't like her?' I asked.

Sissy shrugged impatiently. 'It doesn't matter, with Leona. Like her or hate her, she doesn't give a whit about anybody but her horse. She's so rich, Thea.' She looked at me. 'She can do anything she wants. She doesn't have to care about anybody.'

In fact, though Sissy claimed Leona and Martha Ladue were
the richest girls here, I knew Sissy was wealthy too. Everyone did.
And her family's fortune wasn't new, like Leona's; it had lost that
ugly sheen. Eva told me the funds to build the new riding rings
had been donated by Sissy's grandfather; Sissy's mother and aunt
were alumna, and Sissy's father and grandfather sat on the camp's
governing board.

Yet pretending your family wasn't wealthy, as Sissy did – this
seemed to be part of the game. Sissy played this game so beautifully, moved so easily and naturally through Yonahlossee, was able
to effortlessly wind her way through its hierarchies. She knew
who was on scholarship (ten girls every year, including our own
Mary Abbott), who was smart (she said I'd earned the reputation
as a smart girl, which both flattered and unnerved me), and who
was related (so many of the girl were cousins). She knew who
might be sent away soon, because of her father's financial problems,
despite Mr Holmes's assurances that the country's situation was
improving (Victoria's position at the camp was growing shakier by
the moment). She knew who mattered, who didn't, though she
was kind to both the former and the latter. The Kentucky girls, for
instance, didn't matter, were hillbillies, though I didn't see why.
Molly looked like all the other first years; take away the Atlanta
girls' stylish hair, remove the Memphis girls' gold lockets,
emblazoned with their initials, and we all looked the same.

Sissy's blue eyes were earnest and perfectly round. A child's
eyes. She had chosen me, out of all these girls. I was so grateful.
When I left here, I would remember her always. Perhaps we
would even visit.

I understood, suddenly, how lonely Mother must have been
in Emathla, with only our aunt to call a friend. And I was angry
that she had not ever allowed me my own, that she had not ever
let anyone else in.

The waltzes continued. I danced with three more boys; one complimented my copper hair – he called it that, copper – and another's hands were so wet and slimy they felt like snakes. After we were finished, I excused myself and resolved not to dance again for the rest of the evening. I retired to the chairs set up for this purpose – I had seen earlier that boys could not, or would not, approach a sitting girl – and chatted with Henny, who cheerfully criticized girls' dresses. I let myself daydream, imagined my father would walk through at any moment – after this dance, before this one – no, now, in the middle of this interminable waltz, he wouldn't care about interrupting us: he would want to get to me too badly. Maybe my brother would come – then all the girls could see how handsome he was – or maybe all three of them, Father, Mother, Sam, and I would forgive them right away, be done with Yonahlossee forever.

Mary Abbott was standing alone by the door, nervously tapping her scuffed black shoe on the floor, as if she couldn't wait to make her escape. I felt sorry for her. It would cost me something, I knew, to cross the room and stand with her. Another test, to see what kind of girl I was. It didn't matter if I crossed the room or not; I had already failed, at home, in a way that could not be forgiven.

I had been feeling hopeful, imagining my family coming to retrieve me, and now I felt miserable, the sight of Mary Abbott, my indecision over whether or not to help her – my daydreams of Father interrupting this dance were just that. A fantasy, concocted in my wrong brain.

I looked at the ground, at my nice shoes, worn only once before, at Easter dinner, where I had sat between Georgie and Sam. When I looked up again I had decided I would cross the room, skirt the dancers, and be a friend to Mary Abbott.

But I didn't have to. Mr Holmes was standing next to her,

gesturing at the dance floor, smiling. Mary Abbott spoke, and
Mr Holmes listened attentively. He was so handsome, with his
shock of dark hair, his thick eyebrows. His nose was crooked,
veered a tiny bit to the left, and I wondered if he'd broken it
playing sports.

Mary Abbott smiled now, and Mr Holmes pointed to a set of
chairs, and offered his arm to Mary Abbott; she took it, and
followed him, and I watched Mr Holmes wait for Mary Abbott
to sit, then take a seat himself, and I realized he was kind, that
he had also noted Mary Abbott's unease, but that he had, unlike
me, responded to it. Offered solace. I wondered what he would
have done in Father's position, if Mr Holmes's niceness
would have shredded beneath the weight of a bad daughter.

His kindness made me homesick. It reminded me that I had
once only known kindness. I watched Mr Holmes murmur
something to Mary Abbott, and I wondered what they were
talking about – I knew firsthand that Mary Abbott was not good
at small talk – and *I* wanted to be Mary Abbott, I wanted to be
murmured to by Mr Holmes.

'Don't you think, Thea?'

I turned to Henny reluctantly. 'Hmm?'

'Don't you think the dress is too much for Sissy? She always
does that, parades around in things too fine. She looks foolish.'
Her voice had hardened.

We all look foolish, I thought. Less like girls at a camp dance
and more like ladies at a ball. I think she looks beautiful, I began
to say, but the words caught in my throat. Henny looked at me
closely, like she was deciding about me, too. I had thought
everyone liked Sissy; no, loved her. What could Henny possibly
have against her? Just then Sissy twirled by, still with the redhead,
as if summoned, and caught my eye and smiled enormously, as if
she were the happiest girl in the world.

'Like a fool,' Henny muttered, and then the handsome black-haired boy appeared in front of me, and I remembered where I was. She was jealous of Sissy. And who wouldn't be?

'Thea?' he asked, and offered his arm. He led me onto the dance floor, and my resolve not to dance vanished. He was very direct in how he held me and guided my body; I felt lucky that he had chosen me, but also surprised – he had broken the unspoken chair rule – was I the kind of girl that boys liked?

'I'm David.'

'And you already know who I am.'

He smiled. His shoulders were so broad they strained his jacket. His thick black hair was pomaded back from his broad forehead in the modern style, and his teeth were very big and white and straight. He was almost too handsome.

'How old are you?' I asked. It took him a second to answer, and blood rushed to my face – I had made a mistake, already. But then he spoke.

'Seventeen.'

'And an athlete?'

'Football. Track. I'm stronger than I am fast. Feel,' he said, jokingly, and I touched the muscle that he offered.

The music turned slow, and David gathered me closer. He smelled faintly of cologne. In another world, this would make me so happy, that David had chosen me out of all the other girls. I could feel the admiring, jealous glances of my campmates. And why had he chosen me? Because I'd looked like I hadn't wanted to be chosen. The customs with boys were all wrong. And besides, I didn't want David. I was done with that. I didn't want to be gathered, ever again.

A tap on my shoulder. I opened my eyes and saw Mrs Holmes, then the couples beyond her who had stopped dancing and watched us.

'Too close, Thea.' But surely we were no closer than any of the other girls? Or maybe we had been closer than I thought, and I hadn't noticed? That I hadn't known how close was too close horrified me.

'I'm sorry,' I said softly. I didn't know what to do, what the etiquette was in these situations. Should I leave, or was I meant to stay and bear everyone's disapproval? The music still played, but very few people were dancing. David turned his face to the floor and suddenly I thought of my father, how he had not defended me. He had wanted me to stay, I know he had. But he had let Mother win that battle. Yet the world had not ended, even though it had seemed like it might.

Mrs Holmes watched me. Not very much had changed since the days of white satin shoes that were not allowed to meet the earth. She did not tell me to go, or stay, so I nodded to David and left on my own, made my way through all the warm, glittering bodies. When I reached the edge of the floor, I saw that not everyone was watching. Couples had resumed dancing. Henny chatted with a group of girls. Perhaps about me, but perhaps not. I can save this, I thought. I have to; there was nowhere else to go, at least not right now.

My character was not what it should have been. Nobody had told me that, but I knew. And perhaps I had danced inappropriately; perhaps I was no longer the best judge of what was and was not appropriate. *What is wrong with you?* Mother had asked. And what was? I felt my forehead, flushed and hot. And then I turned to face whoever was watching me – I could feel eyes upon me like a touch.

Mr Holmes. He offered a small smile, and I knew that he was trying to be kind, as he had been earlier to Mary Abbott. And at first I felt a sick feeling rise in my throat, because I did not want to be pitied; but then this feeling was replaced by a hopeful feeling: Mr Holmes did not think I was bad. He watched me for a second more before politely averting his eyes. He did not see me the way all the other adults now saw me: my parents, Mrs Holmes. But he was not a boy, either, like David. He was not drawn to me simply because I was pretty enough, available: a girl at a dance. He liked me, I realized. And I liked him.

I was still more child than adult. I was not a monster but a confused, wronged girl. It would be years, though, before I would understand. In those two weeks at home, Mother had been angry, Father mainly mute, as if there was nothing to be said. They blamed me. And so I came to Yonahlossee a person worthy of blame.

CHAPTER FIVE

Most of the time, my home was very quiet, and my life was constant in the way of happy childhoods. Mother took Sam and me to Orlando once in the winter and once in the summer, where we shopped and dined in a restaurant, perhaps saw a picture, spent the night in a hotel. These excursions were exciting, though I hated to miss a ride, but they, too, were part of our custom.

Sam and I accompanied Mother to town once a month and trailed her from store to store while she ran errands. People knew us; she was the doctor's wife, and we were the doctor's children. Mother was charming in the stores as she told little stories, said funny things while she fingered plain fabrics we would never buy – we bought our clothes in Orlando or from catalogues – and placed orders.

Mother thought gossip was vile. So she did not ever say that the other people in Emathla were beneath us. But we knew anyway. Now I understand that my mother's status was complicated; my father was a country doctor, there was no other woman who occupied the same position as she did. In Gainesville, where there were other physicians, and lawyers, like my uncle, perhaps Mother would have had friends. But what Mother wanted, truly wanted, was, and always would be, a mystery to me. It does not seem possible that a woman so charming and beautiful could find her life's happiness with three people: me, Sam, my father. And once every few weeks, my aunt and uncle and cousin.

But back then I did not ponder my mother's happiness. I was a child. I just wanted the drive to end, so I could get to Sasi.

I rode him once a day, sometimes twice. I never skipped a day. If I was sick, I rode; if it rained, I rode. I spent hours and hours in the barn each day, but only sat in the saddle for a small fraction of that time. The rest of the time was devoted to chores, but they weren't chores to me, couldn't possibly be placed in the same category as weeding Mother's garden with Sam, or helping Idella polish our infinite collection of silver. I cleaned my bridle daily, my saddle weekly; curried Sasi's coat until it shone. Carved the packed dirt from his hooves and squirted iodine onto his tender frog to prevent thrush. I picked manure and spread fresh hay in his stall, changed his water and fed him a mix of sweet feed and oats at eight in the morning, a lighter meal of grain at four in the afternoon. I did these things every day; I took pleasure in them. No one had to remind me.

Mother rode, in her youth. Sidesaddle, which she said she didn't mind, which I'd tried once or twice and hated. Sasi would not take a single step without my asking first. And sidesaddle, one leg hooked over the saddle, rendered me powerless.

Sam could often be found with me at the barn, especially in the afternoons. He didn't ride, but he liked Sasi, and he would arrange courses for us that included elaborate combinations, exact distances between jumps. The trick was turning Sam on to a task; after that he was fully engrossed, a dog with a bone. He would time us and record in his notebook our numbers and how many jumps we had knocked over. And beside that he would write a number, one through ten – his own ranking of how well we had done.

And sometimes, though we weren't supposed to do this, because Mother didn't think it was safe, I would bring Sasi out back and take his saddle off, and convince Sam to sit behind me. I loved riding bareback, though it was painful, less the padding of the saddle: but that was the beauty of it, too – nothing between me and Sasi, like the Indians rode. I could feel every twitch of his muscles, every slight hesitation or surge of interest. Sasi did not think – he simply acted. And in order to ride well, you had to stop yourself from thinking, had to act on instinct alone, and this was something I'd always done well.

Sam would have to cling to me, fiercely, in order to stay on; Sasi, excited by the new weight upon his back, would sidestep and arch his neck, trot elaborately. He knew what was coming, how I would let him go, give him his head and let him gallop until he tired; could he hear Sam as he whispered, frightened, into my hair, begging me to stop? Could he feel me shake my head and turn a deaf ear to my brother? And finally, could he feel Sam relax against me, and, as we swerved to the right to avoid a branch, feel him gasp with fear but also with pleasure?

Fear makes a horse go faster, so I liked having Sam's fear up there with me, goading Sasi on. And this was good for Sam, I thought, I knew – he needed to let himself be scared sometimes, in order to experience the pleasure that risk brought.

Father was usually gone until nighttime, and Mother gardened and tended to the house for most of the day.

Sam and I eagerly anticipated our cousin's family's visits, when Mother and Father would act lighthearted, when Sam and I would spend countless hours with Georgie. But I liked it when they left, too, at the end of the weekend; I liked having my family back to myself again, I liked spending uninterrupted hours in the barn, where I went less when Georgie was here, because he was afraid of horses.

Father saw his patients every day, but even so, he never seemed to particularly care about people. Besides, of course, keeping them in good health, which he cared about deeply. The Atwells on their thousand acres were *almost an island*, my joke with Sam. But it wasn't entirely a joke, for an ocean might as well have surrounded us.

'Thea?'

I opened my eyes, slowly. Georgie stood over me. He had arrived yesterday with his parents.

'Wake up, Thea,' he whispered.

Sam was snoring softly. My stomach ached, fiercely, and I wanted to sleep. We slept in my room, Georgie in my other twin bed and Sam on the floor, though I noticed how Mother had hesitated over the sleeping arrangements this time.

'Thea,' he said again, 'it's almost morning.'

'Yes,' I agreed, 'now go back to sleep.'

'If I'm not tired?'

I closed my eyes against Georgie's voice.

'Come downstairs with me,' he whispered, tugging my hand. 'Please.'

'I'm tired.'

'Come anyway.' His features were softer in the dim light. He looked at me hopefully, and put his hand on my cheek. It felt strangely tender, but good; I could feel my heart quicken. I threw off the covers. I wanted to wake Sam, but Georgie shook his head. Sam and I did what Georgie wanted, mainly. He was older and stronger than either of us.

'Follow me,' he said, and we made our way through the sleeping house that felt dead it was so quiet.

'I should have put on more clothes,' I said, once we were outside in the chilly air. It was fall, almost Thanksgiving, though the leaves didn't change here, instead died suddenly and quickly. Fall was a mixed blessing: I could ride during the day, because of the cool temperature, but I couldn't stay out as late because dark came earlier.

'Aren't you tired?'

Georgie shook his head. 'I can't sleep. Here,' he said, and patted the damp ground. 'Sit.'

I lingered. 'I might go say hi to Sasi.'

'Don't. He's probably sleeping.'

I laughed and sat down next to him, folded my nightgown over my legs. 'Horses only sleep an hour a day.'

'Maybe I'm like a horse.'

'They sleep standing up,' I continued. 'So that they're ready to run, at a moment's notice.'

'Do horses say things like that? A moment's notice?'

'To me. Sasi says all sorts of things to me.'

Georgie nodded, but he didn't smile. I could tell his mind was elsewhere. He seemed pensive, which I took note of because it was so unusual. Usually he moved through the world so easily, was himself such easy company, always in good humor.

'Do you think you'll live here forever?' he asked. We were sitting at the back of my house, the view that was most familiar to me; the porch where we would all sit later, while the adults sipped their drinks. The glass French doors that opened to the less formal sitting room, where we sat in the evenings when we didn't have company.

'I hadn't thought about it.' I lay back in the grass, still sleepy. 'I suppose I'll live wherever my husband does.' The words were strange in my mouth. But it was true; I knew I would live where he did.

'What if he takes you to the moon?' He winked at me, and I thought, there he is.

I laughed. 'Then I'll bring you and Sam along so you can see it, too. But first I'm going to sleep awhile.'

'Then so am I.' He lay down next to me. 'Sweet dreams,' he said, which was what Aunt Carrie always said. He took my hand, and though I expected him to let it go after a second, like he usually did, he did not.

'Thank you,' I murmured. I closed my eyes, I was nearly asleep when I felt Georgie's fingers on my arm, so lightly, running down the length of it. I looked up and he was watching me, smiling; I closed my eyes and tried not to fall asleep, tried to remain in this trance-like state between sleep and waking. The pleasure of my cousin's touch was almost too much, but I did not want it to stop.

Then the sun was bright overhead, and my thighs were sticky with sweat. Even when the air was crisp, like now, the sun was always overhead, following.

'Georgie,' I said, and shook his inert shoulder. 'We fell asleep.'

My uncle and father sat on the porch, a sheaf of papers in front of them; usually my father was making his rounds right now, visiting his patients. We saw them before they saw us; my slender father, his delicate doctor's hands, and my rotund uncle. They'd both had sons who resembled them.

Uncle George looked at me blankly as I approached; I kissed him on the cheek anyway.

'What are you doing out here?' my father asked. He took out his father's pocket watch, which he always kept with him. Uncle George teased him about it, called him nostalgic. And it was true that almost every other man I had seen – not that I had seen many – wore wristwatches. 'It's too early.'

'We fell asleep,' Georgie said.

I was going to elaborate but I could see my father didn't care. When I'd asked my father what Uncle George got from their father that was like the pocket watch, he'd only smiled.

'Why don't you go on inside,' he said, 'it's still early. Don't wake Mother.'

My father, forty years old this June, had started to gray, his dark brown hair turned peppery. Uncle George was balding. They'd both aged, Father more handsomely.

When we were upstairs, I found the blood on my underclothes. I sat down on the edge of the tub and felt; my fingers were covered with a sheen of red-brown, but this blood was different; it clumped, formed clots.

I heard the floor creak outside the door. Sam, getting up. There was only a door between my cousin, who had fallen back into bed, my brother, and me. And there was no lock, either, and I wanted one so badly right now. Sam would knock first, but still – the thin fact of a door was inadequate. I pressed an old towel to my underclothes. I would burn it, later. I would tell Mother, later. My family was progressive in certain ways, and I'd known to expect this. But still, the thought of either Georgie or Sam finding out made me want to die.

Later that day, Georgie, Sam, and I went hunting for a snake for one of Sam's terrariums. I'd fitted one of Mother's belts to myself. Ordinarily I'd be riding, but I'd announced at breakfast that Sasi was lame. Mother had looked at me curiously – Sasi was a sound pony – and I had turned my head. The thought of pulling on breeches over the contraption between my legs seemed impossible. Aunt Carrie was back at the house, with Mother, and they'd told us to be careful, which was advice they gave regardless of activity, and so meant nothing.

'What were you doing last night?' Sam asked, and I knew immediately he was a little hurt we hadn't asked him.

'What do you mean?' Georgie's tone was playful.

'I woke up and you weren't there. Neither was Thea.'

'Georgie couldn't sleep,' I said, 'and so he woke me up! I wouldn't let him wake you up.'

'What are we looking for, exactly?' Georgie asked, oblivious to Sam's hurt feelings. But Sam seemed to accept my explanation.

'Snakes,' Sam said.

'I bet I'll find one,' Georgie said, and grinned. 'I know where they hide.'

'Remember,' Sam said, 'don't kill it.'

Georgie crossed his heart. 'Promise!'

Sam laughed. Georgie had accidentally squashed one of Sam's tree frogs last month, and he was always picking up lizards the wrong way and severing their bodies from their tails. Sam was gentler: he knew how to entice a lizard into his cupped hands, how to pinch a snake by its neck and wind its body around his wrist.

'Poor snake,' I murmured. 'Do you think it really wants to come live with you?'

Sam grinned. 'Better than getting eaten by a bigger snake, or a bird.'

Georgie stopped and unscrewed the cap of his canteen, then tilted it to his mouth. We each had one strapped across our backs. I took a sip from mine, too; I liked how the water tasted cool, slightly metallic. Aunt Carrie let Georgie grow his hair longer than my mother let Sam grow his, so my cousin had a wild look about him now, his brown hair unkempt, bleached in streaks by the sun. My brother knelt and examined a palmful of dirt. Georgie was changing, next to Sam; there was hair when he lifted his arms, and his sweat smelled ripe and musky. From this vantage point, Georgie looked almost like a man, muscle-bound and thick. Sam was still impossibly skinny, in the way of boys, his spine stretched taut against his skin.

'If we're lucky,' Sam said, standing, 'we'll see a coral snake. They're so beautiful. I see some snake tracks, but I don't know which kind. But we're near water.'

Coral snakes lived near water; I knew that from Sam. Or maybe I had always known it.

'Hopefully we won't be lucky,' Georgie said, 'since they're deadly.'

Sam and I gazed at him. Coral snakes *were* deadly, but they were shy. And they had to chew on you for a long time before any venom was transmitted. We knew what to be afraid of in the Florida wilderness, but we were taught to be unafraid of the natural world. The smaller the animal, the more afraid it was of us. And when I was on my pony, my father told me, I was a terrifying creature – snakes could feel our footsteps from miles away, and bears and panthers could smell us before they saw us.

Sam was a very cautious naturalist. His terrariums were full of reptiles that were not poisonous. He only wanted to see a coral snake, not capture it.

'You're such a city boy,' I said. 'You'd have a better chance of choking on your water than being bitten by a coral snake.'

'I'll take my chances with the canteen,' Georgie said, and grinned. He took another sip of water.

Sam started to delve into the specifics of the coral snake's bite, and then he moved on to the pygmy rattlesnake, in order to provide context, and I started to walk again, hoping to move things along. I didn't want to be out here too long. I didn't know how long the belt would last.

'Quiet,' I whispered, when I saw the grass shiver slightly. I pointed.

'Could be a lizard,' Sam said softly. He dropped to his knees, then crawled to the edge of the grass, which came up to our waists.

Georgie and I watched him, trying to stand as still as possible. Sam could move as quietly as an Indian. We could not. I held my breath and Sam reached into the grass and pulled out a long black snake, an orange band encircling his neck. I felt a flash of pride; Sam was quick.

'Good eye, Thea,' he said, and showed us the snake's belly, which was beautifully vermillion. 'He's at least twelve inches.'

We watched the snake writhe around in Sam's net.

'*Diadophis p. punctatus*,' he said.

'Diadophis,' Georgie said, 'this was not your lucky day.'

'But it was mine,' Sam said, happy.

I watched the snake, motionless in the net, as if it had accepted its fate. It was fully grown, an adult, and unblemished. A lucky snake. Sam would not keep him forever in a glass house, but the snake would not know that.

Mother was in my bedroom when I came in from out back, sitting on the edge of my unmade bed.

'There's blood on your sheets,' she said, and I looked to where she pointed.

'I was going to tell you today.'

She stood, and I thought she was going to leave, but then she came very close to me and untucked my blouse before I could stop her.

'Where did you get this?' Her hand lingered on the belt. I looked out the window, at the great oak that hovered over our house like a parent. Father said it kept us cool in the summers, warm in the winters.

'I'm sorry,' I said quickly. 'I'm sorry.'

She nodded, and took my hand between hers, as if entreating me. But I was her daughter, I didn't need entreating. 'Do you know what this means?'

'That I can't ride.'

She laughed. 'No. It means you can have a child now.'

I was horrified. My mother smiled at me very, very kindly and I wanted her to be angry at me, anything but this tenderness. Usually I eagerly received my mother's affection, but I did not want any more attention drawn to this thing that had happened to me, to my body. I had not wanted it to happen. I had not asked for it.

'Of course not now,' she continued, 'but someday. Doesn't that please you, Thea?'

I shook my head. My mother drew me close and pressed my head to her chest.

'Oh, don't cry. I didn't mean to alarm you. I only don't want you to think that this is anything to be ashamed of.'

I sprung back. 'You won't tell anyone?'

'Of course not. This is between us. A woman's matter.' She smiled faintly. 'It's nothing to be ashamed of, Thea. Nothing.'

I nodded. I didn't know what to say, so I thanked my mother, and she responded in kind, out of habit, as she left the room.

'You're welcome.'

I was very good at focusing my mind. That's what Father called it. Mother called it ignoring the consequences. I had bled twice before this, the first time more than a year ago. And I had kept it a secret because I was confused by the thing that was happening to me. I didn't understand how something I had expected could make me feel so ashamed. And I knew telling made a thing real. I flung myself on my made bed, which wasn't something we were allowed to do, and pressed my face into my pillow and wished that I would hear a voice, Georgie's or Sam's or even Aunt Carrie's – just a sign that life went on without me, that my bleeding was not really a great or particularly exciting fact. I was a girl, the only girl in our world. How different I was from Georgie and Sam had been articulated by Mother. I felt, for the first time in my life, apart, adrift. A floating girl.

Now I understand that the relief I could see, faintly, on Mother's face was relief that I was normal. She must have been worried, her daughter fourteen, almost fifteen, and still not menstruating. She's simply a late bloomer – I'm sure Father would have told her this, uttered these exact words or something so close, and Mother would have agreed with him or not, but still she would have gone away and worried.

My father came home later than he had promised, and Mother was waiting for him by the front door. I was afraid she was going to tell him I'd started menstruating, so I waited in the sun porch where I could hear them.

'They're waiting outside,' my mother said, and my father nodded.

'How are they?' He put down his black doctor's bag, which was always with him. 'How do they seem?'

'Fine,' she said, and helped him out of his white coat.

'Fine?'

'Fine, Felix.' Her voice was soft but firm. The conversation of adults was often coded, impenetrable. And though I usually cared very little about the adult matters my mother and father discussed, this was something else, something that involved my aunt and uncle, and, by extension, Georgie. And I cared about Georgie, deeply.

I waited a second and then followed them to the back deck, where the adults went to have cocktails before dinner. I was surprised by my disappointment that Mother hadn't mentioned me to Father. Everyone sat in our low deck chairs, green-painted metal, around a table set with canapés and a bottle of champagne for the ladies, a decanter of whiskey for the men. Though liquor was technically illegal, getting it was like a game everyone played, and won. Uncle George knew someone in Gainesville who kept him, and us, supplied. This was usually my favorite part of the visits, the time when the adults were happiest.

I walked up behind Father, kissed the top of his head. He smiled up at me, and Uncle George winked at me. Georgie and Sam sat on the ground, a little bit behind everyone, watching the snake. Sam had filled a terrarium with dirt and moss and rocks; a miniature of the snake's former home. I sat down next to them.

Aunt Carrie caught my eye and smiled. 'Is your pony better, Thea?'

I looked at my aunt blankly before I remembered. 'Oh yes,' I said. 'He just needs to rest for a few days.'

'Good.' She smiled and smoothed her skirt over her plump stomach.

My father watched my mother as she tipped the champagne bottle to her glass, lifted it away just as the bubbles threatened to flood the rim. We were all watching her, now, and I thought of what she had said earlier, about being a woman. It seemed very womanly, to have everyone watching you.

'Well,' Uncle George said, and paused. He held a pipe in his hand, a thin stream of smoke curling to the heavens. I loved the smell. Idella stepped onto the porch then, carrying a platter of tiny chive biscuits. Sam stood and grabbed a handful before she set it down on the table.

'Sam,' Mother chided softly. She seemed distracted. All of the adults did.

'It's eating. That's soon. The last one didn't eat for days,' Sam said, ignoring Mother, kneeling down and pointing at the snake, which was indeed eating an earthworm. I shuddered.

'Are you going to catch all its food?' Georgie asked. 'Seems like a lot of work.'

Sam swallowed the last of his biscuit. I tapped my cheek, to show him there was a crumb, but he was lost in the world of the snake. He could do this, devote himself completely to an animal; I could, too, with Sasi, but it seemed entirely different. Sasi was warm-blooded, like me.

Sam gently lifted the snake from the terrarium and stroked its head. The snake seemed calm, mollified. Mother said it was Sam's gift, calming animals that frightened most people. He lowered the snake to the wooden ground and it started to slither away, slowly. 'It needs its exercise,' Sam murmured, as he crawled on his hands and knees to follow it.

Georgie looked at me and rolled his eyes, and I smiled. I could not imagine loving a snake as much as my brother did.

'He's a snake charmer,' I said, and Georgie began to say something else, but then we both turned, drawn by the odd, unmistakable sound of someone weeping. My aunt. I felt chilled. I couldn't ever remember seeing her cry. In fact, I'd only seen my mother cry once before, when her horse had to be put down; my father, never.

I turned to Georgie, but he was watching his mother.

'It's worthless now?' my mother asked quietly, 'all of it?'

My aunt closed her eyes, and pressed her fingers to her lips. My uncle watched his pipe, which he held carefully, pinched between his thumb and finger. He would not meet Mother's eye. Neither of them spoke. I turned to my cousin again, and there were bright red splotches on his cheeks and forehead, the redness colonizing his fair skin. He knew.

'Miami,' Aunt Carrie said dolefully, and shook her head. 'Miami.'

Miami was where Uncle George had been going for years, since I could remember. He drove down there once a month, to look after his property, property he would eventually sell.

My father said nothing, sat very still, his hands on his knees, his face blank. But I understood that this blankness meant something: my father was angry.

'Tell her, George,' Aunt Carrie said, 'tell her.'

Uncle George looked at his wife, and she nodded. 'Go on.'

'To put it plainly, as I told my brother this morning, I owe the bank more than it's worth. It was a foolish investment from the beginning,' he said finally. 'But it seemed a sure thing. Bryan himself called the light "God's Sunshine." Everyone wanted a piece, Elizabeth. There were so many people who wanted to live there . . .' He trailed off. 'It seemed a sure thing.'

When my father spoke, his voice was soft but clear. 'Nothing in this life is sure, George.' A bright-red cardinal landed on the railing, and gave a little chirp. My father turned his head in the direction of the sound, gazed at the bird for a moment, and then turned back to his brother. 'Nothing.'

'Especially land speculation,' my uncle said, and laughed nervously.

I felt sick to my stomach. The air was thick, the adults were so distracted they hadn't noticed me and Georgie. Sam was still following his snake.

Georgie stood, and walked off the porch into the backyard without asking to be excused. I waited for an adult to call him back, but they just watched him go, their foreheads creased, and I was suddenly so angry at everyone – my stupid brother, my stupid parents, my stupid aunt and uncle.

I ran after Georgie. My mother called after me – 'Thea!' – but I ignored her.

When I caught up to him, I touched his shoulder.

He spun around. 'What do you want?'

I couldn't say anything. I didn't know what I would say. His meanness surprised me; Georgie was never mean to me.

'Let's go to the barn,' I said quietly. I knew he would follow me. When Sasi heard me, he nickered and swung his pretty head over the stall door. It was nearly time for him to eat. I patted his broad forehead, and waited. I sensed that Georgie would speak when he was ready.

I murmured to Sasi, told him what a good boy he was. I hoped the bleeding would not last too long this time. I hated not riding, hated spending a day or two reestablishing things with Sasi before we could begin again where we had left off.

'My father thought we were going to be rich,' Georgie said, from behind me, 'like you.'

Sasi nipped my hand, lightly, mouthy because he was hungry. 'We're not rich,' I said.

Georgie gave a short, hard laugh. 'You have the oranges.'

It was true. We did have the oranges.

'Do you know what it means to mortgage your house, Thea?' he asked. He stepped closer to me. He touched the tail of my braid, and I shivered. 'It means my father borrowed money from the bank against our house.'

'Why?' I could barely breathe. Georgie's finger lingered on my back, toying with my hair.

'To buy more land, in Miami.' George said. 'He was hoping to sell soon.' He was almost whispering. 'And now the country is doing very badly, and he can't pay the bank back, and he asked for money. From your father.'

I could feel Georgie's breath on my neck. I could smell him: strong, oily, like he had been out in the woods.

'*Very badly.*' Those were our parents' words. Father had said the same thing about the country last week. But our parents' world was separate from ours, another place entirely. Georgie need not worry about the matters of adults. I spun around and faced my cousin, who looked mournful, the opposite of how God had made him to look. I took his hand.

'They'll take care of it. You'll see.'

I could see Georgie wanted to believe me.

'Trust me,' I said.

I would show Georgie I was not afraid. Money meant nothing to me, then. If Uncle George borrowed money from my family, that was fine, because everything was shared in a family, and besides, there was always more money. There was always another set of silk drapes from Orlando, another pony, another ivory-boned knife.

'All right,' he said. The old Georgie had returned to me. 'All right. I'll trust you, Thea.'

He kissed me on the cheek. I blushed, but I was pleased because I had pleased my cousin, because I had cheered him up, because I had shown him that the money did not matter.

I believed all those things I told my cousin that day. I had everything I loved in the world within one hundred feet: my parents, my aunt and uncle, my brother. My cousin and pony within arm's reach. My understanding of our world, I thought, was complete.

CHAPTER
SIX

The rain fell in sheets. Naari and I were halted at the head of the ring, next to Mr Albrecht, watching Leona complete her course. She rode badly today, perhaps distracted by the rain. She and King had nicked several jumps, knocked two over entirely.

'Hold his head!' Mr Albrecht shouted, his voice dulled by the wind. He held an umbrella, which Naari eyed warily. We were to be assessed individually, today, my first time, but I wasn't nervous.

When Leona was finished I nudged Naari into a trot from our standstill: she was distracted by the storm, and her ears flicked back and forth. I murmured to her, kicked her twice, and she gave me her attention for a moment. We passed Leona, who was muttering furiously to King.

'Knees, Thea,' Mr Albrecht yelled. My knees had a tendency to slide upward during jumps.

'One minute.' Mr Albrecht timed our courses, as we would be timed in a competition. I slid my right heel back and asked Naari to canter.

'Time,' Mr Albrecht called, and we were nearly aligned with the first jump, but not quite. I had learned early on, before Mr Albrecht, to forget my mistakes. Remembering could easily ruin a course.

'Now,' I hissed to Naari as we cleared the first jump, but

barely. The rain seemed to quicken, or maybe I was just going faster. The wind whipped. There was no thunder or lightning – camp rules would force us to take cover, then – but I could hear the weak branches of the oak trees snapping.

A pelt of Spanish moss flew into our path, and Naari skittered. I tapped her shoulder with my crop and tightened the reins.

'Balance,' I heard Mr Albrecht yell, but he was barely there.

I directed Naari toward a triple, the most difficult combination of the course.

'Two, two, two,' I repeated to myself – there was room for two strides between each jump, no more no less.

'Yes,' screamed Mr Albrecht. '*Gut!*' I could barely hear him. 'Now,' I heard him yell, and I cleared the first jump. One, two – Naari soared over the second jump, I could barely feel her beneath me, she was a coil between my legs.

And then the last jump. We were nearly done. The wind picked up, then, between the second and third jump, and Mr Albrecht's umbrella flew toward us. Naari swerved to the right, and I lost my right stirrup, and then I heard the unmistakable crack of leather, and my saddle slid to the left. My girth has broken, I thought, incredulously. I looked toward Mr Albrecht, as if to say – look, do you see this?

But then the saddle lurched even farther to the left, and I couldn't believe my bad luck – how could I straighten myself out, move the saddle to the right, when I had lost my right stirrup? It was impossible. I felt horribly dizzy all of a sudden, perched at an angle nearly parallel to the ground.

'Circle her,' Mr Albrecht yelled, 'circle.'

But I was so disoriented I didn't even know which rein was right and which was left. I pressed my right leg to Naari's flank as hard as I could, the only pressure that was keeping me from hurtling to the ground. And I would not fall cleanly. I could see from my vantage point that the girth had not broken completely, so if I fell I would likely be trapped beneath Naari, tied to her by the stirrup I had not lost.

'Do something,' Mr Albrecht called desperately. 'Something!'

Naari galloped by them, and Leona flashed through my tilted field of vision; she was looking at her hand, held in front of her in its navy glove, fingers splayed, palm upturned. Dye streaked her forearm.

In a burst of strength, I somehow threw my arm around Naari's neck, and hitched myself upright again. And then the world was back to its normal order, and I was able to turn Naari in a circle until she slowed.

Mr Albrecht approached us, holding out his hand to Naari, who looked at him warily. 'It is all right,' he murmured, and then to me: 'Are you all right, Thea?'

I nodded. I felt fine, strangely fine. I knew I should have felt relieved, or still scared, but instead I felt blank; relaxed, even. I had been so close to an accident; but wasn't I always that close, whenever I was on top of a horse?

Leona stood in the same place as before, watching us, and I understood that I had witnessed a weakness: Leona hadn't wanted to watch. She had been afraid.

'She's spooky,' Leona said later, at the barn, as we sponged warm water over our horses' backs. Steam rose. 'King's not. He's dull. That's how a horse should be, dull and obedient.'

'I like my horses smart,' I said lightly.

'Too smart for their own good, is that how you like them? You lost your stirrup, you almost fell. She would have dragged you around the ring if you had.'

'But I didn't.' Naari was exhausted, stood perfectly still in the cross ties.

'But you could have,' Leona said. I was about to argue, but

Leona continued: 'The duller a horse is, the better.' She slapped King on the neck. 'People are killed in horseback-riding accidents, Thea.' She unhooked King's cross ties; Naari started at the sound of the metal snaps against the concrete floor of the wash rack. 'You should request a different horse.

'But,' she said, as she led King past us, 'you won't, because you're proud. A horse is a weapon.'

I stopped and looked at her, and I realized that I had something Leona did not. I was fearless. And that counted for something.

'Smart horses will work for you,' I said. 'Once you win them over. Dumb horses' – and here I looked at King – 'they don't care enough.' Leona stared at me, then turned her face away quickly, her long blond braid snapping like a whip; we both knew I was right.

I was currying the saddle marks from Naari's back when Leona appeared again.

'I want to tell you something,' she said. Her tone was neutral. 'I come from a riding family.'

I banged my curry comb against the wall. A curry comb-shaped clump of hair fell to the floor.

'I know.' We all knew.

'Yes,' she continued, 'a family where everyone rides.' She paused. 'My sister walked behind a horse, too close and she was kicked in the head. She died.'

I didn't say anything.

'It was a long time ago. I was born later. She died in three days.' She held up three fingers. 'It was not the horse's fault. It was her fault, she walked where she should not have. It is never the horse, Thea.'

She turned, then, and began to stride away in precisely measured steps.

'Leona,' I called.

She turned. 'Yes?'

'I'm sorry for your sister.' I took a step forward, and though I must have been more than twenty feet away from this girl, this exquisite giant, she took a step back.

Leona shook her head. 'It was before me.'

As I watched Leona walk away, I could see that her disclosure did not mean a door into her soul had opened slightly and forever, as it would have with Sissy. But I liked Leona, in spite of her imperiousness. In spite of what Sissy said. I felt linked to her: we were the best riders here.

Mary Abbott knelt beside my bunk.

'Thea,' she whispered. 'Thea.'

I opened my eyes. There was no moon, and the cabin was dark as coal. I saw Mary Abbott by the flash of her pale skin. My chest felt tight.

Yes, I wanted to say, but my voice would not come.

'Your breathing,' Mary Abbott said, 'it woke me.'

I sat up too quickly and banged my head on the bottom of Eva's bunk, which I hadn't done since my first morning here. My hair caught, my scalp burned. I tried to speak again and my voice came out as a bark.

'You don't sound well.'

I shook my head and began to cry. I couldn't speak, I could barely breathe. When I'd gone to sleep I'd only had a cold. I'd felt a bit achy, but otherwise fine.

Sissy came to me then, and pushed Mary Abbott aside. She took my hand and felt my forehead.

'Fetch Henny.' Mary Abbott disappeared.

Sissy freed my hair from the metal netting. 'Lie back,' she whispered.

'Thea?' Eva's head hung over the bed.

I tried to speak – *Nothing*, I wanted to say – but Sissy shook her head.

'Quiet.'

Sissy wasn't allowed to accompany me to the Castle, where I spent the night in the windowless infirmary. Mrs Holmes checked on me every hour while I slept fitfully, alone for the first time in months, nothing to lull me to sleep but the sound of the wind disturbing the trees. I had become used to the sounds girls made: Gates snored lightly when she first fell asleep, and occasionally Sissy spoke to herself, in nonsense, until Victoria reached down and tapped her. And there was always the heavy sound of breathing to soothe when I woke and believed, for the briefest instant, that I was at home in my own bed where I used to belong.

I fell into a delirium. Mrs Holmes was careful not to touch me when she slid the thermometer in my mouth, held it there with the tip of her finger against my tongue's thrusts.

'Leave it, Thea.' But I would not, my quiet resistance.

'Mother,' I said.

'She's not here, Thea,' she said quietly.

My breathing became more labored as the night wore on; my fever rose. Each time I woke I thought I was home.

Another figure followed Mrs Holmes into the room – by this time, perhaps, I truly was delirious – I saw the sharp, slim outline of a tall man.

'Sam,' I called.

'Hush,' Mrs Holmes said.

Mother would come to me, once she learned that I was ill. She would have to.

When I opened my eyes again, Mrs Holmes and a man – the doctor, I knew – stood over me.

'May I examine you, Thea?' he asked.

I covered my heart with my hand, embarrassed. Even through my stuffed nose, the doctor smelled musty. He didn't wear a white doctor's coat, like my father did when he saw patients. He wore instead a regular suit. It was Sunday, he had made a special trip to see me. He was short and fat, he matched Mrs Holmes better than Mr Holmes did. His wife was probably tall and slender; that was how the world worked.

He took my wrist in his hand and pressed his fingers to it, to feel my pulse.

'She rode in the rain for hours last week,' Mrs Holmes said, 'she chilled herself to the bone. And,' she added, and lowered her voice, 'she's been very homesick.'

'An equestrienne?'

'Yes,' I said. Mrs Holmes went to the closet and pulled out a stack of white towels; I saw a reflection of myself in a mirror that was nailed to the door as it swung shut. I looked very pale. 'All the girls ride,' Mrs Holmes said, as if it were an unavoidable, slightly disappointing activity.

I wondered if she was angry at Mr Albrecht – whom she seemed to like, who sat at the head table with the Holmes family – for letting me ride in the rain.

'I didn't make myself sick,' I said. I wasn't the kind of girl who would do that.

Mrs Holmes said nothing. Mr Holmes had become easy to read, for me; his face was always moving in response to the things girls said, always expressing pleasure or dismay or confusion, but Mrs Holmes was entirely self-composed, a trait I admired in spite of myself. I would like to learn to be that composed. Her clothes were so old-fashioned, of another era: her skirt that fell to the floor, her cameo that closed her blouse at the neck to prevent even the tiniest glimpse of skin. The Holmeses were considered progressive: they'd done away with sidesaddle when they'd taken over, for which I, at least, was grateful. And under the Holmeses' direction, many girls applied to ladies' colleges as seniors, and though some married before they could go, many actually went. And yet here Mrs Holmes sat like a relic of an earlier time.

The doctor felt my neck. 'An illness is a mysterious and often inexplicable event, Mrs Holmes. To know its cause would mean that you knew more than God, Mrs Holmes. Knew more than science.'

Mrs Holmes murmured, but the murmur gave away neither assent nor dissent, and the doctor chuckled and winked at me, asked me to sit up so that he could place the cold stethoscope, warmed by his breath, on my back. I wore only my nightgown, no underclothes.

I was nearly naked in front of this man. My chest ached, and it pained me to breathe deeply, but still I was ashamed.

I closed my eyes and took deep breaths when the doctor asked me to. I was relieved I was not at home, because then Father would have examined me and seen me unclothed. But if I were at home, I would have been well.

'A bad cold,' the doctor announced when he was done. I liked him. He had taken my side.

There was a knock on the door and I put down my book.

'Come in,' I called.

It was Mr Holmes. He was wearing a suit; it was Wednesday, camp life continued without me. Everyone here dressed formally; Mr Albrecht wore a black show coat with his breeches, and the female teachers wore nice, if plain, dresses. I smoothed the covers over my lap.

He folded himself into the chair by my bed, which seemed too small for him.

'Hello,' he said, and smiled. He was too tall to ride horses, it would be hard for him to keep his balance. Maybe if he had learned when he was a child, but it was almost impossible to teach a tall adult how to ride. It should feel strange, I knew, to be alone in a room with a man who was not family for the first time in my life. And yet it did not.

'Hello. How are you today?'

'I'm just fine. I should be asking that of you. Do you feel better?'

I nodded.

'What are you reading?' He gestured to my book.

'*Howards End.*'

'Do you like to read?'

'I love books.'

He picked up the book and examined its cover. 'I love them, too. There's such cruelty and such goodness in Forster's world. But I don't want to ruin it for you. I see you're only halfway through.'

'That could be said of any book, couldn't it?' I asked shyly. But I knew I was correct. 'If the people in them are real.'

'I suppose it could.'

I could tell I had surprised and pleased Mr Holmes. We were quiet for a moment.

'I'm concerned, Thea. Mrs Holmes thinks you are homesick—' I started to protest, but he held up his hand. 'It's nothing to be ashamed of, Thea. Many of the girls are homesick. It always goes away. But you've been here for two months.'

I fiddled with a piece of my hair. It hadn't been washed in almost a week. I must look wild to Mr Holmes, pale and unkempt.

'But I'm not homesick,' I said. 'I'm going home soon.'

He tilted his head, and I could tell he was trying not to look surprised.

'When summer session ends,' I continued. 'Next week.'

Mr Holmes did not speak for a moment. 'Thea,' he said finally, 'you won't be leaving Yonahlossee next week.'

'But I will,' I said, 'there must be some sort of misunderstanding.' This was what Mother had said last year, when an Emathla shopkeeper had ordered the wrong hair tonic for Father. But even as I protested I knew that Mr Holmes would not lie to me. I traced the cover of my book. 'How long, then?' I asked. I could not look at him. Surely they would bring me home for Thanksgiving. We'd never spent a holiday apart.

'Your father reserved a space for a year.'

'A year,' I repeated. 'A year.' The cover of the book blurred. I could not fathom it. Father had not told me himself. He had let a stranger do his bidding. My father was weak. I saw that so clearly now.

Mr Holmes spoke again. His voice was kind. 'You are liked here. This is not a place of punishment, regardless of your parents' intention. It is a privilege, to be here.' He paused, and the pleasure his voice had brought disappeared. I looked at him, and offered a small smile, so that he would go on. 'You'll make of it what you will, but please don't hate it. I imagine you might grow to love it.'

I said nothing. I did not trust my voice. He stood, as if to go. He must think I wanted to be alone. I wanted nothing less.

'Do they know I'm sick?' I asked.

He didn't want to answer, I could see he didn't want to, but he nodded, and pursed his lips together, and I could tell he thought my parents were terrible. He was thinking of his own girls, how quickly he would go to them if they fell ill, and I wanted to tell him that he was correct, my parents were awful, but I also wanted him to know that they loved me, that he did not know what I had done. That he should not judge them. And that none of us knew how we would act, under certain circumstances. None of us, including him.

'They are concerned,' he said hesitantly.

The sound of my laugh surprised him; he looked at me curiously.

'You must think I'm a fool,' I said, before he could go on. 'A rube.' A word I would never have been allowed to say at home. Slang, common.

'Thea,' he said, shaking his head. He was so close I could see the stubble where his beard fought to grow. 'I have never for an instant thought you were a fool. I do not pretend to understand the intricacies of other families.' He paused, and shook his head. 'I'm sorry. I should speak plainly. I do not know your parents, Thea. I do not understand the way in which your family operates. But I know that things have a way of working themselves out, if not immediately, then eventually.'

Before he left, he said one last thing: 'It has always been a great comfort to me that I could bring a book anywhere, to any place. To any part of my life. I'm glad to see you're taking the same comfort.'

When he closed the door and the room was empty again, I sobbed into my pillow. I had not cried like this since home. I must mean so little to them that they had not told me themselves. My chest was on fire, I could hardly breathe. I made it to the wastebasket in time and retched into it. The taste was bitter in my mouth. I'd eaten nothing, but still my body produced enough to expel.

I opened the closet where the supplies were kept and stared at my reflection. I was ugly already, pale and dirty and sharply thin. Now my eyes were swollen and red. My lips were cracked. I looked like some kind of monster; it seemed impossible that my family would ever recognize me. I'd never spent more than a night away from my home, and that was only in Gainesville with Georgie.

When Sam and I were ten, young enough not to be told directly what had happened but old enough to put the pieces together, a woman in Emathla killed herself. She put her infant to bed on a cold night with a quilt; she came back in the morning to find him dead, his face in the quilt. She'd smothered him by trying to protect him, and after she found him, after my father had come and examined the body, after the funeral, the condolences, the stream of calls from neighbors and well-wishers, she'd drunk a bottle of ammonia. My father was called to the house again, though she was already dead when he arrived, and Sam heard him tell my mother that her throat was badly burned, that she'd found a way to punish herself even as she died.

Sam had found me in the tack room, excited by the news, not quite sure what it all meant. I had understood. Not much scared me, but this had: that a person could be so brutal to herself.

There were other stories of people who sought their own death, some successful, some not. I had a closet of infirmary supplies at my disposal. Sharp scissors, a selection of pills, bottles of alcohol and disinfectants. It seemed uncharacteristically careless of Mrs Holmes that she had not locked the closet.

The woman had been young, newly married, probably no more than twenty; not so much older than me. I watched myself smooth my hair, the way my hand so easily clasped and released, over and over again until I stopped. I *would* stop, I would close the closet doors and return to my bed, perhaps start my book again where I had left off.

I wanted to be alive. I wanted to live. I was not weak. And in order to do that, I would make a home here. I would make a home without my family.

★ ★ ★

A slice of light fell upon my bedspread, and I could feel someone looming near the bed. Sam, I thought, half-asleep; here to pull me out of bed like he did nearly every morning.

'Thea?'

'Sissy,' I said, and sat up straight.

'You look like you've seen a ghost!'

'I was surprised,' I said, drawing my covers around me more tightly. Sissy did look like a ghost, pale in the near darkness.

'Mrs Holmes let me come. I'm her favorite,' she said, and framed her face with her hands. She waited for me to laugh, but I couldn't.

I was silent for a moment, and so was she; then I switched on the lamp, illuminating us both.

'She probably thinks you're a good influence,' I said finally, avoiding her pressing gaze.

'What's wrong, Thea?'

I looked at her briefly. She looked so concerned, so upset for my sake.

'My parents aren't coming to get me.' She looked unsurprised. 'You knew,' I said.

'I figured,' she said. 'I hoped.'

'I want to go home.' I was embarrassed by the sound of my voice, thick and overwrought. I covered my face.

'But why?' she interrupted, and gently pulled my hands from my face. 'What's so good about there?'

I looked at her incredulously. 'I miss it,' I said. 'I miss my brother.'

'Your brother, who hasn't written you a single letter?'

'But,' I sputtered, 'it's not his fault. You don't know what I did, Sissy.' Sissy could not understand. I felt sorry for her, that she hadn't ever loved her sister like I loved Sam.

'Try me.' She gazed at me levelly; I'd never seen her so firm.

'But I don't want to try you.' I was feeling desperate. I put my hand to my throat. 'I want to go home.'

She tilted her head. 'The rumor was that you were sent away because of a boy.'

'The rumor?' I repeated.

She gave a short laugh. 'There's always a rumor. Some girl knows someone who knows someone who knows your parents. Something like that.' She tilted her head. 'Is it true?'

'Yes,' I said, and the words that were both true and a lie tumbled from my throat so easily. 'I was sent away because of a boy.'

'Believe me, you're not the only one.' She felt for my hand, through the covers. Her touch was surprisingly strong. 'I'm sorry that you can't go home. But look what you have here – me!' I smiled – I couldn't help it. 'And people who send you chocolates.' She picked up a box from my nightstand. 'What's so good about home? They'd send you away anyway, in a few years, with a husband.' She fiddled with the bow on the box and seemed hesitant suddenly.

'Sissy?'

She looked up. 'I need your help.'

Some people were so easy to read. What would that be like, to wear your heart on your sleeve as Sissy did? My life might be better now, if my heart weren't so carefully tucked away.

'With Boone?' I asked. The cabin had known he was writing her letters, and that she was writing back. She'd shown me parts of them. I could picture his blocky, masculine handwriting.

'I'm in love,' she said very seriously. I wanted to laugh.

'How can you be in love with him?' I asked. 'You've only spent an evening in his company.' Then it occurred to me that this wasn't necessarily the case. 'Isn't that right?'

Sissy turned her cheek, and I noticed a small scar near her ear.

From chicken pox, perhaps. I thought of my own letter, from David, which had been brief. It was a perfectly reasonable letter, one I should have been glad to have received. But boys were trouble. Boys didn't know how to behave. I'd taken it to the Castle and thrown it into the fire when no one was looking. I knew from the other girls that unless I wrote back, David wouldn't send me another letter. It would be the height of bad manners, to write a lady again when she hadn't responded the first time.

I tapped Sissy's wrist. 'Sissy?'

'Only once,' she said finally.

'Sissy.' The disappointment in my voice surprised me.

'Don't scold me.' She took my hand. 'I can't help it.'

'But if you're caught, you'll be sent home.'

'Oh, that would be the least of my worries. My grandfather would murder me. He'd marry me off to some boring Monroeville boy in an instant.' She snapped her fingers, then paused. When she spoke again, her voice was softer. 'He wouldn't think twice about it.' She shuddered. 'If I play my cards right, *I'll* decide who I marry. And I won't get caught. Not if you help me.' She squeezed my hand, as if entreating me, as if it were up to me whether or not Sissy and Boone could be together. And I saw that Sissy was good, that she had learned to move through this world and love people, and let them love her back; that she did not love too intensely, as I did, or not at all, as I imagined Leona did.

'Of course,' I said, 'of course I'll help you.'

She needed me to help her meet him in the woods at night, after the rest of camp was asleep. My bed was near the window, on which Boone could easily signal his arrival with a tap. And I would sleep in Sissy's bed once she was gone, because Mary Abbott, who was the lightest sleeper in the cabin, faced Sissy's bed. This had been my idea – Sissy had told me how good I was at this. That she didn't seem to appreciate the risk she was taking made me want to help her more. One false step and Sissy would be gone, removed from Yonahlossee as quickly as if she had never existed.

Was there something about me that spoke of a receptiveness to this sort of thing? An explicitness in my nature, some quality I was unaware of that made me bad? This was all fun for Sissy. And I wanted it to be that way for her, because she was not like I was.

I thought about the woman in Emathla who had smothered her child with love. I thought about Mother, how isolated she had kept us, how now she had turned me out completely, had thrown me to the wolves. She had known I was sick, and not even telephoned. Father – he had let Mother have her way with us. But knowing all this, how completely I had been cast out, and how Father could not even bring himself to tell me, made being in this place easier. How could I go home, now? What kind of home would it be? I wondered. Would it be any home at all? Yesterday Mrs Holmes had told me I could use the telephone. She felt sorry for me. I had considered her offer for a moment, considered the sound of my family's voices, which I had never heard before except in person. And then I shook my head no.

They had kept Sam, because he had not done anything bad. But my poor twin – there was this world here, among other people, and he knew nothing of it.

CHAPTER
SEVEN

When I left the windowless infirmary after three weeks, the first thing I noticed were the trees, covered now in a brilliant palette of reds and oranges, bright and rich, indescribable, really. The colors, I thought; in Florida the leaves never changed colors, or even died, instead appeared everlasting. I'd read about fall in other places, and Eva had mentioned the colors, but it had happened so quickly; while I had been away, the world turned into a painting; it almost hurt my eyes to look.

I closed my eyes against the electric color. Why should it be surprising that this beauty signaled death? Eva had told me the Indian myth: four hunters tracked a bear into the sky and killed him; he bled scarlet from the heavens, onto the leaves of all the trees as he died.

I had gotten sicker before I'd gotten better, and Mrs Holmes had kept me confined because she had not wanted to risk the health of all the other girls. Thank God for health and happiness, everyone said, or murmured, or shouted, depending on the girl. A chorus as I reentered my camp routine, made my way from Augusta House to the dining hall, clinging to Sissy's arm, out of weakness, but shyness, too: the girls had become strangers in my absence. Henny was engaged to a boy from home. Katherine Hayes's uncle had murdered his wife and shot himself in the

head upon learning that his railroad fortune had evaporated. A
teacher had almost been bitten by a rabid raccoon; Mr Holmes
had heard her screams and shot the animal just in time. Jettie had
been caught drinking, for the second time, by Mrs Holmes; the
real story there was that she had been drinking alone. Like a man.
She was not allowed to ride for a week, which even seemed a
worse punishment than embroidering handkerchiefs. Gossip
abounded. And Augusta House was one girl smaller: Victoria had
left, gone back to Jackson, Mississippi. The clothing stores her
family owned had collapsed all at once, like a house of cards. The
bunk above Sissy was empty now, but she stayed put. She said she
was afraid of falling.

Camp was smaller now, too, by a third: the summer girls had
gone home.

Mrs Holmes left every winter for three weeks to visit the vast
troupe of Yonahlossee alumnae, scattered about the South. Mr
Holmes could not go, apparently, because he was not Southern,
and, as Sissy put it, Southerners liked to exchange money with
other Southerners. Sissy had learned from her grandfather, who
sat on Yonahlossee's board, that Mrs Holmes would double the
length of her fund-raising trip this year. But no one was supposed
to know, lest they think Yonahlossee's fortunes were falling.

'But won't everyone notice when she's gone?' I asked.

'You'd be surprised at how little girls around here notice,'
Sissy said. 'And everyone will be glad to have Mrs Holmes gone.
Mr Holmes's punishments are half as bad as hers.'

I would be glad to have her gone. She knew everything about
me.

I was not allowed to ride. The muscles in my calves had
grown small during my convalescence, my arms had turned
flabby, my shoulders bony. I could hook my hands around my
waist if I sucked in all my breath, hard; I had turned weak, for the

first time in my life that I could remember. For the first time since infancy.

I slipped away to the barn one afternoon, when all the other girls were studying at the Hall. Now instead of bird-watching, botany, and painting we had history, literature, and home economics; math and science didn't seem to exist in this mountain enclave. We didn't have much homework, either, or nothing that took very much time. I liked literature, unsurprisingly, taught by bland Miss Brooks. She became impassioned, though, when referring to books she loved, and watching her I sometimes thought, isn't that always the way? A dull girl charmed by a book?

Mainly girls gossiped in the Hall, or read magazines. Naari did not seem pleased to see me, as Sasi would have; she didn't know me as well. But it was a comfort to see her, anyway, it was a comfort to smell the smell of horses, to smooth her forelock against her broad face, to pet her impossibly soft muzzle. Like silk, I thought, but no, it was softer than that.

I heard footsteps behind me and turned, expecting a groom. But it was little Decca Holmes, holding a short crop. Holding it out to me, it seemed.

'I found this,' she said. There was a smudge of dirt on her cheek. She was very pretty, with her mother's almond-shaped eyes and her father's dark features. Her hair was always braided tightly, in pigtails, but they were loose right now, strands of dark brown hair, almost black, falling in her face.

I accepted the crop. 'Thank you,' I said. And after that I did not know what to say.

'What's it called?' Decca asked.

'A crop.' She seemed to want more of an answer, so I spelled it. But she only looked at me quizzically.

'Crop,' she repeated. 'Crop!' She held out her hand, and I gave it back to her. 'What is it used for?' she asked.

'To nudge the horse along, when he's being lazy,' I said. The quizzical look, again. 'To hit him. To make him go faster.'

'Like a spanking?' Decca asked.

'Exactly.'

The handsome groom entered the barn, and Naari swung her head over the stall door at the sound of his footsteps. It was feeding time. Decca jumped back, and eyed Naari nervously.

'Don't be scared,' I said. 'She's just hungry. She's excited, like you are, for dessert.' I thought it was strange that a girl who had been raised around horses was afraid of them. They were the gentlest creatures in the world. But I couldn't remember ever seeing a Holmes girl ride.

'Do you want to give her a sugar cube?' I asked. Decca pushed her hair out of her eyes and nodded.

I showed her how to hold her hand flat, so that Naari would not accidentally catch one of her fingers. Naari lifted the sugar cube from Decca's hand delicately, and then crunched it between her back teeth.

Decca giggled. 'It tickled!'

We walked back to the Castle together, Decca's small, sticky hand in mine. I was her friend now, it seemed. Being around her had not made me miss my family more, as I had assumed it would; Decca made me miss my family less. She reminded me of Sam, his curiosity, his quiet intensity. She was so observant, and this was how Sam had been, still was: he watched everyone, everything.

Mrs Holmes was surprised to see us enter the dining room together, but then she smiled at her youngest daughter, who ran to greet her. Mrs Holmes tucked Decca's errant hair back into place as Decca spoke. That was what mothers did: they never simply listened. They straightened, and fixed; they ordered their children's worlds while they listened. And if they were good at it, like Mrs Holmes was, like my mother had been, their children never noticed. Decca sat down for dinner, her hair neatened, none the wiser.

I asked Mr Holmes if I could speak to him the next day, then followed him into his office, where I'd last been with my father. We passed Jettie, who caught my eye and smiled. I liked Jettie. There was something unaffected about her.

Mr Holmes's office was full of leather, brass-studded furniture, the brown velvet settee I had sat on when I first came – surely where all the ladies and children sat, behind their husbands and fathers. I wondered if my father had noticed it, or if he had been so focused on the task at hand – transferring the responsibility of my safekeeping to a man he had never met – that the room around him had dissolved.

I sat in the chair my father had sat in, felt the same leather beneath my arms, and I wondered what my father had noticed when he sat in this room. If he had noticed anything at all, or had been so focused on discussing matters – me – with Mr Holmes that the room had slipped away.

'Thea, you're feeling much better?'

'Yes, thank you.'

He folded his hand underneath his chin. He seemed a little too sensitive to heroically kill a raccoon.

'I have an idea,' I began, but that seemed too childish. 'I have a proposition.'

'Please,' Mr Holmes said, and nodded. 'Continue.' He seemed amused.

'Your daughters. I'd like to teach them.'

'Teach them how, Thea?' There was no gray in Mr Holmes's hair, as there was in Father's, and his skin was unlined. He was thirty or thirty-one, nobody knew for sure, and Sarabeth was eleven, which meant he had been very young indeed when he had become a father. A few years older than I was now. While it was rumored that Mrs Holmes was older than her husband, I alone knew her age, approximately the same as my mother's: thirty-six. It was unusual in those days that the husband be younger than the wife – my own father was five years older than my mother – and I liked Mr Holmes more for it. His marriage made him seem generous. It made perfect sense that he and Mrs Holmes had had children as soon as they'd married; age was not kind to women.

'To ride,' I said, feeling bolder; something about the way he watched me so closely, almost eagerly, made me want to continue. I gestured at the framed photograph on his desk, the three Holmes girls all in white. 'Decca said that she and her sisters don't ride, but that they want to.'

'Did she say that?' Mr Holmes asked.

I nodded. 'And Mr Albrecht would help me. I wouldn't be alone with them.'

'I'm not concerned about you being alone with them, Thea.' He looked at the photograph. 'They do need to know how to ride, their mother and I agree. Especially Sarabeth and Rachel. But Decca seems so young.'

I shook my head and inched to the edge of my chair. 'Oh no,' I said, 'the younger the better. It will be second nature to her, if she learns early enough.'

He looked at some papers on his desk, smiled, as if at some private joke. I waited; I wanted this, I wanted this very badly. And was taking advantage, or at least depending on, Mr Holmes's kindness. If anyone would let me have my way in this, it would be him.

'Please,' I said, 'I need to be around horses. And I'm not

allowed to ride until I'm stronger.' I hoped my voice didn't sound too desperate, but knew it probably did, because I could feel the desperation surging through my brain. And what I did not say was that I wanted to be around his girls, that they were a family and I had none here. That his presence brought comfort; that being near his daughters meant being nearer to him. I could never say that.

'All right, Thea,' he said, after a moment. 'You've convinced me. And I will convince Mrs Holmes.'

Did he guess my reasons, which were twofold? Horses and girls, girls and horses. I wanted to be around children around horses; I wanted to see the Holmes girls learn to love a beast. I wanted their father to watch me.

I was distracted during history class, could not remember the site of Grant's great War Between the States defeat.

'Shiloh,' Leona answered when I could not. Sam would have been ashamed – he had all the dates of those battles memorized.

History, then French, then the day was half over; finally, lunch.

'I'll see you,' I said to Sissy, who was chatting with Eva. I ran to catch Leona, who walked alone.

'No running,' a house mistress called; the voice sounded like Henny's, but I didn't look. I slowed and weaved in and out of the girls making their way to the dining hall, masses of them, so many girls! I'd forgotten the sheer size of us when we moved from one place to another. I brushed a little too close to Alice Hunt and she glared at me; I mouthed an apology.

Leona didn't turn around, gave no signal she had heard me. I was out of breath, my feet were heavy, and I could feel a sheen of sweat forming on my upper lip. I felt desperate, suddenly, unwell and crude.

'Thea,' Leona said calmly, when I reached her side.

'Hello,' I said, and settled into her pace.

'I wanted to thank you for the chocolates,' I said, 'they were delicious.' Scrumptious, I had almost said, Mother's highest praise, delivered on rare occasions.

'It was nothing. I told my mother and she arranged it.'

'She sent them from Texas?'

Leona laughed. 'Yes, across the country.' I was so close to her I could see a little crop of white-blond hair on her upper lip, blighting her otherwise faultless face. Leona turned her head to look at me, and I felt as if she'd caught me staring.

I blushed.

'No, they were not shipped all the way from Texas.' She sounded amused. 'They would melt. But they were Swiss chocolates. Could you tell the difference?'

'Yes, of course.'

We were approaching the entrance to the dining hall and Leona paused for a beat, took the open door from another girl, and waved me through as if she were the man.

I found my table and slid into my seat. I looked at the meal: fried chicken, a camp favorite; green beans, roasted potatoes. I had no appetite, but the iced tea was still appealing. Henny, a ruby-and-diamond engagement ring now upon her plump finger, had clearly been told to watch my eating habits, and all her sideways glances made me nervous. I took the smallest piece of fried chicken I could find, a wing, and an extra spoonful of roasted potatoes to compensate. The thought of consuming flesh made me sick. In the infirmary, I had begun to picture my lungs, huge slabs of red meat, throbbing, as if they each contained their own heart, turning black at the edges. On days I felt worse I imagined the black creeping steadily toward the lung's center, approaching. On days I felt better the black receded.

I listened to Molly pester Henny with questions about the

raccoon. Across the dining room, I saw Sissy nodding sympath-etically, murmuring to slender Katherine Hayes, whom I recognized across the room by her curls. I wondered if her uncle had the same curls. I felt sorry for her, but wondered if she'd loved her uncle as much as I'd loved mine. I was jealous, too, because she was blameless.

I turned back to my plate. Henny caught my eye, and I tried to smile reassuringly. In another week I would be just another Yonahlossee girl. I'd been sick, I'd become well, I was here again.

CHAPTER EIGHT

Dear Thea,

We're told you're well. The mountain air is better for you than the air here, I'm sure. And all those girls for you, all those horses. Are your teachers teaching well?

You haven't sent a letter in almost a month. I hope that your silence is a sign of how busy you are, at the camp.

Nothing seems to have changed – Sam and I continue with his lessons, your mother is out in the garden all day, preparing all her precious flora for winter.

Take pity on your parents and send us a letter. Be merciful, Thea, it is a capacity that God has granted only us.

And nary a week until your Birthday. Happy You Day. (I will shout the other half to Sam!) Did you think I would forget? That day was the happiest day of my life, of all our lives.

Love,
Father

It was true, I had not written a letter since I'd been in the infirmary, since I'd learned that I would not be returning home at the end of the summer. I was angry – they'd known I was ill, and had not come to get me – but as my anger dissipated, I saw that I needed to not think of them in order to survive here. I would train myself not to want my family. I needed to live my Yonahlossee life without thinking of how to frame it in a letter for my parents and brother.

I put the letter in my vanity drawer, along with Sam's handkerchief, which I had not been able to bring with me to the infirmary. I had missed it, at first, but then the want had disappeared.

If I had been stronger I would not have opened their letters, which came once a week. Mother and Father alternated the task. They were brief, briefer now that I gave them no reply. I was glum after their letters; Sissy noticed. But I was not strong enough to leave them unopened. There might be some news of Sam inside, or even Georgie.

Thanksgiving at Yonahlossee was a small affair, a more elaborate version of Sunday dinner. Sissy was gone for the week, pining away in Monroeville; that she would miss her weekly tryst with Boone, who came every Thursday, would hang over her week like a cloud. Mary Abbott was the only girl from Augusta House who hadn't gone home, and the atmosphere in the dining hall was solemn, almost.

'Thea!' Decca called out when I entered the dining hall with Mary Abbott. I scanned the room and saw that girls sat out of place. I felt sorry for Mary Abbott, who I knew would have jumped at the chance to follow me, but you did not sit at the head table without an invitation, and Decca wound her hand through mine while thoroughly ignoring Mary Abbott, as only a child could.

Decca led me to the head table, where a few teachers sat along with Alice Hunt, who must have also been granted a head-table invitation. Miss Brooks smiled at me, and I smiled back. Mr and

Mrs Holmes were at either end of the table, as if they were hosting the dinner. Which they were, I suppose. Mr Albrecht sat next to Mrs Holmes; he smiled when he saw me. Sissy told me Mr Albrecht and Mrs Holmes were friends. Nobody cared, though, because Mr Albrecht wasn't handsome and Mrs Holmes wasn't beautiful.

'Here,' Decca said, and pointed to the chair next to her, only sitting down herself after she made sure I was settled, even lifting my napkin from my plate and tossing it into my lap. Mr Holmes watched her with his amused expression.

'Thea,' he said, 'I'm glad that you could join us. You're quite famous in the Holmes' household. Decca especially is your biggest fan.' Decca nodded seriously. Sarabeth grinned at me, but Rachel looked as if she had been crying, her cheeks mottled and pink.

'I'm flattered,' I said, and I was.

True to form, Alice Hunt barely looked at me. I watched the girls file in and saw Leona, her hair pulled back into a tight bun. She looked straight at me, as if she had caught me thinking about her, but her expression revealed nothing. There had been whispers that her family was suffering financially. That was how Sissy had put it – suffering, as if lack of money was a wound. Which it was, the worst kind. But Sissy didn't believe the rumors, and I hadn't, either – Leona's very bearing, the way she carried herself around the room – seemed wealthy, but I wondered why she hadn't gone home for Thanksgiving.

Mrs Holmes wore an old-fashioned mourning cameo pinned at her throat, the hair of the dead intricately plaited behind glass. You had to look closely to see that it was hair at all; it almost looked like a piece of textured fabric. I knew from my lessons that the Victorians had been wild about mourning jewelry, just another way, along with séances, they had tried and failed to reach the dead. Or perhaps they had not failed – Father did not believe in spirits, but how could he know, for sure?

Mother had a mourning locket, passed down to her from her great-grandmother. It was pure gold, designating the loss of her five-year-old son. My parents might as well be dead: the thought sprang into my head, unbidden, and I was ashamed. I was a nasty girl, with nasty thoughts.

Mrs Holmes noticed me looking and her hand went to her throat. It was easy to see how Mrs Holmes could have been pretty before she'd lost her figure.

I wondered who she had lost, or if she wore the piece for fashion's sake. I wondered how she and Mr Holmes had met. It was camp lore that Mr Holmes had defected from the North to the South, though nobody could say for sure why and the wilder speculations involved gambling debts, a lost love (not Mrs Holmes).

I had thought that we would be allowed to dress in our own clothes for Thanksgiving, but even the Holmes girls wore starched white shirts. Sarabeth was almost old enough to be part of the first-year class, but I doubted she would ever live in a cabin.

I had begun to love the Holmes girls, especially Decca, who loved me back. Sarabeth, who so resembled her mother, had turned pretty to me, her inherited stoutness transformed into a charming plumpness. Rachel, quiet and afraid of the world, I hoped I would teach to be unafraid, at least as far as horses were concerned. And finally, Decca; her path seemed already lit by a charmed light. She was the natural rider of the three girls, which was perhaps why I loved her most.

I was needed suddenly, and I liked the feeling, being needed instead of needing. Decca held out her arm, and I noticed a diamond-and-emerald bracelet clasped around her thin wrist. 'That's beautiful,' I said, and traced the rectangular emerald baguettes that alternated with sparkling round diamonds. It was much too fine a thing for Decca to be wearing; even Alice Hunt studied the bracelet attentively.

'The girls got into my jewelry this morning,' Mrs Holmes said. 'Decca chose to ornament herself most exquisitely.' She sighed, but not unkindly; the holiday must have put her in good cheer. It occurred to me that Mrs Holmes had fared better than my mother, at least in terms of jewelry. Mother kept all of her finest jewels in a safe.

Decca beamed. 'I'm exquisite!' she shouted, and Sarabeth put her finger to her lips.

Mrs Holmes touched her husband's forearm, and Mr Holmes gazed at her, lost in thought, and then he stood, abruptly.

The room fell silent, as it always did, but I had never observed so closely how it all worked. Before Mr Holmes's knees had straightened, the room was silent.

'Hand,' Decca whispered, when I kept my hands folded at my skirt, oblivious. Apparently the head table held hands.

Mr Holmes bowed his head, but still his voice projected, deep and melodious. I watched him as best I could with my neck bent. He thanked God for all the normal things: us, health, happiness, and, because of Thanksgiving, the spirit of generosity.

'And please remember those who are not as fortunate as us, in this time of great instability. May God grant them and us mercy.' He stopped, and seemed to want to say something else, but nothing came. A few girls fidgeted. It was hard to hold our attention for very long. 'We are not untouched by the tragedies of late. The girls who have had to return home – hold them in your prayers.' He had our attention, now. It had never been said, by him or Mrs Holmes, that the girls who had left had done so because their fathers could no longer afford tuition. We knew, of course, but not officially. Mrs Holmes frowned, but the source of her displeasure – her husband's revelation or the sadness of the lost girls – wasn't clear, at least not to me.

'Amen,' we chorused. Decca held on to my hand, and smiled up at me. Her two front teeth had a gap between them, only a small space, and though I knew it probably would disappear when she lost her baby teeth, I half-hoped it wouldn't. She tugged on my hand and laughed, inexplicably, before she dropped it. She was always involved in a game, most often played by herself. Children *were* careless and unpredictable, as I had feared, but that was the fun of them.

'What kind of dressing does your mother make?' Sarabeth asked, suddenly, as the food was still being served. The subtext was clear: why are you here, and not there? Sarabeth seemed to have inherited her mother's shrewdness.

'She doesn't,' I said.

'Our mother makes cornbread dressing,' Decca said, 'for our own Thanksgiving.'

'Take your elbow off the table, Decca,' Mrs Holmes said.

'Your own Thanksgiving?' I asked.

'Tomorrow,' Mrs Holmes replied. 'The girls have to learn how to cook, how to set a table. They won't be served all their lives. One would imagine.' She was ladling gravy as she spoke, her eyes darting back and forth from her plate to her girls. Where would all the other girls learn these things, I wondered. I knew how to knead a passable pie crust, how to clean a chicken; this year, Idella was supposed to teach me how to put up preserves. But I didn't much care for cooking, or any of the domestic arts.

'Do you eat snakes down in Florida?' Rachel asked. 'Alligators?'

I blushed. Eva had told me my blushing was the curse of a redhead, though my hair wasn't truly red. Close enough, Eva had said.

Mrs Holmes glared at Rachel. 'Rachel,' she said, 'that is not an appropriate question for the table.' Rachel nodded. She hadn't meant to be inappropriate; it was so hard to know, sometimes, what was and what wasn't.

'That's fine,' I said, and smiled. 'No snakes, but I've eaten plenty of crabs. And crawfish.'

'Crayfish,' Mr Holmes corrected, and winked at the girls, 'we have a Southerner on our hands.'

Alice Hunt perked up at this reference, eager, I assumed, to lay claim to the South.

I laughed. 'Hardly.' But his daughters were little Southern girls, with their smocked dresses and Southern accents and big bows clipped to their hair.

'You're from the Southernmost state. What else would you be if not a Southerner?'

'I'm a Floridian. And we're a different breed.'

'Unbound by the rules of society and civilization, a breed apart?'

We were the only people at the table speaking, and I felt, suddenly, as if on stage. I was drawing too much attention to myself. Alice Hunt patted the corners of her mouth with a white linen napkin, so gently.

'I can't speak for everyone from the state,' I said lightly, but even as I spoke, my voice sounded cold, serious. 'But Florida's a different place. And besides, I don't think we're Southern enough for the rest of the South.'

Alice Hunt nodded, and I had a feeling it was the first and last time she would ever agree with me. Mr Holmes looked at me for a long second. Then Rachel, who hadn't touched her food, began to cry. Her arms were crossed, and she looked fiercely at her plate. We all gazed at her, stupidly, before Mr Holmes broke the silence.

'Oh, Rachel,' he murmured.

Then Mrs Holmes rose. 'Come with me, dear.'

After they were gone, the table was quiet. 'Rachel's had a difficult week,' Mr Holmes said to the table at large, but no one responded. I nodded, and he looked grateful. 'She's quite sensitive.'

Leona found me at the end of the meal, as I slowly made my way out of the dining hall.

'Thea,' she said, and threaded her arm through mine. I looked at her, surprised. 'Full moon tonight.' We were descending the stairs now, and I looked up and saw the moon was, indeed, full.

I waited for her to say something else – isn't it beautiful, makes me miss home – something to account for her arm through mine, for the anticipation that made her voice almost quiver, which was something Leona's voice never did. Leona was steely in her stoicism. Her behavior was rare at Yonahlossee, where there was always a girl crying, a girl giggling, a girl flinging her head from side to side in delight or hysteria or some combination.

'The perfect time for a night ride,' she said, and looked at me; her expression was hopeful, and I realized that she hoped I would go with her.

The barn was empty, but we were silent just in case. Mr Holmes would be disappointed in me if he knew I'd disobeyed the doctor's orders, but there was little chance he'd come down here tonight. Besides, it was more exciting this way, to pretend we might be caught, to pretend that we risked something tonight; there was so little we ever risked at Yonahlossee. We could fail our classes, smoke in the woods, be insolent to our teachers, and all we would get was a warning. It was only boys that were a true risk to one's place at Yonahlossee, one's reputation. For all of Mrs Holmes's talk of education, of carving a place for women in this world, the worst thing we could do here was give ourselves away too easily.

Leona and I tiptoed, did not let the hard soles of our boots meet the ground, though there was no one to hear except the horses – who all watched us curiously, eyes wide, ears tipped forward, their necks pressed against their stall doors. I slipped Naari's bit into her mouth and led her to the front of the barn; she whuffed into my shoulder, nervously, and I murmured soothingly. She was a ball of energy, and after I mounted she danced beneath me like some sort of overgrown sprite, clumsily, her hooves knocking against each other. She was out of practice, too.

Leona led on a trail wide enough for only one horse. Though Naari didn't like it, kept trying to pull ahead of King, I held her back, slid the bit over her tongue, shifted my weight to keep her attention.

We rode on the trail briefly before we came to a large clearing, where we both let our horses go without speaking, stood up in our stirrups and let them fly beneath us. I was so close to Leona our boots brushed; this was how horses raced, neck and neck. The moon was an orb above us, lighting our way; for a while, there wasn't an ending to this, just the blank space of the field for as far as I could see. I gave Naari her head and felt the stinging cold in my ears, the warmth of my calves where they touched Naari's barrel. My hair, which I had not had a chance to braid, whipped my cheeks. I could do this forever, was how I felt; and what else is there to say about galloping? A feeling so close to fear. One misstep and Naari might break a leg, and I would certainly fall, hurtled to the ground with astounding velocity.

You don't want it to ever end. I knew Leona felt the same way. Naari moved so fast beneath me I could hardly feel her move at all. Father had told us that history was a lesson, a way to never forget what had happened before us. And now I knew from my own experience that you could never leave the past behind. But galloping that Thanksgiving night, the first Thanksgiving I had ever spent away from my family, I *was* leaving the past behind. And however illusory this feeling was, the faster we went, the more of it was lost.

Naari and I pulled ahead – she was small and compact, built to be faster than King – but then I sensed Leona at her flank, and without looking I knew Leona was racing us. Before, I had simply let Naari run, but now I pressed my legs around her throbbing sides and touched her lightly with my spurs, which was all it took. She shot in front of King, whom I could hear breathing furiously behind us.

Afterward, Leona and I walked the length of the field, our mounts spent. I had never raced before, only galloped solo on my pony.

'She's fast,' Leona said, which I knew was half a compliment, half a signal that I had nothing to do with Naari's speed. But horses weren't raced without jockeys.

She spoke again. 'Other girls don't like me.' She paused. 'They think I'm cold.' And I knew now she was speaking of Sissy, who had used that exact word. 'I don't care what they think. All I care about is horses.' I watched her profile as she spoke, her square jaw offset prettily by her sloped nose. I looked down at my hands, red and chapped from gripping the reins so tightly in the cold.

'I know . . .' I meant to go on, but I couldn't find the words, let my voice slip into the night. I knew what it was like, to love horses. But I also knew what it was like to love humans. I knew what it was like to want, to desire so intensely you were willing to throw everything else into its fire. There was a reason that I was not at home for Thanksgiving this year. And Leona? Were the whispers true? It did not seem so – she acted the same as ever. Quiet, impenetrable, strong.

★ ★ ★

I lay in bed that night and thought of Mother. I first sat on a horse when I was still a baby, tucked in the saddle in front of Mother, on her old horse, Chikee. He died when I was seven, and that was when Mother stopped riding for good. I used to pity her, quietly, for not riding. Surely she must have missed it, I thought. Surely it was a loss.

I can't remember being told exactly why Mother stopped riding, but I had a vague notion that it related to the pain that sometimes beset her, the pain that was a result of our births. But Mother did not complain.

Mother brought Chikee to the marriage. He was almost twenty-one when he died, ancient for a horse. He was buried where he fell, in the pasture; Father had to hire several men to dig a hole large enough for him. In pictures he is handsome and dark, with gentle eyes. Mother loved him. It is a simple thing, to love a horse.

Mother said that I rode with my head, not with my heart. And that riding with my head would serve me well in many instances, but it would not earn Sasi's enduring loyalty. I always thought that was a romantic view of it.

I rolled over and faced the window. It was like looking into nothing, the night was so black. I had wanted her there, tonight. I had wanted her to see how I floated above the earth. Would she have loved me, then? Watched me and known in her heart that I was her daughter, her daughter who could ride so beautifully, sit atop and not interfere with a horse going as fast as time and space would allow. Mother, it was as if we were floating. Mother, if you cannot love me with your head, then at least with your heart.

And then a face appeared, and at first I thought I had conjured Mother from my thoughts. But no, a boy. I sat up, my heart racing, though by now I had realized it was Boone. I hurried outside, relieved by Mary Abbott's snoring.

Boone looked at me expectantly, and I realized he must not have gotten Sissy's letter. 'She's not here,' I said. 'She's in Monroeville.'

I'd never been this close to him. Usually I saw him briefly, recognizable by his shock of red hair, before I woke Sissy.

But now I was so close I could see his face fall, faintly, as I delivered the news. I knew that he had to borrow a car, drive over an hour, to get here. We stood at the edge of the woods. He took out a slender cigarette case and offered me one with the assurance that I would take it, which made me do exactly that. He cupped his hand around the tip as he lit it, with a silver lighter, and I could see why Sissy liked him. He was quiet and completely at ease with himself.

He leaned against the tree and studied me in his calm way. Meanwhile, I noticed the tip of the cigarette was receding quickly and I tried to take a drag like the stars in the movies did. No one in my family smoked.

Boone smiled. 'You've never done this before?' he asked gently.

I shook my head, embarrassed.

'Just think of it like breathing,' he said, and demonstrated.

'But with a cigarette,' I replied, and he laughed. He wore his clothes casually: a shirt that was pressed, but not crisply; a belt that was cinched around his narrow waist, but not tightly.

I felt suddenly as if we were going behind Sissy's back. She would not like this: me here, with him.

'I should go,' I said, and let my cigarette fall to the ground. Boone moved forward and I thought for a second that he was going to kiss me; he crushed the cigarette into the leaves with his shoe and then retreated, and I was such a foolish girl, seeing signs where none existed; believing, always, that I was an object of desire.

'Thea,' Boone said, and it was a bit of a shock, that he knew my name. 'Does Sissy . . .' Two girls passed by Augusta House. I recognized one of the voices as Jettie's.

I turned back to Boone. 'Does Sissy?'

'Does she say anything?'

'Many things,' I said, and Boone smiled. He seemed earnest. 'She likes you,' I said. 'And you?'

He nodded, slowly. 'I want to make sure I'm doing everything right.'

I smiled. That was impossible. 'I wouldn't worry . . . But you should leave, now. Someone might see us.'

I turned, and he said my name again. I looked back.

'David?' he asked. 'He's my friend.'

I had not imagined they talked about us like we talked about them. But of course they did. I shrugged. 'We'll see.'

Boone was not the type of boy to press an issue. He seemed very kind. Whatever Boone and Sissy had gotten themselves into – and who knew, really – at least he was kind. Perhaps he would not make her regret him.

Dear Sam,

I'm writing in the dark (there's the moon, like a sun, brighter than it ever is in Florida). All the rest of the girls are asleep.

Did you have orange cake? Were there candles?

I would describe how it is here, how different than home, but I don't know where to begin. It is exactly opposite of home. There are so many girls.

I went for a night ride last week. It was pure fun, Sam. Sometimes I forget why I'm here, sometimes all of that just slips away.

I've never written you a letter before. Or received one from you. Not ever. Do I sound like myself, Sam? How would you sound, I wonder. I suppose you might not be reading this at all. You might like to pretend I don't exist, that I won't ever return home, and I can't say I blame you, Sam, I can't say that at all.

I think of you at home and wonder if you do the same things you did when I was there. I wonder if you and Mother and Father have any new jokes, or if Idella has made any new foods. You won't know this until you go away, too, but it is impossible to think that life continues on without me. Does that sound proud? I don't mean it to be. I think you know what I mean.

When you go away you will see that there are other people in the world besides me. And Mother and Father. There are so many girls here. Hundreds of them. They have names I've never heard before: Harper, Roberta, Mary Abbott, Leona. I like them. Not all of them, but many of them. I think once you have seen how many other people there are in the world you won't hate me as much. Although I know you don't hate me – you were very clear on that point. You hate what I did. But is there a difference, Sam?

I'm teaching three little girls how to ride. Well, one isn't that little – she's twelve. But my favorite, Decca, is six years old. She reminds me of you – she's good with animals, horses all like her immediately. She's so young. She doesn't know about anything. She asks the strangest questions. Yesterday she asked why I was a girl and not a boy, as if I had any choice in the matter. I don't remember much from when we were six. I remember you.

You can't know how lonely I am sometimes.

I'll stop before I'm too sad. But before I do, I have to ask – does our cousin continue to heal?

> *Your Sister*
> *Thea*

I knew there was a very good chance that Mother would read any letter I wrote. She might not even give it to Sam. I thought she would, but I wasn't certain; she had always given us our privacy, had called it our autonomy, as if we had any real idea of what that meant. Mother read books on childrearing, and marked passages for Father to read. She considered herself progressive. That Sam and I were allowed to roam freely most of the day was evidence of her progressiveness, of her desire to raise children who thought and acted independently.

Mother had sent me a birthday present, from everyone, though I doubted Sam had any part in it, and a signal from him was all I'd wanted. A pair of drop pearl earrings, with diamond filigree. They were small but beautiful. I tucked them into my vanity drawer without showing anyone. They were her earrings, she wore them on special occasions. It was a mystery, why she had sent them to me. Did she think I'd have a chance to wear them, here? I would, probably, at a dance, but she couldn't have known that. The gift seemed like a gesture, an extravagant one, but I saw it as what it truly was: a way not to see me. They were just earrings, earrings she never wore anyway.

'Happy You Day,' Mother would have exclaimed when she first saw us, at the breakfast table, kissing Sam's temple and then mine. 'Happy Birthday to You and You.'

Last year, for our birthday, Idella had baked a spice cake with orange frosting. She made her own orange extract every year, my great-grandmother's recipe. Last year, my present had been a new dress and two books from Father. I'd wanted perfume from Paris, something I'd seen in a magazine, and I was disappointed I hadn't gotten it. But who would you wear it for, Mother had asked, amused. Sasi?

Last year, things were just beginning in earnest. Sam had received a hunting rifle, and Georgie had been given a matching one even though it wasn't his birthday. Sam had wanted a chemistry set he'd seen in a magazine, not a rifle, and he'd been so disappointed when he'd been handed the long box, clearly a gun.

My parents were always doing that, giving Georgie a present to match Sam's. And my cousin and aunt and uncle were always there, had celebrated all our birthdays with us. As we had celebrated all Georgie's with him. Even his birthday celebrations took place at our house, with a cake baked by Idella, though Aunt Carrie was a marvelous cook. It had never seemed strange. Our house was, of course, where everyone wanted to be. Just the presence of Uncle George and Aunt Carrie's neighbors felt like an intrusion. And we had all the land out back to play on.

I told no one about my birthday this year, not even Sissy, who was pleased that Boone had revealed to me how much he liked her. 'See?' she'd said. 'He loves me.' And I'd had to agree; it did seem that way.

I wondered what Sam had received for his birthday. I should have sent him a book along with my letter; a book where someone makes a mistake and pays the consequences. But that could be any of the books I loved: *Portrait of a Lady, The House of Mirth, The Age of Innocence*. And Sam would not read a book I'd sent him.

At Yonahlossee we celebrated after dinner, each girl took a slice of an enormous sheet cake; but, mercifully, my birthday had gone unnoticed. Perhaps, in the Thanksgiving preparations, it had fallen by the wayside. Or perhaps Mrs Holmes had not wanted me to have a birthday celebration. Either way, I was grateful.

CHAPTER NINE

Last Thanksgiving, I spent the morning in Uncle George and Aunt Carrie's guest room, sleeping and running to the toilet to vomit. I could hear my aunt and mother in the kitchen, cooking; Sam and Georgie up and down the stairs. I loved this chaotic preparation, cursed the illness and my father, who could not fix it though he was a doctor.

I was dozing, half-awake; I opened my eyes and saw Georgie, sitting next to me on the edge of the bed.

'You came to visit me.'

'Yeah.' He grinned. 'Yeah, I did.'

Perhaps because I had just been asleep, had woken, and my brain had not yet reset itself; perhaps because I had been sick, and now was feeling a little better – I can't say why, but my cousin sitting next to me filled me with an intense pleasure. I felt almost buoyant; my hands tingled. His grin seemed like some kind of path to another world.

'I'm glad,' I said, and my voice sounded strange. I touched his hand, above the covers. 'Thank you.'

'Sam came, too,' he said, and I realized my brother was there, sitting in the corner of the room. They had both come to see me, to wake me from my nap. Then Uncle George tapped on the door and told us to come downstairs, and though I'm sure we all went, I'm also sure that I walked around in a kind of dream, still woozy, not completely understanding the pleasure I'd felt with Georgie but greedy for it, not wanting it to disappear.

Aunt Carrie was a marvelous cook, the compliment my father routinely gave her. My mother was not; she didn't care enough about eating her food – picked at her meals, ate half of her plate – to care about preparing it. Her thinness was part of her beauty; her sharp angles carved a space for her wherever she went – my mother was a woman you were required to look at. Mother's beauty was delicate, fragile: a swan's neck, abrupt cheekbones, eyes that could never decide between hazel and green.

Aunt Carrie was plain. In her youth, I imagined, she looked sturdy in that Midwestern way: straw-blonde hair, dark blue eyes, a capable figure. When I knew her, Aunt Carrie was what Mother referred to as stocky, in a constant battle with her figure, and I wondered what happened to her figure after the trouble, whether or not she abstained from food in grief or turned to it for comfort. So when I thought of her at Yonahlossee, I saw her in two ways: as slender and pinched, her full cheeks replaced by dull hollows; or obese and slovenly, her neck folded, her arms ringed with fat. That she would look the same as when I last saw her was impossible.

I woke early the day after Thanksgiving, my sense of time disrupted as it is in illness. I felt completely well. I slept in the bed, Georgie and Sam on the floor; I sat up and saw Georgie was gone. My brother was a lump beneath an old blue quilt.

Aunt Carrie had little flair when it came to decorating. The guest room would have been better plain, in simple solids instead of competing florals. I fingered the duvet cover; burgundy cotton embroidered with gold medallions. Stiff and ugly, the whole room was a study in burgundy – the curtains, the chairs, the

Oriental rug. The brooding, mahogany bedroom set. Mother had been acquiring more and more art deco furniture, which was all clean lines and simple geometry. Aunt Carrie's house looked like it was out of last century.

Still, the house held a certain charm, my family lived there.

The door opened, and a chink of light shone through the curtains and cast a shadow over my cousin's face. I had wished him here and he had come; I felt nervous, suddenly, as I watched him enter the room, watched him shut the door a little too firmly, a thick thud and surely Mother would come see how I was. But no one came.

Georgie was losing his baby fat, developing an athletic posture, suddenly broad instead of awkward. I was still skin and bones.

'Are you up?' he asked.

'Almost.'

I lifted the covers and he got into bed beside me.

'I ate some pie for breakfast.'

'You couldn't wait for brunch?'

'I'll eat again,' Georgie said, 'don't worry.'

He shifted onto his side, and I could feel him staring. I closed my eyes. The cover rustled, and Georgie put his finger on the bridge of my nose, and traced it to its tip.

'Such a pretty nose,' he said, half seriously.

I giggled, and pulled the sheets up over my face. Georgie's hand was trapped, he moved it to my throat and my breath quickened, but it was not unusual for Georgie and me to find ourselves in intimate postures. We had always had an easy affection with each other, the consequence of being children together. But this felt, I knew even then, in that moment, different. I couldn't see Georgie, his hand rested warmly on my throat. His fingers moved, slightly, and I shivered. I rolled onto my side and faced him, pulled the sheet over both of us. His hand was beneath my cheek, now, his eyes were closed. We were so near I could feel his breath on my face, moist and peppery. I could hear perfectly each intake of breath. I put my hand on Georgie's shoulder; he didn't move. I shifted and felt that my nipples had hardened beneath my nightgown. I arched my back, to be closer to him, and in that instant there was a knock at the door, and Mother entered.

'Rise and shine,' she said, and I sat up, flushed, revealing Georgie as well, who had curled into a ball and was feigning sleep.

Mother paused at the foot of the bed, her eyes traveled over me, then Georgie, and I crossed my arms over my chest, though I knew she could see nothing.

'Feeling better, Thea?' Her face was calm and unreadable.

Georgie and I had slept in the same bed just last month. We had done nothing wrong.

'Yes, thank you. Ready for brunch.'

'All right,' she said. 'Georgie, why don't you wake up and come downstairs with me? I think your mother wants you.'

My mother had always been a bad liar. Her voice became thin, turned up at the ends of her words.

I sat in bed after they had gone, a little stunned.

'Morning, sunshine,' Sam said, and I jumped. I had forgotten he was here. He lay on his pallet, his head propped up by his bent elbow.

'You're up?'

'Evidently.' His voice was strange, and he would not meet my eyes, stared at some spot near the door. He had a perfect view of the bed. I wondered how long he'd been awake. The tone of his voice – sullen, brooding – made me feel as if I'd been caught a second time.

We ate brunch, and I watched, relieved, as Sam's sour mood lifted, as he and Georgie competed over who could eat the most crepes. 'Sam,' Aunt Carrie said, 'it's time for *you* to grow.'

Mother had cast her glance sideways at Aunt Carrie at that comment, but that had been the only note of tension I'd noticed. Nobody had uttered the word *Miami*, for which I was grateful. It had been a place I only knew about, because of our orange groves there, but never visited; now it was where Uncle George had been imprudent.

Father made me take a sip of his champagne to settle my stomach. I waved good-bye to Georgie from the back window of the car, stopping only when Sam tugged at my sleeve, pulling me down next to him. I sat down willingly. I felt guilty, though I didn't know why; like I had done something wrong, though I couldn't have said what.

The day after Thanksgiving, Mother and Idella disappeared into the basement and emerged with our decorations: glass ornaments so fragile we weren't allowed to touch them; four hand-carved wooden reindeer purchased from a catalogue; a long, slender Santa whittled from a single piece of wood. A silver nativity set passed down for generations through my father's family, Spanish names engraved on the underside of each figurine: José, María, Jesús.

The next week, as we sat in the sunroom with Father for our lessons, we heard thumping and pounding as my mother and Idella put everything in its proper position.

'Do you think they need help?' Sam asked, his finger planted somewhere on his book so he would not lose his place.

Father ignored him, and I kept reading: we were in the middle of mythology, which I loved. So expansive and lovely, those gods and their heavens. We were supposed to keep quiet while we read. Father was strict about this rule, at least as strict as he ever was.

I raised my eyes and met Sam's gaze; he watched me impassively. I lowered my eyes and returned to the tale of Narcissus.

I wore an old dress of Mother's, a cotton shift with a square neckline. The dress hung on my frame. I was of average height for a girl my age, but almost too thin. Because I only rarely saw other girls my own age, only had Mother to truly compare myself to, I didn't realize that girls were not immediately women once they reached a certain age, that there was an awkward dividing period. I was too comfortable in my own skin, perhaps. I wore Mother's old casual dresses because they made me feel more adult.

Father closed his book, signaling our lesson was over.

'All right,' he said, 'you may go attend to your other, more pressing matters, like helping your mother.' He smiled. Sam and I stood; I went to my father and kissed him on the forehead before I left the room, flattening my dress against my chest with my palm as I leaned over him. Half-girl, half-woman.

Later I helped Mother wind Christmas greenery through the banister on the front porch's staircase, then above the windows. The sun shone directly overhead, mean today; I was hot, my skin felt thin, my underarms and forehead were beaded with sweat. Mother worked hard, and fast. Father said she was more efficient than any man. More and more, Mother liked me to help her with house chores. When I complained, she told me that I had to learn, that keeping house was an art. And, of course, my complaint was oblique: we never challenged Mother or Father, especially Mother.

When we were done, we stood in front of the house and admired it. Mother always liked this part – after she set her table for a holiday she would gaze at it for a few minutes, taken by its beauty, admiring her delicate china and starched linens.

'They look like eyebrows,' I said of the greenery above the windows. 'Thick eyebrows. Like the house is watching you.'

I wasn't happy, out here doing this tedious work while Sam was doing whatever he pleased.

I waited for my mother to finish gazing. She started to say something, but seemed to hesitate, which was unusual: my mother never hesitated.

'Georgie is coming to stay with us for a bit,' she said, finally.

I said nothing. Georgie often stayed with us. Yet I could feel her unease. I thought she was going to bring up the money. I didn't care about the money. 'Damned foolish,' my father had said to Mother, when they thought we weren't listening. But we had been, me and Sam. It was easy to eavesdrop – they'd never seemed to notice that the door to their bedroom blocked no sound – but usually there was no need, their nighttime conversations were of no interest to us.

'Aunt Carrie's mother is ill. She's going there to be with her.'

'There' meant Missouri, the tiny Midwestern town that had always sounded awful: small, flat, plain.

'Georgie's going to be here for a few weeks, then,' Mother continued, 'and he'll sleep in Sam's room this time. With Sam.'

'Why can't he stay at his own home? With Uncle George?' Though I did, in fact, want to see Georgie, I was angry – what did she mean, that Georgie and Sam would sleep separately from me? We had always slept in the same room. Don't cut off your nose to spite your face, I told myself.

Mother didn't scold me for my tone, which was cross; she looked pensive instead.

But then her face resolved itself into seriousness, and I looked down at my shoes.

'Uncle George has to be in Miami.'

That was enough. I understood – she could stop. But she would not.

'To meet with his bank. So Georgie will be coming here, because a sixteen-year-old boy cannot stay alone for a week. He'll bring his schoolwork with him.'

I raised my head and was met by Mother's firm gaze, her stern face. This was how she looked at you when she wanted acquiescence; if Sam were here, he would have kicked a puff of dirt, or shrugged, disguised as putting his hands in his pockets. But I only ever knew how to meet Mother's gaze.

I shifted my eyes and looked beyond her: such a view my home provided. Stands of giant oaks, broken occasionally by orderly groves of orange trees. Miles of thick green growth. Nothing seemed far away, there was so little opportunity for perspective in all the flatness. This lack of distance had always been comforting to me, since I was a child, everything so close even when it wasn't.

'Why can't I sleep in the same room?' I asked. I felt near tears.

She pulled me close before I had a chance to react. 'Don't cry,' she said. She smoothed my hair, which she knew I loved. I relented.

'Thea,' she murmured, 'you're getting older.'

'I'm not.'

'It's natural. It's the way things happen. Do you understand?' She cupped my chin in her hand and tilted my face up.

'I feel the same.'

'But you're not the same. You'll still be close, you and your brother and Georgie. But there are certain things you can't do anymore. Do you understand?'

I nodded.

'Say it, please,' her voice was kind but firm.

'Yes.'

'Oh, Thea.' She patted my cheek. 'Everything will be fine. It's just sleeping.'

I slipped from her grasp and trotted away.

'Be good,' she called from behind me, a phrase uttered so often it meant nothing.

I was mean to Sasi that day. He was sluggish over the cross rails, warming up, and I pointed my toes out and jabbed his flank with my spurs. This was a problem we'd been having for the past few weeks, this clumsiness over the cross rails; there was always a problem, a difficulty, when one rode: that was the whole point of the endeavor, the constant striving. And this reaching depended both on me and my mount, and, more generally, on our natures. I was obsessed, as Father said; at the very least I was a perfectionist. And a horse was a dumb animal, clearly he could not want the same things that I wanted, but he could want to please me, and today I felt no eagerness from him.

And then it was over, quickly, as my fights with him usually were: we fought deeply and briefly.

As I was turned in the saddle, examining the welts my whip had made on Sasi's flanks, I saw Sam perched on the fence, one leg hiked up, his chin resting on it. I wondered how long he'd been there; I wondered if he'd seen me turn the whip over in my hand so that I could wield it more powerfully. Would he have even known that was wrong? Mother would have. She would have made me stop, immediately, no, no, no, her voice an incline.

I nudged Sasi forward. His head hung low. I had exhausted him. He would forget; he might have already forgotten. But he wouldn't forget the fear, and the memory of pain would be replaced by an instinct of mistrust. That was the problem with horses; they were too dumb to remember properly, but there was still a memory to contend with, a memory that could not be reasoned away.

'Georgie's coming tomorrow.'

'I know,' I said. I tried to smile, but the effort felt too great. I watched Sam sitting there with his leg hiked up. I could never hike my leg up like that; even in breeches, the posture would be terrible manners, unladylike. I knew that other twins, the twins I read about in books, were identical; I wondered how it would be if Sam had been a girl, like me. It was the first time I had ever wondered that. We would both have to sleep separately from Georgie, then. We would both have started menstruating.

Sam tilted his head, trying to read my thoughts, and I smiled. Sam as a girl was impossible. I was our only girl.

'I have to sleep separately from you and Georgie,' I said, pulling Sasi to a halt. He stopped willingly.

Sam nodded. 'I know. Mother told me.' He paused. 'All we're doing is sleeping, Thea.'

I nudged Sasi into a walk again so Sam would not see my red face. I was furious Mother had told Sam. We were not the same person, after all.

'Thea?' Sam called, but I ignored him.

Sasi stood still and tired in the cross ties as I sponged warm water over his tense muscles. I traced the cross-stitch of raised lines the whip had left on his haunches. I felt ashamed. I put my arms around Sasi's damp neck and he hung his head low. He loved me. I could feel his enormous heart, pumping in his plump pony's chest. Drawings of his pretty face were in all my notebooks. Sorry, I wanted to say, so sorry, but knew it was useless.

I felt sorry over Sam, too.

Usually I was even and fair while riding, even when I was frustrated. I promised myself that I would not allow it to happen again. That I would not be so easily undone. I told myself I would be different next time, but what good were those promises, made as they were in the calm of the aftermath.

'Go,' Georgie said, and folded laced fingers over his eyes. Sam and I ran in opposite directions, quietly, the air crisp and cool, the sun bright, one of Florida's perfect winter days.

I tiptoed into the barn, so that my heels would not clap against the cement floor. We'd been playing for hours, and I was tired, ready for dinner, but I would not be the one to suggest finishing.

'Hello,' I whispered to Sasi, who stood at his hay, munching impassively. This was a lazy hiding spot, one I'd used before; I was hoping Georgie had forgotten. Or would come into the barn last, like he usually did. I was losing this game. Our rank was figured according to a complicated system. The more dangerous the spot, the more valuable. The rules never changed, but we were always adding new ones, so that the point of the game had unofficially become, over the years, that you were never safe.

We were too old to be doing this, Georgie nearly seventeen, Sam and I newly fifteen. But Georgie had suggested playing, and Sam's eyes had lighted up.

I crouched in the front corner of the stall, underneath the feed trough. This was not a hiding spot worth much, Sam was probably at the top of our oak tree. I watched Sasi's slender, knobby legs; each time he swallowed his entire throat leapt like a wave.

Georgie appeared in the stall window. He'd crept around the side of the barn so quietly I hadn't suspected. I pressed my spine into the cold corner and prayed Sasi wouldn't move.

'Hey there,' Georgie said, and made an uncertain kissing noise with his mouth. Sasi swung his head around.

Georgie waited for an instant more and then he was off. I slunk out of the stall, tiptoed out the same way I had come. When I reached the end of the barn, I peered around the edge instead of making a run for it straight away, and this was my tactical error.

Georgie, creeping along the barn's outside wall, saw me and smiled.

'I knew you'd be in here,' he said.

I took a step backward, out of his sight.

'Don't even try,' he called, 'I don't want to run.'

I ran anyway, toward the other end of the barn, but even though we were matched in speed (I was fast, for a girl), Georgie had the advantage, had me trapped, as long as I was inside and he was not.

'I told you I didn't want to run,' he said, as he met me at the other end; I turned the other way, but it was too late. He grabbed my dress and I tripped to a stop. I expected him to let me go immediately and continue for Sam, but he held my dress and tugged me to the wall.

'What did I tell you?'

I looked at him. This was not the way we played.

'Go get Sam,' I said.

'I told you not to try,' he said.

He put both hands on my shoulders, suddenly, and pressed me to the wall. I could hear Sasi rhythmically chomping hay.

I relaxed under Georgie's grip; his face was so close to mine I could see the faint, scattered stubble of his shaved moustache. I hadn't known he'd started shaving.

'Very bad, Thea,' he said, and smiled, and I smiled, too, and then he was gone, to get Sam.

I was restless, restless. I went to bed at the same time as Sam and Georgie and listened to them talk through our closed doors and then there was silence, and I was still awake. I felt the curve of my breast beneath my nightgown, the swollen tip, the smooth, smooth skin.

Usually I stayed in bed until sleep came, but tonight I wanted out. I stood outside the boys' door and listened for snoring, signs of sleep.

The French doors that closed the living room from the lower landing were fragile, all glass panes and brass fittings, but I knew how to open them quietly. The Christmas tree rose to the ceiling and we'd had to trim the top in order to fit the angel: faceless, hairless, dressed in a luminescent gold gown. Idella's cousin delivered our tree every year. I wrapped my blanket tighter around my shoulders, shivered.

Whenever I see a Christmas tree now, adorned with a mismatched collection of ornaments, I'm embarrassed for it. Mother's tree was beautiful: purple and red glass orbs, handblown, because of this slightly irregular – you could see the place on each where the blower had folded over the hot glass, closing the globe. The ornaments were so thin they seemed almost liquid when the tree was lit.

Mother used candles to light the tree, dozens of them, held by special glass holders. It was dangerous but beautiful. The rage then was to use electric, colored lights, red and blue and orange and green – but Mother hated all that color, thought it vulgar.

Someone was on the landing, then walking down the stairs, then the seventh step groaned and I knew it was Georgie; we all knew to skip that step.

'Shh,' I said, as he came through, but he caught the sharp tongue of the lock with his hip. I drew in a quick breath: the door rattled, a hollow, familiar sound that was likely to wake Mother. If she found us, I knew she would think I had not been good. And my explanation – that I had done nothing, that Georgie had followed me downstairs – well, she would not believe me. I saw all this clearly as I watched Georgie walk past me, toward the front door, and I was chilled, then furious at my cousin.

'Stop,' I hissed, but Georgie was already half outside; he looked back at me and beckoned. I ran to the door, needing to reach it before Georgie closed it roughly.

'What are you doing?' I whispered, as I pulled the door almost closed behind me.

'I'm watching the moon,' he answered, in his normal tone.

'Watch it from inside.'

He shrugged, and turned to me: 'No.' His voice was sluggish, sleepy. When he looked at me, his eyes were off center, distracted.

So I watched the moon, too, full and fat.

'How long are you going to stand here?' I asked.

'Why?'

'I'm cold.'

'You woke me,' he said. He seemed moody, this visit, spent more time in Sam's room, alone. He said he was reading, but Georgie never read.

'How did I wake you?' I had been so quiet.

'I always know where you are, Thea,' he said.

'Only God always knows where I am,' I replied softly.

'Is He watching now?' Georgie asked, also softly. He took a step closer. Another one. And then he was an inch or two from my face, his breath milky and thick.

'Of course,' I said, but I had lost track of what we were talking about.

He touched my hair, and then let his hand fall to my neck.

We examined each other: my blanket had fallen from my shoulders, I was naked and cold underneath my white night-dress. My eyes were large from exhaustion. Georgie's face was swollen with sleep, his features babyish. Sweet – he looked sweet. His hair had gotten long in Aunt Carrie's absence, fallen forward over his eyes and lent him an air that was equal parts raffish and shy.

He put his face closer to mine and kissed me on the lips. Then he touched my cheek, and kissed me again, and parted my lips with his.

I knew that we were kissing, but I had never seen anyone kiss like this. Father kissed Mother on her cheek in our presence. People in my books kissed, but *this* had never been described, how warm Georgie's tongue was in my mouth, how strange and lovely it felt, in equal measures, as if the strangeness made it lovely.

I was not raised in a house where pleasure meant guilt. And this – Georgie's tongue in my mouth, like a live thing, the face that I had known since birth so close now, closer than ever before: this was bliss.

CHAPTER TEN

The Holmes girls waited at my cabin door. 'Hello,' they said, almost in chorus, and claimed my hands. They had stopped curtsying after the first week. Mr Holmes stood with them, watching with an amused expression. His hands were in his pockets, and he inclined his head when I smiled at him. I hadn't spoken to him since Thanksgiving, a few weeks before.

I noticed the other girls' glances. Thea Atwell and the Holmes girls, plus Mr Holmes.

Girls waved to him as we passed, girls I'd never spoken to: Roberta, Laura Bonnell, Hattie. Mr Holmes acknowledged them with a dip of his head, but he didn't take his hands from his pockets.

At the barn, I cross-tied Luther and Bright and the girls curried in a frenzy, stopping only to knock their combs against the wall. Bright was an old, black pony, who had wise eyes: many, many children had sat on his back. I watched and pointed out missed spots. Mr Holmes kept his distance from the horses, especially Luther, which was funny: ponies were notoriously mean, horses gentle. Everyone was eager today; Decca lifted Bright's hoof and pointed to his tender frog, then showed her father how to dislodge the dirt with a pick. Bright's forelock was tangled, and Rachel unknotted it gently.

After we'd tacked the horses, we led them to the ring where we rode; Mr Holmes stood outside the ring and watched, in a pose all men seemed to adopt – his arms rested on the top rung of the fence; one leg hiked up to the middle board, his knee bent.

Mr Holmes watched Decca work through her routine – the same routine I'd worked through when I was a young girl, which Mother had taught me – leaning into the ring like he owned it, like he wasn't afraid of horses.

'Your legs are so strong, Decca,' he called out, and Decca nodded, pleased.

My father's German friend, Mr Buch, once told me I looked Turkish in profile. The comment had delighted me; I liked thinking I looked like someone from another place. I was careful not to let on, lest Sam think me vain. You were supposed to be pretty, you were supposed to be beautiful, but you were not supposed to care.

I wondered what Mr Holmes thought of my profile, if he had ever seen a Turkish girl. Probably not.

'Change beats,' I called to Decca, who was mastering posting. 'Good,' I called again.

We'd developed our own language; or, rather, the girls had become fluent in my tongue. No one had fallen yet, or even come close. I fell all the time, in my youth, and luckily never sustained more than a sprained ankle. But I fell because I was a daredevil, and no one watched me. The Holmes girls were always watched.

Later, after they had dismounted, Mr Holmes praised them.

'Good, girls,' Mr Holmes said, and though Decca and Sarabeth beamed up at him, Rachel wedged herself between Decca and her father and took his hand.

Decca looked outraged, but then Mr Holmes held up his other hand.

'I have two,' Mr Holmes said, and Decca accepted his hand, and I thought how different Sam and I had been from the Holmes girls, who competed with each other, who always, at least in my presence, tried to court their father's attention, tried to walk a little bit ahead of her sisters.

Later the girls stood in the barn's wide corridor, Bright and Luther in cross ties, and curried away saddle marks. I stood in the tack room, where I could keep an eye on them, and cleaned, wiped the sweat off the bridles, the grass off the bits.

'Do the girls do that?' Mr Holmes asked.

I jumped. 'Pardon?'

'I apologize. I sneaked in.' He moved closer, examining my handiwork. 'Do the girls do this usually?'

'They know how and Sarabeth does a good job, but Rachel and Decca are too small.'

'Too small to clean?'

'Too uncoordinated.'

Mr Holmes nodded, and examined my handiwork. He smelled thick, like oil. I was an expert tack cleaner, the buckles on my bridles shone, the brow bands gleamed. He made a sound – a sigh? – and lowered himself carefully on top of a trunk. I massaged balm into the reins and waited for him to say something else. But neither of us spoke. I could see him out of the corner of my eye, and it seemed that he watched me, intently, and I began to enjoy our silence, which felt companionable but not completely neutral: we were both aware of each other.

Mother had taught me how to clean tack, how to make stiff leather supple, how to extend the life of all the equipment you needed for riding. I had always taken good care of my tack, taken pride in this task, which pleased Mother. I was her daughter, in so many ways. We both appreciated order.

Girls came in and out with their saddles. Leona came in, a

saddle blanket damp with King's sweat over her arm, and dipped her head in my direction. She had been warmer to me since our night ride, but almost imperceptibly: she caught my eye more often, tilted her head in a nod when we passed each other at the Castle; at the bathhouse she had even murmured something about how the night ride had done King good. After we had finished with the horses, Mr Holmes escorted us back to the Square.

'I'll be seeing you soon, I'm sure,' he said, and the girls also thanked me, a chorus behind him. It started to rain, lightly.

I waved.

'Such an opportunity,' he said, as I turned away, 'for the girls to learn about horses.'

'The pleasure's all mine.' I remembered my first day here, months ago, Father by my side, Mr Holmes a stranger.

I wasn't as good a teacher to the girls as Mother had been to me. She had always been able to anticipate what I would try next – how I would shift my weight in the saddle, how I would tug the right rein instead of the left – what Sasi would try next, and this prescience had made her an eerily good teacher. I saw that now. I wasn't as good at predicting what these girls would do, but of course Mother had known me better than I knew the Holmes girls. Her prescience had extended beyond the ring: she knew when Sam had rushed through his arithmetic, when I had used a nice towel to clean up a mess. Mother knew everything. But she had not known about Georgie. It had all happened right under her pretty nose.

I turned from Masters – a charming cottage, really, covered with birch shingles – and joined the mass of girls also returning from the ring. Perhaps Mother had sent me here partly because she was angry at herself, for not realizing what was happening in her very own house. For not knowing me as well as she thought she had; for not stopping it.

Sissy ran up beside me, eager to hear about the headmaster watching me teach. I smiled at her, the crowd of girls milling around us. I was one of them. We would stop at our cabins first and change quickly, but we would not be given long enough to wash away the smell of horses.

On Christmas Eve I was the only girl left in Augusta House. Even Mary Abbott's family had scraped together the money to bring her home. Mainly, the girls that stayed were scholarship girls. And then girls who made various excuses: their family was traveling this year; it was too long a trip for too short a time. I had made that excuse, exactly, and for me it seemed at least a little bit conceivable: Emathla, Florida, was very far away from the Yonahlossee Riding Camp for Girls.

The night bell had rung hours ago, but I couldn't fall asleep. It hadn't even been a question in my mind, whether or not I would return home for the holidays; of course I wouldn't. We had sung carols at the Castle tonight, trimmed a giant tree. I had been spared an inquisition by the Holmes girls, because everyone who had not gone home sat together, at a large table; the Holmeses sat at the opposite end from me. Decca had found her way onto my lap by the end of the dinner, but she was too young to care why I had not left.

I heard something outside and thought it might be Boone again, not knowing Sissy had gone home. But of course it wouldn't be him – he was surely home with his perfect family, exchanging perfect gifts.

Someone laughed, but the sound was eerie. It seemed to be coming from right outside my window.

I heard it again, the same laugh, high-pitched. It chilled me to the bone, one of Mother's expressions. I peeked outside my window, very carefully. I saw the back of a girl, dressed in her white nightgown, without a coat, her hair wild. She turned and I recognized her squat profile: Jettie.

I bundled myself up and hurried outside, one of Sissy's extra coats in my hand.

'Jettie,' I whispered, 'why are you out here?' I handed her the coat but she shook her head. Her eyes were glassy, and she held up an amber-colored bottle.

'I'm very warm already,' she said. 'I don't need a coat.'

I put my finger on my lips.

'Why?' she asked, even more loudly. 'What could happen?'

I placed Sissy's coat around her shoulders and took the bottle away. She was moving too slowly to stop me.

'If Mrs Holmes saw you,' I said, 'she'd have a fit.'

Jettie smiled. 'I'd just get Henny to save me. She's Mrs Holmes's favorite. They're cut from the same cloth. May I have my bottle back, please?'

I sat down next to her. 'As long as you keep your coat on,' I said.

'It's a deal.' She took a swig from the bottle, like a man. 'Thea Atwell. You were big news when you came. Katherine Hayes told everyone there was some trouble with a boy.' Jettie looked me up and down, frankly. I pulled my coat more tightly around me. 'But nobody cares about you anymore. That's the way of the world.'

'You're drunk,' I said.

'You're right.' She laughed her odd laugh. 'I know why you're not home, but do you know why I'm not home? I'll tell you,' she continued. 'If you can keep a secret.'

'I can,' I said cautiously. I wasn't sure I wanted to know Jettie's secrets.

'My father lost his job. So now I have to marry. And I don't want to.' Her voice had turned fierce. 'That's the last thing in the world I want. But Mother says I have to. And Henny says I'm selfish. What do you think?' She brought her face very close to mine – I noticed a faint scar on her temple.

'The boy you're going to marry, is he nice?'

'He's not a boy,' she said. 'He's man. He's old. Rich. Tobacco rich. And he's nice enough, but I don't like them. Men. There's something wrong with me. I'd prefer being alone.'

She looked like she might cry. I took the bottle from her and tilted it to my lips. I almost spit, the taste was so strong.

'I'll tell you something else.' She began to cry, then, in earnest. 'I don't want to leave,' she said. 'I don't want to go away from her. From here. I don't understand. It's not as if we're starving. We aren't Appalachians.' Her gaze drifted off to the distance.

Yonahlossee, an island of rich girls in the middle of the poorest. I thought of Docey, her family. We had put together a box of Christmas food for the Mill Girls: ham, pie, potatoes. Mrs Holmes had said it would be delivered in time for Christmas dinner.

'Thea,' Jettie murmured, 'life is so hard once you grow up.'

'Maybe it's better,' I said, finally.

'What?'

'Not to like boys. Men. They're nothing but trouble.'

She looked at me for a long second. 'Don't be a fool, Thea.'

I smiled, then poured the rest of the bottle onto the ground while Jettie watched. More liquor would only make her sadder. She rose then, and walked unsteadily away. She looked like a pony: short and sturdy.

'Remember,' she called. 'It's a secret.'

I traced my lips with my finger, mimed throwing away a key.

I woke the next morning and the world was white.

I slipped on my boots and stepped outside without my coat into a foot of snow.

'Hello,' someone called, and I saw Mr Holmes, walking across the Square, carrying a wrench.

I waved and crossed my arms. I should have dressed before coming out here. My hands were chapped. I needed gloves, but did not want to write and ask Mother.

'Merry Christmas,' he said. 'One of the pipes burst.' He brandished his wrench.

'There's no water in the Castle, and our handyman is home for the holiday.' He stopped when he reached me, a single line of footprints behind him.

'I've never seen snow before,' I said, 'not like this.'

'No?' He looked around, at the expanse of white, white everywhere, on the roofs, on the trees, on the mountains. 'I love the cold,' he said.

He was wearing an old coat, the top button missing. 'I suppose it makes you miss home,' I said.

'You remembered.' He looked pleased. 'Yes, it reminds me of Boston.'

'I've only ever known heat. But this,' I said, 'this is beautiful.' And Sam was not here to see it.

'My mother used to say God was angry when it snowed, but I've never seen it that way.'

'What is He then, if not angry?'

Mr Holmes laughed; a white puff. 'Contemplative.' He paused. 'It seems like you're liking Yonahlossee, Thea.'

I nodded. I was turning colder and colder, but I didn't want to leave. I started to speak, but stopped.

'What were you going to say?' he asked.

There was a little red nick above Mr Holmes's lip, where he had cut it shaving. He and his family would celebrate their own Christmas, before we gathered for dinner in the Castle. I wanted to be there, with him. I wanted him to invite me. I suddenly wanted it very badly. Ask me, I thought, as he watched me expectantly. Ask me.

But of course he would not. I was not a Holmes. I wondered if this would be my last Christmas without my family, and understood in that instant it would not: I could see so many of them in my future, unfurled before me, empty. I did not know where I would be, but I knew my family would be absent.

Mr Holmes was still watching me, curiously.

'I like it here,' I said. I paused. I didn't trust my voice. 'But I miss my home, too.'

He seemed unsurprised. 'Of course you do, Thea. Of course you do.'

My Christmas present from home: a cashmere coat, deep burgundy, with silver-plated buttons. Merry, merry, happy, happy, the card read, the writing someone else's, the saying Mother's. The tag was scripted with the name of an Asheville clothing store. Held to my face, in the mirror, my hair shone against the red. I unfastened my braid and took a handful: it was getting long, growing quickly, thickly. A strange portrait I made in the silvered mirror, my eyes swollen with sleep, my lips dry from the cold, the coat bold and opulent. I touched the mirror. Mother had never even seen the coat, the color. It was an extravagant gift – unlike her, and unlike me. She must have felt guilty, not bringing me home even for Christmas. She didn't know that I wouldn't have gone if they'd offered.

I stuffed the coat into one of my empty drawers.

Last Christmas we hadn't exchanged presents. Mother had told me and Sam about it beforehand, and though I had grumbled at first, Mother had reminded me that Georgie's family was troubled – she'd used that exact word, *troubled* – and we didn't want to trouble them further. And besides, she'd added, we don't need Christmas presents; we have all we need already, don't we? And what was there to say but yes, though I would have liked a new bridle, a smarter pair of breeches.

A few days before Christmas we'd built a bonfire. Aunt Carrie was back from Missouri, her mother better. We stood in front of the fire for what felt like a long time. Father put his arm gently around my shoulders. Mother and Idella came out with mugs of cocoa.

'Oh, no,' Aunt Carrie said, smoothing her hand over her plump stomach.

I watched my cousin while I ate and tried very hard to pretend I wasn't, watching or interested in anything at all, particularly. He stayed close to Sam, deferred to him, it seemed. We never drank cocoa. It was too rich, I felt heavy as I drank and so I tipped my mug into the fire. I felt Mother watching me, so I focused on the fire, the smoke and the sizzle.

We were all quiet, that night. It's tempting to assume we all knew we were on the cusp of something.

Georgie stayed away from me until the fire started to fizzle and the men decided not to add wood. I was over-warm, and seated a foot or two farther away from the fire than everyone else. Georgie left his mother's side and kneeled next to me, but he was silent and I was glad. I uncrossed my arms – the air had a bite to it – and rested my palms on the cool grass, and Georgie leaned back and rested his dry hand on top of mine. We were blocked from sight, it was not a brave gesture. We sat like this for ten, fifteen minutes, and what I felt in that short time, the anticipation, the pleasure, the eerie feeling of bliss – well, this was all still new to me. A week since my cousin had kissed me, and I was another person. Or perhaps not another person, but I suddenly cared about completely different things, and that seemed the same thing.

We had not kissed again, or even spoken of it. But Georgie touched me, now, all the time, held my hand in the barn like it was nothing. We had moved so easily into this; and now I wanted more.

The next day I sat alone on the front porch steps, watching our quiet yard. Georgie had replaced Sasi in my daydreams. I thought about him more than I had thought it was possible to think about something, which was to say, always.

The front door whined. I turned, and Georgie stood in the door frame. This all seemed like magic. I had been hoping he would find me, and he had; there was something so delicious about the way he courted me in my home, the way he seemed to always find me. When I saw him now, when I was close to him, my groin throbbed and then there was a slickness between my legs, which seemed to come almost immediately. He smiled back, but his head was inclined and I couldn't tell if he was shy or smug.

He sat down next to me and put his hand over mine.

'We shouldn't,' I whispered.

'Everyone's out back.' He kissed my forehead, and I drew back, stunned, and I couldn't sort out why: that he would be so bold, kissing me where anyone could see, but also the pleasure of his lips on my forehead.

'Georgie.'

'Can't I kiss my cousin on the forehead?' he asked. He challenged. He seemed so large next to me; if I had seen him as a stranger in town I would have thought he was a young man.

I touched his cheek. I liked how small my hand was next to his face.

'Did you shave this morning?' It felt thrilling, to have the right to ask this question.

'I did.' He stopped my hand and pressed it to his cheek, then kissed the base of my thumb. I wondered where he had learned to do all this. This Georgie was a stranger to me.

I drew my thumb across his lips; he bit it, gently, and my breath caught. I turned my head because this all, suddenly, seemed too much, too good, and I felt dizzy with the pleasure of it. The large bed of ivy in front of my house was blurry, but then a clear spot at the very edge, which gradually came into focus: my brother. I wiped my hand on my skirt and stood; Georgie jumped up next to me, and I waved at Sam, who had walked around the side of the house without me noticing. He nodded in our direction, his hands in his pockets. Take one out, I thought, take a hand out and let me know you saw nothing.

I put my hand over my mouth and turned to Georgie.

'Don't worry,' Georgie said, 'he didn't see anything.' But it was all a guess, whether or not Sam had seen.

On Christmas Eve I sat between Georgie and Sam at the dining-room table.

I wore a gold silk dress that Mother said brought out the red in my hair. It was the last time I would wear it – the bodice had become uncomfortably tight, and by the time I had another occasion to wear a dress so clearly meant for a party, glimmering and unserious, I would be too broad and tall. But I wanted to wear it once more, and ignored Mother's suggestion to choose another dress.

I wore Mother's mink stole also. She lent it to me as if I were playing dress-up, which I was, but now the stole felt more mine than hers. Last Christmas I had been fourteen and all the same people had been here.

Father said grace. Georgie caught my hand under the table and held it, briefly. In my quick inventory of the table, everyone's head was still bowed. The last part of Father's prayer was for the orange groves. This was not unusual. Mother exhaled audibly.

'Amen,' Uncle George added, 'let us all praise citrus.'

My father looked at his wineglass. I knew he was considering how to respond, that the glass simply bought him time. It seemed my father was always buying himself time, had a thousand little tricks he used to think before he spoke.

'Do you jest?' he asked. The word was so formal, like we were reading Shakespeare, and I felt so intensely uncomfortable.

Georgie watched the adults, carefully; I wanted him to pay attention to me, not them. I touched his hand, underneath the table.

'A man can pray for whatever he wants, can't he, Felix?' Uncle George asked.

My uncle was tense tonight, as everyone was. You could cut it with a knife – the phrase lingered in my head.

Then Georgie's hand was in my lap, on my knee. It was hot, even through my dress.

'Please,' Mother said.

'It's true,' Father said. 'I suppose.'

Then Georgie was moving his fingers up and down my knee so gently, so rhythmically, that I wanted to moan. He did it for so long – three minutes, four – that I lost track of where he was. He was higher on my thigh, no, he was lower; he was too high, he was not high enough.

I put my hand on his and stopped him. It was madness, to touch each other in front of everyone, especially my brother. My thighs were trembling. The adults were talking about the Gainesville Christmas Pageant, which my mother had read an article about in the newspaper; something lighthearted, chosen to counter the doom that had settled on the table, and though it wasn't working, though Aunt Carrie still looked like she might burst into tears, I thanked God that something had their attention. Thank God for Christmas pageants, I murmured, and Georgie laughed, quietly, but Sam looked at me strangely.

I'd never put much stock in dreams. Sam used to wake from nightmares, choked and panting, and all he could tell me as I held his hand was that he was falling from a great cliff, that a second before he met the ground he woke.

I never quite believed him, because I couldn't imagine such an insubstantial feeling, rootless, all in my brother's head. After the bonfire I fell asleep quickly and dreamed of Georgie, touching me. He felt through my underwear, gently, then harder, and then he put one finger inside of me. Then two. I woke not knowing where I was, the pleasure so intense I thought I must still be dreaming. I was on the cusp; I put my fingers where Georgie had, was surprised at how firm I felt against the pressure of my fingertips, the pressure that was felt more deeply here. Then I touched outside my panties, as Georgie had. I was wet, soaked through. Bright sparks flashed against my eyelashes. More, and more, then nothing but the tight, quick pulse in my groin. I rubbed my forehead with my wrist, my hands needed to be washed.

This sort of pleasure wasn't yet a secret, like it would become later. No, it was a thing that had never existed, so there was no attendant shame.

Sam woke me the next morning, tapped my shoulder gently. At first I thought it was Georgie.

'If you want to ride,' he said, 'you'd better do it now.'

'All right,' I mumbled.

'Merry Christmas,' he added, as an afterthought.

'Merry Christmas,' I said. He watched me as I sat up in bed, rubbed the sleep from my eyes. I smiled, and he smiled back, but his smile was off, somehow. For an instant Sam was inside my head, he'd seen my dream, knew about Georgie.

Sam tilted his head and I felt a great surge of relief: he did not know.

I shook my head at him, and smiled again, to let him know everything was fine, and though Sam nodded, I knew he did not believe me.

I wanted to try a new jump that I'd built out back. In the ring commands were nearly invisible, it was supposed to seem as if you and your horse were in complete and silent agreement. But out here, the ring behind us, Sasi would only listen if I jerked and threw my weight, slammed my legs against his side, shouted. It was ugly riding, but it felt truer.

I'd left my spurs in the barn. When I squeezed my legs against his sides, normally a command he half-ignored, Sasi exploded into an elaborate trot, neck arched, ears forward, paying attention to everything but me.

I'd come out here for exactly that reason: I needed power, I needed him to clear the highest jump he ever had, not for me but because the jump was pointed into that great and mysterious beyond.

I realized as soon as I turned that I'd given us too much space – too long a straight line, too much time and reason for him to run away, for me to lose control. But I felt him gather his legs beneath him, in clear anticipation of the jump. 'Yes, yes, yes,' I murmured, in rhythm to his canter. My braid thumped on my back, my vision narrowed, and I was only aware of the particular way Sasi's hooves hit the ground – the hard sound that made – and the closing distance between us and the jump. It was all instinct now, there was nothing anyone could teach you about this instant before leaving the ground. 'Now,' I said, and we flew. I wished Georgie were here, watching. Then

Sasi's left shoulder dropped and I was off, on the damp grass, but I still had the rein, I hadn't let go. 'It's fine,' I soothed, 'it's fine.' He half pulled, half dragged me away, rearing backward, scared, but also aware of the opportunity: if he could get rid of me, he could run away, listen to his brain, the deep part that told him to go, at any cost.

But I held on. I loved this pony; I would not let him go for anything. After he calmed down, I remounted. I pointed him toward the jump a second time, and we cleared it without incident, as I knew we would. This was how my mind worked, this is why I was brave in situations where others would not have remounted. The fates wouldn't align to throw Sasi off balance again, not twice in one day. You fell once in a while because that was your due, you rode a horse and expected him to do things he would not have done in nature. You fell once for every hundred clean jumps.

I sneaked upstairs after I had cooled out Sasi and fed him his morning oats. I stood at my brother's door and opened it a sliver.

Sam slept on his bed, Georgie on a pallet on the floor. I was surprised that they slept apart – Sam's bed was large, there was room enough for two.

Sam's arms and legs stuck out at awkward angles, and his hair was matted down to his cheeks by sweat. His brown quilt had fallen to the floor, and his sheet was tangled between his legs.

I looked at him first, almost without seeing him. I looked because he was there. And then Georgie, Sam's comforter draped over his torso. He wasn't sweating. Perhaps it was cooler on the floor. He slept almost primly, his arms beside him in straight lines, his bare feet aligned, toes upward.

Georgie shifted, and I saw a brown flash as he threw off the comforter. He murmured, almost a groan, and then I saw his penis, erect through the opening in his pajamas. It was darker than the rest of his skin, had a purplish tint. I'd never seen a man naked, nor talked to anyone about male anatomy, but somehow I knew that my cousin's penis was erect.

I turned away and closed the door behind me. I felt ashamed, but complicatedly: he should not have shown me that, I should not have had to see, but he had been sleeping, he had not meant to.

Then I felt the opposite of ashamed: I felt a little powerful, like I knew a secret, a moment all my own.

CHAPTER
ELEVEN

'Boone is coming tonight,' Sissy whispered. 'Will you help?'

'Of course.' The stakes were lower now that Mrs Holmes was gone; everyone knew she was the one who disciplined us. She had left last Sunday, after worship, and would be gone for six weeks. When she returned it would be spring, which seemed impossible: everything was dead now, except the evergreens.

Through the window, night was black. We had just entered what Sissy called the doldrums: February. The sun set by five o'clock; we walked to dinner in total darkness now. Sissy said this was the most boring part of the year, when nothing happened. But I liked the calm.

I was riding again. I'd had to gain eight pounds before Mrs Holmes would let me back in the saddle; I might have protested more if I hadn't been riding in secret already.

I still taught the Holmes girls, by my own request, at least for a little while, until they joined Mrs Holmes at her mother's house in New Orleans. Mr Holmes told us to write our mothers and encourage them to attend their Junior League or Garden Club meetings, where his wife would make appearances. It went without saying that all our mothers were members, yet my mother was not. She belonged to Emathla's Camellia Society, but for the flowers.

I watched Mr Holmes and decided that he did not seem any worse for the wear, given his wife's absence.

Mr Holmes watched our lessons once or twice a week, I never knew when he would appear, a specter perched on the side of the ring. Without realizing it, I began to anticipate his presence.

I lay awake that night until I heard Boone's rocks. He threw softly but precisely: from the sound it made, it seemed like Boone hit the same exact spot every time.

At the third rock, I rose.

'Sissy,' I whispered. I shook her thin shoulder. 'Sissy,' I whispered again, and squeezed her forearm. She was sleeping in her clothes.

Her eyes opened slowly, and when she saw me she started.

'It's only me,' I whispered, and put a finger over my lips. Her warm, vinegary night breath rose. You would think that such a delicate girl in such a delicate situation would be a light sleeper, or would not have fallen asleep at all. She rose and left.

We love each other, she had told me when explaining the gravity of the situation: we can't go too long without seeing each other. I smiled – she even kept the love of her life waiting. That girl was not on time for anyone.

'Sissy?'

I quickly slipped into Sissy's bed: there was no moonlight tonight.

'What are you doing?' Mary Abbott's voice was sleepy. I listened until I was sure she was asleep again. Out of all the girls, she would tell. Not out of spite, but because she was odd, had an odd conception of men, boys, the other sex. Whatever one wanted to call them.

They were no mystery to me. I fell asleep thinking, half-dreaming, I was Sissy. They'd only kissed so far. But they would do more, they wouldn't be able to help themselves. Of course

Boone would want it, and this was understood: he was a boy, he had urges, he could not be helped.

When I woke, Sissy stood over me, her hair wet. Rain beat against our roof. We exchanged beds, but I had trouble falling back asleep, could not stop imagining Sissy' and Boone's embrace.

That charged, restless night, the threat not realized: Mary Abbott made no mention of hearing anything.

On our way to the barn the next morning, the Holmes girls' necks wrapped with scarves, Sarabeth spoke. 'Our father's coming,' she said happily, 'to see me.'

I squeezed Decca's hand, which I'd been holding, and she looked up at me curiously. I felt light-headed from lack of sleep, and now, happy. I should be more careful. But careful of what? I wasn't sweet on him; half of camp was sweet on him, the only man for miles and miles, except for the grooms, and they didn't count. But I liked that he spoke to me as if I were an adult.

'Us,' Sarabeth quickly corrected, but Rachel had already taken offense, was staring at her sister with narrowed eyes.

Sarabeth could afford to be nice now, having already revealed her father's true intention. There were moments when Rachel seemed mean, but I could never tell with Sarabeth. They were children, sisters who fought over petty things. Sam and I had never fought; further evidence, according to Mother, of how charmed our life was. She had fought with her brothers, and Father with Uncle George. But we were twins, two sides of a coin.

I was sliding the bit into Luther's mouth when Mr Albrecht told us that a tree had fallen in our ring last night, crashed into a rail during the storm. I paused and the bit clicked against Luther's teeth; he shook his head.

'It's fine,' Mr Albrecht assured me, stroking Luther's muzzle, 'the tree is small. Most of the ring is still usable.'

Sarabeth led Luther, Decca led Bright past the tree.

'Pat his neck,' I told Decca, as she walked Bright by the tree, 'talk to him.'

Bright flung his head up suddenly, the rein snapping.

'There's a bird.' Rachel pointed. I noticed a faint red scratch on her wrist. 'I think it's hurt.'

I kneeled down in the sand. An owl, with its oddly shaped head, was nestled between the branches, so brown it blended into the leaves. It was clearly terrified, had resorted to keeping still because it couldn't fly. If Sam were here he would have known what to do, whether or not the injury to its wing was reparable. I guessed it wasn't.

'What do we do?' Rachel asked, her voice whiny.

'Leave it alone,' I said, perhaps too harshly. My mood was spoiled. Mr Holmes was coming to watch the lesson, and now this. If the owl tried to leave the tree, the horses would spook.

I made a fast decision. Sarabeth was already mounting Luther. Decca was pulling down her stirrups.

'Girls,' I said, 'do not come near this tree. The bird is hurt. It might scare the horses. So stay away.' They all nodded obediently, even Rachel.

I stood at the center of the ring while the girls warmed up. I could see Sarabeth out of the corner of my eye. I focused on Decca, who was mastering posting.

Rachel sat on the fence, her slim legs twined through the slats. At first she sat there quietly as usual, her pale face calm. Her hair was braided in pigtails today, which made her look young. All of the Holmes girls had their father's hair: dark and glossy.

Then, out of the corner of my eye, I saw Rachel come down from the fence to walk around the ring, timidly, as was her style, but also quickly.

'Rachel?'

'I'm going to look at the tree.' Her voice again whiny.

'Don't you remember what I said? You'll scare the horses.' I shook my head in disbelief.

'I just want to see.' I signaled Decca to slow Bright to a walk.

'Rachel,' I said, trying to make my voice a warning. She acted as if she hadn't heard, her thin frame tilted forward. Sarabeth had halted Luther and sat straight in the saddle, watching her sister.

'I'm just looking,' Rachel said, 'I'm bored to death.'

'It's almost your turn.'

Rachel acted as if she hadn't heard me, and continued to walk.

'Rachel.' My voice was high. She looked at me, her head cocked, and I saw she was daring me. My vision was blurry from the cold. 'Rachel, sit down. Now.'

She smiled, and for an instant I was relieved – she was going to pretend she had been joking – but then she took another step.

'Father's coming,' Sarabeth murmured, and Rachel hopped onto the fence, resumed her waiting stance. Mr Holmes smiled; he was thinking of something else, holding out his hand as if to ward off conversation.

I turned to Decca, my mood ruined. I wanted Mr Holmes to be happy.

'Ask him to trot,' I said.

Decca flapped her legs.

'Softly,' I reminded her. 'Gently. What you ask him should be a secret. No one else should be able to tell.'

'I'm bored,' Rachel muttered, but quietly so that her father would not hear. Decca ran through her exercises, and I turned my attention to Sarabeth. I almost forgot Rachel was there.

'Pinch your knees harder,' I called. 'Relax your elbows.'

'Decca's just sitting there,' Rachel called.

'Rachel,' Mr Holmes said, 'that's enough.' Rachel looked as if she might cry. I was pleased by his anger. Rachel deserved it.

'Come, Decca.' And I led Bright to the side of the ring, next to Mr Holmes, so that Sarabeth could practice on the diagonal.

'Rachel,' I said as we passed, 'one moment. And you'll have an extra ten minutes. I want your father to see this.'

Rachel ignored me. I took mean pleasure in making her wait.

'She's learning how to change leads. See how she moves her legs? Right one back, left one forward?' Changing leads was an advanced technique, and Sarabeth wasn't really ready for it, but Luther was so well trained, such an old schoolmaster, that a monkey could have gotten him to do it.

'And he switches.'

'Yes,' I said.

'Like he's skipping.' Mr Holmes drummed his fingers on the fence in rhythm to Luther's canter. Changing leads was something even someone completely unversed in horses could appreciate: it did, indeed, look like skipping. He bit his nails, I noticed. Men didn't wear wedding bands back then, so there was nothing that I could tell from his hands except that his skin wasn't rough from riding or another sport or hard work.

'She's good,' I said. Mr Holmes nodded. I wanted him to take more pleasure in his daughter's trick, in the things she could make Luther do already, but he seemed distracted.

I unclipped the lunge line from Bright's bit.

'Get down?' I asked Decca.

Everything happened at once then. Get down, I asked, but it was more of an order than a suggestion. I had taught Decca to slide both her feet out of her stirrups before swinging one leg over the saddle; this was lucky.

'Rachel,' Mr Holmes said, almost yelled, his deep voice cleaving the cold air. 'I've had enough. Enough!' Now I knew for certain that Mr Holmes was referring to some past wrong of Rachel's. She had been difficult today or for several days.

When I looked over, I saw that Rachel was gone from her spot on the fence, and Mr Holmes was striding toward her. My impulse was to laugh: I had never seen Mr Holmes angry, and it scared me. Rachel backed into the branches of the tree, watching her father, and then she started to speak.

'No!' she said, quietly at first, then louder and louder until her voice had reached a shrill pitch. 'No, no, no, no, no, no!' She looked possessed. She was much too old for a tantrum.

'The bird,' Decca cried as the owl flew straight up, out of the tree, and then faltered, diving unsteadily toward Luther. Luther backed up, quickly, his neck arched, his ears pointed forward.

'Thea,' Sarabeth called, her voice trembling. I could barely hear her over Rachel. 'What do I do?' I dropped Bright's rein and hurried toward Luther, speaking quietly and calmly. Out of the corner of my eye I saw Mr Holmes kneeling in front of Rachel, his hands on her shoulders.

'It's fine,' I murmured, 'it's fine.'

But as I approached the owl leveled out, flying past me so close I might have touched him. His wing was crooked.

'Thea.' I turned and Sarabeth was pointing in the opposite direction, toward the gate I had left open. Bright had backed out of it, and I could see the liquid red of his flared nostrils, the whites of his eyes. His ears were flattened against his head. He backed up, quickly, and half-reared. Decca fell forward onto his neck.

'Slide off,' I yelled. 'Slide off!' Rachel was still yelling, and I had to scream as loud as I could to be heard, and still it wasn't loud enough.

Bright took off then, as I knew he would, and raced toward the barn. It was the worst kind of mistake, a novice's error, to have left the gate unlatched. And I remembered so clearly not having closed it: an instant of carelessness, in the same category as leaving a girth too loose.

'Thea,' Mr Holmes said, and he sounded almost calm. 'Stop him.' I broke into a run as Bright disappeared. When I rounded the corner, I saw that he was running at full speed now, flat out, as horses only do when they are terrified. Decca clung to the saddle. She wouldn't fall off now unless she made herself. But she was frozen.

The riding groups had all halted in their tracks, a dozen still horses, ears forward, waiting to discern the cause of the alarm. Alice Hunt watched me, not Bright, her face a mask of horror. That I had elicited a reaction from even Alice Hunt, who never seemed to react to anything, terrified me. Leona stared directly at me, her face wide and blank: she shook her head, once, as if she'd known my teaching the girls would end in disaster.

Mr Albrecht climbed over the fence, yelling, 'Turn him, turn him, turn him, turn him,' until the words acquired a particular rhythm, until it seemed as if Mr Albrecht was saying, 'tune him, tune him, tune him,' his vowels arched in panic.

'Stop him,' I heard behind me, 'stop him now.' The instruction was useless. Decca screamed, a sound so horrible, so close to a moan, I put my hands to my ears. Just then Bright veered left at the head of the trail; Decca fell the other way, to the right. Her head was not kicked: this was also lucky. It could have been kicked so easily. She fell cleanly, slid out of the saddle almost gracefully.

Mr Holmes caught my shoulder as he sprinted past me, and I fell to the ground.

'Get the doctor,' Mr Holmes called as he passed. 'Now.'

Decca's eyes were closed, as if she were sleeping.

I rose and began to run, in a single motion. I looked back, once, at the girls on their horses, still standing as if statues.

Sarabeth had dismounted, was crying quietly next to Luther, did not turn her head when Mr Albrecht ran in front of her in pursuit of Bright, who might be lost in the mountains forever if he was not found quickly.

I emerged from the cover of the forest into the Square and screamed, 'Henny!' – again and again until she emerged angrily from the house mistresses' cabin.

'Decca's hurt,' I managed, and Henny yelled to Docey, who had followed her outside, to call the doctor immediately. We ran back through the woods, Henny so far ahead of me I lost sight of her brown skirt. Her speed surprised me. My chest felt like it was boiling, I could hear watery sounds when I inhaled. I slowed to a walk, tried to pace myself. I wanted rain, or snow, or wind. Something to make me feel not so alone. I wrapped my arms around myself.

No one noticed me when I materialized from the woods. The girls and their horses had disappeared. Mr Holmes was kneeling next to Decca, had made himself small next to his daughter; Mr Albrecht had his hand on her forehead. The first aid kit was open next to him, the iodine overturned and running into rivulets. Sarabeth squatted nearby, rocking back and forth on her heels.

I focused on the pattern the iodine made in the dirty-beige sand. A complicated design, improbable and random. But I hadn't seen any blood.

I went to Sarabeth and smoothed her dark hair, removed a leaf that had gotten caught in her braid. Someone had taken Luther back to the barn. Her upper lip was covered with mucus, and she was crying, silently. I'd never comforted anyone besides Sam. And that was second nature to me; or it used to be, when we were young and so much a part of each other. Now I went to Sarabeth with Sam heavy in my mind and embraced her, and I was surprised at how eager she was to be comforted: she rested her cheek on my shoulder, and clutched my waist.

'It'll be all right,' I murmured. I don't think Sarabeth heard me, but maybe later the memory of the words would resonate. She would believe me. She was a child. Father had told me things would be all right, and I had believed him.

Rachel was nowhere to be seen. I would have hidden, too. She had hurt the wrong sister. Rachel was the sister who needed to be told it would be all right, that her world and her family had not collapsed. But whoever told her this would be lying. And it would not be me – I did not have the heart for it.

CHAPTER TWELVE

Word spread quickly through the camp about the youngest Holmes girl. There was an unfamiliar car parked behind Masters, where a girl would not notice it unless she looked. The doctor's car, I knew. Decca was hurt, it was just a matter of how badly. She had lost consciousness; I knew this was a bad sign.

On my way back from the bathhouse – for I was filthy, covered in dirt and sand – I saw a gaggle of young girls, Molly among them, whispering dramatically. She waved at me, brightly, and when I half-heartedly waved back she galloped over to me. She was still all arms and legs, like a filly. Her cheeks were bright red from the cold, her hair tied into some sort of knot. If Mrs Holmes had been here to see it, she'd have sent Molly back to her cabin to repair her grooming.

'Thea! They're saying Rachel lost her mind! That she tried to kill Decca!' Her voice was practically a squeal.

I wasn't taller than many people, but I was taller than Molly. I bent down and encircled her wrist with my hand. I could feel her bones like a bird's beneath her skin.

'Molly,' I said, 'that is nonsense. Do you understand me?'

Molly nodded, slowly, and I saw a gleam in her eye that had not been there before. I had handled this all wrong – I should have laughed off the rumor, brushed it away as if it were no more than a speck of dust.

I released Molly's wrist. She stared at me, her eyes wide in anticipation. What would I tell her next? What could she bring back to her clutch of friends, who were all waiting just ahead? Molly wasn't part of a group of girls that mattered, but still – gossip multiplied so quickly here, spreading through our ranks. Katherine Hayes walked by, coolly, but she was listening to every word. She'd rush back to her cabin and disseminate the information thoroughly and coldly. I glared at Katherine, who hid behind her screen of curls. She, who had so recently been the subject of the camp's scrutiny, should have sympathy for Rachel. But now her uncle was two months dead and talk of him and the Hayeses' errant ways had disappeared. I saw Miss Brooks across the Square, her nose in a book. The adults at Yonahlossee were useless.

And there was always truth to the rumors, sometimes just a morsel of it, but still. Everyone must have heard Rachel screaming. And what of me, who had put the girl I loved most in harm's way because I wanted her father to watch me? I turned back to Molly.

'It was an accident,' I said, loudly and uselessly.

The last time something terrible had happened, I had tried to explain myself, also loudly and uselessly. But I was smarter now, or at least not as foolish. I retreated to Augusta House and pretended to sleep, ignored even Sissy, who I could feel behind me once or twice, waiting for me to turn around, to give a sign. Finally she left, all the girls did, for dinner. Life went on, it always went on, and Decca could be near death but still Yonahlossee would feed its girls three square meals a day. It had seemed so cruel, at home, that Mother still neatened my bed in the mornings, that Father still left after breakfast to call on his patients.

I could not force the image of my cousin from my mind, and I was usually so good at precisely that, at living a life at Yonahlossee that had nothing to do with Georgie, or Sam, any of them. I saw Georgie when I opened my eyes, when I closed them: not as he was when I left him, but as he had been when I'd known him best. Mother would be so disappointed in me. I realized that part of Yonahlossee's comfort was that it was a world completely separate from home, and now the two worlds felt like they were eerily merging, and why? Because of me, Thea Atwell, a wrong girl if there ever was one.

'Thea,' Sam had said, over and over and over. 'Thea, Thea, Thea.'

I sat up in bed and pressed my fingernails into my forehead. I wished I could dig through my skin and skull into my brain, remove my memories of Georgie, of that day, entirely. But what of my soul? I knew from Father that though our brains stored our memories, our souls were the reason we remembered in the first place. And there was no way to get at the soul. The pain from my fingernails, though small, distracted, brought relief.

I was still in bed when Mary Abbott brought me a roll from dinner, knelt beside my bed, and unwrapped it from an embroidered handkerchief.

'Here,' she whispered. The other girls filed in: Eva, Gates, and then Sissy, who raised her eyebrows behind Mary Abbott's back.

'Thank you.' The roll was cold and doughy in my palm. When warm, these rolls melted in your mouth. The air ruined them.

'You're welcome.'

Mary Abbott stayed beside me, twirled a piece of hair around her finger, avoided my eyes. There was a faint rash across her forehead, where her wool hat chafed. The sight of her, so peculiar, suddenly enraged me.

'Do you need something?'

She looked at me, unsurprised. 'Aren't you going to eat that?'

I shook my head.

'That's fine,' Mary Abbott murmured. The other girls were preparing for bed; Eva's creamy shoulders, her back dotted with black moles; Sissy's fine, knotty hair, freshly brushed, a pretty gold bracelet on her wrist, which meant Boone would be coming again, two nights in a row. I felt like something awful was going to happen. I could smell it.

'Mr Holmes came out and gave us a speech. I thought you'd want to know. Was I right?' she asked, suddenly bold, her cold, sticky hand upon mine.

I slid my hand from under hers, nodded.

'I knew you would.' She smiled, but to herself, she'd made a bet and won. 'He came out for prayer. He asked us to pray for Decca and his family. And then he asked us to pray for you, Thea.' She paused. 'For you and Decca.'

Sissy watched us, from her bed. But I was all Mary Abbott's now.

'Are you glad he asked us to pray for you?'

'I'm flattered,' I said, and closed my eyes, 'and tired.' Though it was not unusual to be mentioned in Mr Holmes's prayers, right now his request felt like a betrayal. He hated me. Why had he ever agreed to put me in charge of his children? He knew something of my life in Florida. He knew enough to know I shouldn't be trusted. But now he hated me, he had to – since I had hurt one of his girls, what choice did he have?

'I thought you'd be glad, when I was walking over here I thought you'd be happy.' Mary Abbot leaned in, conspiratorially. Her breath was dry and hot. 'Because he's not mad.'

I made my voice as cold as ice. 'Leave me alone.'

Mary Abbott backed away, but not before leaning forward, so quickly I could not shield myself. I turned, and she caught my lips with hers.

* * *

I slept dreamlessly, hot and itchy, woke up dozens of times, unreasonably frightened, the tall bunk beds and the white-clad girls in them unfamiliar, terrifying. Then I calmed myself, it was a trick sometimes, remaining lucid, convincing yourself that the world had not arranged its enormity in opposition – to you, against you. I say I calmed myself but truly my mind was merciful in deciding not to unhinge itself as it had in the days before I was sent away, when I wept until my eyes were ugly pouches in my skull.

'Thea.'

I sat up, startled.

'It's fine, it's fine,' Sissy soothed, 'you're fine.'

'I'm hot.'

'Are you feverish?' She felt my forehead with the back of her hand. 'No. You were talking in your sleep.'

'What did I say?'

'Nothing, babble. Are you all right?'

I nodded. 'Have you heard anything about Decca?'

She shook her head. 'I prayed tonight. I haven't prayed in so long . . .' She trailed off. 'What happened? The mill is saying Rachel tried to kill Decca, that she lost her mind.'

'An owl,' I whispered.

'An owl?' she repeated. When I said nothing, she continued, 'The doctor is here. Mr Holmes must be worried sick.'

'Mr Holmes is alone,' I muttered. Eva stirred above us. 'I'd forgotten,' I said, lowering my voice. I brought my hand to my mouth. My fingers smelled of leather.

'Thea, I have to go. Boone's here.'

'Don't go,' I said, 'please.'

'Oh, Thea,' she whispered, and kissed my forehead. 'I have to. But I'll be back.'

She stood. Her hair was tucked into the back of her coat, her gloves stuck out of her pocket like hands. I felt the unpleasant bite of jealousy: I wanted so badly to be Sissy, going to meet a boy who loved me.

Sissy waited for a second, and then pointed to her bed impatiently.

'Oh!' I whispered, and went to her bed, a little wounded – all of these things had happened to me today, and still a boy was more important.

After she left, I rose, put my coat on, and stepped outside. Then, nervous I might have woken Mary Abbott, peered back into the cabin through the window. Mary Abbott slept almost peacefully. Eva's arm and head were flung over the side of the bed, hanging inertly. I couldn't see Gates, but I knew she slept in a tight ball, like she always did.

None of my sleeping cabinmates needed to concern themselves with the danger outside – as far as I knew, there had never been so much as a Peeping Tom at Yonahlossee. Danger presented itself, every girl knew, from within the family – your father's mistress; mother's thorny relationship with her mother-in-law, your grandmother; the first cousin who had tried to kill himself. But we were no one, nothing, without our families.

If anything happened to Decca, the youngest, the best and favorite of the family, Rachel would have ruined her own life as well as her sister's.

With a brief and distant shock I noticed a light beyond the Square where Masters was, not a part of the Square but not completely away, either; within eyesight, in case something happened, in case a girl needed something.

My boots stuck in the mud as I walked, their soles made a quick, sucking sound each time I lifted a foot; the noise was disgusting, and that was all I could hear, the night was so quiet, so utterly dead: Florida nights were never like this. There was always a chirping, a scuttling, a howl.

It was cold, the air was still, the sky was dark, but it's necessary to understand how dark. The stars were barely there, the twin gas lamps that bordered the Castle burned steadily, always, even during daylight, but they meant almost nothing in the face of so much black. So the small light, illuminating a Holmeses' window; it felt to me like it *meant* something: the light surged, ignited the reptilian part of my brain, and I wanted to move toward it, I wanted to be inside that house, that home, so badly I could feel the desire rise in my throat.

I began to run, clumsily, through the mud, stopping twenty feet from Masters. I confronted it. I was frantic, I knew that I could not trust myself but I also knew that I needed to speak to him.

I turned and retched into the mud. I felt dizzy, suddenly, unmoored. Beyond Masters was the forest, which led to the mountains; I could disappear into those woods. And who would miss me, if I left? And for how long, before my absence brought relief? I was already mostly gone from my family's life. Because I had done this once before, I had been careless. I had let desire dictate everything. I closed my eyes, tried to stop the world from spinning. If Decca were hurt beyond repair, then I would disappear into the woods. If Mr Holmes hated me, if I had ruined another family, I would leave this place.

'I thought we knew one another,' Mother had said, in my parents' room, where I had gone to find her on that other horrible day; she lay on their made bed, the yellow light of the late afternoon illuminating her delicate features, her head propped up at an odd angle. 'You're not the girl I thought you were.'

Who was I, then? When Georgie was pressed against me, I lost all reason. I acted dangerously with him and I would not have cared if both my dead grandmothers were listening at the door. All the various pressures of a boy against my body, the kneading, insistent pressure of his hands; the light, live pressure of his tongue; the almost unfelt pressure of his penis pushing through the fabric of his pants.

'Enough.' I spoke now, startling myself, one of my tricks.

And because I was acting dangerously, I bridged the distance between myself and the Holmeses' front door, noticing how Mrs Holmes or one of the girls had taken care to cover the pots of rosemary that flanked their door with old sheets, then fasten them with a neatly tied ribbon. The door was unlocked, as I had expected; I opened it slowly and slipped through; it was all darkness inside, a warm, dense darkness.

The Holmeses' stairs were spotless, the walls hung with family photos, silver frames dusted, gleaming. The portraits surprised me: to me, the Holmeses were a family without a place or past, even though I knew everyone had a past, and even though I knew specific details of their past: my mother, Boston.

The light came from upstairs.

It had been months, I realized, since I'd climbed stairs in a home – I'd forgotten how noisy they were, and my boots were still on. I half hoped the groaning stairs would announce me. I shrugged my coat off when I reached the top.

I could see the light at the end of the hall, pooling out on the pine floor so clearly.

I passed closed doors. I wondered where Decca and her sisters lay.

I noticed all his books, first, so many books the room reminded me of a library, a place I had been only once, in Gainesville, with Georgie and Sam. Those boys were on the tip of my brain tonight; everything I saw reminded me of them.

Mr Holmes stood at a desk in front of the window, reading a newspaper. He turned a page, and I saw a grainy photograph, but I could not tell of what. It was an impractical place for a desk, where he could not see anyone enter, where the sun would bleach his things, his books, his letters, his photographs. But I understood why the desk was there: he could see everything below, all us girls coming and going through the Square; and beyond us, the mountains. Always the mountains. I touched the doorframe.

'Who's—' He turned and glanced at me, startled. He was fully clothed, in a white dress shirt and herringbone trousers. He wore monogrammed slippers.

'You shouldn't be here, Thea,' he said. He set the newspaper onto his desk, and I thought how different this man was from my father, or Uncle George. Or Sam or Georgie, for that matter. He didn't know me – that was why, and how, he was different.

'How is Decca?' I asked.

Mr Holmes tilted his head, as if he were trying to discern me. I lowered my head; I hadn't been looked at so closely in such a long time.

'Are you worried, Thea? I'm sorry. I would have sent word sooner. Decca has broken her collarbone. The other injury is superficial – a cut on her hand. Her head wasn't hit; the doctor was very grateful for that.'

The iodine had been for her hand. My eyes blurred.

'Thea?'

But I could not look up. Her head.

'Thea? Please look at me.'

His voice was firm; he was still my headmaster. And so I lifted my head and saw Mr Holmes now held a glass in his hand. Whiskey.

'Her personality is intact,' I whispered.

He nodded, slowly.

'I left the gate open,' I said. 'I was distracted.'

He set his glass down and directed me to sit, on an overstuffed armchair next to his desk. He pulled his desk chair opposite me – it looked so small in his hand, so light – and sat down.

'Thea,' he said, 'Decca will be fine. Just a bit of a scare, but nothing that can't be mended.'

'She could have been badly hurt,' I said. I thought of Rachel.

'That is true. But she was not.'

I started to speak again, but he held up his hand.

'She was not,' he repeated. 'It was a series of events, Thea. Thank God they ended well, and leave it at that.'

A door closed in my brain, then, unexpectedly. My understanding of our world shifted: it was a series of events, I thought, all of it.

'And I can't reach Beth. She's somewhere in Alabama, but I don't know exactly where. This day was already bad, to begin with. Our sponsors are not sponsoring. Our donors are not donating.' He smiled, and took another sip of his drink. He was less guarded than I had ever seen him; this must be how he always was with his wife. But perhaps not. Perhaps Henry Holmes was rarely so undisguised.

'And the worst of it is that I don't blame them.' He shook his head. There was a bitter note in his voice. 'Forgive me, Thea. You always strike me as older than your years.'

'Rachel?' I asked.

'Rachel,' he said, and paused. 'Rachel is beside herself.'

'Are you angry with her?'

'Yes,' he said, 'of course I am.'

'Don't be.'

'But how will she learn, Thea, if I'm not?'

'She made a mistake,' I said. I leaned forward in my chair. I could feel a flush creep up my chest, across my cheeks. 'A mistake!' I thought of my brother and cousin as I had last seen them. It was all a mistake. 'If it is a series of events, then let her be. She's learned her lesson.'

Mr Holmes seemed surprised. He finished his drink and set the glass on the floor, next to his feet.

'Has she?' he asked. His speech was looser. The alcohol, combined with his wife's absence. 'I'd like to think so. But as a parent you never quite know what your child is learning.'

Mr Holmes turned his head at the sound of a door closing. He started to stand, and I caught the edge of his sleeve. He looked at me. 'Don't hate her.'

'You never hate your child, Thea.' He gazed down at me. I made myself meet his gaze.

He did not look away, so I did. I stood, then, and put on my coat. I realized all of a sudden how improper it was, me in front of a man I was not related to without even a robe to cover my nightgown. And yet I did not want to leave. I wanted to stay, to be with him, to go wherever he went, to be enveloped by Mr Holmes and his books.

'I should leave,' I said, 'I'm sorry to come here like this.'

He nodded, and took a step forward and he was so close I could smell him, the pomade in his hair, and it made me think about the time he had visited me in the infirmary, and told me I would grow to love Yonahlossee. He had been kind. It was only now, months later, that I was able to see how kind he had been.

'Rachel isn't bad. She made a mistake. There is' – here he looked at the ceiling, as if deciding how to phrase it – 'a difference.'

He departed then, mumbled something about checking on Decca, leaving me to quietly observe his office and all its books: neatly ordered, in bookshelves; stacked on his desk, with little slips of paper sticking out of their pages; one open, on the sofa.

I went to this book, and picked it up. I touched the pages he touched, the spine. I could see how Mr Holmes lost himself in other worlds in here.

CHAPTER
THIRTEEN

Dear Thea,

Did you like the coat? How was Christmas at school? Your father says we need to go away somewhere for a while but where? Here is where I want to be. I'm not lonely. Your father is working more than ever, even if everything else is changed there are always the sick and dying. And there seem to be more of them here now, the sick and dying.

I wish I could see you, Thea. I wish things were not how they are. You should have been my child longer. All three of you should have been children longer. I'll stop with that. Does it surprise you to read a letter like this, your mother so maudlin?

I cut back all the roses, mulched all the beds, hacked away everything dead. I worked for days, perhaps did too much. Sam helped. Your brother is still your brother. There is more to say, surely, but I can't think of it. I know you wrote to him. I know he has not written back. He is still reeling, Thea; I hope I am right in telling you this. I mean not to hurt your feelings, only to explain his.

Georgie is fine. Sam said you asked.

Bundle up in those mountains. Don't ride too long or hard. Remember your health.

Love,

Mother

I sat in the Hall with Sissy, in our usual spot, on a threadbare red velvet sofa, and read Mother's letter. I was exhausted. I'd been sleeping poorly since my nighttime visit to Masters, three days ago.

We weren't supposed to have roses in Emathla, in that humid, hot climate, but Mother loved them. She worried over them, and when they bloomed in the spring they were beautiful; you would not have known they did not belong.

My feelings were hurt. She had known they would be; I felt stung, crumpled. It was one thing to think of my family separately, going about their lives; another entirely to think that an alliance had been formed against me.

Katherine Hayes started playing something cheerful on the piano. Decca's accident had hushed Yonahlossee – girls had cried into each other's shoulders, and sported grave expressions, and looked sadly at Masters – but only for a day. Jettie stood at an easel, painting a watercolor of the view of the mountains from the window. I could see from here that Martha Ladue, who sat next to her, was idly flipping the pages of a magazine, and that Jettie's painting was very bad. Martha Ladue seemed to be interested in only two things: speaking French and being beautiful.

The day after I had gone to Masters, Mr Holmes had told everyone during morning prayer that Decca had broken her collarbone, that she was recovering nicely. He seemed exhausted as he spoke to us. His eyes were tired. Since then he had appeared at most, but not all, meals. In his absence, Miss Metcalfe, the French teacher, presided. This was the first time I'd paid any attention to Miss Metcalfe. She fell into the boring category that most teachers and girls here did: plain but not ugly, nice but uninteresting. I knew she must go to Masters and speak to Mr Holmes. I knew she must lend him her sympathetic ear. *I* wanted to do that. I wanted to bring him comfort. I felt a little like he belonged to me, now. He had let me into his office in the dead of night; he had comforted me, and I wanted more of that: more letting in, more comfort.

Henny had left with Sarabeth and Rachel yesterday, to chaperone them on the train to New Orleans to their grandmother's house, where they would be reunited with their mother. Decca stayed behind, because of her injury. Before they left, though, both girls had eaten their meals at the head table when their father did, and though I watched carefully for signs of distress, Rachel seemed unchanged. She seemed happy, even, and I understood that her happiness was an accident: it could so easily have turned out worse. I tried to be glad for the happy Holmeses. I tried to swallow the envy that rose in my throat like tar.

I was glad Sarabeth and Rachel were gone. I knew the feeling was base, petty, but I wanted to be closer to Mr Holmes, and their absence would make this easier. He thought that I was good. Or at the very least he did not think I was bad. And that he thought so made me wonder: perhaps I was not as bad as I had thought.

It was so easy to be here among these girls, who knew nothing of my visit to Masters, who knew nothing of the intensity of my thinking, which I could feel hurtling toward obsession.

'I'm bored,' Sissy said, and drew a stack of Boone's letters from her schoolbag, which was what she did when she was bored.

There were a few girls who studied at the Hall – Gates, from our cabin – but most of us didn't; our classes didn't require it. We knew boys at boarding school received grades, which meant something in their lives, though *what* grades meant remained vague. We learned in class, were lectured to about wars and famines, ancient kings and queens, the habits of the presidents. But the lectures were cursory. We needed to know what had happened, because we were the well-bred daughters of men who could afford to educate us – but not why, or how. Not any of the stories that made the facts interesting.

We were ranked according to our equestrienne skills, but none of us would compete professionally, or do anything besides ride as a diversion once we left Yonahlossee. And many of us would go back to places where we couldn't sit astride a horse.

The few girls here who did truly care about learning – Gates, in our cabin – were not popular. It meant you were too hungry, that you sought something unappealing and vague. It was better by ten to be charming and witty, like Sissy, than to care about books.

I watched Sissy hold the letter to her face, then draw it back again as if she were trying to trick her mind into seeing it for the first time. I wondered what she would be as an adult, whether or not she would still seem so young. Sissy's charm, her thin wrists, her easily tangled hair, her long, awkward neck, seemed so clearly and profoundly childish to me. She was lovely, Sissy, anyone could see that. But she was lovely because she seemed harmless.

What would it feel like to be Sissy? I thought of Boone gently and urgently kneading her breasts. Sissy smiled to herself, serenely, and I saw Boone's hands and felt a familiar sensation in my stomach. I turned my head and watched Jettie paint a disfigured mountain peak until the feeling went away.

Sissy would never have gone to see Mr Holmes in the dead of night. The idea wouldn't even have occurred to her. She had chosen a normal beau. Boone came from a good family; the *good* implied that his family was wealthy. Their biggest hurdle would be that they were too young, that Boone was not Southern enough, not Alabama royalty. He was from Asheville, which Sissy had told me was fine, but not wonderful. But I gathered he had enough money to smooth that particular wrinkle. All of this seemed so ridiculous, the nuances of hierarchy, the subtleties of position, and though Sissy sometimes made fun of all this fuss, with me, I could see she took it seriously.

Outside I hugged myself against the cold, my old coat too small. I squinted my eyes against the sun until I entered the woods, and then it was dark, the light dappled onto the forest floor and the effect was eerily beautiful, a pricked pattern engineered by randomness.

There was no trace that Decca had fallen. The iodine had been absorbed by the earth long ago; Bright was back in his stall, chomping hay; the felled tree had been cleared away. I lingered at Bright's stall and he whuffed into my hand, curious. He had no memory of what had happened, no idea at all. I envied a horse's dumbness, not for the first time in my life.

We took turns jumping the combination Mr Albrecht had devised. I went next to last, and I watched girl after girl fail, go either too fast or too slow between the second and third jumps, then nick a rail.

'Well done, Thea,' Mr Albrecht murmured as I passed him.

Just then I saw Mr Holmes walking alongside the ring, toward me, and I was hot and panicked but also terribly eager.

'Hello, Thea,' he said, and smiled.

'Mr Holmes.'

'Well,' he said, after a pause, and rested his arms on the railing in the posture that was so familiar to me, 'Decca is feeling better.' He looked beyond me, at the other ring, and I knew he was in front of me only briefly, before he continued his tour of the riding rings, before he would stop and chat with other girls. Jealousy was still such an odd feeling. At home, there had been nothing to envy, nothing to want that I didn't already have, or could get.

'Is Decca lonely?' I blurted, and then tried to speak more slowly. 'I mean, does she miss her sisters?'

'I think she must. She's the youngest. She's never been alone before.'

'I know that feeling,' I said.

'You're the youngest?' he asked.

'No.' I shook my head. I was relieved that he did not know as much about me as I had thought; and then also disappointed for precisely the same reason. He looked at me expectantly, waiting for an answer.

'I'm a twin,' I said. 'Fraternal.'

'Ah,' he said. He seemed neither interested nor surprised. He must hear so many things about us girls, all the time. He took his hands from the rail, preparing to leave.

'May I visit Decca?' I said, before I lost my chance, 'sit with her?'

He paused. I could tell I had pleased him. Parents liked when you were interested in their children. I wondered if Mother and Father had felt the same pleasure when people complimented me and Sam. But no one had, except occasionally, in town.

'She would like that, Thea. Thank you.' He began to turn around, but then he stopped. 'I almost forgot – I wanted to tell you that Rachel is fine. That everyone is grateful Decca was not seriously injured.'

I wondered what his memory of that night was. I had been so bold, and he did not seem to mind.

I watched him walk away, his slim, busy hands swinging by his sides, then folded behind him, then in his pockets. I knew what the feeling was, now, that had embroidered itself in my brain. Knowing made me feel less horrible. I had what so many girls had: a crush. It was as simple and harmless as that. I had never had one before. With Georgie, things had simply happened, one after the next; I'd never had any control. But this time, I had control. This was just a crush.

I turned Naari around and saw that Leona stood at the gate, watching, and I got rid of the stupid smile that had been on my face.

The Holmeses' housekeeper met me at their door that afternoon, when everyone else was at the Hall studying, or feigning studying. I stepped into their house and unlaced my boots.

'There's no need,' the housekeeper said. She was young, with golden-blond hair coiled into a braid. A smattering of freckles dotted her cheeks. When she spoke, I could see that her teeth were horribly crooked. Still, she was pretty. She had that Appalachian look, wan, thin. The mountain families were large, I knew, and inbred. Sissy told me that they thought nothing of marrying their cousins. But who else were they supposed to marry, I wanted to point out, isolated in hollers and valleys unreachable by automobiles and trains, places that never saw outsiders. When the only boy there for you happened to also be your cousin.

'I'll make a mess.' I pried off my boots and handed them to her; she returned a moment later and led me up the stairs.

Decca's room was chilly. I was glad I'd kept my scarf and jacket. I felt Sissy's gloves in my pocket, lent to me for the winter, but to put them on would be impolite, even if I were only in the presence of a housekeeper and a child.

'Is she warm enough?' I whispered, because Decca was asleep.

The housekeeper paused a moment, as if considering whether or not to answer me.

'Hot-water bottles,' she said, finally. She left, then.

I sat by the bed in a chair clearly meant for this purpose: Mr Holmes must sit here, too, I knew, for hours, days if the hours were added together.

Decca was swathed in pink blankets.

Her long lashes rested dramatically on her pale skin. Her hair – so dark it was almost black – was shiny with oil. I wondered if Mr Holmes knew anything about washing girls' hair, about tending to a child of Decca's age. I touched her soft forehead and though she stirred she did not wake.

If he came into this room while I sat here with his daughter it would be happenstance. I could not be accused of being bad. I could not be accused of being forward. It would simply be a meeting engineered by chance. I wanted to be close to him again, I wanted him to speak to me, to ask me questions, to answer mine.

I would come again tomorrow, and the next day. I drew my gloves on and rested my head on the back of the leather chair. It was big and comfortable, meant for someone larger, a man's easy chair. The furniture in this room was the same as ours: washstand, desk, and vanity.

A homely embroidered mat hung between the beds, the Lord's Prayer stitched in green. Mother would have hated this room. It was clean, spotless, but looked mean. I took off a glove and fingered Decca's bedspread – made of some rough linen, with a thick border of dark red. There was a timeless quality about this room, perhaps due to its sparseness; except for the lamp, I could have been sitting in a bedroom from a hundred years ago. Was this house an accurate representation of Mrs Holmes's taste, or had it always stayed the same, Mrs Holmes only changing small things, grace notes? Pictures, maybe dishes. That would undo Mother, to live somewhere that was not her own.

At the end of the hour I was taken to the front door and shown outside by the housekeeper, who managed to lead me through the house and hand me my boots while ignoring me. Decca had spent the whole visit asleep.

I looked up at the house, for some sign of Mr Holmes. The drapes were drawn against the cold, and even if they hadn't been, it was impossible to see through a window lit by daylight.

Mr Holmes had still not appeared. I asked the housekeeper where he might be – I had come three days in a row and seen neither hide nor hair of him. She shrugged. 'You'd have to ask Mr Holmes.' I thought there was a note of challenge in her voice. Insolence. Or a note of satisfaction – of course I could not ask him, because he was gone when I came to the house. Because he was distant when we met in the dining hall – or did not meet, he made sure of that. He stayed away, it was not my imagination. And so I began to imagine that he also wanted to see me, that there was something that existed between us. I could not yet say what – I did not know. If I were a better girl according to Mother, I would stop all this, reinsert myself into Yonahlossee life, go to the Hall with Sissy instead of coming here every day. But I no longer knew what kind of girl I was.

I played with Decca, or read to her, or sang her songs. She had not slept after that first visit. I lay awake at night and rose when Boone threw his rock and shook Sissy awake, hard. Boone, so handsome and nice; he waited outside like a trap, waited for Sissy to fall. I lay in Sissy's bed and listened to her tiptoe out – she was so loud! – and hated her, hated Boone for making her furtive.

I hated the girls in Augusta House, who thought my visitation arrangement strange. 'You only sit there?' Mary Abbott asked that night, sidling up beside me on the way to the bathhouse. 'Why do you?' Wasn't that very apparent? Achingly clear? But no, it was not. Only to me, only I knew.

Now I was awake and knew I would not get back to sleep, and felt so hot, so ready.

'Do you love me?' I imagined Sissy asking. 'Do you love me? Me?'

'Do you love me?' He would ask me that.

'Why did you stay away for all that time?'

'Because I loved you,' he would say. He would put his hand on my breast, underneath my dress. Those slim, long fingers inside me, touching me, feeling parts of me, the odd pressures, the closeness.

Oh. I bit my pillow and there were sparks against my eyelids. If only this could last – longer, longer. If only, but it never did.

My breaths were quick but deep. My limbs were heavy against the sheets. I wiped between my legs with my handkerchief and left it there.

I could fall asleep now. I closed my eyes and was not ashamed. Mr Holmes, Mr Holmes, Mr Holmes. When I closed my eyes, he was all I saw.

Dear Mother,

I do like my coat – thank you. It's so nice I don't know when I'll wear it. It's cold here, but beautiful. I think I prefer the cold to the heat. You can ride forever in the cold. I'm riding again, did you know? I don't know what else to report. There's nothing to report, I suppose. It's cold and I'm riding and camp life is the same. We do the same thing every day, exactly, except for Sunday but then our Sundays are exactly alike so everything has its order.

You wouldn't like it here, I don't think. There isn't any green in the winter except for the evergreens and they don't really count, do they? Everything dies and the world is all one color – white – until spring. I never knew anything but colorful, humid Florida and I thought that was what I preferred, but truly it was simply what I knew. I wonder what the desert is like, or up north. Who knows what I prefer?

*Mrs Holmes was your friend? I didn't know. I didn't know you
had friends. I would write more but we're kept so busy. Don't worry
about me. Don't even think about me.*

'My father spoke on the telephone,' Decca said. 'To my mother.'
I was reading to her from a book she loved, called *Winnie-the-
Pooh*; she should keep still, the housekeeper told me. But Decca
was back to her old self, a sling she had to wear to keep her right
arm immobile so that her collarbone could heal the only evidence
she had fallen. There was no need for me to come like this, I
knew that, and though I told myself, and everyone else, that I
came for Decca's sake, really I came for my own. I wanted to see
him.

'Oh?' I asked.

'Yes. Father sounded angry.'

I tried to hide my surprise. Mr Holmes should speak more
carefully. But clearly Decca did not know what this all meant.

'Why was he angry, Decca?'

'When will my sisters be here?' Her voice was plaintive. She
missed them, I realized. She didn't understand their absence. I
understood. Boone had told Sissy that a boy at Harris Academy
had been sent back to school with a suitcase full of money, and
told to hide it. He'd stored it in his mattress. It was such a dumb
hiding place I didn't know if the story could be true, but the banks
were failing, we all knew that; a girl's uncle was president of First
National, Charlotte's bank that had closed in December. Yet the
Harris boy's family had money – he was at Harris, after all, not
beneath the earth working in some mine. His father didn't know
what to do with their money, though, how to keep it safe, how to
ensure that it would protect them.

There was enough money in the world for all of us to be here,
to ride our horses, to wear our white clothes. I wondered if

Mother's citrus fortune was in a bank. Surely it was. I couldn't imagine Mother hiding money among her furniture, her things. But I didn't know, I realized, I didn't know anything at all about how my family was handling their financial affairs. I had never known. The citrus income had shadowed us, all my life; it was impossible to imagine the Atwells without it: I saw now that it gave us an edge, a little way to feel better than people who did not have wealth from a distant, exotic source.

Mother would never have used the word ' "better".' We were simply different. Unique.

'Thea?'

I gazed at Decca, who looked at me curiously.

'They'll be back soon,' I answered. I hated how vague I sounded, but I didn't know how else to sound.

Mr Holmes sounded angry on the telephone. I would have given my left arm to know why. But Decca was just a child – she might have misheard. Perhaps Mr Holmes had sounded upset, not angry.

I wondered how much she remembered about the accident. It seemed a mercy, that she was too young to understand Rachel's part in it.

Decca picked up her doll – its hair was patchy, its clothes smudged. It must have belonged to Sarabeth, then Rachel; finally, Decca. I had never had to share anything with Sam. I'd never liked dolls, but still I'd had at least half a dozen.

Decca whispered to her doll. I tried to listen to what she said but then drew back, embarrassed, a sixteen-year-old girl straining to hear the mutterings of a child. I should let Decca have her secrets.

If our lives had not been so blessed, if we had not had Mother's money – if, if, if. But this particular line of possibilities had never occurred to me. Then Father would have had to live in a city, where there were more paying patients. Then Mother could not have kept herself, and us, so apart from everyone else. We might have lived hours from Gainesville. We might have only seen each other once a year, for Christmas.

We would not have had money to give them. We would not have been able to help. We would not have been better. We would not have been lucky.

Did my parents hope I'd been taught a lesson? They thought they'd sent me somewhere safe. Away from men, away from cousins. Georgie, Georgie must be – I tried not to think of Georgie here. I stood – Decca was still playing with her doll, the room was still ugly and stiff, I was still alone in this house with his child.

I thought we knew one another, my mother had said, and then, later: This will all be fine, do as you're told, do as we say and this will all be for the best.

If my parents had kept me at home, I might have learned their lesson, I might have wanted to please them more than I wanted to please myself. In my head, I thought, if I can make Mr Holmes love me, it will all be all right.

CHAPTER
FOURTEEN

It was bitterly cold the next time we went to Gainesville. Aunt Carrie's mother had taken a turn for the worse and died very suddenly, and we were going to offer our condolences. I'd wrapped a scarf around my neck and head and face, left room for only my eyes. I watched the landscape speed by, punctuated occasionally by houses: they all looked the same to me, splintering wood, windows that were glassless black squares.

Since Christmas I'd only seen Georgie three times, which was, I thought, less often than we usually saw the Gainesville Atwells. But how often we saw each other was never something I'd tallied before. But now – now I wanted to see my cousin more than I could ever remember wanting anything.

Mother was concentrating on driving, which was new to her. There weren't many things that Mother wasn't good at, but driving was one of them. This new car had a backseat, which I thought was the height of luxury; right now Sam sat in front with Mother, and I was sprawled across the mohair seats in back. Sam sat tensely. He was a little afraid of how fast we went in cars.

That morning I'd gone through Mother's handbag looking for the little pot of perfume she kept there. I'd found a blank envelope, unsealed, and inside a check made out to George Atwell for the

largest sum of money I'd ever seen. Father's nearly illegible
signature bit into the thin paper.

I dabbed perfume behind my ears, as Mother always did.
Georgie would be George Atwell one day, lose his nickname, and
what would he do then? Would I be his wife? I steadied myself on
the counter. I didn't think I wanted to be his wife. But I knew
from books that that's what you did, when you kissed.

There were no houses on the final stretch of our drive, as they
would have been sucked down by the bog. It seemed so near on
either side: if we stopped, the animals would emerge from the
groves of cabbage palm and the thick stands of maiden cane. The
bobcats hid – we almost never saw them – but the alligators often
sunned themselves on the edge of the road when it was warm,
their gnarly, muddy skin, almost black, their improbably white
teeth that were visible when they lazily snapped their jaws, as –
what else could it mean – a warning.

It was perhaps my imagination that Mother sped through this
stretch, that the automobile shook violently, that she did not slow
down as she normally did for dips in the road. Father loved this
leg of the drive; he thought central Florida possessed the most
beautiful landscape in the world: a little bit of swamp, a little bit
of forest.

At Georgie's, we stepped out and waited while Mother gathered her things – a book for Aunt Carrie, a big crate of food:
beans, Idella's bread, preserves. Surely Georgie's family did not
need our food? I touched the sack of beans, and looked at Mother
curiously.

'Just some extra things we had,' she said. I walked toward the
house: was it my imagination, that it looked grim, in need of
sprucing up? It was a matter of fact that paint flaked from the
windowsills, that a gutter was hanging by a thread. But things
could not fall apart so quickly.

'Georgie's at a neighbor's,' Aunt Carrie told us after she had shown us into the living room. 'He'll be back soon,' she said, when she saw my face, which I tried to make look happy again. But I felt devastated. I'd waited for weeks!

'I'm sorry for your loss,' I said – Mother had coached me – and Aunt Carrie put her arm around my shoulders and pressed me to her. She felt sturdy, next to Mother, who was all angles.

'Both my parents are gone,' she said, her voice pitched as if she was asking me a question, and I realized she was close to tears.

'Carrie,' Mother said, and led my aunt to a chair, 'it will be fine.'

'Will it, Elizabeth?' She offered my mother a thin smile. 'You sound like our president.' This had all turned Aunt Carrie mean, I realized.

Mother laughed nervously, and Sam and I slipped away.

'Want to go out back?' he asked, but I did not. I did not want to observe the natural world today; I did not want to follow Sam around.

'I'm tired,' I said, even though I wasn't. Sam looked at me for a second – I always went with him – and I didn't meet his eye.

'All right,' he said, hurt. 'I'll go by myself.'

I was sorry, but not sorry enough to go with him. I went to my aunt and uncle's bedroom, where I could think. Their bed was unmade. Beds were so rarely unmade in my world.

I pressed my forehead against the window and watched until Sam disappeared into the woods. Last night we'd stayed up far past our bedtimes and took turns reading to each other an Agatha Christie mystery we'd read a thousand times already. I spent nearly all my time with Sam – he should not be hurt now. I looked at my hands, my nails that I had carefully trimmed last night, painted with oil. They were not a child's hands. I stood and gathered my hair into a knot. I'd worn it down, brushed it ten different ways, decided on a side part.

I fell asleep in Aunt Carrie and Uncle George's bed; I opened my eyes and Georgie was there, and I felt as if I'd summoned my cousin through a dream.

I held out my hand. Sleep had calmed me. My fingers gleamed in the soft lamplight.

'Where is Sam?'

'Outside. Mother is showing Sam and your mother her first azaleas.' He paused. 'We'll hear when they come back in.'

He rubbed my hand, I watched him, he rubbed my hand gently with his thumb and I wanted to moan.

He traced my eyebrow with his finger, lightly. 'So pretty.'

'Do you think Sam knows?'

He shook his head. 'I'm almost certain he doesn't.'

That was enough, in that moment. I looked out the window and was surprised to see that it had turned dark while I slept.

'You look so old,' I said, and he did, standing there with one hand in his trouser pocket, the other over mine, kneading slowly but insistently. I sat up and kissed him, he leaned down and opened his mouth, put his tongue into mine.

'Open your mouth, Thea, like this.'

I did what he said. He turned his head away and I didn't know what he was doing but then I saw he was taking his jacket off. The idea thrilled me: he was taking his clothes off, he was going to stay. He faced me again. I watched him for a moment. He was breathing heavily, his face was flushed. I knew that I was calm – calmer, certainly, than Georgie.

'Come here,' I said.

'Yes,' he said, 'yes, yes,' and he climbed on top of me, propped himself up with his elbows. I wanted him closer, I pressed my hands hard against his back and at first he resisted but then he relented and he was pushing into me, and I wanted it, he was pushing into me and I reached down between us and felt for the hard pressure of his penis. I knew it would be there. It felt not like I expected it would, it felt swollen and very soft. I reached—

'No, no,' he whispered, 'not yet. Just feel me from the outside.' So I touched him like he wanted, gingerly at first, but he kept pushing himself into my hand, harder and harder, and so I touched him harder, ran my fingers firmly along the length of it, and Georgie moaned while he was kissing me, moaned and moaned.

I ached. I pressed him to where I ached, shifted so that it touched more, harder, and I pressed and pressed and when it happened it was different, it was quicker, and when I was finished Georgie was still moving on top of me, kissing me, kissing my neck, my chest.

'Oh.'

'What?' he asked.

I shook my head. He didn't know what I had just done. Georgie stood up suddenly. His pants were tented at his crotch. I'd done that, too.

'We should go down,' he whispered, 'they'll wonder.'

I sat up and unknotted my hair.

'You're so pretty,' he said, and kneeled in front of me, put his head in my lap. I combed his hair with my fingers. We heard the screen door slam, and then footsteps. 'What if they catch us?'

'I thought you weren't worried?' I asked.

'I'm not,' he said, 'not really.'

'I'm not either.' In that moment I was so certain that they wouldn't. This was nothing they could conceive of, I felt. That we were in his parents' bedroom seemed to prove the strength of our secret.

And it was true, neither of our mothers had seemed to notice anything when we went downstairs, Georgie first, me ten or so minutes later, counting the seconds aloud because Uncle George and Aunt Carrie's clock wasn't wound.

By the time I came down Mother was gathering her things. Sam looked bored. But I caught his eye and smiled, and he smiled back.

On the way home I pretended to sleep in the backseat, so that I could think freely about my cousin.

'Are you all right, Sam?' my mother asked. So she could feel it also: Sam seemed too quiet.

'Sam?' Mother asked again. She turned to look at him, and the car swerved. 'I hate this contraption,' Mother muttered, shaken. 'Sam, why so quiet? If you don't tell me I'll have to look at you again.'

I smiled. When Sam spoke, I knew he was smiling, too, from his voice.

'Georgie—' I bit my lip, hard. He could tell Mother right now, and this would all be over. And in that instant, Mother and I both waiting, poised for Sam to speak again, I almost wanted him to tell her. 'He ignored me, today.' His voice was plaintive. I felt relieved that his malaise had nothing to do with me; then guilty. Georgie and I had both ignored Sam today.

'Things are a little tense right now, in your cousin's family,' Mother said, finally. I could tell she was thinking of how to frame it so that Sam would best understand.

'Why?'

'They might lose their house, Sam.'

My eyes flew open. I wanted so badly to speak, but I did not want to enter this conversation. To do so would feel like a betrayal, of Georgie.

'They won't,' my mother continued, 'because this family is

generous, and we're glad to help. It's what family does. But it's hard for your uncle to accept charity. And it's hard for Georgie to know all of this. He shouldn't ignore you, but put yourself in his shoes. It must be hard for him, to see you.' It made sense, suddenly, why we hadn't seen them in almost a month.

For as long as I could remember, we'd had more than my cousin's family. We were two children; one child, in those days, was noticeable. My father was brighter. And my mother won, in every contest, when put next to my aunt. My mother was from a wealthy family, with connections. And she was beautiful; my aunt was plain. I felt all this, but I didn't think much of it. And I did not have a girl cousin to compete with. I did not have to be prettier, or more graceful, or brighter.

But of course I knew my mother was wrong: Georgie had ignored Sam not because he was embarrassed or petty but because he only wanted me.

'Yeah, well,' Sam said. 'He didn't ignore Thea.'

And I smiled: Sam was right. But then Mother spoke.

'Thea's a girl,' Mother said.

For an instant I thought she meant that I was too pretty for a boy like Georgie to ignore. But then she spoke again.

'She doesn't matter like you do.'

I felt as if the wind had been knocked out of me. My heart beat so loudly I was sure Mother would hear it. But I calmed myself: I knew how to do that, because of Sasi. Horses could smell fear.

The shacks we had passed on the way up were lit by firelight, now. I tried to find some sign of poverty, but I didn't know what to look for. I was angry, suddenly, that my parents had kept me away from everything real.

Mother was wrong. I mattered, I thought, and tried to let the sound of the wind against the car lull me to sleep. I mattered. My name was Theodora Atwell, and I mattered to Georgie Atwell.

CHAPTER FIFTEEN

The news came through an old house mistress, who lived in Dallas and was friends with Henny. Leona's family had lost everything. Her father's oil was sour, we kept hearing, though no one knew what it meant. It was now worth less than drinking water. We knew what this meant. *Everything*, Henny said, but even she seemed to take no pleasure in this gossip.

'Where will they live?' I asked Sissy, on our way to the bathhouse, both of us swaddled in our winter robes.

She looked sideways at me. 'They'll still have their house, Thea. Just not their lives.'

When we arrived at the bathhouse, I scanned the room for Leona, who I sometimes saw around this time, but saw only a gaggle of first-years, Molly among them. We were required to bathe every other day during the summer, but only every third day during the winter. Mrs Holmes's standard of hygiene was high.

As I waited for Docey to draw my bath, I wondered what sort of life Leona was left with. Leona had done nothing wrong, nothing unforgivable. She would leave this place. She would give up horses, or at least horses like King, who had cost a small fortune. She would not go to a ladies' college, perhaps.

Docey motioned that the bath was ready and took my robe as

I stepped in. I'd completely discarded any remnants of modesty after the first few weeks here. Docey's hand was red, from testing the water so many times. Leona's life might be limited, now, in a way that it hadn't been before, but she would not be a maid, like Docey. She would never go hungry. There was surely a rich relative who would help.

Victoria, Leona, all the girls who had been sent home – their lives would change in subtler ways. Rich suitors would not abound. They would have to choose more carefully. All the *Ladies' Home Journals* mothers sent us were now full of articles about little jobs women could take in to support the household: laundry, sewing. I'd almost laughed. As if Leona's mother could save the family fortune. As if Aunt Carrie could have doubled the size of her garden and paid back the bank. That wives could earn even a fraction of what their husbands had lost was a fantasy.

I understood that our teachers, who we had previously pitied, for they had none of our advantages, were lucky. Miss Brooks had a salary, and room and board; she talked about books all day instead of worrying about keeping her family afloat. It must feel like a relief, not to be saddled with a family right now.

In the days that followed, everyone watched Leona, for signs that she had faltered, would falter. But she acted no differently. And, gradually, the girls, as girls are wont to do, lost interest. If anything, she acted more imperiously. Watching her guide King over jumps as if they were playthings, clear the course beautifully, perfectly, then pass us on her way out of the ring without so much as a nod – well, it made us wonder if it was really true at all. But still she reminded us of our own precarious balance in the net of fate. If Leona's father could lose everything, what of our own fathers? What of us? The question floated above us, now, a cloud.

★ ★ ★

In Augusta House one night Eva switched off the lights and lit candles, brought out a Ouija board, which she had borrowed from a first-year cabin. The first-year girls were consumed by them. We had been trapped indoors almost all day, unable to ride because of the rain. It almost felt like hurricane weather.

'Those,' Gates said, as soon as she saw it, 'are forbidden. And foolish, besides.' But even so, she joined our circle, placed the tips of her fingers very lightly on the wooden, heart-shaped piece of wood. We sat on the faded Oriental rug that lay in the center of the cabin. I absently combed its fringed edges. They covered the floors of all our cabins; I knew how expensive they were. Mr Holmes should sell all these, I thought, and pay a girl's tuition.

'My father says those are demonic,' Mary Abbott said, from her bed. 'You shouldn't.'

'Oh, Mary Abbott,' Eva said. 'Don't be so grim. It's just fun.'

'Who are we contacting?' Sissy asked.

'My grandmother,' Eva suggested, 'but she was so boring in real life. I can't imagine death has made her more interesting.'

'Eva!' Gates said. Eva raised her eyebrows, lazily, and smiled. I stifled a laugh.

'How about you, Thea?' Sissy asked. 'Is there anyone you'd like to contact? Do you know anyone dead?'

The question rang out like a bell, sounding clearly in my mind. Was Georgie dead? Tears came to my eyes, that old, familiar wetness. But no: Mother had said in her last letter he was fine.

'No,' I said, and smiled, weakly, 'no one I can think of.'

Sissy tried to meet my eye. 'How about an old Yonahlossee girl?' I asked, to interrupt the stillness.

'Which one?' Gates asked. She sat primly, her legs folded beneath her, the way we had been taught to sit in etiquette class if we ever found ourselves without a chair.

'Lettie Sims,' Eva said. 'She's why we can't swim in the lake anymore. Drowned,' she added.

'When?' I asked.

'In the 1800s,' Sissy said. 'A long time ago.' She smiled reassuringly. 'A very long time ago.'

I smiled back, to show her I was fine. But Sissy did look a little otherworldly in the candlelight; all of us did. I was not so fragile that a drowned girl from the previous century could alarm me.

We all touched the wooden heart, lightly. Mary Abbott turned off the electric lights, so all we had were candles. 'Spirit of the occult,' Eva began, and Sissy giggled. 'Spirit of the occult,' she began again, 'please let us speak to Miss Lettie Sims, who we know the girls called Simsy. We want to ask her a question. Respectfully.'

The heart moved, of course it did, one of us pushed it. I watched the faces of these softly glowing girls and wondered what I would ask if I could ask anything at all and know the answer would be true.

'A-S-K-O-N-E-Q-U-E-S-T-I-O-N-I-F-Y-O-U-M-U-S-T-B-U-T-O-N-L-Y-O-N-E.'

Gates's freckled fingers, I thought; she wanted to get this done with.

Mary Abbott whimpered, from her bed, 'I'm scared.'

'Shh,' Eva whispered. 'She doesn't want to hurt us.'

Sissy's hands were shaking. Did they really believe this? We had read an essay about the occult with Father, how it was simply a way not to believe all the soldiers from the Great War were dead. I tried to meet Gates's eye, but she was watching the board.

'This is foolish,' I said, 'it's one of us moving it.' I started to take my hands away, but Sissy shook her head.

'Please, Thea,' she whispered. 'Wait.'

'Hurry, then. Ask a question.'

The wind whipped against our cabin, which felt unsturdy,

suddenly, like a house made of paper. A branch hit the window and Eva gasped. Sam had briefly been afraid of Kate the Bell Witch, when we were seven; he said she could disguise herself as anyone or thing, recognizable only by green eyes. A snake, a bird, a little girl. Georgie had told him the legend, scared Sam silly. Mother blamed him, he had let the outside world in. For years Sam looked carefully at the faces of people we encountered. But we didn't encounter many, and none of their eyes, to his relief, were green.

'A question?' I asked.

'I have a question,' Gates said, which surprised us all. She closed her eyes and took a deep breath.

'Will we be all right?' Her voice wavered, ever so slightly, which it never had before and never would again, at least not in my presence.

That winter I got better and better on a horse. The cold seemed to agree with me. At the very least, you could ride longer without fear of overheating your horse. Faster and stronger, I jumped perfectly any course Mr Albrecht arranged, usually on the first try. My legs no longer ached after I finished a ride. My arms were stringed with muscle. Eva had cut my hair off; now it fell to my shoulders, and I looked less like a child. When I examined myself in the mirror over my washstand, I liked what I saw, I liked what I'd become again: perhaps it was my imagination, but I looked in the mirror and saw that I was superior to the old Thea, I was more powerful than she'd ever been.

I cleared my plate most mealtimes. Henny watched and sipped glass after glass of cold water. Not fat, not yet – she was plump, very round, but anyone could see that she would be fat soon. It was her fate.

Sometimes I asked about her wedding. She was pleased with me then – oh it was so easy to put myself into Henny's good graces. She talked less about her fiancé than about her flowers, the rolling cart of desserts, her dress from New York. Martha and Jettie were going to be bridesmaids. I wondered if it pained Henny to think of beautiful Martha standing next to her. Miss Metcalfe was silent when Henny spoke of her impending matrimonial bliss, and I realized with a shock that she was jealous.

I asked a question about their new house, the one they would move into after they were married, and Henny turned to me, excluding all the other girls at our table.

'You'll know what it's like, Thea, you'll know how much joy there is.' Her hot breath smelled faintly of chocolate. What an odd way to phrase it, the joy floating somewhere, an infinite quantity of it, as if you only had to stand in the right place to catch it.

When Mr Holmes did appear, a week into my visits with Decca, it was nothing extraordinary. So many things were like that: you waited and waited and waited, and then it happened, and you were still you. I wasn't yet sure if this was a disappointment or a relief. It seemed to be a little bit of both.

We were downstairs, playing dominoes on the coffee table. I was drinking tea and watching Decca's milk – her glass rested very close to the edge of the table and I was afraid she'd knock it over with her elbow. I'd already told her to be careful, twice, and there was a limit, I'd learned from spending so many hours with Decca, to how many times you could warn a child.

There were expensive pieces in this room: a collection of tiny Limoges boxes in a glass case, six silver calling card cases on an end table, all engraved with various initials. An oil painting of a girl sitting in a field, a sheep in the distance, that reminded me of *Tess of the D'Urbervilles*. There was nothing personal except for the initialed card cases; again I wondered if any of these things belonged to the Holmeses. Was there a discretionary fund that each headmistress was allowed to draw from? But that fund surely would have been stopped now, with the trouble. Even if the money in the fund hadn't been affected, it would be in poor taste to use it.

'Go.'

'Sorry,' I said, 'sorry, let's see . . .' But I didn't see. I'd never played dominoes before and apparently the Holmes girls had played since birth. It was a dull, endless game.

Decca wore a summer dress, evidence of a father's hand. Decca could be obstinate, and she was picky about her clothes. I imagined she'd insisted on this, and Mr Holmes had given in to his daughter's seasonally inappropriate whims.

I was wearing the Yonahlossee uniform but I didn't mind it. I had gotten used to the sight of us, all alike at first glance. I wore no jewelry.

Decca stood; I interrupted the caressing of my hair.

I was vain, I was sixteen years old and would never again feel so watched.

'Father's home,' she announced, and twirled in a tight circle.

'Decca,' I scolded, 'behave.'

There was always some tragedy that accompanied his arrival: the milk, this time.

'Decca!' I was furious. All this waiting, all my calibrations, and now the milk was spilled and Emmy unavailable – how to call her without sounding coarse?

Decca ran to her father and I busied myself with soaking up the milk with my skirt.

'An accident?' Mr Holmes asked and lifted Decca on his hip. He offered his free hand to me and I accepted it and stood.

'Emmy,' he called, and she appeared so quickly I knew she must have been waiting.

'We were just . . .'

'Playing?'

I nodded, looked to the right and out the window. Everything was blank, still and cold. 'Playing.' I felt defeated. Decca sat curled and small on her father's hip, Emmy scurried on the rug, patting and feeling.

'That's fine, Emmy.' And although he sounded distracted, he spoke gently to Emmy, who stood and curtsied and backed out of the room without ever meeting his eye.

I wasn't going to say a thing, I wanted him to speak next, after I'd waited and waited.

But it was Decca who spoke: 'I'm winning at dominoes.'

'Don't boast.'

'She's not. It's true.' I smiled at Decca, who grinned back.

Mr Holmes put Decca down but she clung to his leg. He rested a hand on the top of her scalp, carefully extricated his leg from her grip.

'Is that right?' He smiled.

Decca nodded, unsure; there were adults laughing and sometimes that was fine and sometimes it was not.

'Go upstairs, now,' he told Decca. 'Please,' he asked, anticipating her refusal, 'I'll be up in a second.' And we were to be alone, now! I wondered if he thought I was pretty. I willed him to look at me, to notice me, but he seemed distracted.

Decca kissed me on the cheek and my cheek flamed scarlet, she was so close to me, her scalpy smell and her thin shoulders.

Mr Holmes patted Decca's head as she passed and smiled after her, and I knew that if she had not been his favorite before she would be now.

There was one thing in this room that did not belong, I thought, and it was me: I was intruding; surely Mr Holmes thought I was a bother. Sometimes the house mistresses met here with Mrs Holmes, but mainly the Holmes house was private, theirs, not a place for girls. As Mr Holmes arranged himself in a chair, I knew that he did not want me here.

'Well,' I said, ready to make my excuses. What had I thought? That Mr Holmes would fall in love with me? This was how crushes made fools of girls. I resolved to never have one again, to never love someone until they loved me first: to control my heart.

'Sit, sit,' he said, 'please,' and gestured toward a chair, and I had been wrong. He wanted me here. He seemed genuine. I had not imagined everything.

Just then Emmy reentered the room carrying a tray, which she sat on the coffee table. She refilled my teacup in careful, measured steps: first pick up the teapot, support under its belly as well as by its handle. Angle your wrist, do not allow your arm to tremble. Pour. Straighten your wrist now, quickly, so that you interrupt the stream of tea decisively, so that no drops of boiling water leap from the weakening stream and land on the porcelain tray – or, God forbid, silver, which shows everything and more – or even worse, on the lady for whom you are pouring.

Emmy did not once raise her head or glance at me. Her hand was perfectly still. She was here in Masters for a reason.

She handed Mr Holmes a tall, clear glass and left. My mouth felt chalky. More tea was exactly what I wanted least.

Mr Holmes took a long swallow from his narrow glass, halfway done already. He was pale, but that could have been the quickly dimming light, orbiting us into darkness.

A bell rang. Everyone would still be at the Hall; I thought of Sissy, who was probably expecting me. I was going nowhere.

'Class time,' Mr Holmes said, but so informally, as if I needn't worry myself. He swallowed the rest of his drink.

I heard water run upstairs, Emmy drawing Decca a bath.

'Excuse me for a moment, Thea,' he said quietly, and left the room.

Mr Holmes returned with a glass decanter. We kept similar ones in our formal room.

I've gotten into a bad habit since Mrs Holmes left, I imagined him saying.

He seemed very far away, at the other end of the room mixing a drink on top of the piano, his sweaty glass on the bare wood – it would leave a ring, he was a man and did not think about rings – but no, he picked the glass up and smoothed away the dampness with his coat sleeve.

He sat down and examined his drink. We heard a noise from upstairs and both looked up. I caught his eye and smiled, he smiled back, this was how to be easy and natural with a man. I looked up again but Mr Holmes was looking down, stirring his drink with his finger.

'Thea,' Mr Holmes began, then paused. He flicked his spirit-sopped finger and then smelled it, and I was suddenly and unbearably embarrassed – these were private gestures, I was not meant to see them. He took a long swallow of his drink.

And because I was nervous, the first thing that came into my head popped out, like one of Sam's tree frogs.

'Mrs Holmes is still gone?' And it was precisely the wrong thing to say. It sounded like I sat in judgment of Mrs Holmes's absence, when truly I was grateful: if she were here I would not be, that was certain.

He nodded slowly. 'I'm of half a mind to send Decca there, brace and all, but I think I would be too lonely.'

I smiled – it did not seem possible that an adult's loneliness could be relieved by a child. But I supposed we had relieved Mother's loneliness.

'Only a month until her return,' he continued. 'Hopefully I can hold the camp together for another month.' He took a sip of his drink and grimaced the way adults did when they drank hard liquor. The grimace meant the taste was pleasurable. I knew from watching Uncle George.

'Are there more donations?'

He looked up at me, surprised. 'You mentioned before,' I explained, 'that people were not donating as much as you'd hoped.'

'Yes, yes. You have a very excellent memory, Thea.'

'Not really,' I said. 'My brother is the one with the excellent memory. He knows all the names of all the plants and animals, hundreds and hundreds of them.'

'Your twin,' he said. 'I remember some things.'

I could feel my face flush with pleasure. He could remember one detail about my life and make me so, so happy, more happy than I could remember being in ages.

He finished off his drink and cradled the glass in his lap.

'Beth is having better luck, yes. Better her than me. I'm no good at separating people from their money. Do you know what has made everyone more willing to contribute?'

I shook my head.

'Horses.' He laughed in disbelief. 'For the women, at least, this seems to be their soft spot. There are girls here, girls on scholarship, girls who will be sent home if their scholarships are not funded. The women are unmoved by the plight of such girls. But mention the plight of horses and' – he snapped his fingers – 'the check is signed.'

'The plight of horses?' I did not want to align myself with the women he so obviously held in contempt, but I wanted to know what he meant. If I couldn't ride, I didn't know what I'd do.

'Oh, I didn't mean to alarm you, Thea. The horses aren't in any danger of being taken away.' He sighed. 'No one would buy them now, anyway. It's their expense that's daunting. Grain prices have shot sky-high, thanks to the drought. I never thought I'd be so familiar with the agricultural economy. Horses eat a great deal, as I'm sure you know well.'

'Yes. They're big creatures.' I understood the impulse, to protect the animal that had no voice, no parents to look out for it. I would certainly be more willing to donate to a horse fund than a girl fund.

'I shouldn't bore you with all this,' he said.

'I'm not bored.' And I wasn't. I've never been less bored, I wanted to say, for this adult world, where I was not someone's daughter, or niece – well, this was entirely new to me.

'Thea Atwell, from Florida. So serious. Were you a solemn child?'

'I don't know.' Usually Mr Holmes held something in reserve; his current sociability seemed an act, bought with a drink.

He laughed. 'I don't know what's gotten into me. Look here,' he said, leaning forward, twisting his glass around and around, 'thank you for all your help. You've been a blessing.'

'In disguise,' I said, and Mr Holmes didn't laugh, as I had intended, but nodded, as if he agreed.

Walking to my cabin, I savored the quiet campus. I savored his hand that had glanced my shoulder as I left, lingered – was that my imagination? – no, it had lingered, it had not wanted to leave. He leaned forward and thanked me and it was such a thrill, such a feeling of grace.

After dinner that night – a thick, dull stew, surprising for something so bland to emerge from the Yonahlossee kitchen, but I ate it anyway – Mr Albrecht stood as we were eating our dessert of standard shortbread (rich but also a little dull) and told us to find our riding groups. Mr Holmes sat next to him.

'But why?' I asked.

'The Spring Show,' Molly answered, 'it's soon.'

'It's still February.'

'There's a lot of planning. And then there's the Spring Fling, right afterward.'

'You haven't heard of it?' Henny asked. 'Everyone competes, everyone watches. It's splendid. If you're a house mistress you sip champagne with the adults and watch the rides.'

'It is splendid!' Molly said. 'There's a picnic lunch and then you get all pretty afterwards for the dance.'

The dining hall was a swarm of Yonahlossee girls as each of us tried to locate our group. I saw Leona from across the room, walking in a straight line. Girls moved out of her way in a neat sort of folding when they saw her coming, as if she were a thresher and they were the wheat. Her family's troubles only made us more careful of her. I remembered Leona's picture, on the wall outside Mr Holmes's office. Most people were not themselves in a photograph: the camera rendered them too solemn, too straight-lipped, too unknowable. Sam used to say that the way people stared at the camera made it seem as if they were watching something awful. But Leona was not any more discernible in the flesh. She passed by me without acknowledging my presence and I fell in line behind her.

We found a table and sat down. My group, advanced, was responsible for designing a course for the intermediate girls. Gates sketched a triple, and we all leaned forward to watch, her pale hand flashing against the white paper. Jettie watched closely, murmured approval.

This was perfect: Mr Albrecht still sat with Mr Holmes at the head table; Mr Holmes was close enough that I could see the details of his person – his crisp collar, his watch, the blunt edge of his hair – but we were arranged at such an angle that he could not see me.

Mr Albrecht drew something in the air, Mr Holmes nodded,

his elbows rested on the table but that was fine, everything was cleared and men sometimes did that. Mr Albrecht crossed his arms against his chest and listened to Mr Holmes; then they were done speaking, for Mr Albrecht was not the type of man who was good at speaking about nothing. Both their chairs had arms and ours didn't, because we were girls, not headmasters, not men. I watched their faces but they were like masks, neither looking at anything, staring past each other into the deep space marked by Yonahlossee girls.

It didn't occur to me then that it might be difficult to be a grown man surrounded by hundreds of girls, so certainly out of their reach that we could flirt, we could playfully take Mr Albrecht's elbow in the tack room, let our hand linger in his when he helped us dismount, and he could do nothing in return. Mr Albrecht wasn't a man, not to any of us, I don't think, because he wasn't handsome or rich or young. But we flirted with him because he was there and so were we. He probably touched himself at night, when we were ensconced in our cabins, he at home in town. He would hold himself and think of Leona's white hair against her naked back, the curve of Eva's breasts, contained by her white blouse – he cupped his hand against one, then the other, she wanted to unbutton her shirt but he wouldn't let her, liked to feel how her nipples stiffened against the cotton. She wouldn't be wearing her thick undergarments, there would be nothing except the thin, stiff cotton between his hand and her breast.

'Thea?' Leona asked.

'Yes,' I said, hopefully authoritatively, though I had no idea what they wanted.

'Does a triple meet with your approval?'

I shrugged, then tried to still my shoulders, nodded instead. Last week I'd had trouble with a triple. 'It does,' I said, and wondered at her composure. Her world had altered dramatically, her family no longer what it was, and she acknowledged nothing.

Then Martha passed by our table, holding her group's sketch (she was in Sissy's class, and though she was a better rider than Sissy, Martha's tranquility did nothing for her on horseback). She had little diamonds in her ears tonight, and I watched her and she was a sparkle, a glimmer, a flash; something not of this world.

Mr Holmes seemed to be studying Martha, too. His face was very calm. I did not want to admit to myself that Martha was more beautiful than I was, though of course I knew she was, I knew almost everyone at the camp, if asked, would point to Martha as the most beautiful girl. But I also knew there wasn't any real way to measure beauty, and perhaps something specific about my face was something Mr Holmes might love.

Mr Holmes turned his head, and it was a second before I realized he had caught me staring. I looked away, quickly, flustered.

'How does this all sound to you? Thea?' Leona again.

'I think,' I said, and glanced at the sketches laid upon the table, 'I think this all sounds perfect.'

Leona smiled. 'Are we distracting you?'

My cheeks flamed. Everyone watched me. Leona turned in her seat and looked pointedly at the table where Mr Holmes and Mr Albrecht sat. I shook my head. I didn't want to submit so easily to Leona, but it seemed like the quickest way to stop her.

'Well, good,' she said. 'We wouldn't want to do that.'

Gates trailed beside me as we gathered our things and left, her sketchbook tucked neatly beneath her arm.

'Thea.' Her voice low. Her cheeks red underneath her heavy freckles. 'Leona won last year. She was the youngest girl to ever win.'

'I know,' I said. Didn't everybody know?

Gates nodded slowly. 'Then you must also know how badly

she wants to win again.' She touched my arm. 'Just be careful,' she whispered.

I was surprised that Gates cared. She didn't usually involve herself in camp pettiness.

We watched Leona, who sat alone at the table, reviewing Gates's sketch. She seemed to be giving the piece of paper all her attention, which is how Leona moved through the world: whatever she did received her full attention.

'Who knows if she'll even be here by the show,' Gates said, and what I felt was disappointment, not relief. Leona was my only true competitor.

That night I opened a letter from Mother. Sissy was gone, with Boone. I had been impudent in my last letter, I knew; addressing Mother as if she were my equal, when of course she was not.

Dear Thea,

You sounded angry in your last letter. I understand, of course. Yes, I was friends with Beth Holmes. She was Beth Babineaux, then. Her family was a great New Orleans family. Rich as the day was long. I don't suppose they're rich like that now, but who knows. I lost touch with her; I lost touch with everyone, and would you like to know why? I had all I needed with you and Sam and your father. I could have had twenty friends; I could have had thirty. But your family is your greatest friend, Thea. I didn't tell you I knew Beth before you left because there were so many other things on my mind. It wasn't a plot, Thea. I honestly wouldn't have imagined you'd cared.

We sold the house. Astonishingly, someone wanted to buy it; I hadn't thought there would be any takers but your father was right: there are still people with money. We are among them, luckily. I am packing up all our things now. We are moving to Orlando, where your father will work. We might eventually move farther south, to

*Miami. It's all up in the air. We needed to get Sam away. We
needed a fresh start, as you have there, at Yonahlossee.*
                   Love,
                   Mother

I tore the letter into tiny bits as soon as I was finished. I was not
astonished that someone else wanted my house; it was beautiful,
perfect. What shocked me was that my parents would do this.
That it was gone. I truly hadn't thought that Mother would ever
leave.

I knew even as I was ripping the letter that it was foolish, a
gesture no one but myself would see. I'd have to get on my hands
and knees tomorrow to gather any stray pieces from beneath the
bed. And the other girls might notice, they might wonder what in
the world I was doing, and then I'd have to come up with a lie, yet
another one, to make my family seem like a different one.

My next thought was Sasi. I had known he was going to be
sold, since I was getting too big for him anyway, but I had pushed
the thought from my mind. Would we live on a farm in Orlando?
Or a place where you could see your neighbor's house, or both
neighbors' houses, from your own? Would they sell Sasi to a girl
or a boy? Would Sam go to school in Orlando? And did she think
I was dumb? That Yonahlossee was anything but a place to get rid
of me? If it was a fresh start, I was a monkey's uncle.

A year ago and I would not have believed any of it: Father
leaving his patients, Mother leaving her house. But I believed it
now. The worst thing I could do, I knew, the thing to hurt her
most, would be to not write a letter in return.

I was afraid he wouldn't come back, but he did, the very next day,
sent Decca upstairs just like the last time, and I felt both grateful
and fearful.

'Decca's doing well?'

I nodded. He was looking around for another drink, had already polished off the first. I waited for his voice to waver a little, for his gestures to become less precise. Alcohol turned Mr Holmes into a boy.

What I noticed about him in the flesh – that his pinky joint was swollen, rubbed raw by something, that there was a dry patch of skin on his forearm – was not what I noticed when I imagined him. It was the same with Georgie. I would dream about how blissful it would feel when he touched me, but then when he did I would notice strange things: how bony his elbow was, how he smelled faintly of stale hay.

'Have you heard about Leona's family?' he asked.

I was surprised. He'd never mentioned another Yonahlossee girl to me; he was breaking a rule.

'Yes,' I said, 'everyone has.'

'Have they?' He smiled, and fiddled with a cuff link. They looked old. His father's, his grandfather's. 'And what has everyone heard?'

His tone unsettled me. 'It's none of my business,' I said. I didn't want him to think I was nosy.

'Has that ever stopped anyone before? It would be unnatural, in a place like this, not to care about other people's concerns.' It was all happening so quickly, this shift from fine to horrible.

'I don't know what you mean,' I said, but I did. I tried to keep my voice light, so that we could talk about something else, but the sound of my light voice irritated him, and he shook his head.

'Oh, of course you do. You're always watching, aren't you? All these silly girls, you watch them, don't you? They come to you with all their worries and you listen and tell them nothing in return.'

'They don't come to me that often.'

'You watch, I know, because I watch *you*, sometimes, I see how you slink, how you creep around all the other girls and *notice* things—' He stopped. 'Your face doesn't move, Thea. You hold yourself apart. What must the other girls think of you?'

I willed myself not to cry. 'I don't think they do, much.' I felt fragile, Mother's letter a week old but still every word fresh and stark; if I ever saw my home again I would see it as a stranger. It was lost to me. Would Sasi's next boy or girl love him as I had? It did not seem possible. I'd spent more time with Sasi than I had with Sam. I knew from the way he cocked his ears if he was frightened or simply excited; I knew from the way he nipped my shoulder if he was angry or playful.

'And I don't think you really believe that.'

If he had been my friend, I would have asked him: Why are you being so mean? So cruel? But he was not my friend.

I stood. 'I have to be going now.' I had been so, so stupid. I wasn't Mr Holmes's confidante. I wasn't his friend. I was no more, no less than a gossipy Yonahlossee girl. But I was even worse than that: Mr Holmes believed I thought I was better than everyone else. Nothing could have been further from the truth – that was my first thought. And my second, which came so quickly I wondered if it was the truer thought, was that I *was* better. I didn't let myself get too involved with the camp because I felt, somewhere deep down, that I was better than all of those girls. That I knew more, had understood more, was destined for a different sort of life.

I walked past him to the coat closet, fiddled with the knob, I didn't know how to open it, I had never opened it before. Where was Emmy, she should be here, she should have interrupted us, stopped him. I wanted to tell him that the different sort of life I was destined for was not a better sort of life. That in some dark moments I would give anything to take back everything I had done.

My ears roared and I didn't hear him until he was right behind me. I stayed where I was; for the world, I wouldn't have turned and faced him. He drew a finger along my spine.

'Always hold yourself so straight, even when you're slinking. Did I ever tell you that was the first thing I noticed about you, when your father came here? That your posture was perfect.' His finger traveled down my back, stopped at my tailbone. 'I suppose I wouldn't have told you that, would I? Wouldn't have had the occasion. Leona will have to leave, Thea. It has all fallen apart, it is all falling apart. I can't get my tenses straight.' His voice had turned soft.

I turned to face him, and he touched my cheek. 'I'm sorry, Thea. I have a mean streak, it seems. It is all wrong,' he said, and then he was gone.

I didn't open the coat closet until I heard him upstairs, above me, in Decca's room. I tried to button my coat but my hands shook, both of them, terribly. And my hands never shook.

I left and went to my cabin. I was alone, and even though I knew everyone else would be at the Hall, I was still grateful. Everything was in order, our nightgowns folded and tucked into drawers, our lotions and perfumes carefully capped and lined on our washstands, our beds made in the morning and then straightened by Docey after rest hour. There were personal effects: framed photographs, pictures from magazines, velvet purple jewelry boxes. Ghosts lived here, we haunted this cabin, we hadn't ever truly claimed it.

I felt tricked. I had liked his kindness, and now his kindness had disappeared, but I still wanted him. I wanted him more, if that was possible.

I didn't bother to pull the covers up. No one was here, no one would see that I hiked my skirt up over my waist, put my dirty shoes on the quilt, moved my hand so roughly that I was raw afterward. No one heard me. No one saw the smear of blood, no one asked why I stared so long out the window, what could I possibly be watching for that long? Nothing, nothing.

When I sat at my dressing table I straddled my chair like I was riding. I was riding, even when I wasn't, a horse was always in my head. I spent at most two hours a day on a horse, the rest on the ground like a girl, but even so, when I walked on my own two feet my gait was vaguely, constantly unsettling, as if I were always stepping onto dry ground from a ship.

I was on a streak, I cleared every jump with an inch to spare. With two inches. Mr Albrecht had me lead demonstrations for the other classes. This is what it looks like. You are not a pretty rider, he told me once, you are not graceful but you are technically flawless.

I wanted to win. Leona was making it easy, to want to beat her. I saw now that her friendliness toward me coincided with my convalescence. And now that I was a threat, her only real threat, she ignored me when she saw me in the Castle. At the Hall last week I'd seen her giggling with Jettie. I'd smiled at Jettie but she'd turned her back, and Leona had looked over Jettie's shoulder for a long second, assessing me, until she'd whispered something else into Jettie's ear and Jettie's sturdy back was shaking from laughter. I'd looked down quickly and checked myself, but nothing seemed amiss; my cheeks burned and I'd turned to Eva, asked her a dumb question, and tried to look like I didn't care.

I realized that other girls probably wondered what was said about them all the time. But I had never before known the peculiar sensation of both wanting to know and then never wanting to know what someone else thought of you.

Being so close to Sissy had served me well; I was liked because she was liked, I absorbed some of her radiance and passed it off as my own. Mostly, though, I was not well known.

At dinner, Molly had once teased me about being too solemn. When I had said something funny in the Hall, the group of girls Sissy and I were sitting with had laughed and looked a little stunned that I had a sense of humor. Now Mr Holmes told me that I slinked. What else slinked? Animals, criminals.

Did Leona and Jettie make fun of how solemn I was? Did they think I was proud?

During practice Leona cut me off, twice. And then I did a strange thing: I trotted Naari directly in front of King, passing them so closely King left a trail of spit on my boot. I polished it off later, still surprised.

It was unusual for two third-years to be the best. And it must have been doubly unusual that Leona had been the best last year, as a second-year. Besides me, Gates, and Leona, the rest of our class were seniors. And though Gates was a very elegant rider, she was too fussy, too appraising on the back of a horse, to ever be excellent.

But now I wanted to be inserted into Yonahlossee history. I wanted to be admired, I wanted my photograph to hang on the wall outside Mr Holmes's office. I wanted him to pass by me a dozen times a day, every time he came or went. I wanted people to see me and think I was pretty, yes, but that I was more than pretty: that I was good at something the way few people are good at anything in their entire lives.

Was it too much to want that? Was it too much to want him? Yes and yes. In the back of my mind, the nasty thought always lingered that I would be happier if I did not want so much.

CHAPTER
SIXTEEN

'When are we going to Gainesville?' I asked Mother, as we were stripping my bed.

'I don't know – let's move a little faster, hmm?'

I tugged the sheets from Mother and threw them on the floor, adding them to the pile of dirty linens. 'All right,' I said, 'can we go soon, do you think?'

Mother glanced at me, but seemed distracted.

'Maybe Georgie could come here?'

She unfurled a sheet, tucked it beneath her chin, and smoothed out wrinkles with her palm. All in one motion, she was so deft at these chores, she could fold a complicated blouse in a second, iron my father's shirt in under a minute. We hadn't seen Georgie's family in three weeks, nearly a month. I understood that there was a reason we had not seen each other in so long; Mother had made this reason clear to Sam. But I wanted to see my cousin. I wanted to see him badly.

'Why isn't Idella doing this?' I resented my mother's quick, able hands, scurrying over my bed, my private bed, tucking in corners and picking up invisible specks of lint, dust, something.

She ignored me. 'There, all done.'

'Is Father eating with us tonight?'

She turned from the curtains, which she had been shaking – particles of gleaming dust were suspended in the air.

'I don't know that, either.'

'I guess nobody wants to see us.'

She turned from the curtains. 'What do you mean?'

'I'm lonely.'

She sat down next to me; her breath smelled like coffee and the lavender toothpaste she used. She looked around my room, then finally spoke. 'This house charms people. I've always thought that. It's so beautiful. It's so . . . lovely. You'll never live in a place like this again, Thea. You should love it.'

'I do love it,' I said.

'Someday you'll meet a man and fall in love and want to go where he goes,' she said, as if she were reading aloud from a fairy tale, as if she were hardly listening to me, 'and you'll have to make a new home for yourself.'

'Mother!' I tugged at my hair. I hated when she did this, changed what you had said you wanted. I thought about my cousin's thick, sturdy hands. *That* was all I wanted. Not a husband. But she continued, trancelike.

'You will meet a husband, Thea.' Mother stood, and I saw the crow's-feet that framed her eyes, the worry lines that creased her forehead. I said nothing. I gave her nothing.

'And you'll have to be careful to choose the right one. It will seem like fun and games, but it's not. Not at all.'

'It was like that for you?' I asked. 'Unfun?'

She smiled, and shook her head. '*Unfun* isn't a word, Thea. It was fine for me – look at the result.'

She gestured around the room, grandly, and stopped at me, as if to say – you, you are what I got. Which I suppose I was.

★ ★ ★

But then Georgie's family did come, the very next week. Mother told us over breakfast, as if it was nothing unusual. And perhaps it wasn't. The money Uncle George had borrowed had fixed whatever needed to be fixed, like a paste, like the hay I stuffed into a crack in the barn's wall.

Greetings were exchanged on the front porch, I was kissed, exclaimed over.

'Perfect weather,' Mother pronounced. It was perfect weather, the brief stretch of spring we would have before descending into the maddening heat of summer. But Mother thought it boring to talk about the weather. She was trying to be cheerful, I saw, trying to distract.

I kept my eyes trained away from Georgie as I spoke to my aunt and uncle.

The adults left us and then it was only the three of us, as it usually was. I smoothed my hands across my bottom to make sure I hadn't bled through, a movement so practiced it was unconscious. I wasn't menstruating right now, but I wasn't regular, as Mother put it, and so I could start any time, really. I wondered if other mothers kept such close track of their daughters' bodies.

'Let's go out back,' Sam began, 'I'll bring my tent, and Idella will pack us lunch, and . . .' While Sam was explaining his plan, I met Georgie's eyes for the first time. He met mine, I should say. I watched for a glimmer of something.

I felt almost insane with desire. Should I call it that? Lust. A specific yearning. I didn't know how this would be.

'Sam,' Georgie said, taking his eyes away, 'no. None of that for me today. I'm going to stay inside and work on homework.'

Georgie's voice was cruelly casual. In an instant, I regretted everything; I wanted Georgie to be nice, I wanted Sam not to be hurt, I wanted it all the way it had been.

'Why?' Sam asked, crestfallen. He looked to me, then Georgie, like he was trying to put the pieces together. But I did not want to be a piece of this puzzle. I was furious at Georgie, suddenly. He should not goad Sam. He should not try to make him wonder.

We both waited for Georgie to speak. I did not want to say anything; speaking would mean choosing a side, and which side would I choose? I looked at Sam, his auburn hair cut just yesterday, by Mother. Then Georgie, who watched Sam calmly.

'Why?' Georgie said, mimicking Sam. My stomach turned, it truly did – a flip beneath my skin. 'Because I don't want to pretend to camp. I don't want to pretend anything, today.'

'Georgie!' I said, and they both looked at me, my brother and cousin. I shook my head. 'Nothing. I'll go with you, Sam.' I stood.

Sam shook his head. It was too late. 'No,' he said, 'I'll go by myself.'

'Thea,' Georgie said, after Sam had gone inside, but I was so mad I felt sick with it.

'Why did you do that?' I asked. 'Why?'

He began to answer, but I didn't want to hear. I slipped inside the house, quietly, in case the adults were near; I meant to follow Sam, but he had already disappeared. I could have found him if I'd wanted to, I knew all the likely places he had gone. But if he didn't want to be found, there was no point in looking.

I sipped Mother's champagne while the adults visited. Uncle George had said it was four o'clock in the afternoon, cocktail hour somewhere. Aunt Carrie's one sister was doing poorly; her other sister had responded to the death better than anyone had predicted. Wasn't it always a surprise, my mother said, how a person acted after he had lost someone.

'Where are the boys?' Uncle George asked.

'Out back, I think,' I said, though I didn't know. They had both disappeared after this morning's squabble.

'Hunting,' Father said. He looked at his glass, which he held with two hands, a child's grip.

'Maiming the defenseless and innocent,' Uncle George said, and then dropped the glass decanter stopper he had been holding on the mahogany coffee table, the one that was particularly hard to keep unblemished. Its surface had been buffed and varnished until you could see a blurry reflection of yourself in the reddish wood. That hadn't been what Father had meant. He meant they were hunting animals for Sam's terrariums, not hunting animals to kill. But they were doing neither.

'Oops,' Uncle George murmured, and spilled a little whiskey onto the rug. Mother moved to help but he waved her away. He was quick with his napkin, blotted the spilled alcohol instead of rubbing it, which would smear the dyes.

'You do that well,' I said.

'Thea,' my father said sharply. I turned my face. I was not myself right now, and it was difficult to be kind to Uncle George, who looked so much like his son. I didn't think this was possible, but somewhere on the edge of my mind an idea lurked: Georgie would find Sam, tell him about us, and it would all end.

Uncle George laughed. 'It's fine. I might as well help myself to another while I'm here,' he said, and poured a neat glass.

We were all silent for a moment. My father stared into his drink. Mother watched the carpet; I knew she wanted nothing more in the world than to be able to properly clean it. I knew well the idea of self-preservation, from Sam and his animals. Georgie would not tell, because telling would mean something bad for him, too.

'Thea,' Uncle George said, and my father's glass trembled when his brother spoke, 'Thea, you're getting awfully pretty.'

'Thank you.'

'She looks exactly like her mother did at that age. She's the spitting image. Wouldn't you agree?'

My father glanced at me briefly, and shrugged. 'No, I wouldn't know. I didn't know Elizabeth at that age, remember? Neither did you.'

'She does,' my mother said, and touched the end of my braid. I knew she was trying to distract my father, but I didn't want her to touch me. And besides, I didn't look like her. I wasn't ever going to be as pretty as she was. Which was fine – what had it gotten her? A house in the middle of nowhere. 'My hair, mainly. She has Felix's forehead, more and more.'

Father smiled, as if at a private joke.

'It's interesting,' she continued, 'to look at photographs and see how you change year to year.'

'Is it?' Aunt Carrie asked. 'I've always thought looking at pictures of myself was an exercise in vanity. And boring, besides.' I looked at Aunt Carrie, shocked. I'd never heard her speak to my mother like this.

Mother furrowed her brow and pretended the rim of her champagne flute was the most interesting thing in the world. She was close to tears. Aunt Carrie stared intently at the fireplace, empty, swept clean, and the men did nothing.

My father broke the silence. 'You are quite pretty, Thea,' my father said. 'A smart, pretty girl.'

'The whole world's at her feet,' Uncle George said, his voice picking up again, eager to help his brother relieve the pall that had settled over the room.

'I'll bet you have twenty suitors by this time next year,' Uncle George said. 'Thirty.'

'I don't think so,' my father said humorously. 'Not in my house.'

'I don't want any suitors,' I said.

'That will change,' Aunt Carrie said. Her voice was strange. I wondered how much she'd had to drink.

'It will!' Uncle George said. 'Of course.'

I heard the distant slam of the screen door.

Sam came in first. He walked to the coffee table and took a handful of cheese biscuits, then flipped the tail of my braid, and the relief I felt – it felt like another chance.

'One at a time,' Mother said, and Sam nodded but continued to stuff himself.

Georgie came in and met my eye and smiled, then sat next to Sam – at his feet, because there wasn't another chair – and they continued a conversation they'd begun elsewhere, chattering about a swimming hole in Gainesville. And then the adults began their own chatter, about nothing, about everything, and I was so grateful Georgie hadn't told I wanted to weep.

But the quality of the adults' chatter was off; they sounded tense, distracted. I noticed that while Georgie was pretending to listen to my brother, his attention was elsewhere. He was watching the adults, very carefully. He caught me staring, and grinned in a way that chilled me. Something about the way he had turned his attention from them to me, as if we were connected.

I understood then that my family could never know my secret. Money, money where money did not belong, had almost ruined us. I understood that loving, where loving did not belong, would be much worse. No, they simply could not know. But that did not mean that I would stop.

After I had lain on top of the covers for an hour, the rest of the house asleep, after I stopped feeling impatient and entered into desperation, my door opened, and Georgie motioned for me to follow. He was wearing his regular clothes, thoughtless, my brother would have noticed. The stairs were mercifully quiet. The remnants of a key lime tart had been moved from the dining room onto the kitchen table, a tacky, grotesque mess now.

He almost let the screen door slam, and I felt a flash of anger. I caught it and eased it shut.

A fog had come and made the outside world impenetrable. I slowed, walked more carefully; Georgie plowed ahead, almost disappeared into the white.

We were both barefoot, and as we walked blindly to the barn I was half-afraid I'd step on something sharp. But not afraid enough to turn around and get my shoes, or to have paused as we left the house and slipped them on. Not afraid enough to make Georgie wait.

He dipped in and out of the fog, in flashes; I saw a hand, an elbow, then nothing at all. He was a stranger to me, that's how I could do this, behave like a girl who would shame her family so easily.

When I reached the barn, I went first to Sasi. Before my brain caught up with my heart, I thought he was missing. But then I saw that he was lying down, asleep, his knobby, thin legs tucked carefully beneath him.

'Thea?'

I turned and put my finger to my lips, but Sasi was already hoisting himself up, illustrating in a second how improbable a horse's body was, how dainty and inadequate his legs were.

'Why did you do that?' I asked.

'Do what?'

'Don't play dumb,' I said. I put my hand flat against his chest, and I could feel his heart thumping against bone, through blood.

'Oh that.' He touched my finger. I wondered if he could also feel his heart, through my hand. 'He's such a child sometimes.' I started to speak and he touched my lips, then put his finger inside my mouth. It tasted like dirt, and I liked it. 'I'll be nice to him, don't worry.'

And I didn't worry. I had other things to think about, now. Sasi pricked his ears toward us, curious, and then Georgie was kissing my neck, then licking it, and there was a roar in my ears, and he roamed over my breasts with his thick hands, and the roar subsided, turned into a distant buzz. Georgie combed his fingers through my hair, tenderly, and I thought of my mother, who was the only other person who did that.

'You are certainly,' he said, and then paused, and undid the top button of my nightgown and put his hand down the front, 'very beautiful.'

He led me to a stall, and slid the lock open and pushed me inside. There was a blanket from the house already draped over the packed-dirt floor; a good blanket, from Mother's stacks.

I pointed to the blanket. 'Don't leave that here. Mother will notice.'

He shook his head and relocked the stall door, the familiar sound of metal against metal. He turned back to me, his erection pushing against his pants, like a tumor, a growth. He backed me into a corner and thrust his groin into me. His pants were thick, wool – winter pants. My nightgown was thin cotton. I felt everything, his sensation was dulled. I closed my eyes and unbuttoned Georgie's pants on the second try, I reached inside and was surprised again by how soft and tender his penis felt.

There were little flashes where my brain should have been, as if it had receded for this. We were on the blanket, Georgie was on top of me, my nightgown was hiked to my waist, and Georgie's penis was touching me, was slippery because I was wet and he had parted me and put his penis against the slickness. Then it felt very big between my legs, almost painful, and I didn't want this to happen, not yet, not in this way, so I flipped him over, in one smooth motion, and he was surprised. *I* was surprised, but I wrapped my legs around his thigh and moved while I also moved my hand fast over his penis. The same rhythm in my legs and my hands, and I couldn't get it quite right, the rhythm, I was doing two things at once and neither was right. So I moved faster, and the intense ache between my legs subsided briefly before it exploded, and then I stopped touching Georgie altogether for a second. I could see more clearly now, could see that Georgie was watching me, his hands folded beneath his head as if he were looking at the sky on a clear day. I smiled at him. I began again where I had left off.

I remember feeling very adult, for the first time in my life.

I came in from hitting golf balls with Georgie and Sam around lunchtime and saw Mother, who had been upstairs all morning. Uncle George was off with Father, but Aunt Carrie had made herself scarce on this visit.

Mother smiled at me and returned to her paper, the glasses she used when reading small print slipping down her nose. I took three sandwiches from the platter Idella had left on the table.

'Aren't you going to ride today?'

'We're playing golf.' Mother nodded slowly. I didn't want to tell her I had started menstruating this morning. It was private. 'We're not very good,' I added.

She reached underneath the table; I didn't know what she was doing until I noticed that her arm was now weighed down by the blanket.

'This was out,' she said. She pushed her glasses up. She hated to wear them, but Father said she would wear out her eyes if she didn't.

'Oh?'

'In the barn. Maybe Sam and Georgie were using it, for their hunting? Not you? Sam should know not to use the good blankets. This is an old carriage blanket, it's older than you, you and Sam together.'

I nodded, and after I gave Sam and Georgie their sandwiches I went to the front, muttered something about the mail, and sat on the steps. I looked at the road that was only traveled twice a day: my father going, my father returning. I had been stupid. Stupid, stupid girl. I felt very desperate. This is what it feels like to be desperate, I whispered to myself. Stop it.

If Sam suspected, if he could no longer keep the secret and had confided in Mother, if, leaving Sam out of it, Mother had seen something on her own, peered through one of the hundreds, thousands of windows this house boasted – we did not shirk when it came to glass, Father said, your mother loves the light – if she had looked into my world with Georgie, and if in that moment in that world he had touched my cheek, kissed me, bitten my thumb . . . if, if, if.

CHAPTER
SEVENTEEN

The next time I saw him it was the same thing: he sent Decca away and accepted a drink from Emmy. We sat for a moment before he spoke.

'The girls are starting to apply for next year.'

'Is it a rigorous application process?'

He smiled. 'It can be.'

'Are we handpicked from thousands?'

'You weren't,' he said, 'but yes, there is some handpicking involved.'

From upstairs we heard Emmy's sharp warning, Decca's hysterical giggle. She often acted this way in the afternoons, like a horse who had been pent up in his stall for days. A few moments later I heard the front door open and close. Through the window I saw a glimpse of Emmy leading Decca across the Square.

Mr Holmes sat in his leather chair, I sat on a couch, two, three feet away from him.

'How do you pick?' I put my hand on the couch, as if to make smaller the distance between us.

'Family connections. If your sister went here, or your cousin. What kind of family you come from. We try to have some parity among the states. Though St Louis is as far north as we ever get. And then after all that I suppose we look at the girl herself. What her parents want her to achieve while she's here.'

'What her parents want,' I echoed.

'Yes. They write the letter, they answer the questions on the application. Her father, usually. Did you think it would be otherwise?'

I was silent.

'To have all your decisions made for you is a curse. But it's one you know well, I assume.' He had known exactly what I had meant; he had articulated what I meant better than I could have. But he seemed distant, today.

'It wasn't always like that for me.' I smiled at what I had said – why was I defending my father? But Mr Holmes looked at me expectantly, so I continued. 'I never felt like that, like everything was decided for me, until they sent me here.'

'Here,' he said, and seemed lost in thought.

'Do you like it?' I asked. I was losing his attention.

'Yes,' he finally said. 'In the end I do. What I tell myself is that this world is changing quickly, that female education is becoming vital. But truly I fell into this position, and it's a nice enough life, a nice enough place for the girls. Though most of the time I think I'd rather be reading a book.' He closed his eyes and rubbed his temples. 'You don't think, when you are young, that you will simply fall into your life. But that,' he said, and raised his head and looked at me, 'is exactly what happens.'

I stood and went to him, quickly, so that I wouldn't convince myself not to. I sat down beside him, in the small space the chair allowed. And what compelled me to do what I did next? If I had moved away, or simply done nothing – well, I feel certain Mr Holmes would not have touched me. He had touched me last time, yes, but today it felt as if he would not; today felt as if we were going to erase the sins of yesterday. And I did not want them to be erased; if he erased how he had touched me – well, then he erased me, Thea, what small stake I had eked out in his life. And so I put my hand on his knee, and turned my face into his coat.

He did not move away. The pleasure of that moment was so extraordinary it felt almost unbearable, a gift too large. At first he was tense, but then I felt him relax. If a Yonahlossee girl walked in and saw us, she would be shocked, briefly, but then she would think that Mr Holmes was comforting me; that I had been upset, that our headmaster offered solace.

Or perhaps I was fooling myself. Perhaps she would know exactly what she saw.

'It's a beautiful place.'

'Yes. Thea.' He put his palm on my cheek. His voice trembled. 'We can't,' he said.

'It's all right,' I murmured into his shirt. I had been right in divining his feelings.

He stood, and looked down at me. 'You have brought me comfort. I don't know why. It shouldn't be this way. Do you know how bad it is out there?' He wore a pained expression, now. 'This place might close, Thea. Let's hope Mrs Holmes works magic out there, but we are asking people for money they do not have, or money they want to hold on to.' He shook his head. 'But let's hope that's not true, let's hope that this is simply the worst year in everyone's life. And lucky you, to have the worst year come so early. You have nothing except hopeful years ahead.'

I laughed, and then I stood so that we faced each other, Mr Holmes and I. He raised a hand and I thought he might touch me, but then he brushed his hair from his forehead, and I saw that his hand shook, and I was thrilled, I was unnerved, I was exhilarated: his hand shook because of me.

'Why are you laughing, Thea?' he asked softly. 'Everybody's life is falling apart. What do you want? I know what I want, right now. If things weren't so bad outside of here maybe I'd want it less. But desperation leads men to do desperate things. Isn't that right? Tell me it's right.'

Instead of answering I kissed him. Even in that moment I was shocked at my boldness, but grateful for it, too. He was so much better than Georgie, so firm and gentle. Georgie was sometimes rough. Mr Holmes stood, and looked down at me, and took a step backward, and I couldn't tell if he were stepping away from me or asking me to follow him.

'Take me somewhere,' I whispered. He looked at me for a moment; then turned his head and looked out the window, and I knew he was deciding.

'Where would you like to go?' His voice was so solemn.

If I did not answer, it was because his question didn't seem to require an answer. Because I knew precisely where I wanted to go. With him, anywhere.

In the end, after one hundred seconds, two hundred, he led me upstairs into his library. He moved quickly, almost clumsily, as if he were surprised by the course of this afternoon. He closed the door behind us and I glimpsed all the books that lined the walls before he laid me on the couch. He drew me to him and the way his hand rested on my back almost undid me; I moaned, and he kissed me. By the end, he lay on top of me. He kissed my mouth, my face, my neck. I'd never been kissed like this. I felt helpless, my arms pinned to my sides by his weight, but helpless in a very lovely way.

Mr Holmes offered solace. But so did I. We took comfort in each other.

★ ★ ★

Leona caught me as I was leaving Masters, en route to Augusta House. I tried to ignore her, but she did not want to be ignored, today.

'Weather's turning,' she said, and sidled up next to me. I said nothing. 'I'm going to visit King,' she said, when we were almost at my cabin, 'do you want to come?'

All the other girls disappeared into their cabins. I only had on a light sweater, and now I buttoned it against the chill. A storm had threatened all day but never come; one of those days that felt like a menace.

I could still feel the full weight of Mr Holmes on top of me, even as I walked through the Square, even as I stood here, deciding what to say to Leona; as if some trace of what we had just done was mine to carry with me, now. I felt changed.

'Why?' I asked.

'Why? I just thought you might enjoy it. I just thought—'

'Stop. I thought that at least you, of all people, would have no tolerance for artifice. So stop, please.'

Something shifted in Leona's stance. 'All right,' she said coolly.

She eyed a group of passing girls. That she could be so casual while we were having this discussion infuriated me. Again I felt the impulse to touch her, to hurt her.

She tilted her head. 'I guess you're kept busy,' she said, 'by other things, now. You're such a busy girl, Thea.' She paused, and I knew she was going to say the worst thing to me now, the reason she had sidled up beside me in the first place. 'Why was it you were sent away again?'

I stood there speechless, foolish, aware of how helpless I must seem.

I spotted Sissy coming down the steps of the Castle, and walked, half-ran past Leona to join her. She had undone me. Leona called out: 'But I forgot. You're not a girl anymore. You're very adult now, aren't you? You spend so much time with adults, lately.'

Aren't you leaving soon? It was on the tip of my tongue to call out. But I couldn't. It seemed too bad, even for me.

We watched Leona walk away, disappear into the woods.

'Off to see King,' I muttered.

'Did you hear?' Sissy asked.

'Hear what?' I thought she was going to tell me that Mrs Holmes was returning.

'About Leona.'

'No.' I felt light with relief. I still had more time.

'She'll be gone by the beginning of summer. And when she goes, King stays here.'

'Oh, no,' I said. I was horrified. To have to leave her horse when she had done nothing wrong. I had had to leave Sasi, but I had nearly outgrown him anyway. And still, it had been miserable. But there was some small part of me that took pleasure in Leona's misery. She was so awful; perhaps that's why awful things happened to her. 'That's awful,' I said, because Sissy seemed to expect more of a response.

'Not as awful as everything else that's happened to her family,' Sissy said, and looked at me curiously, and though I did not agree I said nothing. *This* was the most awful thing to happen to Leona, of course it was.

The next time I saw Mr Holmes he led me to his library again, and closed the door, and I reached for him, but he stopped my hand in midair. Even that, his hand on mine, was thrilling.

I could feel what he was doing, the way he held my hand, as if stopping a child. He was asking if I wanted to stop. But I did not want to stop.

'Emmy's gone?' I asked.

'Gone,' he echoed. 'With Decca.'

I kissed him, then, and the idea that we were going to stop, that we would not touch each other again, disappeared, a puff of smoke.

He kissed my neck, and unbuttoned the first button of my blouse. His hand shook, and I touched it.

'You're so lovely, Thea,' he said. His voice was sonorous, trembling.

He brought my hand to his cheek, and held it there for a moment while he watched my face, and I had never before felt so observed, so carefully accounted.

Then I took my hand back and began to unbutton my blouse, began the process by which I would reveal myself to him, and the moment felt so tender, so utterly unlike anything I had felt before. Mr Holmes touched my breasts, and then pressed me to him and slid down to the floor, so that he was kneeling in front of me.

The world today was dark, wintery, the kind of day we never had in Florida. I could only see the mountains from his window, the rest of camp below my line of sight.

'Thea,' he said, and took my hands in his, 'you want this?' And his voice was so kind, gentle. I wanted to please him; I wanted to be pleased by him.

I nodded. 'Yes,' I said, and I almost didn't trust my voice. 'Yes.'

He put his hand under my skirt and slid it up my thigh until he reached the line of my panties.

'Take these off,' he murmured, and I let him peel down first my stockings, then my panties. I felt very relaxed, sleepy but not tired. He stroked the inside of my thigh.

I put my hands on his shoulders to steady myself, and he looked up at me, and I saw this was going very quickly for both of us, now.

'Open your legs.' I did. He put one finger inside me, and I tensed.

'Does it hurt?'

I shook my head.

'Here,' he said, and pulled me down next to him, on the rug. He lay down next to me and undid his trousers. He put his finger back inside me, then another, and pushed up my skirt.

'There,' he said, 'I can see you. You're so . . .' He stroked my forehead. His voice was so soft, so loose.

'Beautiful.'

He smiled. 'Are you supposed to give yourself compliments? I was going to say something else. You're so . . .'

I waited. He pushed his fingers farther into me, and it was such an odd pressure that I loved.

'Exceptional,' he said. 'Beautiful, too, but there are so many beautiful girls. Be something besides that, Thea.'

'All right,' I said, 'I'll try.'

He took himself out and I touched him, but he shook his head. 'No, just lie there. Just lie there.'

'And be exceptional.'

'Yes.' He kept his fingers inside me as he touched himself and looked at me until he came, and then he seemed like he was in great pain for an instant, closed his eyes and cursed.

We lay there on the rug together afterward.

'Can I ask you something?'

'Nothing too complicated, please,' Mr Holmes said. He patted my hand. I smiled. Everything was so easy, now. If I could lie right here forever, shut the door on my life and everything it held, I would. In that moment, I would have.

'Thea?' His voice was gentle.

'Mr Holmes—'

'Jesus. Please call me Henry. I'm begging you.'

I turned and faced him. He placed his palm on my torso. 'So strong.'

'You know Mrs Holmes knew my mother?'

'Yes.'

I waited for him to tense – he rarely spoke of Mrs Holmes – but he didn't.

'Do you think you'll ever leave?'

He was quiet for a long time. 'I'm sorry,' I finally said. 'Never—'

'No, it's all right. In a way. Will I ever leave Yonahlossee? It's a question I ask myself, of course. In a way I like it here. When I was young all I wanted to do was leave Boston. I hated it there. And then I left.' He seemed lost in thought.

'Where did you go?' I asked.

'New Orleans. And then we ended up here. I thought the South would be different. And it was. But not different enough.' He turned to me. 'But you can never really leave your home, can you?'

'I didn't want to leave,' I said. 'I loved my home.'

He lifted a handful of my hair and inspected it. 'You had such long hair when you came here. And then you cut it off, like everyone else.' He smiled. 'You should remember that the sins of youth seem very far away when you're no longer young.'

I said nothing. I thought of my mother, my father, my brother. Sasi. My first pony, before Sasi, dead for years now.

'Do you see your family at all now?' I asked.

He shook his head. 'After my father died, Beth and I met my mother in Philadelphia, when Sarabeth was a baby. But since then, no.'

'What did you do?'

I must have sounded stricken, because he propped himself up on his elbow and touched my cheek. 'Thea, Thea. I didn't do anything. My parents wanted me to be a certain person, and I wasn't that person. I was a great disappointment. But – and this took me years to realize – they were a great disappointment to me as well.' He watched me. 'Thea, I don't know what you did, but you came here so that your family could forget. So that you could forget, so that when you leave here what happened will have disappeared.'

'I ruined my family.'

'I doubt that,' he said quietly. 'If your family was ruined, it wasn't because of you.'

'They trusted me.'

'Who?'

'My parents, my brother.'

'Your brother may have trusted you, but your parents never did. Parents never trust their children. I don't know what happened exactly, and you don't need to tell me. I believed for a long time that I had shamed my family. But it's in a family's best interest to make a child believe that.' He spoke quietly, but also firmly. He taught a single class at Yonahlossee, an advanced literature seminar that the senior girls took. I wondered if this was how he explained the characters in books to his class. It seemed so important to him that I understand what he meant.

I nodded, but said nothing.

'Do you really see? You're sixteen years old. What your family thinks of you seems like everything. But it's not. They have their own interests to protect. I wish I'd known that, how much a family has to protect, how sometimes a child interferes with that.'

'You know it now.'

'Was that a question? I do. Yes, I do.' He paused. 'You have a brother, correct? Did they send him away, too?' But they weren't really questions, none of them.

'I have a cousin, too,' I said.

'And where is he?'

I shook my head. 'I don't know,' I said finally.

The light was becoming dim behind the curtains. Mr Holmes kissed my forehead and held me very close. 'So your brother is home. Your cousin is some place unnamed. And you are here. With me.' He drew his finger across my lips. 'They traded you, Thea. They sent you here and kept your brother.' I started to speak, but he shook his head. 'Don't believe them,' he said very softly. 'Don't ever believe what is said about you.'

I took his hand and put it in between my legs, and he looked at me uncertainly, and then he understood, and his fingers were cold at first. He knew better than Georgie what to do. He knew how to prop himself up on his elbow, so that he could watch me. He moved his fingers slowly, and I was not embarrassed, or shy to look at him, as I usually was.

'You're very wet, Thea. And exceptional.'

There was something in his tone that I couldn't quite place. 'Faster, please.'

'Certainly.'

I touched my breasts, and closed my eyes. He knew how to lead me very carefully up this path; he would not go too quickly, or slowly. I moaned, which I could do because the house was empty. I bucked against his hand, and he pushed me down, gently. My eyes were closed but I saw anyway – in quick flashes I saw my mother, my brother, Sasi, and then Georgie, Georgie, Georgie – and his hand disappeared, everything disappeared, and there were only bright flashes and my cousin's face.

I opened my eyes and stopped his hand. He was watching me very carefully. I pulled his head onto my chest, and we lay there like that for a while, until I heard the bell ring, and I tried to hold Georgie's face in my mind. It was the first time in a long time I had thought of him and not felt pain.

* * *

So: I knew this would end, I knew Mrs Holmes would return. It was the end of February. She would be back by mid-March. But I had always been expert at ignoring the unalterable. Sometimes it was as if God was watching, had narrowed His vision until Yonahlossee appeared, nestled in the mountains. I had wanted something very badly, and then I had gotten it, and the getting kept getting better.

Winter began to disappear. Lifted, like a second skin. Docey took away our comforters from the ends of our beds. Our yellow and blue scarves disappeared from our closets, along with our sweaters. We thawed, too; everyone seemed prettier, nicer, fresher in the spring air.

I spent every afternoon at Masters, and our days began to feel like years. It began to feel like we had known each other for a very long time. Mr Holmes peeled away the layers of Yonahlossee in a way Sissy couldn't. She was one of the girls, she didn't have the vantage point he did. He told me Jettie's drinking was a known problem, that Mrs Holmes would have sent her away years ago but for Henny, who convinced her that keeping Jettie on was their Christian duty. He told me Yonahlossee was keeping King in exchange for Leona's tuition, which hadn't been paid in over a year. He told me Katherine Hayes's father wasn't doing as well as Katherine thought, that her grandfather had stepped in and paid her tuition; that her uncle had shot himself because he was about to be arrested. He liked the Kentucky girls best because they were the least mannered. And the Florida girls, he'd said, and grinned. I like them, too.

I came back early from French class because I didn't feel well. My stomach was troubling me – cramps, it was that time of the month.

Docey was mopping the floors, her back turned. She was humming some tuneless melody, but I was certain she'd heard me. I waited for her to turn around, acknowledge me, but she drew the mop around and around, over the same spot. From the back she almost looked like one of us.

'Docey?'

She turned then, but said nothing.

'I'm going to lie down for a bit.' I stopped short of asking her if this was fine.

She nodded, and watched me while I stepped out of my boots, tiptoed across the damp floor. She didn't offer to help. My stockings were wet, now. I lay back on my bed and peeled them off, surprised by the feel of my bare legs against the quilt. I closed my eyes and pretended to drift off.

Yesterday Mr Holmes was melancholy, told me I'd forget this place. But I couldn't imagine.

Mr Holmes's breath tasted like gin. Juniper berries, he'd told me, the perfume of the evergreens. If we had been married and a wedding portrait taken, we would not have seemed an unusual couple. Mr Holmes was thirty-one. Women married men twice their age all the time. His hair was thick and glossy – Eva had joked she'd die for his hair – his carriage boyish, his lips very red. I carried my youth in the way I moved, in my speech and furtive gestures. But I didn't look young when I stood still.

A sharp sound. I sat up, disoriented. My mouth was dry.

'You were saying things,' Docey said. She was cleaning under Mary Abbott's desk.

'Was I?' I got up and poured myself a drink of water. 'What?'

'Nonsense. Nonsense words.'

For a second I was frightened I'd revealed something. It had been a week since I'd seen Leona in the Square. Now we avoided each other, as if we had come to some mutual decision. I'd gone

over and over my comings and goings from Masters. There was
no possible way she knew anything. I'd thought of Emmy, too,
but Leona wasn't the kind of girl to ever talk to a servant. I liked
to think that there was some sort of mutual understanding
between the two of us, that she knew I knew about King, that I
felt sorry for her, a pure form of pity. But Leona wouldn't want to
be pitied.

'Do you know Emmy, Docey? From Masters?'

She smiled, almost smirked. I was about to ask again when
she answered: 'She's my sister.' She turned to face me, then
looked me in the eye for the first time that day. Her lazy eye
darted crazily.

'I didn't know.'

Docey went back to her work. 'I didn't know,' I repeated.
I should have known. I watched Docey drag her rag over the
desk, carefully, paying attention to the finials and knobs –
carefully, but quickly – and knew suddenly that they spoke
of us.

'But your hair is brown.' I paused. 'You don't look alike.' And
this was true: Emmy was pretty, and Docey wasn't.

'Do you look like your sister?' Her tone was pointed.

'I don't have a sister.'

'None?' She seemed surprised.

I shook my head. 'I have a brother. And we do look alike, we're
twins.'

'A twin?' she asked. It was the first time I had ever heard her
sound pleased. 'What's that like?'

I smiled. 'It's all I've ever known,' I said. 'It's like there's
another you, out there.'

'I don't know if I'd like that.'

'You wouldn't like it or not like it, if you had it. It would just
be . . . how things are.'

Docey said nothing. I watched her lazy eye. I wondered if it could be fixed, if there was some corrective method available, or if people with lazy eyes simply had to live with them. I wondered what she saw, right now – did my face stay still? Did it move, wildly? But of course Docey would never be able to fix her eye.

I realized I'd been staring. 'How many siblings do you have?' I asked, and then thought she might not know what that meant. I flushed. 'Brothers—'

'Twelve,' she said. 'Twelve,' she repeated.

I was astonished. I couldn't even name twelve relations. Between Georgie's family and mine, there were only seven.

Docey smiled at the shock on my face.

'What do they do?' I asked.

'What do they do?' she repeated. She shrugged, and I understood how vile Yonahlossee must appear to Emmy and Docey. Mary Abbott's father, the preacher, had written of two little boys who lived not far from here, up in the mountains. They had died from eating poisonous berries. All the other girls thought they simply hadn't known they were poisonous, but of course they had; in Florida I had known exactly which berries I could eat, which would send me straight to death. And surely these boys had spent as much time outside as I had, or more. They'd eaten them because they were starving. I wanted to apologize to Docey, but for what? Luck, fortune, fate.

She'd turned away from me anyway, bent down, and rolled the woven rug beneath the desk into a tight roll. She seemed to linger. I helped Mother clean, I was familiar with the desperation it entailed, born of futility. It was a fixed system of entropy, like Father had explained by tossing a coin.

'Do you like to clean?'

Docey laughed. It was a stupid question. Mother liked to clean, enjoyed ordering her world like that. But this wasn't

Docey's world; it was ours. I turned to slip my shoes on and then leave, but then she spoke.

'I don't mind it.' But she was lying, we both knew that.

He was quiet today, sat almost mournfully with his gin. His shirt was buttoned crookedly, and though Mr Holmes was somber, his shirt made him seem playful.

'Let's go out back.' I rose and Mr Holmes followed. I knew he would, he was in his passive mood.

It was a little bit thrilling to walk through the parts of the house I'd never seen – the dining room, to a formal sitting room whose French doors opened onto the porch. There was a table next to the window, heavy with glass bottles, their necks slender. I went to it. The sight, up close, was a marvel – various exotic plants that I'd never seen before, growing in bottles like model ships.

'Beth's.' Mr Holmes had come up behind me. I remembered that Mrs Holmes loved to garden. He picked one up. 'She sends away for the seeds.'

I imagined all the attention they must require, the special tools, the careful nurturing. I had not thought Mrs Holmes capable of magic like this.

The back porch was clearly built for entertaining – there was a bar in the corner, and clusters of small tables surrounded by chairs. I imagined fathers of alumna who came out here with Mr Holmes to admire the view and talk – about what? The purpose of a place like this. The goal of women's education. Things that none of us girls ever spoke about.

I didn't want to be here anymore, where fathers came and spoke of their daughters with Mr Holmes. 'Let's go outside,' I said.

'I have such a headache.'

'The fresh air will help,' I said.

He opened the screen door to the woods that lay beyond the porch. Outside the footing was rocky, but it was fine because Mr Holmes had to offer me his hand, and he seemed reluctant to touch me, today.

'I come up here sometimes on Naari,' I said. Mr Holmes said nothing. I was still careful about mentioning horses around him. 'It's easier when she does the climbing.'

He laughed.

'Are you feeling better?' I asked hopefully.

'It's not a horrible one. When I was a boy I had to lie in a dark room on the floor. Always the floor, for some reason it felt better, and wait until it went away. There was no logic to it. Sometimes it went away immediately, and other times it took days.'

'And you had to lie on the floor for days?'

'Mostly, yes.' He stopped, and leaned against a tree. 'My governess would sit outside the door and forbid anyone to come close. I couldn't stand any noise.'

I closed my eyes and pictured a small Mr Holmes, laid flat by pain, his English governess barring the door.

'You had a governess?'

'Yes. You sound surprised. My family was very wealthy. Is very wealthy. Well, less wealthy than they used to be, I imagine, but I'm sure they've survived.' He gave a hard little laugh.

I hadn't been surprised. I knew he came from money.

'My family was very wealthy, my mother and father lived in Europe for most of the year, I had a governess. I failed out of Harvard, twice. Then I met Beth.' I opened my eyes. 'And the rest, they say, is history.' His voice had changed, was stiff and distant.

'And the rest, they say . . .' I trailed off.

'Is history,' Mr Holmes finished. 'I was very disappointing to my parents.'

'So was I,' I said.

'Yes. But there are worse things.'

I was silent.

'Thea, when you're young, disappointing your parents seems like the worst thing in the world. But it's not. Believe me, it's not.'

I nodded. We walked in silence for a moment. The air was warm, felt like spring. Sometimes I resented always having to wear a skirt – I could never play as wildly as Georgie and Sam – but right now a skirt was convenient, allowed me to take giant steps to keep up with Mr Holmes. I thought pants – especially wool pants, like Mr Holmes was wearing – would have constricted me, been too hot and smothering.

'What is the worst thing, then?' I asked tentatively. 'If not disappointing your family?'

'Disappointing yourself,' he said quickly. 'Disappointing yourself,' he repeated. 'And it's such an easy thing to do.'

I turned this phrase over and over – the thought had never occurred to me. Why should my disappointment matter? My parents were disappointed in me. And my brother, and my aunt and uncle. The word seemed to come unhinged, the way that words always did when you lingered on them too long – *disappoint*. What did it really mean? How was it even possible to disappoint myself? I was just myself. I was Thea, I was a girl, I was a daughter and a cousin and a sister and now a friend.

'Did you disappoint yourself?' I asked.

He laughed. 'In too many ways to count.'

I watched the back of his head, he was silent for a second. He was so strong, Mr Holmes; we were climbing a steep incline and his breath remained even, his footing sure.

I thought he was done with the subject, but he continued. 'If I could do it all over again, relive my youth, as they say, I would do things differently. But so would everyone, I think. The trick is not to get mired in the muck.' It was an expression Father used. He turned, and I watched his profile as he spoke. 'The past is the past, Thea. I hope somebody's already told you that. But if they haven't, well – it's something to remember.'

Mr Holmes stopped at a stand of trees and went through an opening I hadn't seen. A secret opening, I thought as I followed, for our secret affair. The idea thrilled me. The trees opened and I could see straight through to the sky. I think half the transgressions here were committed because of weather like this. And the other half – in the memory of the weather. I touched his jacket, soft against my fingertips.

'Where does Emmy think we are?' I asked.

'I don't know, Thea.' He shook his head. 'You should be at the Hall, with all the other girls. You should not be here with me.'

'But I want to be here.'

We were quiet for a moment, and I knew that when he spoke again he might very well end this, send me back to be with all the other girls.

But instead he bent down and delicately picked up a transparent snake skin. 'Snakes are coming out again.'

I reached for the skin, a long tube, dirty and translucent. 'This is old.'

He looked at me, surprised.

'There are snakes all over in Florida.'

'You're not scared of them?'

'Not particularly. Leave them alone, they leave you alone.'

I turned my face up and kissed him. I kissed him hard, directed his tongue; drew him closer to me.

'We can pretend we're all alone out here,' I said.

'Because we are.'

Mr Holmes kissed my neck, and suddenly we were on the

ground, he was on top of me. My skirt was unbuttoned, and his jacket was off. I reached for his pants. Mr Holmes above me, framed by the bluest sky I thought I'd ever seen, and I felt so lucky, that he was here with me, that I was getting again what I knew I shouldn't have.

'No,' he whispered, and instead he licked my breasts, then my stomach, and continued down. His mouth was over my panties, and I started to sit up. He raised his head and pressed his hand into my shoulder and pushed, hard, until I relaxed. What are you doing, I thought of asking, but I felt if I spoke I might end this. My thighs quivered, and his tongue felt like it was inside me. Which was impossible, wasn't it, but it felt so large and it moved and I put my hands on his head as if in a blessing.

CHAPTER EIGHTEEN

Sissy caught up with me on the way back from the barn. I usually waited for her, but lately I had been scurrying out of the cabin after rest hour before the bell had even rung; and then, when I was done with riding, rushing through cooling out Naari. It was easy to evade Sissy, who was always late. I had started to do whatever I wanted to. Sometimes I didn't even bow my head during prayer, but watched Mr Holmes. He made small motions with his hands, even though he kept his eyes closed while he was speaking. I tried it once in the woods, closed my eyes and spoke to the trees. But it felt as strange as walking blindfolded.

'You're always hurrying,' Sissy said, 'I can never catch you.' She sounded irritated, her raspy voice high.

I shrugged. There were girls all around us. I opened my mouth to speak but closed it again; I didn't really have anything to say.

Sissy shrugged, and I realized with a shock that she was imitating me. I stared at her.

'What?' She shrugged again. 'I never see you, and you don't seem to care. You haven't asked about Boone in weeks.'

So this was what this was about. I was relieved, and, strangely, disappointed.

'I know he still comes,' I reminded her. 'I'm the one who helps you. Takes your place in bed.'

She drew me to the side of the path, into the woods. 'Stop, Thea.' Her voice cracked. 'You've been walking around with your head in the clouds. You never come to the Hall anymore.'

'Nobody studies, anyway.'

'That's not what I mean.' I started to defend myself, but Sissy continued. 'You're in Masters too much. Girls are talking.'

I waited for her to go on. But she didn't. 'What are they saying?' I asked.

'They're saying you're obsessed with Mr Holmes, that you're lovesick.'

I laughed, but the sound was strange in my throat. 'Sissy,' I said, trying to sound incredulous. 'I go there for Decca. She asked for me, you know.' I offered this as if it were proof of something. And then there was also a feeling of relief, that what Leona had said in the Square was gossip, nothing more.

'Thea, don't!' Her voice was high. 'I'm your best friend. Don't.'

I was touched, even in that moment, that she considered herself my best friend. Sissy stood so rigidly; I took her hand, drew it from her side. 'I just like being there. With Decca. With Mr Holmes, too. We talk. He understands me.'

'What does he understand about you?' She gripped my hand tightly, now, and looked at me plaintively. 'You were sent away because of a boy.'

I nodded. I had told her this, so long ago it seemed like another life, when I was settling in at Yonahlossee and wanted so badly to have a friend.

'Mr Holmes isn't a boy.'

I took my hand away. 'I know that.' I paused for a moment. If I were brave enough to trust Sissy I might have asked her what she meant, exactly, what she had guessed.

'What about David?' Sissy asked.

'David,' I repeated, confused. I'd nearly forgotten about him.

Sissy watched me. Eva walked by, with Gates, and I smiled at them over Sissy's shoulder. 'He's not . . . I'm sorry.'

'Oh, don't apologize. It's just, it would be so easy, to like him. So fun. Just come around more,' she said, and her voice had returned to normal. 'Please?' I'd seen Sissy do this before, decide that a quarrel was over and end it just like this, snuffing a candle. It was one of her gifts, never deigning to fight with anyone. But she had never acted like that with me. She had never needed to.

I thought about David the rest of the day, as I walked from place to place and nodded at various girls and knew that I was not like them, did not want the same things, had made my life unnecessarily hard, and would continue to do so. And why? Why Thea, why, Mother's voice ringing, ringing.

I knew why, though. I was a smart girl. David was a boy, and he reminded me of Georgie, as any boy would. I was done with boys.

Suddenly Yonahlossee was a haze of color: candytuft carpeted the fields beyond the riding rings in all manner of pink; grape hyacinth lined the Square; and finally daffodils, my favorite, circled our riding rings in carefully planted beds. Mrs Holmes had supervised their planting before she left. She has a genius for flowers, Henny said one night, and I had to agree.

There's no future in this. I kept waiting for Mr Holmes to speak these words, but he never did. I knew this would end. I knew the date. I knew how. Mrs Holmes would come back, and we would simply stop.

There's no future in this, Mr Holmes might have said, might have prepared me for the inevitable. But I wasn't naïve. I could have been called many things – shameful, cowardly, cunning – but not naïve. Why did I act this way, first at home, then at

Yonahlossee? I risked everything when I was old enough to know better. But there was always this: the hard kernel of want in my throat. I could not push it away. I did not want to.

Mother would be so disappointed in me. She would hate me, if she learned what I was doing. Yet if my family could cast me out so easily – out of their home, out of their hearts – shouldn't I be able to act in the same way? I wasn't weak. There was so much want inside me, there was so much desire. I felt it exploding when Mr Holmes touched me, I felt it multiplying.

With Georgie I had felt desire, yes, but a fraction of what I felt with Mr Holmes. He taught me that desire is divisible, that it changes in relation to its object. I wondered if Mother knew that. I wondered if Father did. Because you couldn't know, if you had only ever desired a single person, if you had been kept away from everyone else.

I thought about what Mr Holmes had told me, that my parents had made an exchange. He didn't know them, he didn't know my father's tenderness, my mother's lovely home. He didn't know how we had loved each other.

CHAPTER NINETEEN

Georgie was in Missouri, with his mother and father. Mother had said that we might see him next week, but I couldn't confirm the date without calling attention to myself.

I'd woken and gasped for breath the air was so thick and soupy. The clock on my bedside table read three-thirty; in another hour or so it would be light enough to ride.

In the summers you had a second skin, a layer of moisture and sweat that was always with you. And this was only the beginning of it.

Outside, the world looked dead and disinterested; there was no breeze to rustle the grass, no crickets rubbing their legs together to interrupt the stillness. I sat on the steps and unbuttoned the first button of my nightgown, which made no difference. I closed my eyes and thought of my cousin, the way he had touched me last time, the way I had touched him, how we were learning.

'Thea,' Sam called, from behind me. I knew without looking that he was sitting in a rocking chair.

'Sam.'

'You weren't scared?' he asked. He sounded like he had been up for a while. He had always liked to startle others, to jump out from behind doors, to wait in a bush and spring up, suddenly, a surprise.

'Who else would it be?' The question hung in the air for a moment, two. I spoke again. 'Can't sleep?'

'Who can? It must be a record, this heat. It feels like it.'

'It never is. A record.'

'No,' he agreed, 'it never is.'

We were silent for a few moments. Sam sighed.

'You'll be tired tomorrow,' I said.

'I'll just sleep tomorrow. I won't miss anything.'

'I guess not.'

'I want to go away, Thea. I want to travel.' His voice was strange. I turned and looked at him. He was barefoot, sprawled in the rocking chair in his normal day clothes. His head was turned, in profile, and I saw how handsome my brother was becoming. He was going to be more handsome than I was beautiful, our features more suited to a man's face; but I pushed the thought from my mind. I was fifteen years old; I wanted to be beautiful. I did not want anyone else to be more beautiful, even my twin – or especially my twin. 'Don't you?' he asked again, and turned to me. Mother said some twins looked less and less alike as they grew older, but that didn't seem to be the case for me and Sam.

'Where would you go?' I asked. My brother had never spoken to me of leaving before. Not ever.

'I think I'd like to go somewhere on a ship,' he said, and I couldn't help it, I laughed.

Sam wouldn't look at me.

'I'm sorry,' I said, 'it's just the picture of you on a ship. Would you be a sailor?'

He said nothing.

'Sam,' I began, 'I'm sorry—'

'No you're not. Anyway, wouldn't you be glad if I left?' His voice was high, and I understood that Sam did not really want to go anywhere, that he wanted nothing about our lives to change.

'Why would I be glad, Sam?' I spoke quietly. 'I need you.'

'Need me?' It was his turn to laugh. 'Need me for what? You spend all day on Sasi. You don't need anyone.'

'That isn't true,' I said. But, strangely, my feelings weren't hurt. I felt they should be, I expected them to be, but they weren't.

'No,' Sam said, 'I suppose it isn't true. You need our cousin.'

I lay back against the hard brick, suddenly exhausted. I could feel Sam stand behind me; I thought he would go inside now, but instead he sat down next to me. I watched his back: he was growing broader as I was growing narrower.

'No moon tonight.' His voice was dull.

I shook my head, even though he wasn't looking at me.

'Do you remember when you thought an Indian lived out there?' I asked.

'You believed it, too.'

He lay down next to me, and I knew the coolness of the brick was a relief to him also.

'Thea?'

'Yes.'

'Do you ever wonder what it feels like to be dead?'

I considered the question. Sam passed his hand lightly over my eyes. 'Close them.' I did. 'It feels like this,' he said.

'No it doesn't.'

'Try and fall asleep. You might as well be dead, when you're sleeping.'

I tried to push all my thoughts away and make my mind go blank. I tried not to think about Georgie, I tried to lull my mind into stillness. I wanted to please my brother.

'I don't think this is working.' Sam didn't respond, but I could tell he wasn't sleeping, only trying. 'I wonder which one of us will die first.'

'Me,' he said, 'it will be me.'

I said nothing. To be alive without Sam – would that be any life at all, I wondered. I knew Mother and Father would die first, though I didn't know in which order; this made sense. They had lives before me, and I would have a life after them. But Sam and I had never existed alone, and now this existence seemed as much a burden as a pleasure. Or perhaps it was neither. It was merely a fact.

'Thea. Try again.'

I listened to Sam. I closed my eyes. And what did I see? Mother's old carriage blanket, weighing down her arm like a stone. I tried to think of other things, put them on top of the blanket: Sasi, Georgie, the usual things. But they all led back to the blanket. Usually I was so good at plucking from my brain what I did not want to consider.

I almost fell asleep. The sun rose very slowly, by increments, and I kept my eyes shut against it, tried to make myself drift into oblivion. Then suddenly I could taste what it would be like to become nothing. And it was an absence so large I couldn't quite conceive of it, except to be terrified.

I opened my eyes and sat up, turned to Sam, who slept peacefully. My hand hovered above his shoulder. I needed to wake him, I needed to tell him I was scared. He would help me understand it. But then I let my hand drop, onto the brick. I wanted to be separate from Sam. I wanted to experience something he did not. And so I stayed on the porch for another hour, the sun turning us hotter and hotter as it rose.

I should have woken Sam to prevent the burn that we would sport for the next week, our forearms and faces bright red, then pink, then peeling. But I did not. My face was redder on my left cheek, almost like I had painted it with rouge; it had been turned to the sun while I had watched my brother. He had wanted me to follow him there, to wherever he was, and I hadn't. I could not. I watched him and saw very clearly that there were places I would not follow Sam, where he would not follow me.

What Sam said rang over and over – you need our cousin. We love him differently. Georgie, his thick waist, his broad chest – what Sam could see. What Sam couldn't see: the trail of hair that split his navel, the taut surface of his stomach.

We love him differently, but what was the difference? My mother and father loved each other, shared a bed; I loved my mother, my father loved me, they both loved Sam. Marriage meant you included someone, permanently, in your family. That kind of marriage made sense. In the Bible, Jacob married two first cousins, Rachel and Leah, and it was a joyful occasion. Occasions. I didn't want as much as that – I only wanted a single person, a solitary being.

But that was so long ago. At the beginning of time, everyone must have been a cousin. Cousin-marriage, then, was a modern term, applied to pairs like Charles Darwin and Emma Wedgwood, their marriage an anecdote, woven into Father's lecture in order to entertain, trick us into caring. I'd wondered if Emma was related to the porcelain manufacturer. Neither Father nor Mother had known, and there was no way for me to find out at that time in my life, no matter how badly I wanted to.

And so the story of Emma and Charles lodged itself somewhere in my young brain. Mr Darwin had carefully considered both the benefits and detriments of marriage, committing himself to Miss Wedgwood for as long as they both would live. Marriage meant less money for his work, less time to catalogue all the unknown species of flora and fauna in the great beyond. Miss Emma Wedgwood was already catalogued, already *known*, and Mr Darwin couldn't have been less interested in what he already understood. In his huge, unrelenting brain, Mr Darwin's capacity for love had already been filled by the vast inhabitants of God's earth.

If Mother found out what I was doing, she might want me to marry Georgie. And I did not want to marry my cousin. I did not want to live in Gainesville. I did not – and this thought shamed me – want to be poor. But still I wanted my cousin. I wanted him very badly. I tried to separate the two things in my mind. I could not make sense of it all, how I could want one part but not the other.

It was the longest Georgie and I had been apart. I didn't think of it this way then, but that night in the stall must have worked on my conscience, because suddenly I saw what I was doing clearly, and I was terrified that someone would know. I was still hungry for my cousin – I wanted him to touch me, I craved his touch – but my hunger was tempered by caution. Perhaps it was as simple as this: I was older. I saw my mother unfurling her precious carriage blanket, pulling it from beneath the table, and it unlocked the possibilities in my brain. If I had allowed things to go further I would no longer be a virgin. That was the first thing, and then the second was that if anyone knew, I wouldn't be marriageable. I could have conceived a child, *we* could have conceived a child. It was a possibility. I shudder to think of my life had that happened.

My mother held up the blanket, and in Georgie's absence it had revealed itself to me like a flare in the night sky that had come into view suddenly and terrifyingly.

Then Georgie was back, and we went to Gainesville for tea, just me and Mother, Sam was busy with something. His absence would have seemed like a blessing a month ago. But now I wished he were here. Georgie had tea with us, stared at me in a way that was obvious, but Mother and Aunt Carrie didn't seem to notice. I ate a scone and it was dust in my mouth.

I followed him upstairs later. He patted the space next to him on his unmade bed; I went reluctantly. I'd never liked his room.

'Did you miss me?'

'Yes.'

'My cousins there aren't like the ones here,' he said, and I looked at him strangely; it suddenly struck me that that was exactly the phrase his father had used, over dinner. But of course father and son meant it differently: Georgie leaned in to kiss me, his eyes already closed, and I turned my cheek.

'You left the blanket in the stall last time.'

'I did?'

'Mother found it. We could have been caught.'

He smoothed the sheet between us, and though he came close to touching me, he didn't. I could hear my own heart. He kept drawing his hand in a pattern that brought it close and then away again.

'Georgie,' I said, my voice nearly a whisper.

'My cousins in Kansas City aren't doing very well. Everyone's moved into my grandmother's house.' He gave me a sidelong glance. 'It was good that she died.'

'Don't say that.'

'What? It's the truth. They're all farmers, they don't have professions they can depend on, like our fathers. Well, like your father. People are always sick, aren't they? But it hasn't rained in months there. They're desperate.'

I stilled his hand and held it between both of mine. This was the Georgie that was mine, who no one else saw.

'I'm sorry.'

'Do you know how poor everyone is now? Father says it's just starting, that it'll be worse before it's better. The cows in the pastures are starving. You can see their spines.'

I shivered. 'They should shoot them, put them out of their misery.'

'They can't. Then that would be the end of things. Think Thea – they need their cows.'

'It will rain again. It always does.'

'Only God can say that.'

'Or the ocean. The ocean decides when it rains.'

'Tell my uncles. Tell them to ask the ocean.'

I hadn't meant to be flip. 'I'm sure it's awful.'

'It is.' He rested his head on my shoulder, which he'd never done before. It was usually I who leaned against him. I stroked his forearm, watched how the fine hairs stood at my touch.

'All I thought about was you, when I was gone. How much I wanted you to be with me.'

'Well, here I am.'

'I mean be with you differently.' He drew his finger across my lap. 'Do you want to be with me like that?'

I looked around the room – the ratty bedspread, flung on the floor; the uneven floorboards; the secondhand desk; the framed photograph of a man I did not recognize, someone from Aunt Carrie's family. There was a small lockbox beneath the bed, which held his treasures: a silver dollar, a smooth stone from Ormond Beach, a postcard from Toronto.

These were all his things in the world. And now me, he had me, too.

'You don't need to answer,' he said, into my neck. 'Just stay here with me.'

I came to Yonahlossee in late July, the summer nearly over. In Florida this was always the worst month, the heat so vicious it claimed lives, a dozen every July. The bugs were unbearable, biting, buzzing, trying to get at you any way they could. When I undressed, I found mosquitoes in my undergarments, nestled between my thighs.

Georgie was visiting, for the Fourth. I looked forward to seeing my cousin with a distinct combination of dread and exhilaration.

My uncle bought fireworks from a stand in Gainesville, a box full of them, on a whim. We'd never lit fireworks before. I saw my father's expression as Uncle George revealed his surprise, and he was not pleased, anyone could see that.

'A gift,' Uncle George said, 'a gift,' and my father said nothing, and I pitied Uncle George, and I was so angry at Father for his meanness.

'A fine one,' my mother said, splitting the silence, 'a fine one.' But it was too late.

Sometimes when I think of that weekend – and I have thought of it often, wound and rewound the scenes – I am not impressed. What happened seems, if not normal, inevitable, unsurprising. My family emerged a different family, but that would have happened anyway. Sam and I would have gone to college, Georgie would have married. The children would have left.

And other times I think of that weekend and I am a young stranger, that weekend is impossible.

I did have the sense that someone was watching us. I was very careful, I diligently ignored Georgie when we were in front of anyone else, including Sam. He looked at me as if we had an understanding when I didn't laugh at a joke Georgie made, when I refused to even smile; it was so simple to please him.

We watched the fireworks late at night, when it was darkest. My uncle kept praying to the moon, in jest, to go away. Sam and Georgie carried the box to the end of the field, past the barn. Georgie did a little jump and clicked his heels in the air, gave a holler, and Sam smiled and so did I, in spite of myself, but then I went cold. The fireworks had not excited Georgie. *I* had, and what he imagined we were going to do later. I looked at my mother, who watched my brother and uncle and cousin disappear into darkness.

'I hope he'll be careful,' my mother said, and I wasn't sure who she was referring to. If only she knew; then she could tell me to be careful, she could stop things before they went any further. We couldn't see them anymore but I heard Georgie yell something to Sam, probably some instruction, and his voice ricocheting off my brain thrilled me, amplified some desire I hadn't known I'd had.

'I haven't seen fireworks in years,' Father said quietly. I put my hand on top of his. He turned it over and held mine. He was very easy to love.

'Did you have them when you were little?'

'I don't remember.'

I thought that odd – whether or not you'd seen fireworks in your childhood seemed like a thing you'd remember – but I sat quietly because I sensed that Father wanted to sit quietly. I would remember this night, I thought, but perhaps one day all of this would have faded into a vague, barely recalled memory; that seemed unbearable, that all of it could simply disappear.

We heard a whoop and Mother stood, terrified, and then we heard the bang of a firework, and the rays of color spread across the sky.

'It's fine, Elizabeth,' my father said, and my mother sat back down.

'Do you like them, Thea?' my mother asked.

I looked at the sky. 'Yes.'

Aunt Carrie was quiet. I looked at her and wanted to scream. You should know, you should have stopped your son from falling into all of this.

I left before the men came back, went to check on Sasi, who was, as I'd anticipated, frantic. I stayed with him for a while, but he wouldn't be soothed. I walked him around the ring, let him graze, but he wasn't interested in grass. The air smelled scorched, and there was no way to explain to him that it had all been for fun, that there was no real threat.

Back inside, Mother told me she was putting the house to bed – a phrase I'd never heard her use before. She must have read it in her book. I found her in the living room, drawing the curtains, and told her I would be outside for a while, tending to Sasi. She told me not to stay up too late, and I promised I wouldn't, though I planned to sleep outside if Sasi wouldn't calm down. Perhaps Georgie was in the next room – in the kitchen or the hallway – and heard, or he went to find me in my bed and guessed, correctly, that I was in the barn. That was where we had met before. It was not inconceivable that I would wait there again.

I was dozing – not fully asleep, but nowhere near awake, either – when I heard him. I watched my cousin while he looked for me. Sasi was exhausted from working himself up, stood very still, his head in the corner over me. I loved him. The feeling rose in my throat.

Georgie walked by the stall. His face was sweaty. A moment later he walked by again and stopped at the stall, propped his elbows on the door and smiled.

'Found you.'

Sasi started, jerked his head up and walked over to the door; Georgie backed away.

'I wasn't hiding.' I stood by Sasi and stroked his neck, ran my fingers through his knotted mane. I hadn't been taking good care of him lately.

'Thea?'

I turned my head and looked at my cousin, and he was so eager. He motioned for me to come, and I went, it was what was expected of me, after all we had done together. I followed willingly, and as soon as I was outside of the stall he pushed me against the cold brick wall, which felt good through my dress. He smelled of sweat, and he bit my lip. I turned my face and he began to gather my dress around my hips. He pressed his erection against my bare leg, and I turned back and saw that he was watching himself, that he was aroused by the sight of his erection pressing into my leg.

'Georgie,' I said, 'wait.'

'Why?' He took my hand and led me into our empty stall. His voice sounded deeper than it had a moment before. I smoothed the hair away from his forehead and smiled at him.

'All right.'

'You,' he said, 'you are so good.'

I would have done anything, then. I turned away from him and unbuttoned the front of my dress, and he was behind me, sliding the dress from my shoulders. He kissed my neck, and felt my breasts, and then he turned me around.

He put his finger beneath my chin and lifted it. 'Are you all right?'

'No.'

'I'll make you better.' But I wanted him to ask *why* I wasn't all right; I wanted him to feel this risk half as much as I seemed to. He appeared so careless, Georgie, so careless about all of this. He didn't take his eyes away. Ask, I screamed, inside my head; ask, ask, ask. Instead he put his hand between my legs while he watched me, and he was gentle. He stopped, a little half-smile on his face, and I knew he was goading me. It worked.

'Don't stop,' I said, and he unbuckled his belt, and it all felt so good, and then I wanted him, I *needed* him, because what I felt in this instant was not pleasure, exactly: it was the promise of pleasure, an itch that needed fingernails raked across it. And maybe, I thought, as I felt him next to me, as he guided my thighs apart while he traced my nipples with his fingertip. Maybe, I thought, as he pushed himself into me, it was enough, that Georgie would try to understand me later, that right now there was a need and when we were done the need would not exist anymore.

'Loosen,' he said, and I tried. It hurt, now, but the pain, I saw, was a part of the pleasure. I should not have done this, I had been very bad, and now I was being punished. It was all so clear, now. I looked out of the stall window into a black, black night. I felt the cloth of Georgie's shirt, I put my hands on his shoulders and brought him closer to me. If a door had slammed, if Mother had stepped onto the back porch and called my name.

Sam's face flashed in my head, not as he was now – angry, hurt – but as he used to be, a little boy who felt the world too deeply. 'We should switch you!' Mother used to say, as if little girls were better suited to feel the weight of things than little boys. Georgie bent down and licked my breast like an eager dog and I shuddered, pulled him up – I felt excluded from what he was doing right now, he was inside me but he was enacting a private fantasy, one that required my presence but not my love.

Mother had been right. I was too much like a boy, too dumb to the consequences. I remembered the tent Mother let us make between our beds when we were little. Sam clasped my face between his fat hands: 'Thea,' he said, 'Thea!'

Georgie heaved against me, once, twice, and he seemed so large inside me, impossibly large. Then he put his head on my chest and breathed deeply. It was over very quickly.

What had Sam wanted? I couldn't for the life of me remember.

I slid down the cold wall until I was sitting. Georgie stood over me, tucked his shirt into his pants, fastened his belt. It was something about seeing him do all those things, those normal, everyday gestures, that made me feel very alone. I put my head in my hands.

'Thea?'

'What have we done?'

'Don't you know?' There was, outrageously, impossibly, laughter in his voice.

'I don't mean that.'

He sat down next to me. 'It's all very natural,' he said.

'It doesn't feel like it.' I shook my head.

'Doesn't it?'

'We should have waited.' I looked away.

He laughed. 'Why?' he asked. 'There was no reason to wait, for us.'

I was naked and my cousin was completely clothed. He traced a pattern in the sawdust and seemed to consider what to say next, which was unlike my cousin, to think before he spoke.

'We were wrong,' I said.

'I didn't make you do anything.'

I shook my head. He understood nothing.

'I want my dress,' I said, and pointed to it.

He retrieved my dress from the middle of the stall, and it seemed to me that he moved like a stranger. Then he stood over me, watched me.

'Didn't you think that would happen?' He sounded genuinely curious. I wanted very badly to be alone.

I felt very keenly that I had given up too much for ninety, one hundred seconds. And that minute, those two minutes, had been painful for me, it had all been for Georgie's pleasure. I saw very clearly our future: we would do this a dozen more times, two dozen more times, and then Georgie would be finished with me, with our arrangement. Boys could do this, I understood now, watching my cousin, how he stood over me, so carelessly, so confidently. Boys were meant for this world. 'We're not the marrying kind,' he said. 'Thea? Did you think we were the marrying kind?'

'I don't know what I thought,' I said. 'Not this.' I gestured at the stall, the walls brown with mildew; they needed to be scrubbed, one of my summer chores. Georgie followed my hand, followed it to where it stopped: him, in clothes my parents had bought him, the only nice things he had. My cheeks burned. 'It's dirty.'

He knelt next to me and touched my cheek. 'It's not like that.'

'It is,' I said, and removed his hand. 'It's exactly like that. It's what you do, in your family.'

'In my family?' I felt all the words forming in my heart, ready to tumble out; I clutched my dress to my chest and saw how I would end this. I pitied him, now. He stood so dumbly; he was so confused. I didn't want to pity him. I didn't want any part of him. I wanted to wash my hands of him, and in this moment that felt possible: I could be done with him forever.

'You're like your father.' I was speaking quickly; I pictured my kind, mild uncle and felt like a nasty, nasty girl but I had no choice. 'Your father came to my father like you came to me, begging. You're just like him, shameful.'

I held my dress to my chest and wished for nothing more in the world than to be clothed. My cousin looked out the stall window, into the night, black as pitch, here where the lights of town did not reach. I felt sick. I wanted this to be over. But I watched my cousin's profile and knew it would never be over; we were family, we could not be rid of each other.

I looked down. When I looked up again, Georgie's face was mean. And what choice did he have? I ask that question now, years later, too late, everything a ruin. 'Look at yourself,' he said, and his eyes roamed over my body, the dress that covered me so inadequately.

'If you don't leave,' I said, 'I'll scream.'

'You'll scream?' What if I had waited a beat before I'd threatened to scream? Or, better, if I had stepped back in time and said nothing at all and kissed him good-night and acted as if everything was the same, and let our arrangement end slowly, as Georgie said, naturally. He could be thick and clumsy and cruel; he was also kind and funny and sincere. And anyway, none of that mattered. He was mine. He was my cousin. I wanted to take everything back. I wanted *him* to take everything back. For the first time in my life, I understood that certain words were brands, etched onto the brain. 'Who will hear you?'

'Everyone.'

'I don't think you want everyone to hear you.'

We watched each other. God knows what you were thinking, Thea. Only God knows. I could hear Mother's voice. Georgie watched me, but I wouldn't meet his eye. Finally, he left.

I slept in the barn. I felt unclean, but not unclean enough to wash. It seemed natural to fall asleep in this empty stall, to stay in the barn until it was light.

I slipped upstairs at dawn and bathed, thought of Georgie, who slept in the next room. I might as well not have bothered with closing the door. He had seen me naked. But there was Sam, who hadn't. I pressed my fingernails into my forearm. I had been used by my own cousin. I was a young woman when young women were powerless. You would think I could have predicted what would happen. But I never felt powerless in my home. I hadn't known to be careful in that regard.

When I went downstairs to breakfast, Georgie wasn't at the table, and neither was Sam. I assumed they were still sleeping – it was early, not yet seven.

'Has your pony calmed down?' Mother asked.

'Yes.'

'Are you all right, Thea?'

I wanted so badly to tell her. I wanted so badly to be comforted. I'm so ashamed, Mother, I've done something so awful you won't believe me.

She tapped my wrist. 'Thea?'

Her voice was so soft, so lovely.

'Yes,' I said. 'Only tired.' She looked at me, her head tilted, and I knew I could never tell, not in this life.

After breakfast I saddled Sasi, headed out into the orange groves. I rode all morning, turned around and let Sasi canter back in the direction of the barn. I felt careless today. There would be consequences – Sasi would fight for his head the next time we went toward the barn – but they felt small, and I felt large and bad. And I felt scared, though I tried to ignore the feeling of fear as it rose, tried to dampen it, send it back; I had always been so good at being fearless. I'd felt near tears all morning; now the cantering lulled me into some sort of trance and I flopped around in the saddle like a rag doll. I began to cry, like a girl, like a child.

Then Sasi swerved to avoid something – I couldn't see what – and I gasped and grabbed Sasi's short mane and righted myself in the saddle, just barely, while I tried to murmur soothingly, while I tried to pick up the slack in my reins. It was always like this when you rode, doing a million things at once, all by instinct.

'Sorry,' Sam called behind me, and I wished I had fallen, so that I would have an excuse for my tears.

'Thea?' Sam asked. 'Are you all right?'

No, I wanted to say, no, I am not, and then I started to sob. I had let Georgie do things to me that had turned unimaginable in my mind; I had done things to him that I could never speak of, not to anyone. Not to Mother, not to Father, not to Sam, not to – and this occurred to me only now, on the back of the pony I loved, in the middle of an orange grove I had ridden through thousands of times, no, millions – my husband. I felt sick and dizzy.

'Thea?' And this voice belonged to Georgie. Of course. Georgie was being nice to Sam, perhaps because I was no longer his favorite. 'Thea?' he said again, and then Sam was beside me, holding Sasi's rein, speaking quietly to him. Sasi nipped Sam's shirt, nervously, but then calmed down. I remembered what Mother always said, that it was in our blood to love horses. And what else was it in our blood to do?

'Why are you crying?' Sam asked, but I could only sob harder. The beauty of the day amplified my misery; if it were raining, I would have not felt so alone, so wretched.

Sasi panted heavily, and for a moment or two that was the only sound – his grave, rhythmic breaths.

'Thea?' Sam asked again. Stop saying my name, I wanted to scream. Stop. I turned my face so I wouldn't have to look at him and saw Georgie, sitting on a rock. He had not come near me. I noticed then that both he and Sam had guns slung over their shoulders. I wondered if Sam had shot anything. Surely not. You did not raise orphaned squirrels only to hunt them as adults.

'I'm sorry,' I said, 'I'm sorry, I'm sorry, I'm sorry.' I wiped my face, thick with sweat and snot and tears. I felt slimy, like a monster.

Georgie rose and walked toward me, and before I knew it he had put his hand on my thigh, braving his fear of Sasi, and I screamed at him, 'Don't touch me!' I had never felt like this before. I saw sparks against the clear blue sky. I felt hot, so hot. 'Don't touch me!' I screamed it over and over, until my voice was hoarse. I could feel both boys watching me, in wonder.

Sam turned to Georgie. 'What did you do?'

'What did we do,' Georgie said, and his voice had turned mean. 'What did we do together.' And then he began to walk away, and

Sam lunged after him, and pushed him to the ground. It took Georgie a second to get up he was so surprised.

Sasi, wound up, trembling beneath the saddle, started to trot, but I was still looking back, so I saw Sam – the back of his head, which I knew so well, his thin shoulders, his graceful pose – raise his hand and slap Georgie across the face, his palm open, and then Georgie respond with a punch to Sam's face, and Sam began to bleed from his nose, heavily.

'Stop,' I cried. I leaned forward; Sasi gave a small rear and I slammed down onto the pommel of the saddle because I wasn't paying attention. Now there was a sharp pain in between my legs, and I was almost glad for it, because it made things real again, Sam and Georgie were no longer surreal figures backdropped by a giant orange grove, hitting each other sloppily.

'Stop,' I yelled once more, and waved my hand, as if that would help. When I turned back again, I saw Sam raise the butt of his rifle and strike my cousin – his cousin, our cousin – on the shoulder, and Georgie, stunned, fall backward, regain his balance, and lunge at Sam. He looked like a child trying to throw an adult off balance. Georgie was scared of horses; I flailed my legs against Sasi's side and directed him to gallop straight toward my brother and cousin. I wanted to stop their fighting. And as I was galloping, I was most aware not of what might happen – that any one of us might be terribly injured, that I was putting into effect a course of action that would almost certainly leave one of us damaged – no, I was thinking of how sloppily I was riding, how ugly I must look on top of my frantic, overheated pony, and I was ashamed for Georgie to see me this way.

Georgie looked up at us, his mouth bloody, an expression of terror on his face; I shifted my weight in the saddle so that we would gallop right in between my brother and cousin. Sasi flew, I'd never gone so fast with him, the orange grove was a blur.

There was a bitter taste in my mouth. I wondered if it was fear.

I did not divide them, as I'd hoped. Instead, Georgie panicked and ran in front of us to Sam. He thought that I meant to run him over, he thought he would be safe with Sam. He didn't know that a horse would never do that; a horse would rather stay in a burning building than trample a human. Sasi stumbled; his hoof hit something hard – the rock, I realized, that Georgie had been sitting on – and in that instant I saw Sam raise the butt of his gun and hit Georgie on the side of his head, but Sasi regained his balance and he was going so fast, he would not slow down. I put all my weight against the bit, but Sasi was an electric wire beneath me, so I slid off while he was still cantering and hit the ground hard.

I picked myself up and turned and there was Georgie, Sam shaking him by the shoulders as if he were a doll. I could see how Georgie's head flopped, I could see that he was not well.

'Sam,' I yelled, 'you'll kill him.' Sam looked at me, aghast, and I saw that he was in shock. I was not in shock. There was blood all over his face, smeared across his cheeks and neck like paint; Georgie was bloody, too, and so was the ground. There was so much blood. I had never seen so much of it, but it occurred to me that surely Father had, that surely he would know what to do.

I motioned for him to come to me, and he ran wildly, his limbs unrestrained, like a child. 'Go get Father,' I said. Saliva glistened around his mouth. 'Go get Father,' I repeated.

I was alone with Georgie while Sam ran to the house. I smoothed his hair from his forehead. His skin was hot. His hair was matted with blood; Sam had hurt our cousin with his gun, his gun which he had never before used against a living creature.

I kneeled beside him and arranged him so that he did not look so disheveled. I straightened his vest and used my handkerchief to dab the blood from his lips, but his mouth was still too red, so

I tilted his head back and ran the handkerchief along his teeth. He looked better when I was done. I smoothed his forehead again. He was breathing and I half expected him to open his eyes and smile at me, as if last night had never happened. But he would open his eyes and smile at me and I would not be able to smile back. I would not have forgotten.

I heard a shout from the house – Mother, or Aunt Carrie, I couldn't tell – and I noticed Sam's gun, which lay next to me. There was a little blood on it, and so, without thinking, I wiped it on my breeches, which were bloody already, and threw it away from me, as far as I could, which was not very far at all.

He was still lying like this when my father appeared, with the rest of the adults. I held his hand, and my father looked at me strangely for a second before I was pushed to the edge of the circle that surrounded Georgie – my mother and father, my aunt and uncle.

Sam looked at me. I took his hand, impulsively, and he shook it off. His eyes were glassy. He looked like he did not know me.

'Sam?' I said softly. I tried to ignore the circle of adults in the periphery, tried only to focus on my brother's bloody face.

He looked at me briefly and then squatted on the ground, wrapped his arms around his legs, and began to rock gently, back and forth. I squatted next to him, and put my hands on his shoulders, and he looked at me again, and again he did not seem to recognize me. Then I wanted to die, I wanted Sam to smash *me* in the head with his gun.

Mother peeled herself away from the circle and came to us. She looked to Sam, then to me, then back at Sam. She leaned down and grabbed each of our upper arms, like she used to do when we were children, my right and Sam's left, like we were a single person, and leaned down to see us at eye level. This was also reminiscent of childhood.

'Go to your rooms,' she whispered, and her breath fanned across our faces. She squeezed our arms too tight, dug her nails through fabric, but we said nothing, Sam did not even seem to notice her, and Mother did not seem to notice how odd Sam looked. 'Go,' she whispered again, and released us with a nod toward the house.

Sam stood, and I watched him from the ground. I rubbed the place where Mother had gripped my arm. He wandered away, his gait unsteady, but then he turned around and stared at me. I looked away.

'Thea,' he said, 'Thea, Thea, Thea.' He kept repeating my name. He sounded possessed; he was not himself.

'Stop!' I cried, 'stop! Now!' I put my hands over my ears. This was what he did when we were little, when he wanted to bother me. I'd hated it, hated how my name turned into nothing more than a sound when it was strung together. I'd almost forgotten. He hadn't done it in years.

He stopped then, his lips parted. I wanted very badly to say something else, but knew there was nothing to say. Sam pointed behind me; I turned and saw Sasi, who stood at the entrance to the barn, his sides heaving. I'd forgotten about him. I went to him, took the reins and smoothed his neck, and watched the graceful figure of my brother disappear. I couldn't return Sasi to his stall like this, he would colic and die, and so I was hand-walking him around the ring when I saw Uncle George in the distance, trailed by the other adults, holding his son in his arms, his inert, damaged son.

'Is he dead,' I shrieked, 'is he dead?' and Mother hurried to me, stopped when she reached the railing.

'No,' she whispered, but in a shout, 'no, he's not, but he's hurt, and what happened, Thea?'

I said nothing.

'Thea,' she said again, and her voice was so sympathetic. I didn't deserve that voice, and I knew it was the last time she would ever offer it to me. When she spoke to me again, her voice would have turned ugly.

She couldn't stand there forever, and as the other adults passed she reentered their assembly. I turned my face into Sasi's slick neck, I felt his dusty sweat on my forehead and tried not to look at my cousin.

CHAPTER TWENTY

I sat on my bed with a letter in my hand. Mr Holmes was expecting me; if I waited any longer he would start to wonder.

I touched the handwriting on the envelope. *Theodora Atwell*, it read. *Care of the Yonahlossee Riding Camp for Girls*. The letters my mother sent were perfunctory, and she never addressed me as Theodora. She told me that she was packing all our things, that she and Sam and Father would live in a hotel while they looked for a house, that Father would go early to set up his new practice. I suppose I was glad for the letters, that she was preparing me for my new life, that I was able to imagine their life while I lived my own, here. She implied, but never stated, that I'd live in this Orlando house with them.

But this letter, which I held in my hands, bore Sam's handwriting. It seemed sometimes that God was toying with me. The day before the show, and a letter from my brother, who hadn't sent a single word since I'd been here.

Dear Thea,

I know you want a letter from me but why? By the time you read this it will already be old. You know we're moving. Everything is the same here but without you. But it won't be the same soon, because we'll be gone. The family that is going to live in our house has five children. Five. Think of it. You would like some brothers and sisters and like others less. That would just be the way of it. Father has given me more work to do. I think he thinks the busier I am the better. I don't know what to write, Thea. You said you wanted a letter but what do you want it to say?

There is something wrong with Georgie. Mother and Father won't tell me but I hear them talking. It's not hard, they think I'm a fool who doesn't know how to listen at a door but they're the fools. Father has said the same thing about him for months – 'that he is not quite right.' What do you think that means? Do you know that the police interviewed me? I wasn't scared, but Mother and Father were. We haven't seen Aunt Carrie or Uncle George since you left. I think Father has seen Uncle George, but I don't know for sure. We're paying for everything. I know that. The Orlando house will be smaller. That's what Mother says. But we haven't bought one yet. They're still looking. They wouldn't tell me this but I think we can't afford to buy a new house just yet. I think they have to wait.

I am bored here. I wish I had a friend.
Your Brother
Sam

I folded the letter into a hundred squares, until it wouldn't fold anymore, and then I unfolded it and looked at all the words, read it and reread it until I had it memorized. By accident; I would have preferred my brother's voice not be stuck in my head, a record playing the same song over and over and over until I wanted to scream. But I did not want to scream. I wanted to cry. To weep, like heroines did in novels. Mother had lied. Georgie was not fine. But I had wanted to believe her, and so I had.

I didn't know what it meant, his letter, except that he was lonely and angry. He hadn't been an angry person; all of this had made him angry, changed him into a different boy. I felt selfish, small, mean: I'd been sent away to a place where it was impossible to feel lonely. And Sam, well, he'd been made to stay, to be the only child in that world. And Georgie – how long had Sam known? How long had he borne that burden alone?

His letter, I decided, was a way to ask me to return. And at first I had wanted to go back. But now I did not. There was no future for me at home.

I rose and took Mother's earrings out of their red velvet box. They hurt to put in, but I had expected that. I hadn't worn earrings in months, not since I'd tried on Sissy's rubies. And then I hurried across the Square to Masters, where I knew Mr Holmes would be waiting.

At Masters, Mr Holmes led me to his library, but I did not follow.

'I want to go out back,' I said, 'like we did last time.'

'All right,' he said, 'whatever you wish.'

I led him through the house, and out the back porch. It was sunny, like it had been that other day, and I hoped the sunlight wouldn't be ruined for me forever. I hoped I would someday be able to not remember that day so clearly.

We walked up a steep trail, and I felt Mr Holmes touch the back of my thigh. I turned and smiled at him but kept walking. I knew he was wondering about my silence. But he needn't. I knew where I wanted to go. I knew what I wanted to do.

With Georgie it had felt like a violation, a thing we should not have done. A violation of what, I did not know. I knew that Georgie would never be the same again. I had known all along; Sam's letter had simply confirmed what I had suspected. A series of events. At first I thought I might have changed things, prevented the Atwell tragedy: there were so many ways it could have all been stopped. If I had not ridden, that day. If I had simply taken another route. If Sam had refused to go hunting with Georgie. If I had not cried like a little girl.

But I saw now that it had all started before I was even born. With two brothers, and their sons. A daughter, the odd girl out. And then we were all pressed on by circumstances that, at first, had nothing to do with us. Circumstances we responded to, badly, but did not create. The Miami land boon, which preyed upon my uncle's hopefulness; the Depression, which amplified my family's sense of being better than the rest of the world.

So to say it could have all turned differently: only God could say that. It was like saying I should never have been born, which was the only way, I saw now, that all of this could not have happened. One of us would have had to go: me, Georgie, Sam.

I stopped at the clearing and turned to face Mr Holmes. 'Thea,' he said, 'Thea.' He touched my earrings, the earrings that had been a gift from my mother. That Mother and Mr Holmes had touched the same thing without knowing seemed outrageous, sad, but also comforting.

Nearly a year ago, what had he seen when he approached the car? He had been waiting for us, for me. Watched my father, who seemed hesitant; watched him hesitantly wind his way behind his automobile, filthy from the journey; then me, I sprang out of the car before Father could open my door. Did he think that I was bold? That I was impertinent? Theodora Atwell, from Florida, who behaved indiscriminately – worse than that, very badly, and so was sent away. First my legs emerged from the car, a girl's legs. Then me, smaller than he thought, and pretty, with perfect posture. Or if not pretty, interesting-looking. Saw all this through the gloom of dusk. And then realized he had watched too long and hurried outside to greet us.

'Thea,' he said again. That was all he would say. Everything came to me by some sort of instinct I hadn't known I'd possessed.

I had done things, of course, but never this confidently, this easily. There was an ease between us, now, that felt so correct, and it seemed impossible that anyone other than he and I had ever felt like this before. I had never wanted Georgie like this.

I kissed him, hard, held his cheeks between my hands.

Then I pointed to the ground, and he understood, he understood exactly what I wanted and he lay down on the ground, on the dirt, and I unbuckled his belt and helped him slide out of his trousers.

I lowered myself onto him, and he was so large and solid inside of me, and I didn't want the feeling of that to end. The feeling that seemed to give me a reason for everything that I had done, starting with Georgie: for this, for this feeling that I was not alone. And even while the feeling burned bright in my brain I was sad, for I knew that this would be the first and last time we ever did this. And it did not seem possible, in this moment – I gripped his shoulders, and he pushed up my blouse and sucked my breasts, and pressed me to him – it did not seem possible that I would ever feel this way again. I stilled my hips for a moment, leaned down and kissed him. Both our bodies were slick with sweat.

'Don't stop,' he murmured, and I promised I wouldn't.

I watched his face, his half-lidded eyes; what had he loved when he was a child? Had he held his mother's hand as they navigated an icy street and been comforted by her touch? Had he loved his father's voice as he recited the blessing? He must miss these things now, the touch and sound that slipped so quickly from memory.

I moved faster, and he put his hands on my hips and pushed me down, down, down, into him; and then I was angled differently on top of him and closed my eyes against the pleasure of it, that feeling of hopefulness.

I didn't want to remove Georgie from my mind. I wanted to

remove that night, the following day. And that, I saw now, was impossible. The pain was part of the pleasure, and both were my memory of my cousin.

It was a beautiful morning the day of the show, the kind of morning that anticipates a beautiful day. If I often call the days here beautiful it's because they were, because I can think of no other way to describe them accurately except to simply call them beautiful, like a postcard, a painting, a thing not real.

I walked into the forest path with Sissy on one side, Mary Abbott on the other, her breeches sagging at her knees. Sissy had wound her limp hair into a tight knot. My show coat felt tight across my back when I lifted my arms. In two months I would have outgrown it. But I wasn't thinking of that, I wasn't thinking about a year from now, or even a day: I was thinking about the next hour, when I would jump in front of all these girls, and Mr Albrecht, and Mr Holmes.

Mr Holmes was standing at the gate with Decca. My body responded to him, now; it felt like there was a magnet embedded in my skin, telling me to go to him. But of course I would not, could not. I held my hand up in a wave, and looked away. I saw Leona's blond hair, woven into her tight braid; she counted the steps between a double.

I fell into place behind Leona, who was walking the course a second time. This irritated me; etiquette dictated it was someone else's turn. I counted the strides between each jump and tried to see the course from Naari's perspective, tried to anticipate what might frighten her – the potted plants that bookended each jump, the tents at the far end of the ring that shaded our lunch tables, the mere presence of all the people – so many things.

I was sore between my legs, but I knew from last time that the soreness would disappear quickly. And then all I would be left with was a memory, which would fade and fade and fade until I only had a memory of that memory. But Mr Holmes had changed me. I was a different girl, because of him.

I tried to focus on the jumps. I was impressed by the course, which Sissy's group had designed. The trickiest jumps in the advanced course were a water jump, which led into an oxer; and a triple combination that ended with a wall of bricks. The wall was the tallest and last jump of the course, designed as a final test. The bricks were fake, made out of lightweight wood, but the horses didn't know that: to them it was a solid obstacle.

Mr Albrecht blew his whistle, and I had to leave the ring before I'd had a chance to measure anything. I wanted to be angry with Leona, I knew the anger would help me win, but I couldn't. This would be her last time on King. She passed by and her cheeks looked pinker than usual, and I was actually shocked – she didn't seem the type to wear rouge.

I knew I should let her win. Sissy had even hinted as much. And I had laughed, told her that Leona would probably beat me fair and square. But I hoped that wasn't true.

Qualifying rounds went quickly. I warmed up in the adjoining ring and watched as the water jump claimed three girls before it was my turn: two third-years from Louisville and Martha Ladue. I'd drawn the third-to-last slot. Mr Holmes still held Decca; I couldn't see them very well, only their profiles, Mr Holmes's blocked by Decca's. There had already been one fall, a girl I didn't know well tossed after her horse refused the oxer.

There was a break halfway through the qualifying rounds. I tried to make my breathing even, tried to relax Naari with consistency. This was not a speed round – I needed to focus on accuracy. I closed my eyes and pictured each jump, counted the strides in between them.

When it was my turn, I timed my start perfectly; when Mr

Albrecht's whistle blew, I was lined up with the first jump. Naari rolled her eye at one of the pots, but I pushed her through my legs and she cleared it. I jumped like I always did: everything, everyone else disappeared. All the people watching were a blur. I focused on the sharp smell of Naari's sweat, her trembling movement between my legs.

I *knew* we had the last jump, I knew it for a fact, but then the bricks tumbled beneath us and I cursed Naari under my breath. She hadn't picked her legs up high enough. But we'd been fast.

Leona flew by us in a trot, so close she created her own private breeze as she passed. Naari wanted to trot, too, was nervous and wound up. I wanted to ask Mr Albrecht what my time was and I spotted him, his back turned, gesturing. He was talking to someone but I couldn't see who until I walked past, and when I did I saw that it was Mrs Holmes.

I watched Leona from a safe distance. My head throbbed, and my mouth was bone-dry. It's over, I whispered to Naari as we watched, but even then I did not quite believe it. Perhaps my eyes had deceived me. Perhaps my mind was playing tricks. But I knew the truth, which was simple: Mrs Holmes had come home a day early. People came home early all the time.

King cleared every jump, including the last combination, as if they were tiny playthings. His legs were miles long; he barely had to exert himself.

Sissy found me in Naari's stall, where she stood with her head hung low, exhausted. Sissy slipped in and swung the gate shut behind her. I patted Naari's rump. She would have a few hours to rest. The advanced class went first, and then last, so that their horses would have the most time to recover.

'Why are you down here?' she asked. Her cheeks were red, and her hair had fallen out of its bun. She was dressed completely in white, like we all were. I wasn't competing against Sissy, but she wasn't a threat to anyone. She wasn't good enough. She didn't care enough.

'I'm tired.'

'But there's lunch. Aren't you hungry?'

I followed Sissy's finger and saw girls in white, milling around. 'What kind of lunch?' I hated how plaintive my voice sounded.

'Sandwiches. But they're good.'

'Mrs Holmes is back.'

'I know.'

I held my throbbing forehead in my hand and would not look at her.

'I'm sad,' I said, finally.

'But you knew she would come back.' Her voice was soft.

'Yes,' I said. 'Yes. But isn't that always how it is? You can see it coming, but you can't stop it.'

She drew me to her in a hug, and I noticed how fiercely she did this, as if she was afraid I would refuse her. But I didn't. Nobody had hugged me last year, after Georgie. Nobody had touched me.

The three top finishers – me, Jettie, Leona – were in the jump-off. I was first, not an enviable position, but I was glad to go. We had to be fast. I knew it would be between me and Leona; I had always known that. King was bigger, a more gifted athlete, but Naari was faster, as she'd proved that night long ago; and more than that, she was smarter. King was dull, unflappable. But if I could make Naari nervous enough, she would go as fast as she had that night, and we would win.

In the warm-up ring, I kept my eyes on the tips of Naari's ears and walked her in circles, smaller and smaller until she was practically pirouetting. I wouldn't let her trot – I wanted to reserve every bit of her energy. I hadn't looked at Mr Holmes but oh, how he watched me. I could feel it. Mr Albrecht looked at me curiously as I passed him. I should have been warming her up slowly, gradually working into the course, but in the end rules were rules, and we both understood that. I could handle my horse however I pleased.

I wrapped the reins around my hands, something I had only heard about. It was stupid; if Naari refused a jump at the last instant, I would be pitched over her anyway, still attached to her by the reins; at the very least, I'd break both my arms. But I felt my old fearlessness rising up, as I always did before a difficult course. As I always did, when people were watching. And now this crowd included him and I felt so reckless; reckless, as I wrapped the reins so tightly around my hands the leather bit into my skin; reckless, as I heard Mr Albrecht's whistle and pressed Naari into a gallop.

I liked the fierce leverage wrapped reins brought; I bent my elbows and Naari slowed, quickly, and then I turned my toes out and dug my spurs into her sides, and I had her trapped, I had all her power harnessed between my legs and hands, beneath me. I'd never felt such energy, roiling beneath me like a violent wave.

We were going much too quickly; in a lesson Mr Albrecht would have shouted at me to reduce our speed by half. All the white-clad girls were a blurry crowd, interrupted every few feet by a house mistress's hat. If I'd wanted to find Mr Holmes in the crowd I couldn't have.

I splashed through the water jump, felt Naari change her footing, and knew, as she collected herself in preparation for the oxer ahead of us – and then as she soared over it, her ears flat against her head in concentration – that we understood each other: I wanted to win, and she wanted to be rid of me, this confusing girl on her back, goading her forward with sharp pains on her flank, then holding her back with a terrible pressure in the corner of her mouth; she tasted blood from the pressure of the see-sawing bit, which flattened her tongue against her teeth, made it difficult to breathe.

Naari snorted in frustration. 'Good,' I whispered to her, in beat to her canter, 'good, good, good,' and as we approached the last combination – it was a dirty trick, to put the tallest jump last – I flapped my legs against her sides and moved my hands up her neck, and she felt the relief in her mouth, in her brain, and leapt forward.

This was a speed round, so knocking down jumps didn't count against us, but I *needed* to clear this wall of bricks; I needed Mr Holmes to see me do it. As we were suspended above the last jump – for a second, two seconds – I closed my eyes and for an instant imagined I was at home again, on top of Sasi, jumping out back, jumping into the great and unknown beyond.

I had to circle her five times before she finally walked. The crowd was utterly silent. I had cleared everything.

Leona trotted in on King, ignored me completely. But Mr Albrecht caught my eye, and I noticed that all the girls around the ring were also watching: me, not Leona. I slapped Naari's neck and she flinched.

'Cool her down well,' Mr Albrecht murmured as we passed.

I nodded. I tried not to notice that everyone was staring. Mary Abbott stood by the entrance, and as I passed she grabbed my rein.

'No,' I said, furious, 'let go.'

'What a ride,' she said, in a singsong voice, 'what a ride. Good girl,' she said to Naari.

'Don't touch her.'

Mary Abbott looked up at me, unsurprised, blew her bangs out of her face as she considered me. 'If there's a jump-off I bet you'll win that, too. You'll win everything today, if I had to guess.'

'Leave me alone,' I whispered, and nudged Naari into a trot, pulling her back into a walk when I had passed the crowd. I slid off her back and began to walk her in a circle again, watching Leona from a safe distance.

'You're fine,' I murmured to Naari, but she didn't respond, hung her head low, almost to the ground. I tried to dry the sweat from the raw places I'd spurred into her sides, each the size of a dime, but she flinched at my touch. I felt so horribly sorry, suddenly. For all of this.

A first-year I didn't know by name – Holly? – scurried past, stared at Naari with wide eyes. When I tried to catch her eye, she looked away. Naari shuddered as a breeze swept past us, the air cool on her hot skin. The gentle, rushing sound of branches was all around us, and I felt suddenly calm, empty, free of whatever violent force had possessed me. I stroked Naari's neck and wanted nothing more than to be magically transported back to my bed, a soft quilt pulled to my neck.

It was hard to tell how fast Leona and King were going – he was so lanky he always seemed to be moving slowly, as if through water. They were a beautiful pair, Leona and King; I couldn't help but admire them, the sheen of Leona's navy boots a glossy contrast to King's burnished coat. They were like royalty, I thought. Yonahlossee royalty. And soon they would mean nothing to this place, a barely remembered girl and her horse.

Again King cleared the final combination as if it were nothing.

The top three finishers – me, Jettie, Leona – filed into the ring. No one knew our times. I spoke softly to Naari, who pranced and arched her neck; Leona glared at me as Naari tried to overtake King.

'Check her!' she commanded. Leona would be fine, I knew; it seemed as if she could weather any of life's storms.

'Why do you always have to be first?' I asked. This was easily becoming the second worst day of my life but the flash of shock on Leona's chiseled face was satisfying. 'I think I'll go first, this time,' I said, and pushed Naari ahead of King.

I saw Henny next to the entrance of the gate, chatting excitedly with someone I didn't recognize until she turned her head and looked at me. Mrs Holmes. Everything about her was shorter: her hair, which hung in a loose, small bun; her skirt, which no longer brushed the ground; her shirt, which was no longer fastened shut at the neck with a cameo but revealed a little bit of her pale skin. I felt dizzy, leaned forward in my saddle too quickly, as if I might faint.

'Are you well, Thea?' Mrs Holmes asked. I looked at her, my mouth open. I could not hide my surprise. She looked fresher, as if she had returned from a spa. I could see how she had been pretty in her youth. Not beautiful, but pretty in a pert, compact way. I felt sick to my stomach.

'Yes, Thea,' Henny said, and her voice was cold. 'Are you well?'

I nodded and walked past, avoided meeting Mrs Holmes's gaze, ignored Henny's admonishment.

'Thea,' she called, 'have you forgotten your manners entirely?' But I couldn't face Mrs Holmes; I couldn't, not for anything, pretend to like her.

I had forgotten, of course, I'd forgotten everything. I'd forgotten she would return, lay claim to her husband, her life here. And yet, as I followed Jettie into the ring, I still wanted to win.

We all turned our horses to face Mr Albrecht and Rachel, who was awarding the garlands to our class. She smiled at me, her face freckled by the sun. She'd been gone for a month, but I guessed being the headmaster's daughter afforded you certain privileges. Mr Albrecht had his arm around Rachel; protectively, I thought. She was still loved, here. Her cheeks were rosy and she looked hopeful. Of course she was hopeful. Her parents reunited, her family of one piece again. I saw Molly in the front row, chattering excitedly with another first-year. All the first-years still seemed like fillies, their wispy hair and long limbs. They didn't seem to know where to put their hands and feet when they walked, how to control their legs that had grown so long so quickly.

'In a moment,' Mr Albrecht announced, and the crowd fell silent, 'we will have our results.'

Jettie was muttering to herself, furiously, and I turned and looked at her.

'Always staring,' she said, when she caught me looking, which was something Henny had said to me once. I was silent, closed my eyes against all the people watching us.

When I opened them again I saw a mass of faces, all watching solemnly. This meant so much to all of us. I saw Martha conferring with Henny, and quiet Alice Hunt watching attentively. Molly, chewing on a fingernail. I knew so little about any of them, except Sissy. I knew enough about Eva to call her a friend.

Rachel caught my eye and then looked away, quickly, and I knew that I had won.

'And this has never happened before,' Mr Albrecht began, standing in front of us, addressing the crowd. He could have been any man, from the back, his heavy English the only clue that he was not like the rest of us. 'We have never before given the prize to a new girl.' He paused. I saw Henny whisper something to Mrs Holmes, who shook her head. Everyone knew it was me now, of course; Mary Abbott beamed, and Katherine Hayes eyed me with interest. I watched Mrs Holmes so I would not look at her husband, who I knew was standing near the back of the crowd, Decca on his hip. Mrs Holmes watched me as well, a calm expression on her face.

'Horseback riding,' Mr Albrecht continued, 'is, if I may say so, a true partnership between human and beast, between the power of a person's mind and the sheer force of a horse's strength.'

'Get on with it,' Leona muttered quietly.

'And all is fair in the jumping ring, where there cannot be favorites, where what matters is skill and speed, in that order. Girls, it is a lesson that is well suited to life: in all your endeavors strive hard, and honestly, and great rewards will be yours.'

He took the simplest garland from Rachel, where they hung on her arm in a neat row. He pinned the garland of greenery around the neck of Jettie's horse, who flattened his ears and bared his teeth. Then a garland around King's neck, who stood patiently as Mr Albrecht fiddled with the clasp.

'And our winner today, Theodora Atwell from Emathla, Florida, who has impressed us all with her daring and skill.' Mr Holmes entered the ring, passed by his wife and Henny with a nod of his head.

He pinched Rachel's cheek after he took the garland from her arm, and she turned her face in embarrassment. Panic swelled in my throat. I didn't want him so close, but then there he was, so near I could see the part in his dark hair. Another Yonahlossee tradition.

'Thea,' he murmured, 'well done.' He patted Naari's neck, gingerly, as only a person unacquainted with a horse would do. Then he fastened the garland around Naari's neck. Forsythia dotted with purple creeping phlox, the first bloom of each. And who would have thought that such an unlikely combination – the former so startling, almost electric; the latter so delicate – would have been beautiful? Mrs Holmes would have thought of it. Mrs Holmes was back in time to tend to her garden.

She was tending to Decca now, in the crowd, dark and lovely Decca. Mrs Holmes did not deserve what I had done.

King backed up, suddenly wary of the garland, and Leona dug her spurs into his sides. Mr Holmes hurried Rachel over to the side of the ring. My mouth was very dry; to deny myself water was a punishment, the best one I could think of right now.

'It is fine, King,' Mr Albrecht said, and King's ears darted in his direction, and I felt so sorry for him, his master turned cruel over a loss he could not comprehend. I clucked, and King turned his head in my direction, eager for comfort, and Leona's face, for the first time, was easy to decipher: I should not have won. I knew in my bones that this was all over.

In books it was more of a gradual dawning, a slow and painful recognition. But I knew in an instant that Leona wanted to do me harm any way she could. I had gotten in the way of the one thing in the world she cared about: her last chance.

And I would not take it back. I would die before I'd lose. I was so good on a horse because I was fearless. I had always impressed people with my willingness to try jumps that were too high and wide for such a small girl. And now I licked my chapped lips and sought out Mr Holmes. He held Rachel's hand at the edge of the ring. Everyone was watching Leona, who was making a spectacle of herself, spurring King into a frenzy. But Mr Holmes watched me, as I knew he would. When I met his eyes he shook his head, sadly, and if I could have turned a knife in my heart, I would have.

Instead I waited, like a good girl, waited for Jettie, then Leona, to complete her victory lap, then took my own, the applause thunderous, like a warning; waited for the photographer to take my picture, waited for Mr Holmes to disappear with his family into the woods. Waited while a hundred girls congratulated me, my ugly riding forgiven.

'Oh, how pretty,' they said, and touched Naari's neck, one by one.

Then I guided Naari out of the ring, walked past the barn and up the mountain on a trail that wound its way through the forest for a few miles before you came to a clearing. It was the only trail that didn't take you back, eventually, to the barn – it went all the way to Asheville via an old mining road. Or so I'd heard.

I gave Naari her head and untied my garland, the forsythia already bent, the phlox bruised, and dropped it somewhere in the woods. I'd ridden my horse too hard, with everyone watching. I didn't regret that. I'd ridden too hard for this particular competition, but I'd won.

I came to the first clearing and dismounted. The air was so sharp and clear it pinched my throat to breathe deeply. Naari rested her muzzle in my palm, an unusually affectionate gesture for her. I knew it was an affection borne of exhaustion, of uncertainty – we weren't anywhere she recognized – but I was grateful. I put my palm on her wide forehead, traced a circle around her liquid eye.

I was fearless. It was a trait that served me well in the ring, and badly in life.

I chose one of Sissy's dresses from her closet, which was bursting with this season's fine silks and satins. Her mother had just sent them. Sissy was embarrassed by the riches, but she shouldn't have been. A new dress would make her an object of envy, not scorn; it meant she was safe. She would not be plucked from this place, like Leona. The dress I chose was formal, hit my ankles.

'Do you want a necklace?' Eva asked.

'I don't think so.' I watched myself in the mirror, which was too small to see my entire reflection at once. My hair was dirty, I hadn't washed it in almost a week, but it looked very heavy, dully auburn. I took a step back and addressed my body, the green satin clung to my hips in a way Mother would have considered immodest. The dress was tight across the chest, flattened my breasts. I wasn't sure if the effect was strange or attractive. The straps were off the shoulder, and I couldn't get rid of the feeling that they were falling.

I wore Mother's earrings again. For the first time I wore jewelry that competed.

I left the cabin before everyone else. They were still applying the bits of makeup they hoped Mrs Holmes wouldn't notice: swipes of rouge and powder, light lipstick. I hadn't wanted any, and I was avoiding Sissy; that I was able to slip out of the cabin unnoticed seemed like an extraordinary bit of luck. I was buoyed by this feeling as I walked through the Square, lost myself in the crowd of girls headed to the Castle. It was seven o'clock in the evening, twilight, and the light softened us. The Holmeses stood at the entrance, which was festooned with navy and yellow ribbons, but I was calm. The girls were with them, clustered around their father.

I ached with a sadness that had nothing to do with him: they were a family presenting a unified front, even with their secret divisions and sorrows. Suddenly I wanted my twin very badly, was moved almost to tears by jealousy. I straightened myself, felt to make sure my hair was in place, those straps. What would our reunion be like, when it came? Would he be happy to see me? It didn't seem possible.

'Our champion,' Mrs Holmes said at the door. And because Mr Holmes stood behind his wife, she could not tell how he avoided my eyes.

'Thank you,' I said, even though she hadn't exactly congratulated me. I looked at the girls. They all watched me, Rachel especially.

'Are you glad to be back?' My voice was surprisingly steady. 'To see your father?'

They all nodded. 'We had fun with my grandparents,' Sarabeth said.

'So much fun,' Rachel echoed.

'They all had a grand time,' Mrs Holmes said. 'And I met with so many old Yonahlossee girls.' She smiled. 'There are so many of you, scattered across the South.'

It took me a minute to identify the you to whom Mrs Holmes referred – but of course. I was a Yonahlossee girl now.

Seeing them was not as hard as I had thought it would be. In fact, the sight of them brought relief: I had not ruined the Holmeses.

'Well,' I said, and turned my head to see if another girl was coming, to look away so that I would not see Mr Holmes so calmly ignoring me. Molly and Henny were at the bottom of the stairs, Molly chattering, Henny half-paying attention. I turned back to the Holmeses, curtsied, and slipped through the doors held open by Docey and Emmy, the first time I'd seen them together. And there was a resemblance, in the way they each held themselves, in the way their heads sat on their necks, the way their hands darted quickly about. I smiled at them. Docey smiled back, but Emmy pretended she hadn't seen me.

The dining hall was beautifully decorated, the flowers from the show transported here. Mrs Holmes had only been back a day, and already she had organized things, put everything back into its proper place.

The boys all stood at the other end of the dining hall in suits, colorful bow ties at their necks, and I felt very conscious of the length and formality of my dress. Everyone else wore shorter, more formless dresses – Sissy had raised her eyebrows at my choice but I had chosen it anyway, and why? Why had I wanted everyone to look at me? I felt their eyes, a hundred eyes, track me across the dance floor. Yet it was not an entirely unpleasant feeling. I imagined Sam in their midst, waiting to dance with a girl. They should have sent him away, too; didn't they know how

unfair it would seem, to let me go someplace but not him? They
were fools, like Sam had said.

Sissy came through the doors with Eva. She glanced over at
the crowd of boys, quickly, and I wished she weren't so obvious,
I wished her heart had been a little less on her sleeve that night.

'Is everything all right?' Sissy asked when she reached me. I
noted her earrings, the ruby studs that I had found while I sneaked
around our Augusta House, almost a year ago. How time flew.

I nodded, and bit into a tiny berry tartlet, hot from the oven,
and the butter melted on my tongue. The music started, and boys
began to approach. We stood there awkwardly, Sissy watching me
closely, me pretending she wasn't. Why did she think I could so
easily transfer my affections to someone else? Then, as if
summoned, David appeared, as tall and handsome as the last
time.

'Thea? We meet again.'

'David.' He was the kind of boy who refused to be refused.
'You're here.' An idiotic thing to say. Surely I could have come up
with something better than that.

'I am.'

I let him lead me into the throng of dancers, fold my hand into
his, place his other hand on the small of my back. Mr Holmes was
taller than he was. Katherine Hayes was wearing a bright red
dress, had painted her lips bright red to match. That was bold, to
so flagrantly wear lipstick. But Katherine was nothing if not bold.

David was silent, led me fairly gracefully around the dance
floor.

'Do you like this song?' he asked when the band finished the
first song and started another.

'I like it well enough,' I answered. He looked away, and I
thought my tone was too harsh, but then I felt his fingers fan
across my back.

'How has this year treated you?' he asked.

'Let's just dance,' I said, and smiled to soften my request.

He pulled me closer, and I wanted to rest my head on his shoulder, close the little distance left between us. So I did. I rested my head on this strange boy's shoulder and let him pull me, guide me around the Castle, that place where I'd eaten hundreds of meals, said a hundred prayers. I wasn't afraid of being caught this time. The lights were dim, we were surrounded by dozens of other dancing couples, it wasn't a risk. He smelled faintly of cologne.

The song ended and he stopped and held me by the hand, seemed reluctant to let me go. I smiled apologetically, turned toward the last place I had seen Mr Holmes, and instead I saw Mrs Holmes, who stared at me without the slightest trace of kindness. I had to look away, finally, because she would not. I caught David's jacket sleeve.

'Another one?' I asked, and he seemed surprised. I threw myself into the rest of the night, took only one break from dancing, followed David and Boone and Sissy into the far corner and sipped from a flask of whiskey. Sissy took one swallow; I took as much as I could handle. After the whiskey I felt lovely, I felt like a lovely girl with a smooth neck and bright lips. I could feel David watching me as I tilted the flask to my lips, and I was glad I'd worn this dress.

Leona wasn't there. I'd looked, and she wasn't easy to miss. And maybe it was the whiskey, but I felt bold enough to forget about her, to put her out of my mind. Perhaps I had imagined the threat: she didn't know anything, not for certain, and could she really bring a rumor about me and Mr Holmes to his wife? She would have to have proof.

'What are you doing?' Sissy whispered, when we switched partners, but she grinned as she said it.

'Nothing,' I mouthed back. I fell into Boone's grip, then; he swung me away from Sissy. Boone and I were both a little drunk. Up close, Boone looked a little startling, with his shock of red hair. But more than his hair it was his skin, translucent in that redhead way. Thin green veins framed each eye.

'Are you having fun?'

'Yes,' he said, and turned me out for a twirl. He was a good dancer.

'Sissy's made quite the catch.'

He smiled. 'Has she? Funny, I was thinking the same thing about my own catch.'

It was a strange thing, to be held like this, close enough to smell the pomade Boone used in his hair, but with the implicit understanding that this was all quite platonic. Boone had on his face a bland smile he must reserve for girls who weren't Sissy. I looked at his beige trousers, light enough that I could see clearly where they wrinkled, and I wondered who clothed this boy. His mother, when he visited home? Did she bring him to a seamstress, wait while measurements were taken, then carefully flip through swatches of fabric? Did she think that by clothing him well she sent him out into the world prepared?

'Do you love her?'

He smiled and the skin around his eyes multiplied. 'Yes,' he said, and paused. 'Are you all right Thea?' He looked concerned. 'It's only – that's such an odd question.'

My cheeks burned. He was so nice, Boone. My heart ached against his niceness. He looked across the dance floor at something, and when I followed his gaze I saw he was looking at Mr Holmes, who was helping Mrs Holmes cut an enormous sheet cake, decorated with sugared rose petals; she slid a piece off her serving knife onto the plate he held, and then he had another plate ready in an instant. Boone looked from him to me, and I bowed my head.

'It'll be all right,' Boone said quietly, and I said nothing, just let Boone hold me in his kind, chaste embrace.

He gave me back to David, and I danced with him until it was time to leave. The band played a slow song, something with a melancholy tune, and David was telling me how much he liked me and I looked beyond his shoulder and watched the other couples.

Sissy was pressed into a corner by Boone, and I was surprised they were being so bold; Sissy must have been drunker than I thought to throw her decorum to the wind like that. Or maybe it was a Yonahlossee effect, throwing one's decorum to the wind.

I felt Mr Holmes staring before I turned around to acknowledge him. There was only one corner of the room where I hadn't looked, and that was where he would be, and then I turned so I could see if his expression matched the one I had imagined for him, if he stood casually, also like I'd imagined, and just as our eyes met he turned his cheek and left the room. I was stung. It was still mid-song but I muttered something to David about collecting my things.

He held on to my hand by the fingertips again and I yanked it from him, more forcefully than I'd intended, and his face hardened.

'You're a tease,' he said loudly, and I realized that he was both drunk and angry. It was on my lips to apologize, but then I spoke.

'You're just a silly boy,' I said, and David's face crumpled, and he did look like a silly boy, but I couldn't worry about him now. I hurried away and realized I had no things to collect, nothing to keep me here so I wouldn't have to go outside, where Mr Holmes would be waiting. Or worse, wouldn't be. The room looked dismal, the refreshment table littered with dirty glasses and plates, a wedge of cake disfigured on a stand. Docey was cleaning up, swaying to the tune of the sad song.

'Good-bye, Docey,' I said, because there was nothing else to say, because I felt horribly out of sorts and embarrassed.

She smiled at me and held up her hand in a wave, a wistful expression on her face.

I hurried down the stairs and I would have left, but Mr Holmes called my name. I knew then that Mrs Holmes was gone. He drew me into a shadow, outside the light that the gas lamp projected.

'What do you want?'

He looked taken aback but then he gathered himself, visibly, a slow rolling of his body, as if he were preparing to give a speech. 'Did you have fun tonight?' This was the public Henry Holmes, not the one I loved. His tie was neatly tied, his hair combed flat. I noticed that his hair had been trimmed, and of everything that had happened this day, this was the worst, by far, to see his hair resting in such straight lines against his skin, to know exactly who had trimmed it, that it would be months before his bangs fell into his eyes again.

'What do you think?'

He shook his head. 'No.' He stopped, rested a palm on the wooden shingle behind him so that he stood in a contorted position. I wanted him, but I could never have him again.

He started to speak, but I stopped him.

'There is nothing to say,' I said. 'Not really.'

He smiled. 'There are so many things to say, Thea. Too many.'

'Then let's not say any of them.' I looked at my hands, still red from my ride today. I should wear gloves, but they dulled my connection to the bit. 'I am leaving,' I said. 'I have to, now.'

'You don't—'

'No,' I said, and just then Miss Brooks emerged from the Castle, and saw us immediately. Mr Holmes waved, and Miss Brooks looked at us curiously, and I wondered if everyone knew or if the idea of it was too unimaginable for someone as nice as Miss Brooks.

Once she had disappeared into the Square, I turned back to Mr Holmes.

'You were right,' I said. 'I grew to love this place. I do love it. It's so beautiful.'

'Then stay, Thea. Let it continue to be beautiful. Don't punish yourself by leaving.'

'I'm not. I've been punished enough, I think. It was a punishment, to be sent here, but that's not the way it ended up, is it? I came here under such bad circumstances, and now I'm leaving under such good ones.'

'Are you?'

'Yes,' I said, and I wanted so badly to touch him, but knew I could not, so instead I repeated my answer, and tried to make my voice emphatic, so that he would remember that he had helped me: 'Yes.'

'Where will you go?'

'Home,' I said. 'Home.'

CHAPTER
TWENTY-ONE

When I returned from the party, the rest of the girls in Augusta House were up, in various stages of preparing for bed. Sissy was gone, was fearless, at least for tonight. I slipped under the covers with my borrowed dress still on. Mary Abbott watched me, but no one else noticed.

'Did you have fun?'

I nodded. My eyes were closed, but it sounded like Eva was hanging her head over her bunk. 'Did you?'

'Yes . . .' She trailed off. I thought she was finished when she spoke again: 'I'll be so sad when we go away from here, no more dances.'

'I see many more dances in your life.'

'But they won't be like these,' she said.

For better or worse, I thought. 'No. You're so dreamy, Eva. Always dreaming about someplace else.' That wasn't quite what I had meant to say, but I couldn't articulate what I felt. 'You'll always be like this.'

'Like what?' Mary Abbott asked.

'Young and beautiful,' I said, and Eva laughed. I had pleased her. 'Young and perfect.'

After everyone's breathing had reached a steady pitch, I went to Sissy's bed and lay there for an hour or so – of course I was fooling no one. I must have fallen asleep, because I opened my eyes and was startled, then relieved by the darkness. I walked heavily across the room and poured myself a full glass of water, drank it and poured another.

Before the lights had been turned off, Mary Abbott had asked where Sissy was, if we ought to tell a house mistress. Eva had laughed, and told Mary Abbott not to worry. After all our precautions, I felt a flash of anger; even I was being more careful than Sissy. She was taking foolish risks.

The next morning I came to the Castle just as prayer was ending, and picked my way through the throng traveling to classes. Girls seemed to part in my presence, as if they were a herd of horses and I was a snake. Katherine Hayes and an Atlanta girl whispered to each other; Katherine raised her eyebrows as only she could as I passed. But Leona, who stood alone at the edge of the crowd, watched me impassively, and something about how she stood gave me hope: perhaps this was all my imagination.

I felt a hand in mine. Rachel.

'Hello,' she whispered, and squeezed my hand. 'Are you going to teach us again?'

I gathered her in a hug and kissed the top of her forehead. 'I missed you.'

Rachel smiled up at me, abashed, and I told her that we'd see about the lessons. She left and I saw that Mr Holmes was watching me from his place at the lectern.

He looked at me sadly, and all the girls and their eyes disappeared. I would never be alone with him again.

I felt someone at my side: Sissy. She looked to where I was looking, then back at me again.

'Come,' she said. 'Let's go to class.'

Later that afternoon, on our way to the barn, Sissy seemed giddy, and it was not hard to guess why.

'Boone and I are engaged,' she told me as we walked, me with my hand shading my eyes, 'secretly.'

I squeezed her hand. 'That's wonderful. I wish you all the happiness in the world.' And I did, that was true – Sissy's shining eyes seemed proof of something.

There were only a few girls outside but it was not my imagination, now: Sissy did not seem to notice – the soothing effects of love, I supposed – but they all stared. I tried not to look but that was impossible. When I waved at Molly, she hurried away like a worried mouse. I almost laughed; as if I were in a position to frighten anyone.

'People are looking,' I said to Sissy.

'Are they?' She surveyed the Square. 'I don't think so. Maybe they're just glad to see you.' But there her tone was off; she was lying, clearly.

When we were almost at the barn we saw Gates, leading her pretty chestnut to the ring.

'Gates,' Sissy called, and Gates turned. When she saw us, her face tautened; she looked stricken, as if she had seen a ghost. Her horse looked at us attentively, his ears flipped forward.

'Hello,' she called out, her voice tremulous. Her horse whuffed into her shoulder, and Gates gave a small smile before she walked on. But Sissy spoke again.

'Wait,' she cried, 'wait!'

'Sissy,' I whispered furiously. Other girls were looking, now. I saw Henny eyeing the situation curiously, her head cocked, Jettie at her side, always at her side. I watched them for a second. It dawned on me that Jettie loved Henny. But then I hurried after Sissy, who was marching toward Gates.

'Is there something I should know, Gates?' she asked, her

voice steely. 'Some reason you're ignoring me?'

Gates shook her head, and I felt sorry for her. She wasn't ignoring Sissy; she was ignoring me. She was kind, Gates – right now she kicked at the dirt and looked like she might cry. I smoothed her horse's red forelock down between his eyes, and he looked at me warily. 'It's okay,' I murmured.

And to Sissy: 'It's not you. Leave her alone,' I said. 'It's me,' I added, in a whisper.

'But we walk together!' Sissy cried furiously, and she made me glad I had come, still, willing to be confined in this place if it meant finding Sissy. I looked at Gates and saw what Sissy did: a spineless girl.

'I've known you since you were twelve, Gates Weeks! You should be ashamed.' I saw Mr Albrecht coming toward us and pulled Sissy away. We almost ran into Alice Hunt, who led her giant bay; she managed not to acknowledge our presence.

'Sissy,' I said, after I had pulled her into Naari's stall, and she had brooded silently for a few minutes. I was untangling the knots in Naari's tail to give me something to do – whatever else happened in the world, there were always knots in a horse's tail. 'I'm going to leave, but you'll stay. Don't make an enemy out of everyone.'

'You can't leave,' she said. 'And why would you want to?'

'It's time.'

Sissy looked like she might cry. But when she spoke she was angry.

'It's not that simple. You can't just pick up and leave.'

'I'll think of something,' I said.

'I wish you'd never met Mr Holmes,' Sissy continued. 'I wish Mrs Holmes hadn't left. I hate him,' she said, and looked up at me, her cheeks burning. 'I know you don't hate him, so I hate him twice as much.'

'He's—' I started, but Sissy shook her head.

'Please don't,' she said. 'I'll always hate him. It's wrong,' she said. 'All wrong. You could have loved someone else.' I watched her for a moment, my good and true friend, her brown hair tucked behind her ears, her cheeks still scarlet, her forehead creased in anger. She meant I could have loved David; she meant I could have been more like her.

'I loved another boy before I came here.'

'I know that,' she said impatiently. But she didn't know. I had never even told her I had a cousin.

'You don't know the boy was my cousin. And not a cousin I never knew, a cousin twice removed who lived in another state.' I spoke quickly – I had to say it all at once, or not at all. 'He was like a brother to me.'

Sissy said nothing, only watched me, so I continued, half out of fear, half out of relief, because the telling felt so good, and as I spoke I remembered that telling had this power, this sweet release I had not experienced in such a long time. When I was little, my eardrum had burst from an infection, and though the pus and blood that streamed down my neck horrified Sam, who had run for Mother, I had felt nothing but relief from a pain that had come upon me so gradually I hadn't even known my ear was hurt. And this was the same, but with the heart.

'My brother found out.'

'Sam,' Sissy said softly.

'Sam. My cousin told him. There was a fight, between my cousin and Sam. A horrible one.' My voice broke. 'That's why I was sent away.'

'Was Sam sent away, too?' When I didn't answer she lifted my chin up with her finger, like Mother would have.

I shook my head. 'I'm not a right girl.'

'A right girl,' she said. Her husky voice was soft. 'I wonder what that is, or where we would find her.'

'You don't understand,' I said, finally.

'No?' she asked. 'I understand enough, I think. We don't choose who we love, do we?' She smiled, and I knew she was thinking of Boone. 'We don't choose our families, either. But you can choose to be angry at least.' She took my hand and squeezed it, hard.

'Ow,' I said, but she would not let go.

'Don't let your family decide the rest of your life.'

'That's what Mr Holmes said.'

'Then we agree on something, he and I. What do you think you're going to do?' she asked. 'You're just a girl.'

'I know,' I said quietly. 'I'm just a girl. But I'm his sister, too. I need to see my brother. He did nothing wrong.'

'Neither did you.'

She dropped my hand, and drew me to her. She smelled unusual, of sweat and dirt. 'You've been unlucky so far,' she whispered into my ear, 'but luck changes, all the time. God grants happiness only to those who seek it.'

Mary Abbott came back to the cabin while everyone else was at the Hall. This was when I would be with Mr Holmes, at Masters. It wouldn't be long until Mrs Holmes noticed my absence, observed that I wasn't studying enough. I needed to leave before that happened.

Mary Abbott looked at me for a long time, her head at an angle. 'What's the matter with you?'

'Why do you care?' I snapped.

She looked away and said nothing.

'I'm sorry. I'm tired. I need to sleep.'

'But that's all you do now. Sleep. We are friends, aren't we?'

'Yes, Mary Abbott.' Why had Mary Abbott chosen me? Why

not Eva, or Gates? Or Sissy? Sissy surely would have been nicer, would have known how to handle her. 'What do you need?' I felt like I was daring her to tell me that everyone knew about me and Mr Holmes, that all of camp was talking.

She lowered herself onto the edge of my bed. 'Someone saw Sissy in the woods last night,' she whispered, even though we were alone. 'Did you know she was there? With a boy. Everyone's talking. The rumor's that Mrs Holmes knows.'

I sat up, so that my face was only an inch from hers. 'Who, Mary Abbott? Who saw Sissy?' Today played quickly through my mind: all the girls turning away, but not from me; all the girls staring, but not at me.

But Mary Abbott didn't know, or wouldn't tell me. She looked worried, and I wondered if she was afraid of Leona. Because I knew who had told. Leona, who hadn't been at the dance, who had probably been at the barn; walking back, she could have so easily seen Sissy and Boone. She was the only girl I knew here who would tell on Sissy. Who would hurt another girl so terribly in order to hurt me.

But anyone could have seen Sissy last night – she had been so careless. I felt a flash of anger, again. How could she have been so careless? I looked at Mary Abbott, who picked at my bedspread. Could it have been her? I didn't think so – I had always been her focus, her eyes burning so consistently into my back it felt like a strange sort of plague. Me, not Sissy.

I took Naari into the mountains that night while everyone else was at dinner. The light lasted until eight o'clock these days, and so I stayed out until I could see the faint outline of the stars.

It was so easy to close my eyes and see Sissy's fine brown hair, her wide-set eyes; I could see her face more vividly than I could my mother's, my brother's, my father's. When I left I would ask for a photograph. Mary Abbott said Sissy would be sent home in the next day or so, now that word was starting to spread, and though I didn't particularly trust Mary Abbott, I knew she was right. Mrs Holmes would find out; she always did. And if Sissy were sent home because of a boy, she would never be allowed to marry that boy, the one who had shamed her, marked her otherwise pristine reputation. All her plans, all her life, in shambles. She who had been so sure just yesterday of how my family should have acted. Who could say what her family would do, would think of her, regardless of how she might defend herself? Certainly not Sissy herself. Not having permission to marry Boone might be the least of Sissy's troubles.

I saw Mr Albrecht's silhouette in the barn as I dismounted. It was too late to remount and ride around until he disappeared.

'Thea,' he said, and nodded.

'Hello.'

'No more classes for you. Just the nightly trail rides.'

I shrugged. His accent lent such a strange rhythm to his speech.

'I don't think I've had a chance to congratulate you on your success,' he said, and extended his hand, 'well done.'

I let him shake my hand, his coarse palm around my small, relatively soft one. 'Thank you.' And I felt near tears again, inexplicably. I placed my other palm on Naari's broad forehead. It would be as if I had died, once my scent disappeared, once she learned to stop expecting the sound of my boots against the floor in the afternoons, once she became used to the noises and smells of another girl. But I would always remember my first horse. I would never forget.

Mr Albrecht looked at me for what seemed like a long moment. 'You're a talented horsewoman. You could stay with it.' He stressed the word *stay*, because of his accent.

'And do what?'

'You could do things that have not been done before,' he said, still holding my hand.

I looked away. 'Perhaps.'

There was still kindness in the world, at Yonahlossee. It almost seemed irrelevant.

CHAPTER TWENTY-TWO

I rose early the next morning and dressed carefully, tucked my shirt neatly into my skirt, polished a scuffmark from my boot. I looked over at Sissy, who was sleeping on her back, her arms flung out beside her. I smiled. Last night she had told me that girls knew about her and Boone; she didn't seem worried, though. She'd seemed a little bit proud. I'd acted surprised. She clearly had no idea of how far the rumor had traveled, how it had snaked its way through camp to Mrs Holmes's ears.

As I examined myself in the mirror I was nearly certain I could feel Mary Abbott watching me, but when I turned around and looked her eyes were shut, her mouth closed in a thin line.

I got to the Castle early, to catch Mrs Holmes before breakfast. The dining hall was nearly empty, except for a few second-years sitting at a table. I took the long way around them, and as I was passing the kitchen, the door swung open.

'Hello,' Emmy said, and looked away, down to a spot on the floor. She carried a tray full of glasses, a dishtowel slung over her shoulder. The door swung shut behind her.

I said nothing, and began to walk by when she spoke again.

'Aren't you going to say hello to me?'

'Hello,' I said. 'Hello, hello, hello. I'm on my way to see Mrs Holmes.'

Emmy gave a short laugh. We had never really spoken before. She held herself more elegantly than her sister, didn't have the wandering eye, but their voices were the same, high, so thickly accented I had to pay attention to understand them.

'Docey feels poorly for you.' She shifted the tray in her hands.

'Pardon?'

'My sister. She feels poorly for you.' She spoke quickly, almost impatiently.

'Oh,' I said, at a loss.

'But we have a different feeling about this,' she continued, 'I was there. You can say what you will about Mrs Holmes, and girls always do, but she's a good soul. A good soul,' she repeated firmly, almost primly.

I thought about all those afternoons in the library, Emmy lurking behind closed doors. I leaned against the wall, a cold sweat on my brow.

'Does she know?' I asked quietly. I turned and stared at the table of second-years watching us; nobody conversed with the servants here. But this table I could handle – these girls were from Kentucky, and they looked away quickly.

'Isn't that something you should have thought on before?' She shifted the tray again. Her arms trembled, and I almost reached out to take it from her.

She waited, as if for an answer. I looked from the tray, crowded with glasses, to her face, watching me imperiously.

'Thought on?' I asked, and Emmy lowered her eyes. I had shamed her, and it had been so easy. 'This isn't any of your business.'

As I began to walk away for the second time, Emmy shrugged. 'Not from me she doesn't. Know,' she added.

I was glad no one had heard me mock Emmy, a servant, born with none of the advantages I had known since birth. I'd never once thought of her as someone who could be cutting. But just now I could have been sparring with Leona, or Katherine Hayes.

I turned around before I entered the stairwell and saw Emmy setting out the glasses on the table where the second-years sat, her eyes downcast, her face expressionless. Then I saw Henny, sitting at our table, a book in front of her. She saw me and I instinctively held my hand up in a wave, before I could think better of it. Henny only raised her eyebrows.

Even though I had more serious problems than Henny's cold shoulder, I still cared. If Yonahlossee had taught me anything, it had taught me that it was impossible not to care, not to marvel at the mysteries of girls' affections, which were hard won and easily lost. If no one knew about me and Mr Holmes, then why was Henny acting so coldly?

It was a question that occupied my mind as I climbed the stairs, slowly, half-hoping she wouldn't be there. But then I'd just have to come back.

'Thea,' Mrs Holmes said, and looked up from her desk as I passed through her door. She pointed to the chair as if she had been expecting me. Mr Holmes stood behind his wife, looking out her window, but when he heard my name he turned around, his hands in his pockets, always in his pockets, a confused expression disfiguring his handsome face. I stood in the doorway for a moment, noticed that my own hands were trembling. I clasped them behind my back and went to the chair.

'You wanted to see us?' Mrs Holmes asked, absentmindedly pruning the potted ivy that sat on her desk, snapping the dead leaves away with a flick of her fingers.

You, I might have said, *I wanted to see you*. I lifted my head. 'Yes.'

'About what?'

'Sissy.'

She gave a little gasp. It was satisfying to shock her. He watched me impassively. Did he know me so well that he had predicted what was coming? Had he felt it this morning, had he insisted on accompanying Mrs Holmes to her office? That would have meant that he knew me better than I knew myself, because I hadn't even known I would go this far. And no one knew me that well.

'I know someone says she saw Sissy in the woods. With Boone Roberts from Harris Academy?' I couldn't stop my voice from lilting into a question. Mrs Holmes had stopped her pruning, now held a leaf in midair, her mouth parted. 'But it wasn't her. It was me.'

Now she looked confused, an expression I had never seen cross her face before. She looked mystified, for an instant, before she composed herself. She should have been headmaster, not her husband. And for all practical purposes, she was.

'Yes?' she asked. 'And? Tell us.'

I hadn't been sure I'd be able to do what I had to do next. But the way Mrs Holmes used 'us,' the way she gestured at me like I was harmless, nothing more than a girl – Mr Holmes caught my eye, and I suddenly felt so exhausted. So reckless.

I looked Mrs Holmes in the eye. 'Ask Eva,' I said. 'My bed was empty.' I paused. My voice wavered, and I took a deep breath. When I spoke again my voice was clear. 'Sissy is loved. Her family is loved. No one will want to see her go, least of all her father, her grandfather.' I didn't need to spell out what I meant; if nothing else, Mrs Holmes was a shrewd woman. 'Especially if they think it might be a mistake. And I'll see to it that they think it's a mistake. People won't care as much when I am sent home.' I shook my head. 'Do you see? It won't get you anywhere, punishing Sissy.'

'I see,' Mrs Holmes said. 'I see perfectly well. How interesting all of this is. But let me ask you this: have you thought about what got *you* here? Have you thought that perhaps it is best for Sissy to be sent to a place where she will not be tempted?'

I looked at her in wonder. 'Where would that be? We're already on the top of a mountain.'

Mrs Holmes turned briefly to her husband, as if to say, do you see this girl in front of me, so impudent, so presumptuous? She shook her head, gave a hard little laugh. Mr Holmes looked outside the window again, and I knew he wanted nothing more than to be absent from this. He would never help me; he was not capable of it. Mrs Holmes had always handled the disciplining of the girls, the unpleasant parts of keeping order.

'You're so lovely, Thea, just like your mother was. So lovely. Do you think you own the world? Do you think you have any say in what the world does with you? So lovely, so naïve.'

'Beth,' Mr Holmes said, a warning, but she acted as if she hadn't heard him.

She crumpled the dead leaf in her fist and flung it into the wastebasket.

'Your mind works in ways I do not understand, Thea. Usually I understand all my girls. You will pretend to have gone behind Sissy's back with her fiancé?'

I must have looked surprised – and I was – because she continued.

'Yes, I knew they were engaged. I know everything, Thea.' She smiled, and pressed a finger to her lips. 'I don't think you really want to go home.'

I thought of how regal my house looked on a gray day, its stately lines illuminated by the sky like ash behind it. I wanted to go to *that* home, the home of my childhood, the home that included Georgie, the home where my family loved me without reservation. But that home was gone now, sold to strangers.

'How could you want to go home?' she asked, her voice softer. 'Do you know why they sent you here?'

Mr Holmes's hand encircled his wife's upper arm, gently, as if she were a child. 'Enough, Beth.'

But of course I knew why they had sent me here. I almost laughed.

Mrs Holmes ignored her husband. 'They thought you might be carrying a child,' she said. She stared at me, but it was she who looked stricken, not I. 'They would have known soon enough, but your mother always was a worrier,' she said, and turned her head sharply. 'Henry. You're hurting me.'

I could see how tightly Mr Holmes gripped his wife's arm. 'That's enough,' he said quietly. 'There's no use in all this.'

'She'd rather I deal with the poor child, I suppose. I was always the problem-solver, between the two of us. I used to think that pretty girls didn't have to worry so much about the mechanics of life, the simple procedures. But your father, what of him? He's a doctor, he would have known soon enough whether or not you carried your cousin's child.' She gave a little gasp, and put her hand over her mouth. Mr Holmes let go, then, and Mrs Holmes massaged her arm where his hand had been, a faraway look in her eyes. Her face had softened. I thought of all her plants in their slender bottles. It seemed incredible that she felt any sympathy for me. It was so easy to deceive people.

'She needed to know,' Mrs Holmes said, breaking the silence. Then she turned to me. 'She should know what awaits her at home.'

I shook my head, though no response was required of me. I remembered Mother checking my sheets every day before I left. I remembered what Mrs Holmes had said when I first met her, to see her if I noticed anything about my body. Of course.

'It's not a surprise,' I said softly. It would have been a surprise if Mrs Holmes had told me that Georgie was well again, that Mother had forgiven me. That my parents had considered and acted upon the worst possible scenario was really no surprise at all.

'I'll have to make an announcement, you know. I'll have to make an example of you.'

'I know,' I said quietly.

Mrs Holmes spoke again, softly now; I had to strain to hear her. 'Do you know why your mother was friends with someone like me? We didn't travel in the same circles, no. You'd never even heard of me when you came here . . .' She trailed off, then shook her head, quickly, and continued. 'Your mother was something of a fast girl at Miss Petit's. Not unlike you, Thea. I was Miss Petit's favorite. Your mother was given a choice: leave in disgrace, or align herself with me. She wasn't stupid, your mother. She fell into line. But I like to think that we were friends. I like to think that eventually she loved me as I loved her.' She did not know about me and Mr Holmes; of that I felt certain. A small mercy.

'My mother was fast?' I asked.

'Oh,' Mrs Holmes said. 'The fastest.' Her faraway voice had returned.

In the dining hall the tables were still being set. Docey looked at me curiously, and I smiled at her, eager to be kind to someone. Emmy was nowhere to be seen. I sat on a bench out of everyone's way. The smell of frying bacon was so pungent I felt sick to my stomach. More girls streamed in, their eyes small from sleep. They barely glanced in my direction as they passed by; strangely, I felt a vague sense of disappointment. I didn't matter anymore. I glanced at the clock; I had only spent ten minutes in Mrs Holmes's office, which seemed impossible.

What were Mr and Mrs Holmes doing right now in her office? Perhaps assigning blame, deciding whose fault it was that a girl, two girls, if Sissy was counted, had slipped from their grasp. Or perhaps Mr Holmes was soothing his wife, had drawn her near, was telling her that this strange thing that had just happened, with Thea Atwell from Florida, was fine, would be fine.

I closed my eyes against the movement in the dining hall and put my head in my hands. There was a dull ache at the nape of my neck.

I had destroyed one family, and then come close to destroying another. The pain in my head deepened, I didn't know how I would be able to rouse myself when Sissy came in.

Sissy was late, of course. I would wait. I saw Katherine Hayes walk in, chatting with Leona, which was odd. Alice Hunt gaped at them. I almost smiled – I'd never seen a person look so astonished.

Mrs Holmes burst through the stairwell, her face red. Mr Holmes followed close behind, speaking urgently under his breath. Girls turned in their chairs, startled. Leona and Katherine stopped in their tracks. We'd never seen Mr and Mrs Holmes exchange a harsh word. To see them fight, openly – this was unheard of. Everyone started whispering, all at once, the hum of all those voices torture. I shut my eyes, put my hands over my ears.

'Thea?' A tap on my shoulder. I opened my eyes. Docey, with her darting eye. 'Are you all right?' she whispered.

Beyond Docey I saw Sissy enter the Castle with Eva. Everyone turned in her direction, the whispering died down, and I watched Sissy notice – scan the room, slowly, put her hand to her throat. I put my own hand to my throat. I'd never seen Sissy frightened before. I saw Henny whisper something to Jettie. She was so typical, Henny – I understood then that's what I'd always hated about her. Of course she would look smug. She was too dull to seem any other way.

Mrs Holmes raised her voice at the other end of the room, and everyone looked away from Sissy.

'Thea,' Docey said, more urgently, 'you should go. Go!' she said again, and tried to pull me up.

Time was operating according to a different clock. Everything was moving too slowly. Mrs Holmes watched Mr Holmes wind his way through the tables, now set with platters of thick fried bacon, tureens of oatmeal; he was searching for something, as he walked, quickly checking each table, girl after girl averting their eyes. He stopped at my table, and Mary Abbott pointed behind him, and Mr Holmes followed her finger to me.

Everyone was deadly silent, the hum evaporated. He tilted his head to the door, as if we were alone, back in his library, surrounded by all of his books. *Have you read all of them?* I'd asked. *Most*, he'd said, and laughed. *I'm old. I've had plenty of time to read.* I'd smiled, because he was so young, we both knew that. Then I'd accepted his hand, let him pull me from the couch.

Now, in this dining hall where I'd eaten hundreds of meals, Mr Holmes still seemed young, if being young meant you seemed untouched by the world. He *wasn't* untouched, I knew that better than anyone, but he didn't seem haunted, there was no eerie look in his eyes. He looked like an immortal.

He pointed a thumb to the door, and Martha Ladue, who was sitting a table away from me, gasped, a flush spreading over her white skin.

Follow me, he'd said that afternoon, but that was just a formality, a thing he said. I would have followed him anywhere. He took me upstairs, to a room I'd never entered. All done up in pink, with a narrow white bed. Sarabeth's room. I didn't understand why he had brought me here. He retrieved something from her dresser, a pretty marble-topped piece, while I was hungrily taking in the room, and put it in my hands. *Look*, he'd said, and he'd seemed suddenly shy, his hair falling over his eyes.

But now, in the dining room, I knew it was no longer true. I would not follow him anywhere. I would have, for a moment, and that's how it had been with Georgie, too. I would have followed him anywhere for a moment, and then the moment ended.

I shook my head, and Mr Holmes watched me in that fierce way of his, as if he were inventorying my soul, and then he left. I looked to the head table; his children weren't here. He would have taken them away had they been. He would go to them now. This was where he would always be. I would leave, but he never could.

'Girls,' Mrs Holmes said, and stepped up to Mr Holmes's lectern, where he usually led morning prayer, 'your attention for a moment. An announcement.' She was flustered, her voice unsteady, her hands fluttering in front of her. That I had undone her brought me no pleasure.

But the view, always the view: she stood in front of the window, the same window I had touched nearly a year ago, when Father had dismissed me from Mr Holmes's office. She was framed by the mountains; despite everything, I could still sight a marvel. Both then and now.

'Theodora Atwell is leaving us. Tomorrow morning. It is all very sudden, of course.' Girls started to whisper again, as I'd known they would, as I'd known what Mrs Holmes would do as soon as I'd seen her enter the dining hall. It was an odd sort of comfort, to know all this and not be frightened.

'For an infraction. Involving a young man.' The din grew louder, and Mrs Holmes raised her voice. 'I expect that there will be no more talk concerning this matter. You are ladies, and ladies do not gossip.' She looked at me then, across the room.

In Sarabeth's room, I'd looked at what he'd handed me. A

photograph of a much younger Henry Holmes in a silver frame that needed to be polished, Mrs Holmes's absence wrought in little ways like this. *Me*, he'd said. *Me when I was your age.* He stood in front of a lake, holding a paddle. He looked directly at the camera, as men always did. He looked the same, except his face was fuller, not chiseled into handsomeness by time. I touched the glass. *So handsome*, I'd said. But what I'd meant was this: so new.

'And let this be a lesson, girls, to act your age. To obey the rules.'

Sissy looked at me from across the room, along with everyone else, a slow dawning illuminating her delicate features. She knew. She looked away, out the window, touching the diamond horseshoe that rested in the hollow of her neck, and for an instant I thought that what Mrs Holmes had predicted might be the case: Sissy would believe I had betrayed her. She backed out of the door, everyone watching.

Mrs Holmes watched me. Then I felt Docey's hand on my shoulder. I took it, and held it, and though Docey's hand was tense at first, she didn't take it away. I could tell by feel that we had matching calluses – mine from riding, hers from the constant work of putting things in order. Our hands felt the same.

I found Sissy in the woods, where she and Boone went. She sat on a fallen log, crying into her hands.

I told her what I had done, and gradually, her crying stopped. I sat so close to her I could smell her. That's what sleeping in her bed a dozen times had earned me – recognizing the scent, surprisingly pungent, she left on her pillow.

'You'll sleep in the infirmary tonight. That's where they'll put you, before they send you away for good.' Still she wouldn't look at me. I tapped her shoulder, and she turned to me, her wide-set eyes swollen.

'Thank you,' she said, her voice even more jagged, from the crying. 'It was a brave thing to do.'

'There's proof. Eva noticed that I was gone that night. I told Mrs Holmes to ask her.'

'Eva wouldn't tell.'

Of course Eva would tell, if it was me versus Sissy. 'It doesn't matter. She won't ask.'

'No,' Sissy said, 'she believes you, along with everyone else.' Her voice broke.

'Mrs Holmes doesn't believe me. She saw right through it. Through me.' I took Sissy's hand. 'I'm sorry.'

'I know.' She flung her hand in the air, as if to say, we're done with all that. That gesture never left me. In my darkest hours I would recall it, extract it from the recesses of my mind. 'But who will I talk to, now that you're leaving?'

I thought then that it was always a matter of exchanging one thing for another, losing one kind of love for a new kind.

'And why do you want to go home, Thea? I don't understand.'

I smiled. She was right to ask that question: why did I want to go home? My family didn't want me. 'I want to help you. And my brother. I need to see my brother.'

She nodded. 'But your reputation. What will your parents think?'

I looked away. That was what I feared most, but I couldn't tell Sissy. I would be leaving this place in shame, which was exactly the opposite of how I wanted to leave it. I wanted my parents to love me; no, they had always loved me, I was their child – I wanted them to like me again. And leaving this way, in the midst of a scandal – I had made sure they would not. But better me than Sissy, who still had a chance; in my heart, I knew I was ruined in Mother's eyes; one scandal or twenty, it didn't truly matter. The Thea I had been had disappeared, a puff of smoke.

'I think I am a lost cause, to my parents.'

Sissy looked like she might start to cry again. She grabbed my hand. 'That is awful, Thea. The most awful thing I've ever heard.'

'It's not the most awful thing I've ever heard,' I said. 'There's worse. I need to do what's good, Sissy. I need to help my brother. I need to be a right girl.'

I went to the infirmary after I'd packed all my things, which took almost no time at all. A kitchen girl I didn't know by name brought me lunch and dinner. I tossed and turned against the hard mattress all night. I was going to see my parents soon. My brother. What had they been told? I was doubly bad, returned to them for the same sin for which I had been cast out.

The door opened. There was no lock, and for an instant I thought Mr Holmes had come to see me, and I was so happy.

But the silhouette belonged to a girl. I sat up and turned on the lamp. Mary Abbott.

'Why are you leaving?' she asked in a normal tone of voice.

'Shh. Because I was bad.' I sighed. 'You shouldn't be here.'

'But you weren't bad!' She knelt down next to my bed. 'I know who was bad.'

My stomach dropped. I remembered the night I'd lain in Sissy's bed and Mary Abbott had called out.

'She shouldn't have done that. She shouldn't have sneaked away all the time.' She paused. 'But don't be mad at me.'

'I won't,' I said, 'I promise. Just tell me everything.'

'I didn't tell Mrs Holmes.'

'Who did you tell?' I whispered slowly, as if I were coaxing a small child.

'Henny,' she whispered, her eyes wide. 'Henny.'

'Oh,' I said, and lay back against the iron headboard. 'Oh.'

'She asked!' Mary Abbott said defensively. 'She heard rumors, it was something all the girls have been talking about for such a long time, and then I saw Sissy.'

'The night of the dance,' I said.

She shrugged. 'Lots of nights. I know where they go. I've known for a long time. Sometimes I follow them.' She seemed proud.

'You watch them?' I asked incredulously.

She shook her head quickly. 'Just for a second, two seconds. Just to see Sissy's safe. I love her, too,' she said. 'Like you.'

I nodded, assembling all this new information, which was, after all, unsurprising. Unsurprising that Mary Abbott should have followed Sissy and Boone into the woods, unsurprising that she had been an instrument of Sissy's demise without the malice that such action usually called for. She was lonely. That was all.

'You were bad at home, weren't you?'

'Yes,' I said, without thinking. 'Very bad.' I felt my eyes warm.

'Oh, Thea,' Mary Abbott said, and then she hugged me, fiercely, and whispered into my ear. 'It's all right,' and whatever spell she had cast was broken. I pushed her away, hard.

'Ow,' she cried, and rubbed her shoulder, drew her arms to her chest as if to protect herself – she did need to protect herself. I recognized something in her, a certain deviancy, a certain need. A yearning she knew she needed to hide without knowing how. She hadn't the slimmest idea. She was too much like me; I could not be kind to her. The only difference between us was that I did not seem as strange, on the surface of things.

'It's better,' I said, 'not to be strange. Not to be noticed.'

Mary Abbott looked pained, but she nodded. She reached for my hand, and this time I let her take it. She was always reaching for my hand; but this time would be the last time.

'Take care,' I said, 'take care of yourself.'

★ ★ ★

I found Sam that night after I had confessed everything to my mother, almost everything: I would never tell her that my cousin and I had slept together. I thought I was being merciful; I never imagined that she did not believe me, that she had her own ideas about what had happened. But she was right, in the end; she was correct not to trust me.

I believed, as I searched the house for her, finally finding her out back pruning roses, that telling might relieve me. I believed foolishly.

Sam was in our old nursery, reading a magazine, sitting Indian-style on the bare floor. He shook his head when I walked in; his eyes were glassy, and the room was very dim.

'Do you want more light?' I asked, my hand on the switch.

'Leave it.'

Sam turned a page, and I saw an advertisement for roller skates, which neither of us had ever used.

'What are you reading?' I asked.

'I'm reading an article about people with unnatural desires.'

'I'm sorry.' My face was swollen from crying, it felt as if there was sand trapped underneath my eyelids.

'I should have stopped you.' He looked miserable, his eyes swollen and red, veins I'd never seen before at their surface. His left eye was black from a bruise.

'You couldn't have,' I said quietly. 'It wasn't yours to stop.'

'They're going to send you away.'

I was stunned. 'Who?'

'Who do you think? Mother and Father.'

'Where?' I thought to my mother's brother, in south Florida; that was the only place they had to send me.

'To a place I've never heard of. It had an Indian name.'

'I won't go. Sam,' I said, my voice rising. I didn't stop to think how he knew this. He must have overheard something. 'Don't let them take me.'

'Why, Thea?' he asked. 'Why did you do it?' He began to sob. 'They'll send you away, and I'll be alone. Did you think of that? Did you? Did you think that you would go away and I would be all alone?'

I threw myself on him. I felt my twin relent, and this relenting made the next two weeks, before I was sent away to Yonahlossee – the utter awkwardness, the turned heads of my family, the acknowledgment of my deep betrayal – my brother yielding against me in that moment made all of this bearable.

'I should have known,' he murmured into my hair. I could barely understand him.

I held his face in my hands. His cheeks were hot and sweaty.

'You did know,' I said.

I wandered the Castle the afternoon before I left Yonahlossee, sneaking out of the infirmary, which wasn't at all hard to do. No one watched me. I knew by the bells that it was rest hour. Sam would know I was coming home, by now. Mother would have told him. Surely he would be glad to see me, in his heart if not in his head.

I'd left a book in one of my classrooms. But the book didn't matter so much. I had become attached to this place, and I wanted to see where I'd gone first when I'd arrived almost a year ago, once more before I returned to Florida.

I knew what to expect, now, the rapid process by which Yonahlossee would turn alien.

The dining room was clear of the chaos of this morning. I tried to memorize each detail as it lay: the table where I had eaten hundreds of meals; the space where Mr Holmes had stood and talked to us of God.

I climbed the stairs to the third floor, to see it for the last time, but perhaps I knew, somehow, that Mrs Holmes would be in her classroom.

She leaned against the window in an odd posture, her forehead on glass, her open hand pressed against the wall, as if she were trying to push her way through. I knew the view very well: she was in the mountains, only a window between her and them. I thought she might be crying.

And then she turned and I drew back, certain she had seen me. But she went to a desk, where Decca sat, drawing. Mrs Holmes smiled, and pointed to something on the paper. Decca nodded. I watched them for too long, Decca engrossed in her drawing – she kept looking at the window, and I realized she was drawing the mountains – and Mrs Holmes watching, her face constantly moving – her lips, her forehead – in response to Decca's work. She looked pleased. They both did.

When I left, I wound my way behind the cabins – I was meeting Sisty – so that in case Mrs Holmes returned to the window she would not see me.

My father had been in his study. I knocked and his voice sounded the same as always, giving me permission to enter: quiet, firm.

'Thea.'

'Father.' He was in the middle of writing a letter. Now he tapped his chin with his pen and waited. 'How is Georgie,' I blurted, because either I said it now, and quickly, or not at all.

'Georgie is in the hospital. Did you know that?'

I shook my head. 'He was breathing when I saw him last.'

'Yes. Unfortunately one can breathe and still be badly damaged. It seems his brain is injured.' He paused. 'When your mother told me what you had confessed I was sure she was wrong.' His voice was even. 'Was she wrong?'

I shook my head.

'I wish with all my heart that she was.' It was strange, for my father to use a sentimental phrase like that. All my heart. 'But your brother is involved in this, too. Georgie's wound –' and here he lay his pen down and put his hands before him as if he were cradling a melon – 'is consistent with violent injury. Do you understand, Thea?'

I nodded, not understanding.

'Georgie was either hit, by your brother, or he fell. Either way the result is the same. But there is a great distinction between the two, as you must know.'

I said nothing.

'It is plausible that Georgie fell on a large, blunt object. I told the hospital the rock. They relayed this information to the police. That your cousin had fallen and hit his head on the rock.'

'All right,' I said, because he seemed to require a response. 'All right.'

'Your brother did not know who I was when I found him later. He had been sitting under a tree for hours. He had wet himself. His recounting of what happened is faulty, at best.' He looked at me like he was surprised to find me there.

'I just wanted to find out about Georgie,' I whispered. His name was dirty in my mouth.

'Well, now you know. He is not well.'

'But he will be well again?'

I should not have asked, clearly

My father shrugged faintly. 'God willing.' I made to leave, but my father spoke again. 'Did you see, Thea? Can you tell me what happened? Can you be honest?' He looked so pained, my father, so undone. The top button on his shirt was undone; it was never undone.

'It was the rock,' I said. 'The rock, not Sam.'

It seemed an easy thing, to let my father believe what he wanted so badly to believe. The least I could do.

My mother found me in the barn later, untangling the knots in Sasi's tail. It was something to do.

'Thea.'

'Mother.' I held the tail loosely; I did not want to let go of it completely.

'I was out for a walk.' She gestured toward the wide expanse. My mother never took walks. She was either in the garden or in the house. She had spoken to me three times in the past week. Once she had asked me to sweep the front porch, which I had done, twice, even though it hadn't needed it.

She rested her forehead against the stall door; she looked tired, vulnerable. Perhaps she would have news of my cousin.

'We've decided to send you away from all this.'

'I won't go.' I looked my mother in the eye, and though she was surprised, all the rules of how we behaved with each other had disintegrated, as if into thin air.

She closed her eyes. 'You have no choice. It will be better for you, to go.'

'No. I'm fine here. I'll stay out of everyone's way. You'll see. I'll sleep out here. I won't be a bother. Please, it won't be better for me.'

She laughed. 'You'll sleep in a stall? You're not an animal, Thea. Are you?' She shook her head. 'You will go.'

'Oh.' I wound Sasi's tail around my wrist. 'I see.'

My mother watched me for a moment. 'Why, Thea? Why did you do it?' Her mouth was screwed into a small, ugly knot. She did not look so beautiful, in this moment. She looked betrayed.

'Why was it so bad?' I asked. My voice cracked. 'You loved Georgie.'

It seemed like she was ready for the question, like she had already asked it of herself.

'I wanted more for you!' she cried. 'Don't you see, that Georgie is not enough? And even if he was, it's all a horrible mess now, Georgie in the hospital, your brother the one who put him there. Uncle George and Aunt Carrie cannot forgive. And I'm so angry at Georgie . . . and at you.' She gestured outside the barn, at our thousand acres. 'We had everything, Thea. Everything. This place is ruined.'

'Please,' I cried, 'where are you sending me? Don't. Please don't.' I touched her arm. 'Please keep me here. I'll be good.'

She looked at her forearm where I had touched it, then up at me again.

'I'm afraid it's too late for all that,' she said, calm now.

We settled into a semblance of routine in my final week at home. I woke up early in the morning and rode until Sasi was exhausted. I made jumps that were higher and higher, and Sasi cleared them because he could feel how reckless I was. Mother busied herself with chores, and I helped her by making myself scarce. I knew I was the last person she wanted to see. Sam disappeared for hours at a time out back. Hunting, I presumed. Father left before I rose and returned after I was in bed. He made some mention of a sickly infant that would not nurse when I passed him in the hall. I did not ask again about my cousin. I assumed that Father would tell me if his condition changed for the worse. I was naïve, I thought my parents' silence meant that Georgie was getting better.

I was supposed to be packing my clothes. Mother had been vague about what I'd need. I had gotten as far as emptying my drawers onto the floor. Now I combed through these piles of all my fine things: shimmering dresses, stiff cotton skirts, smooth silk scarves. I didn't deserve them. I couldn't imagine a future in which I'd wear them again.

A knock. I'd been keeping my door closed to spare my family the sight of me.

'Come in.'

Idella's brown hand, first. I went back to my things. The disappointment was nearly unbearable.

'Your mother sent me to help pack.'

I gestured at the piles. 'I've made such a mess.'

'Let me.'

I watched as she made better piles, put skirts with skirts, breeches with riding shirts; deftly folded all the things I'd unfolded.

'Your mother says to pack lightly.' Idella glanced at me. 'She says there will be a uniform.'

'A uniform,' I repeated. 'Do you know why I'm going away?'

Idella smoothed the collar of a blouse. I knew so little about her. She wasn't married. She lived with her mother and two sisters; they were all deeply religious.

'I'm sure it's all fine.'

I nodded, close to tears. 'It's not,' I said.

'God willing,' Idella said. 'God willing.'

CHAPTER TWENTY-THREE

The train from Asheville to Orlando was half-empty. There was another girl my age who sat in first class. We ate together in the dining car, at separate tables. I studied her. She did not look at the waiter when she ordered, and when her food came she ate in a hurry, shyly, as if she were in danger of offending someone by dining. She wore beautiful, teardrop-shaped emerald earrings, which she touched constantly, in the same way that Sissy touched her horseshoe pendant. The horseshoe pendant hung around my neck now, and I found myself tapping it constantly, as Sissy had, but not for the same reasons: I touched it because Sissy had, because I missed her.

I could not eat the tomato soup the waiter brought. It wasn't very good, but I should have been hungry; I hadn't eaten very much in days. I forced myself to eat the roll. As I sat here, on this train, this bland food before me made everything real again. I could feel my resolve scattering like dandelion fluff. It was so green outside the train window, so green and alive. The beauty of North Carolina lay in its austerity, the mountains so far away, so cold, so distant. Once we crossed into Florida, everything was alive, at you. I knew as soon as I stepped off the train the heat would greet me like an old friend, even though it was only spring.

I was jealous of the girl, whose name I didn't even know, who

I would never see again. I had never wanted to be someone else so badly. I wanted to begin again: at birth, without a twin, without a cousin so close he was a brother.

'Do you know the next stop?' the girl asked. She stood before me. I hadn't even noticed that she'd left her table. For a moment the name would not come to me. But finally it did.

'Church Street,' I said. 'Orlando.' The girl seemed nervous, and I wanted to take her by the shoulders, say look, please, you have nothing to be nervous about. But I didn't know that. I didn't know what or who she would meet when she stepped off the train, which was beginning the slow process of stopping. I could see the station, where I would soon be, and it seemed impossible that I could be here on this train but that in five minutes, ten, I would not be. And that I would not be by my own volition. Why, Thea, why. Why had I wanted to return to all this. To my brother who hadn't written me a single word for months, to my mother and father who had sent me away so quickly it was as if they'd known all along how they would handle a crisis, a tragedy, a thing Mother hadn't planned: send the girl away, keep the boy.

And then I saw them, my parents, waiting on the platform, my father in a suit, my mother in a wide-brimmed hat. And I knew why I had wanted to come back. Yet I was not ready to see them. I faltered. I put my head in my hands.

I looked up again and saw the girl was watching me. At Yonahlossee she would not have been popular; she was too nervous, too needy.

'Who are you meeting?' she asked.

'My parents.' I looked outside the window. My mother stood in front of my father; my father's hands were clasped behind his back, his head bowed. My mother looked agitated. My fast mother, who had once been beautiful and shameless. She looked thinner. Sam was not there.

I watched my parents as the train pulled in, stayed in my seat as the other passengers disembarked and my mother peered anxiously into their faces.

I stood. I could already feel my legs weakening, atrophying ever so slightly from disuse. I hadn't been on a horse in days.

When I finally emerged from the train, the last passenger, my mother was visibly relieved.

'Thea,' she said, her voice high. Her eyes roamed over my body, and lingered on the necklace; then her eyes hardened. But she couldn't help this; I saw that she was trying to be kind.

My father raised his head and I saw with surprise that he had aged. He had gone completely gray in my absence. Even his eyebrows were gray. We waited while a porter gathered my luggage, while my father tipped him and my mother wrapped a scarf around her hair for the drive. Passengers for the next train milled around, and I was glad. They were someone else. The women wore pinks and purples and greens, a surprise to my eyes after so many days of white. And nobody watched them. Nobody made sure they got to classes on time, or turned off their lights at nine, or rose at seven. Nobody cared.

My mother and father turned to go, and they expected that I would follow. My mother turned first, then my father, and I waited for them to say something.

'It's time to go,' my father said. 'Come.'

My father held out his hand; my mother's eyes were desperate. 'Yes,' I said, 'let's go home.'

But still I stood where I was. I had misspoken. We wouldn't be going home. I looked behind me and saw my train leaving; another giant machine poised to take its place. There would be other trains. I smiled at my father and allowed him to take my hand. I had not wanted to let go of his hand so many months ago, and now I had to make myself touch it. We were all being very brave.

My father opened my door, and waited until I was settled to shut it. We were silent while my father navigated our car onto the road. Orlando looked so busy – I had not seen cars, or roads, or any other tall building besides the Castle for so long. Then my mother turned so that I could see her pretty profile and I knew that I didn't have to try at all to love my mother and father; I hadn't known how easy it would be. They had my heart on a string, and I saw that they always would, until they died. Then I would truly be free, except for Sam. One string, instead of three.

I watched Mother's profile, that old familiar view. It was sharper, now; I had done that. I waited for her to speak.

'Thea,' she began, and I could smell her, even from here; I could smell her old familiar smell. I leaned forward in my seat.

'Yes?'

Then she turned and faced me, closed her eyes and lightly touched her forehead with two fingers, a new gesture. 'This headache,' she said. 'It won't leave me.'

I wanted to say something before she spoke. I wanted to tell her about the strangeness of all this, the utter strangeness. So much had happened in this last year, the busiest year of my young life; I felt so old, now. I wanted to tell her, and Father, too, about the strangeness of all those girls at first; then how all those girls had not seemed strange any longer. How now *they* seemed strange, my own parents, even though I loved them, even though I wanted to please them. I wanted to say: you can't ever imagine a moment, it seems like it will never come, but then it does, and there you are, Thea Atwell from Emathla, Florida, the same girl you thought you were.

'Thea,' my mother said. 'We've been living in a hotel for the past month, but we'll be leaving next week. We've bought a house. There are so many here, abandoned.'

'Sasi?' I asked. I couldn't make complete sentences; all I could manage were words.

'He's sold, Thea. You were going to outgrow him anyway.' Her voice was soft. She was again trying to be kind.

'Who has him?'

'A little girl,' my father answered. 'She loves him. The truth is, Thea –' my mother made a small noise of protest, but my father shushed her, which was shocking; more shocking was that Mother did as directed, and fell silent – 'the truth is that we can't quite afford a horse for you right now.'

'He was a pony,' I said quietly.

'Pardon, Thea?'

'Nothing,' I said, 'never mind.'

I looked at my hands, these hands that Mr Holmes had held. My mother turned around and leaned her head against the window. 'This headache,' she said, 'is murder.'

It wasn't hard, not crying. My mother, after all, was a liar, a liar who I loved, but still a liar. She had promised me that Georgie would be fine, that she would write if he were not. I had been foolish to believe her, but I had wanted to believe her. I watched the street, and saw a dirty little girl and I wondered if she was poor, if her parents had abandoned their house; or perhaps she was only a little girl dirty from her backyard. Her dress looked nice enough. I would never know.

The hotel we stayed in seemed grand to me, with red plush carpet and an elevator. A bellhop accompanied me and Mother to my room. It was going to be mine alone, I saw as soon as he opened the door, my brother not anywhere in sight. The room smelled moldy, but rooms often did in Florida.

The bellhop was young, and handsome, with thick brown hair and long, lean limbs. Of course, I thought, of course I would get the young and handsome bellhop, not the old, wizened one. I told him where to put my things, and when he was done he waited.

'That will be all,' Mother said.

'Mother.' I looked at her purse.

'Oh yes,' she said, 'I'm sorry, so sorry.' She seemed nervous, and I knew why. She was about to be alone with me. And that I had just spoken to a man, and told her what to do in regard to this man, could not have helped. She would rather I hid in the corner until he left, even after he left. Well, I was not going to do that.

He closed the door behind him, and I turned to Mother and looked her in the eye; I waited for her to speak.

'Well,' she said, 'camp worked wonders for you, Thea. You look well.'

'It was not a camp, Mother.' She stiffened. But I wasn't going to get into all that. 'No, it's all right. I'm glad I was there for so long.'

She watched me for a long time, the electric fan the only noise in the room. She wore a dress I had seen a hundred times before. She was still beautiful; the bellhop had paid more attention to her than to me. I felt my nerve weaken. She was my mother, I was her child, and this was a fact, and this was unchangeable. I waited for her to scold me, to express her displeasure, to tell me she knew all about how bad I had been, for a second time.

'Well,' she said finally, and took my hand, 'what are we going to do with you now, Thea?'

I began to speak, but she hushed me.

'No, please. We'll talk about all that later. I'm tired.'

'Sam?'

'Sam is in the room next door. I suggest you let him come to you. But you will do what you wish, I'm sure.'

I nodded. I would. She was correct.

I had meant to stay in the infirmary my final night. But I couldn't. I rose after what seemed like hours of tossing and turning, which had followed Mary Abbott's visit. I *wanted* to fall asleep, to take advantage of the brief respite slumber provided. But sleep would not come and I began to feel panicked, hot; my scalp burned on top of my brain. That's what it felt like, anyway, that my brain was thinking too many agitating thoughts, that it was on fire. I hoped I would not regret leaving. I hoped Sam would be glad to see me. I hoped Sissy's life would turn out exactly as she wished it to.

The Square was deserted. There was a full moon, which was so, so pretty. There wasn't a single light on at Masters. Augusta House was quiet, all my friends fast asleep. Boone would not come anymore, now that Sissy had almost been caught. It didn't seem that Boone's identity had been revealed, a bit of luck. I'd made Sissy promise to write him a letter, to be more careful.

I thought of Kate the Bell Witch as I walked to the barn, the woods deep and black on either side of me. It would be so easy, to disappear.

Most of the horses didn't bother to swing their heads over their stall doors. It was late, not near feeding time. But Naari did. She recognized my footsteps. And she would forget them, and not ever know what she had forgotten.

I held her muzzle to my face, breathed in her softly pungent smell and let her breathe in mine. Who knows what I smelled like. Like a girl. Like Thea.

I heard the sound of metal on metal behind me, and jumped; I thought I'd been caught. But what else could they do to me? I had nothing to lose, nothing left to give them.

It was Leona, emerging from King's stall, closing the gate behind her. She wore her nightgown, which fell only to her knees where mine hit mid-calf. Though I had changed into my day clothes before I'd come down here. I noticed her feet were bare. It was the height of foolishness, to walk in bare feet around a horse. Her hair was wild. Or nearly wild, as wild as Leona's hair ever got. King put his giant head over the gate and looked at me. Leona reached behind her and patted his muzzle, absentmindedly. I'd thought her capable of such treachery. But really my first instinct about her had been right: she only cared about horses.

'Thea Atwell,' she said. 'You beat me. Nobody has ever beaten me before.'

'Sorry,' I said, and in that moment I was: I should have been kinder, I should have let her win.

'Don't be. I would have done the same thing, in your shoes. In your boots.' She smiled, and I did, too.

'I'm sorry about King,' I said, and gestured behind her, at his big, handsome face. Leona turned and buried her face in his neck, and King relaxed into her embrace, like a child. In the ring he was fierce, but on the ground he was gentle. I thought she was crying, I knew *I* would be crying, but when she looked at me again her face was dry as a bone.

'There will be other horses,' she said, 'but not like this one. And not for a long time.'

I nodded. I believed her. If anyone could find her way back onto a horse it would be Leona.

'You'll have to leave her, too,' she said. There was no malice in her voice.

'Yes.' I looked at Naari's small, dainty face. 'But she was never mine in the first place.'

★ ★ ★

Sam did not come to my door. I lay in my bed for hours and hours. I fell asleep; when I woke, the window was lit by streetlights, though I could tell by the way the darkness hit the windows that it was nearly dusk. My mouth was dry. There was no Docey here to pour me water, no other girl to tell me what time it was.

I poured myself a glass of water from the sink and drank it, quickly, then poured another and drank that, too. My eye caught a slip of white; a note, slipped under the door. My heart caught; Sam. But no, Mother, telling me they didn't want to wake me for dinner. They. Had Sam been with them? I saw how sad it all was; my family living in different rooms in a hotel. I heard something outside, in the hall, but I wasn't familiar enough with this place to know what it was that I heard.

I opened the door slowly, and there he was, my brother. The back of him, but I knew, the same way I would recognize my hand if someone brought it to me.

He turned and in the bright light of the hallway I saw that he had indeed become more handsome than I was pretty, as I'd predicted. He was a man, now, his shoulders broad, a head taller than I was, at least. It was so amazing, this life: it took a person I knew completely and utterly and made him into a stranger.

'Sam.'

'Thea.' His voice was deep. I'd never hear it again as I'd left it, soft and pretty. He had a voice that asserted itself, now, that directed other people, that made itself heard in a crowded room. A man's voice.

I put my hand to my throat. 'What time is it?'

'Late,' he said.

'You couldn't sleep?'

He said nothing, would not meet my eye. 'Come in,' I said, and opened my door, 'please.'

He hesitated. 'Please,' I said again, 'don't make me beg.' And then he came inside without a word, and sat down on the bed; I sat down next to him. The bed was unmade, and I was embarrassed, suddenly, that a boy was in my room and the bed was unmade, which was vulgar. But then I remembered that Sam was not a boy but my brother.

We sat in silence for a long time. It was familiar, though; I preferred it to our conversation, which had been stiff, awkward. Sitting down, he did not seem so tall; he was my brother again.

'So much has changed,' I began, but Sam interrupted me.

'For you,' he said. 'For you more than me. I didn't leave.'

'I came back,' I said. 'For you.'

He looked at me then, and he was astonished, utterly. When I left him his face was bruised and beaten; now it was perfect. He laughed.

'For me?' he asked. 'For me?'

'For you,' I said, but my voice wavered.

'Let's not pretend that any of this was for me. Can we not pretend, Thea?' His voice had turned plaintive.

I shook my head. 'I thought you wanted me to come back. I've said sorry so very many times.' I touched my necklace, and Sam's eyes went to it, and I saw he was hungry for me, as I was for him; he wanted to see all the ways change had wrought itself in his twin, as I did.

'You left.'

And I understood he was referring to both times: I had left him for Georgie, and then a second time, for Yonahlossee.

He smiled at me sadly, and I wanted so badly to touch him. Just his hand, his shoulder.

'Oh, Sam.' I knew I would remember this moment for as long as I lived. I could live to be a hundred and this moment would never leave me. 'I'm sorry,' I said, 'I'm so sorry,' and I meant I was sorry for all of it; for all of us, forever apart now. A sob caught in my throat, and that was all it took: Sam turned and hugged me, fiercely, and I knew then how impossible our lives had gotten. And Georgie, whom we had not spoken of, had not been mentioned by name. There was no need. He was between us, as real in his absence as he had been in his presence.

After a while Sam released me, then stood, and walked to the window. Because he was not facing me I felt bold.

'Where are they?'

He continued to stare out into the night. 'They moved to Missouri.'

'And the Gainesville house?'

'The bank owns it. Uncle George let them take it. They wanted to leave.' He tapped his fingers on the glass. 'I haven't seen them since . . .' he trailed off. 'Only Father talks to Uncle George. That's all. Father sends them a check every month. "It is our Christian duty,"' he intoned, using the voice he always used when he imitated Father: deep, slow. But now he sounded just like Father.

'They said that?' It was unlike my parents, to be so frank.

'They had to say something, Thea. We had to sell the house. And besides, I think they want me to know that our life is not exactly the same, now. They want to prepare me.'

He turned his head to look at me, to read my face, and then he turned back to the window. 'There's enough money, don't worry.'

'I wasn't worried.'

'Just not as much as there used to be. And no one knows how long this will go on.'

He meant the Depression, of which he had known nothing when I left. My brother knew so many things now. He was no longer a child.

'Do you remember what happened, Sam?'

He stared out the window; night in the city was so bright, so different from my Yonahlossee nights. He stared outside so long I thought he must not know what I meant, but then he spoke.

'Yes,' he said, 'like I remember a dream. Mother and Father blame the rock.' I watched his back. He placed a palm on the window. 'Do you remember how Mother used to say that our lives were blessed, that we had our own private patch of paradise?'

I nodded, and met his eyes in my reflection on the window.

'Well, she doesn't say that anymore.' He gave a short laugh. 'I thought God was watching us.' He was quiet for a moment, and it was all I could do not to interrupt. I had never heard this before. I didn't quite believe it. 'I know it's silly. But I thought that God knew we were special.' He smiled. 'I didn't mean to hurt him, Thea. It would be better if he were dead.'

'Hush,' I said. 'Who can say that?'

'I can say that!' he said, almost shouted. 'I can!' He shook his head. 'I can,' he said more quietly, 'because I have been here and I have seen all of it. All of it, Thea.'

'All of it,' I repeated, surprised by the sound of my own voice. 'You should leave, Sam. It's not your mess.'

'Whose is it, then?'

'No one's. Just a series of events. A series of events,' I repeated.

'No, Thea. It's ours.'

'It's not mine.' I rose, and walked over to the window, peered over his shoulder. The sun was rising, and street sweepers were making a neat job of clearing the sidewalks. 'There's all these people in the world, and we are only two of them. Mother and Father thought they were punishing me, by sending me away. It was a reward, to stay here. But they were wrong. It was not a punishment.'

'You learned so much, at camp.' I could smell his breath, the particular tang it had whenever he hadn't slept long enough.

'I learned enough,' I said. I took his hand, and squeezed it. 'You should leave, too. Our lives are elsewhere.'

He laughed. 'Where?'

I shrugged. 'Who knows. But God grants happiness only to those who seek it.'

The next morning there was a knock on my door at noon. I was awake – I'd fallen asleep as the sun rose – but not dressed. I opened the door and found Mother, Sam behind her. He looked fresh, alert, and I wondered when or if he had slept after leaving my room. He caught my eye and looked away, and then Mother did, too, and I realized neither she nor my brother wanted to see me in my nightclothes. Of course.

'Shall we dine?' Mother asked, eyes averted, and I told them I'd be dressed in fifteen minutes, though it only took five. I waited on the edge of the bed, in a dress that was too small for me, covered my knees just barely and pinched my arms. It was pretty, though, white polka dots against brown fabric. I had picked it out from a catalogue last spring; it had arrived after I'd left. I had forgotten the dress existed. But there it was, hung in my closet by Mother, the plain fact of it greeting me after nearly a year. It had been expensive, and I'd wanted it so badly because of Georgie, because I wanted him to see me in it. Georgie's face came to me so quickly, then. It was all another life, I told myself while I waited on the edge of the bed, because I sensed Mother wanted me to wait for her, did not want me to come find her. All of it another life.

'Your hair,' she said, in the elevator, held her hand flat and brushed the bottom, blunt edge of it, where Eva had cut it straight across. 'It's pretty, Thea. Very pretty.' I felt my cheeks flame; I couldn't help it. I turned my head, but Mother had already seen.

She and Sam and I ate a mainly silent meal in the hotel restaurant, which felt cavernous because it was so empty. Sam seemed distracted, watching the one other patron – an older man, dressed in a suit – reading and rereading the menu. Mother was subdued. She had not seemed subdued in her letters.

She barely touched her food, but made Sam finish what she could not, for fear the restaurant staff think her greedy, wasteful. I had never before seen her want so badly to place herself in the good graces of strangers, and I realized that this was one of the rewards of hiding herself away from the world: she did not have to care. And it was exhausting, caring. I had gotten used to it, at Yonahlossee, but all the wondering of what other people thought of you – it could weigh on your mind. But sometimes it weighed pleasantly, when someone admired or wanted you. Mother had starved us, in that way.

I sipped my iced tea, which was not as good as Yonahlossee's, which Mother and Sam had never tasted, would never taste. Mother watched Sam closely as he gobbled down her sandwich – his appetite seemed to have doubled in my absence – and her eyes darted back and forth from the waiter to her son. I almost could not believe it, except that I did. Our lives were unimaginable to us; if a year ago a fortune teller had read our future to Mother, she would have laughed, uproariously. She would have closed the door, then, and sealed us off again. But here we sat, our home dismantled, and Mother cared, deeply, about the opinions of a waiter, a waiter whose name she would never know.

'That was filling,' she said, when our table had been cleared, 'I think I'll go rest my eyes,' and I realized that she worried about small things now because the big things had turned her sick. Which might be, I saw, to my advantage: no one had mentioned my disgraceful exit from camp.

I knocked softly on Sam's door after lunch, but he didn't answer. I thought perhaps he was sleeping. I hoped so, hoped that he wasn't avoiding me. He had been nice enough at lunch, bu distant. I spent my afternoon writing letters: to Sissy and Eva and even a brief one to Mary Abbott. I was trying to be kind to her, as so many girls had been kind to me at Yonahlossee.

Father knocked on my door at six o'clock, promptly, the same time as the church bells down the street rang out, reminding me of Yonahlossee. We ate at six o'clock there, too, though Father of course would not know that.

Sam stood behind him, just like before.

'Your mother is not feeling well,' Father said, and stepped aside so I could walk by, as if I were a lady. I met Sam's eye and understood that they were taking turns with us.

After we had ordered, Father asked me what I had learned at camp.

'Learned?'

'What did you read? Who did you study?'

I laughed, and Father looked at me strangely. 'I learned to be around other girls,' I said. Father nodded. This is what they had wanted, after all; he had told me so in his first letter. *You will learn how to behave around other children there, Thea. I hope that is not too much to ask.* I would never forget it. But Father did not remember what he had written; he looked vaguely disturbed, as if I were mocking him. Which I suppose I was, but not in the way he thought.

'Did you like it?' he asked, 'after you settled in?' Sam looked at me, too; they wanted to know. They wanted me to tell them a story. But I would not. Yonahlossee was mine.

'I grew to love it,' I said.

The next morning, both Mother and Father appeared at my door, Sam behind them in his normal place.

'We thought we'd go for a drive,' Father said. He smiled faintly, in his way. 'And see our house.'

Mother clung to Father as we made our way through the hotel, and shielded her eyes against the sun when we stepped outside. Sam looked out the window, at the shops we passed, at Church Street Station, where I had arrived just the day before yesterday, at the groves of oranges the city eventually gave way to. The country, I thought; we'll live in the country again, because Mother couldn't bear to live in town. No one spoke in the car, not a single word, no one even tried, including myself. Now I was used to chatter, to noise, to the constant hum of girls' voices; I felt ready to burst, to explode this silence.

After a little while Father turned down a narrow road, and then turned again, after a minute or so, and I saw where my family would be living. It was pretty, Spanish-style, white stucco topped by a red tile roof. Thick palm trees surrounded the house in a neat square. It was half the size, I estimated, of our home, but that house had been so big, too big, really, for the four of us.

'Is there a barn?' I asked, though it didn't matter.

'No,' Father said, and led us up the front steps inside. The door was locked. We had never, in all my life, locked our doors. But now it would be done, from this point on. We stepped inside the empty house, into an empty room, the walls stark white. I could see how it would be pretty, though, with Mother's touch. The ceilings were high, the staircase wrought iron, the wood floors even and richly brown.

'It's pretty,' I said, turning to Father, and I could see that he still wanted to please me, us, that he hoped the house would be some sort of salve.

'Yes,' he said, 'isn't it?' And my mother did not seem to realize he'd asked that question of her.

'Yes,' she said, finally. 'Quite.'

Sam and my father went to look at the garage, and my mother went back outside, to the car, I thought, to rest. I waited for a moment, tried to gather myself. It would not be easy; it would never be easy, and waiting would not change a thing. I went to the window and saw that Mother had not gone back to the car. She sat on the front steps, her legs folded neatly to the side of her.

She looked pitiful, and I was so angry with her, because I did not want to feel pity, which is the worst kind of feeling, for my mother. She should be beyond pity. Father seemed the same, quiet and kind. Sam was distant, but the elemental way he moved through the world, easily, naturally, was unchanged. But Mother was ruined. She had been taken away from her home. She had belonged to a place, not people.

I remembered a woman, a friend of Uncle George and Aunt Carrie's, coming to Emathla to see our house. She and her husband were going to build their own house, soon, and had heard ours was magnificent. And it was. But so easily destroyed: a fire, a hurricane, an old oak felled on its roof. A daughter behaving inappropriately.

I remembered Mother showing them all our rooms, even mine and Sam's, and the woman, who was very tall and thin, like a bird, saying, over and over, 'Exquisite.' I remembered her so clearly because we did not often have visitors. Aunt Carrie trailed behind; I closed my eyes against the image of her, trailing. I put my head in my hands; all these memories, of home before the mess, of Yonahlossee, flooding from my head like so much vapor.

'Exquisite,' the woman kept saying, 'exquisite,' and I realized that our home was exquisite; I had never thought of it in any way before except to call it our home. By the end of the visit Mother seemed bored. And this woman *was* boring; she kept saying the same thing over and over, at each room. But Mother was bored because the woman was stating something so plain it did not need to be spoken. Like calling Mother beautiful. Like calling us lucky.

We stood on the front porch until their car had disappeared in a puff of dust and Mother took my hand.

'Well,' she said, 'let's get back to our exquisiteness, shall we?'

Now I watched her sit on the front steps, pretending to look at a yard that she would never love, in front of a house that would never be hers. Her house was her child, I realized; but no, that was wrong. Her house was her mother, her father; she took comfort in it, expected it to shelter her from life's slings and arrows.

I slipped through the front door quietly. The heat was at me immediately. There was no color in the yard, only the palm trees, and shrubbery. Surely my mother would add color.

'A nice yard,' I said, from behind her, and she nodded but didn't speak. I sat down next to her, and she patted my knee, lightly.

'Mother,' I said, 'I want to leave again.'

She turned to face me, languidly; she seemed to be moving underwater, and it occurred to me that Father might have given her medicine, for her headaches.

'Why not, I suppose,' she said. 'Why not?'

Her answer felt like a punch, a blow. I expected reluctance; no, I had *wanted* reluctance, some sign from her that she needed me. But I would have gone anyway, so wasn't I being a foolish girl? I was getting what I wanted, more easily than expected.

Tears came to my eyes. But then she spoke again, and her voice was firmer, like I remembered her voice. 'I thought you might want to go away again. Once you had a taste of what it was like.'

'You were right,' I said, and began to cry, and hated myself for crying.

'Oh, Thea,' my mother murmured, and pulled me close, and if I could have stopped time, stilled all the clocks, I would have.

But I could not. I was just a girl. My mother was just a woman. 'Beth mentioned something about a boy you were meeting.' She laughed. 'I thought there were no boys there, but of course, there are boys everywhere. You'll go somewhere else, and my advice to you, for whatever it's worth, is to find a kind boy.' She stroked my hair. She sounded like her old self. 'Find a kind boy, like Father. I was once in trouble with a boy.' I tried to lift my head, to look at her, but she pressed it back to her chest. 'Long before your father. It is such a wonderful kind of trouble to be in. As long as you can get out of it. And you couldn't quite.' She paused. 'Get out of it, I mean. Could you?'

She let go of my head, and I sat up, tried to look at the blurry world through my tears.

'I didn't leave because of a boy. You might not believe me, but I wanted to come back. I wanted to come back and see my brother.'

'So that you could leave again?'

'What is there for me here?' I asked. 'There is not even a horse, here.'

Mother gazed at me for a moment. 'It's true,' she said, 'it's true. There is nothing for you here, not anymore. I wanted something else for you and Sam,' she said, her soft voice returned. 'But that was my mistake, wasn't it? To think I could fiddle with your natures.'

The week leading up to the Fourth of July had been our last together, mine and Sam's, before what I had done was laid bare. There was something between us now, we both knew that, though of course neither of us had any idea, really.

It was pouring outside, in buckets. I flung myself from chair to chair, bored to death. I wandered into my brother's room, opened the door without knocking. He looked afraid, but he turned back to what he was doing when he saw it was me, not Mother.

'A nest,' he explained, as I stood over him, 'of baby squirrels.'

'Only two?' Sam had raised squirrels before, but usually there were more of them. They were so ugly, the size of mice, hairless and pink, their eyes sealed shut. Sam had nestled them in an old blanket. It seemed impossible they would grow to be squirrels.

'A raccoon got the rest.'

One of them shifted, and I reached my hand down to touch one—

'Thea!'

'Sorry,' I said. 'I forgot.'

'Mother would kill you,' I said, after a moment. She didn't allow Sam's animals in the house.

Sam smiled. 'No.' He shook his head. 'If she saw, her eyes wouldn't believe it.'

But chances were Mother wouldn't come to Sam's room again; she'd already made the beds and straightened the upstairs.

I watched Sam try to feed one of the squirrels with one of Father's syringes, absent the needle.

'Is it milk?' I asked.

Sam shook his head. 'Cow's milk would kill them. It's sugar water, warmed. They're doing better now, I think.' The squirrel opened its mouth and began to suck, and even I was excited, in spite of myself. 'There,' Sam said, 'there.'

I watched him for a few moments. 'There, there,' he said, over and over, a refrain for the nursing squirrel.

'Why do you love squirrels so much?' I asked.

He shrugged. 'Why do you like horses so much?'

There were so many reasons, but when I tried to name one good one, I couldn't.

'See?' Sam asked. 'And besides, I don't love squirrels. I just . . . I like being outside. I like the natural world.'

'The natural world,' I repeated.

'Yes,' Sam said. 'The natural world.'

He began to murmur to the squirrel again, and I fell back onto the bed, and closed my eyes against the sound of his voice.

I lay there, close to sleep, hearing my brother's pretty voice, still pretty even as it turned deeper and deeper, as it had over the past few months, changing to match his increasing height. My brother was a flower, unfolding, shooting toward the heavens.

That night I went to his hotel room. It looked lived-in, unlike mine. There was a jam jar filled with flowers on the bureau, and three snake skins, almost completely intact, with tiny holes where eyes used to reside. I touched one of them, very lightly.

'What happened to your terrariums?' I asked.

Sam perched on the edge of his bed, watching me.

'They're gone.'

I nodded. 'I'm leaving,' I said.

'I know.'

'You could leave, too. They would let you.'

My voice sounded too urgent. But he should leave, too. He should not let this swallow him whole.

When he finally spoke, his voice was a challenge.

'But I don't want to leave, Thea. I don't want –' and he paused, but no, it was more than a pause. He stopped himself from saying whatever terrible thing he was going to say. But I knew.

'To be like me?' I asked.

He looked away. I knew I was right. It was not fair, of course. I had been made to go away. I had not abandoned him on purpose. But in the end I got the better deal. There were so many accidents in the world, some happy, some not. I would take what I had gotten.

I went to my brother and sat down next to him on the bed. My twin would not leave because he was a better son than I was daughter; he could not leave because he could not imagine life without them. Sam wasn't brave. He never had been. He was loyal and true and still belonged to my parents in a way I never would again. He wasn't brave, but one person could only be so many things. He was still my parents' child, and perhaps he always would be. Only time would tell.

'You're a Florida boy,' I said. I reached into my pocket and pulled out the handkerchief I had taken with me to Yonahlossee. It looked no worse for the wear. I put it in his hand and closed his fingers around it.

He looked at it, and then at me. 'Yes,' he said softly, with his new voice. 'Yes I am.'

That night I lay in bed and tried to summon Sissy's eyes, Mr Holmes's elegant hands. Naari's dainty face. But I could not remember. Everything was slipping from my mind. I rose and dressed in my Yonahlossee uniform; it was the only thing that fit. The clothes still smelled of Augusta House, and I tried not to cry, I tried not to want something I could never again have.

Outside the air was thick with moisture, the moon hung over us like a fat face. There were a few people, scattered on the sidewalks. A door swung open and I glimpsed a crowded, smoky room, a man in front of a piano.

'Excuse me, miss,' someone said, and I realized I was in someone's way. I stepped to the side and a man walked in front of me, and I recognized him as the bellhop my mother had almost forgotten to tip. A woman was on his arm, but I could only see the back of her, her sheer dress, her black hair. He gave no sign that he recognized me. I watched him slip away into the night, off to another place, or perhaps his home, where he would touch his girl, she would touch him, and the night would open like a flower.

I walked and walked. An hour, two. I lost track of time. I thought, foolishly, that I might see Sam. I knew he wandered at night. I knew he roamed. But there was no sign of him. I walked away from the streetlights, in the darkness. Mother had not taught us to fear the world; she had taught us to scorn it.

I finally arrived at Church Street, visible from a block away. I knew it would be busy here, or if not busy, alive in some way. There were people going places, people returning, always, always.

The sky zippered open, as it did in Florida, suddenly and violently, and the lightning lit the sky in a way that was beautiful and fierce. I was unafraid. Nothing in the natural world scared me. This lightning was far away, and I was surrounded by things taller than me, where the lightning would strike first.

I sat down on a covered bench, next to an old woman who was clearly waiting for a train. She asked me for the time and I looked at the giant clock above us and told her. She did not thank me; she was agitated, and I understood why.

'I'm going to Miami,' she said. 'And my train is so very, very late.'

I almost laughed. Miami. Sam had told me there were thousands of acres of land there, abandoned by their owners, our uncle just one piece of it.

I understood the woman's agitation. She was waiting to be taken away from this place. She was dressed like someone from another century, long, long skirts, a blouse that hid even her wrists. And she was from another century, I realized. She had been born long before me, and I knew someday some impetuous girl would think the same of me: that I was old and foolish, dated, born too long ago to matter anymore.

I sat there and waited for the train with this woman. I tried not to fear the future. I hoped it would be kinder than the past.

On my way to Yonahlossee, all those months ago, I had watched my father's profile as he drove and felt ashamed. I hoped I would not always feel this intensely. But then I knew I always would. It was my nature.

I sat on the bench and felt the strong wind whip my ankles and tried to keep a hold of all my memories. I touched Sissy's necklace. I saw myself in future trains and wondered who I would travel with. I wondered where we would go.

I would travel nowhere with Georgie, who died six days short of his twenty-fifth birthday. I never saw him again, I never saw Aunt Carrie or Uncle George or their home in Gainesville. Georgie would never be himself again, a curse worse than death. If he had died, the circumstances surrounding his death would surely have been examined more closely; mercifully for us, Georgie lived. However briefly.

Mercy eluded my aunt and uncle, who tended to Georgie for the rest of his life. At Yonahlossee I only remembered Georgie and his family in the past tense, I tried never to think about what my family, especially my cousin, was doing in the present. It was perhaps a flaw in my character that I could forget so easily about my wounded cousin. That's what I thought then. Now I'm glad I was able to put it out of my head, to survive. We did not speak of him often, but my father revealed to me, one night when he was very drunk and old, long after my mother had died, that Georgie often succumbed to terrible rages, that the part of his brain that controlled anger was damaged in the accident. The accident.

My mother became an invalid, locked herself in her room most days and tended to her migraines. I was sent to a proper boarding school, in the Northeast, a place of my choosing. There was a stable nearby, where I continued to ride. I exercised the horses of the rich, which was a good way, I learned, to put myself on a horse when I couldn't own one. I thought of Leona in those days, wondered how exactly she had found her own way on the back of a horse again. I was certain she had; how was the only question.

I left the South. My brother stayed put. He lived his life with my parents, who stayed in Florida but did indeed move to a foreign and strange south Florida, to a busy, bustling Miami, where my father continued to practice medicine.

My father never saw his brother again, but he continued to send him money. I saw the letter once, folded around a check: to George Atwell in Centralia, Missouri. Citrus continued to be good to my family; it kept us afloat in the thirties, and in the forties it made us wealthy again. It saved us, allowed me to go away to school, allowed us to live some semblance of the lives we had imagined for ourselves.

After Georgie died, Aunt Carrie sent us his obituary, cut from a newspaper. There was a note folded over the clipping, in Aunt Carrie's hand: 'He has left us.' She and Uncle George thought that there had been a fight between the male cousins; I'm fairly certain they never knew my part. I would have cut my tongue out of my mouth before telling them, and Georgie – well, if he even remembered what had happened, he was not quite right, they would not have, I am almost certain, believed him. I have lived my life and Georgie is a shadow, Georgie is a person who I once loved, whose death I had a hand in. He is a ghost. My ghost.

I am certain Sam did not mean to kill Georgie. He was a boy, turning into a man. He did not know his own strength. It was a series of events, Sam. A series of events.

I never told a soul about what I had seen, my brother raise his rifle and strike Georgie in the head. Did my father know? He was a doctor, surely he could have told the difference between a wound from falling and a wound from force. But only God knows this.

I came home twice a year, two weeks for Christmas and two weeks in the middle of the summer. One twelfth of the year. In a way our relationships remained the same – my father was still distant, my mother difficult. But the qualities of those feelings were complicated now by what I had done, by what my family had done to me. It's difficult to say what Sam thought about everything – we were twins, we never had to articulate our feelings to each other, we just knew. But not anymore, Sam and I didn't know each other, it was safe to say, any longer. He was distant and pleasant when I was home, which was the worst punishment I could think of, to treat me like a stranger. I never cried again in his presence, nor he in mine.

I came back and was able to eat meals with my family, discuss matters of no consequence, sleep in the same house as they only because of Henry Holmes. Only because he made me understand the exchange my parents had made. Me for Sam. But I had made the first trade: my brother for my cousin.

I experienced true love, joy when my children were born, grief again when I lost a child in my fifth month. I had a life, separate from my family and what had happened when I was a child. And horses were always a part of my life, a blessing; taking comfort in them had always been something I'd done by instinct, and it was an instinct I never outgrew. I took pleasure in how good I was in the saddle, how well I knew my way around a horse. I was good at something in a way most people are never good at anything in their lives. They were a gift; how many people have such a constant in their life, separate from the rough and often beautiful mess that is their family?

At Yonahlossee I learned the lesson that I had started to teach myself at home: my life was mine. And I had to lay claim to it.

When I returned from Boston, I was always surprised by the palm trees, the blunt heat, the moisture in the air so heavy it was almost sickening. My parents lived in a neighborhood where they could see other houses from theirs; they lived in a house that was beautiful and cold.

Sam decided to be a doctor, like Father. He stopped exploring the natural world. He spent all his time inside, now, and when I was home I would study his cheek, made pale by his preference for the indoors; when he turned toward me, there was a flash of skin, a succinct feeling of desperation. We were lost to each other. At Yonahlossee I learned to live a life without my brother; I learned that what once seemed impossible was not. And my life all to myself was easier, in many ways. Lonelier, but a twin is as much a burden as a pleasure. I did not know life without him, we had a language all to ourselves in infancy, we shared a womb. When everyone else expected one – my mother, my father, my grandparents – we were two. And it is not easy to be two people where there should have been one. If there had only been one person, then Georgie would still be alive. Because no one else besides Sam would have cared so deeply, so irrevocably, about what his other half had done.

My parents had sent me away because they saw I was a girl who wanted too much, wanted badly, inappropriately. And back then all that want was a dangerous thing.

Woe be to you, Thea, Mr Holmes said. We were in his library, surrounded by his books. My blouse was unbuttoned. He took my hand and kissed my thumb. Woe be to you for wanting too much. He kissed my wrist. For wanting so much. He lowered me down onto the couch, my uniform hiked over my hips.

I wanted everything. I wanted my cousin. I wanted Mr Holmes. I was a girl, I learned, who got what she wanted, but not without sadness, not without cutting a swath of destruction so wide it consumed my family. And almost me. I almost fell into it, with them. I almost lost myself.

But I was too selfish. I wanted, as Mr Holmes put it, too much. And none of it was a decision, a list written out, a plan articulated. We have no say in who we love. And woe be to all of us, for that.

Woe be to Sam, who never left Florida, who never lived in the world beyond its shores. He had a wife, he had a family. He did not have his twin. Woe be to Mr Holmes, who I never saw again, who surely felt me as a loss, as I felt him. Woe be to Mother and Father, who allowed what I had done to unravel their lives. Woe be to Georgie most of all, whose first love was his last, who has turned to dust now, a stone in a Missouri cemetery the only evidence that he existed, proof that he lived and left some mark. Evidence that he existed, but not that he loved. I am proof that he loved. And perhaps that was my most important task, in this life: living a life for both me and him. Seeing things that he never did. Doing what he could not.

But woe be to Thea – no. Take it back, Henry. And surely he would, if he had continued to know me. Surely he would have seen that my life was full, and rich, and my own.

A photograph would hang on the wall outside Mr Holmes's office, though I would never see it. I would never return to Yonahlossee, or my home in Florida. The photograph would serve as a reminder to him. A reminder to everyone that Theodora Atwell and Naari had won the Spring Show in 1931. I had left in disgrace, but still my picture would go up. It was tradition.

I heard a train in the distance, the familiar whining. The woman next to me stood, my presence forgotten. Woe be to us. The memory sprang up, unbidden. One of the countless afternoons we spent with each other, all flooding out now, flooding out of my head and turning into so much vapor. I faltered. I put my head in my hands.

But no. I looked up again. The train made its slow ascent into the station, and the woman marched into the rain, though it would be minutes and minutes until she was allowed to board. But she didn't care. She simply wanted to leave.

I thought of my picture in the Castle, which neither my parents nor Sam would ever see.

But what would future girls see when they looked at the photograph during their daily comings and goings, peered closely? Not the shade of my hair, rendered colorless by the photograph. Not Mr Holmes, who stood beyond the frame. Not anything, really. Just a girl on a horse, like so many other girls.

Acknowledgments

A deep debt of gratitude to my agent, Dorian Karchmar, who took on *Yonahlossee* when it was barely a manuscript, and guided me through many revisions. It would not be a book without her.

Thank you next to my editor, Sarah McGrath, whose care and insight made the book so much better. At Riverhead Books, thank you to the entire amazing team and especially Geoff Kloske, Sarah Stein, and Jynne Dilling Martin. At Headline, my UK publisher, thank you to Claire Baldwin.

At William Morris Endeavor, thank you to Simone Blaser, Tracy Fisher, Catherine Summerhayes, and Eugenie Furniss.

I owe many thanks to the creative writing departments of Emory University and Washington University, respectively – the former, where I took my first creative writing class; the latter, where I received my MFA and then taught while I wrote *Yonahlossee*. At both schools, I studied under many fine professors. A special thank-you to Kathryn Davis, who has always been my most enthusiastic cheerleader; and Marshall Klimasewiski and Saher Alam.

Thank you to Tim Mullaney, David Schuman, and Curtis Sittenfeld, for support while I wrote.

Thank you to my mother, for teaching me to love a home. Thank you to my father, for driving me thousands of miles to and from the barn. And for not letting me go to law school. Thank you to my sister, Xandra, who has always been my biggest champion. As I grow older, I feel increasingly lucky for the love and support my parents and sister have always offered.

Finally, thank you to Mat, my husband. This book is for him; it couldn't be for anyone else.

Bonus Material

Adriana Trigiani in conversation with Anton DiSclafani

Anton, you captured the beauty, mystery and peril of the Appalachians in your novel. Why do you think the mountains of North Carolina make for such an evocative setting?

Even now, when I see the Appalachians after any period of time, I'm taken aback by their loveliness. I think the Appalachians speak to something very human in all of us – I'm amazed by how many communities and homes are tucked into the highest hillsides, and then think of the people who settled those areas, when there weren't things like pavements and cars! There's such rich history in the Appalachians, both past and present.

You are a true southern belle – you grew up in Florida, spent summers in North Carolina and studied in Georgia. I'll bet you get your thank-you notes out immediately. What is it about growing up in the South that makes storytelling so delicious and inspires truthful and beautiful prose?

I think southerners have a real gift for sitting around and gabbing. So I grew up around my family, and friends, who just knew how to spin a tale, and took real pleasure in telling a story. The South prides itself on hospitality – I think we might rival Japan in how welcome we try to make guests feel in our homes – and part of making a person feel welcome is including her in your stories. Entertaining her. And southern women, especially, have such brilliant turns of phrase. My mother, who is from Alexandria, Louisiana, still surprises my sister and me with little jewels: wound tighter than Dick's hatband; I'm gonna do whatever trips my trigger; Pinkie thought he had two heads till he cut one off.

Aside from Yonahlossee, do you have a favorite Southern spot to visit or somewhere full of memories that you might share with us?

This is an easy one: Atlanta. I went to college there, at Emory, and I love the whole city, and would move back in a heartbeat. It's the perfect marriage of old Southern charm and a very progressive arts and political scene.

You attended a camp similar to Yonahlossee, which was an actual riding camp for young women operating up until the 1980s. What was your camp experience like?

Nothing like Yonahlossee! My camp experience – I went to Camp Greystone, in Tuxedo, North Carolina for two summers – was pretty tame. The food was delicious – I have such a memory for food! – and so Thea's meals were inspired by my Camp Greystone meals.

What scared and titillated me about camp is what I try to evoke in *Yonahlossee*: the utter absence of parents. There are adults, sure, but they're not attached to you in any sort of meaningful way. There's such energy created by the absence of adults: it's like a pressure cooker for girls. And lots of drama happens, naturally.

Let's talk about your heroine, Thea Atwell. She's a total original – strong, feisty, determined. How did you imagine this headstrong, wild young woman? Is there any of you in Thea or is she based on someone you know?

She is definitely not based on me! Or anyone I know. I am a pretty cautious person, and have never, ever been accused of being fearless, so I wanted to imagine myself into the brain of someone who isn't scared of anything, really. So in a way Thea is the opposite of me.

Horses are as much characters in this novel as humans. Even if you aren't an equestrian (and I'm not) I fell in love with your descriptions of the horses. They were so real to me as characters. Do you ride horses? What role has riding played in your own life?

I do ride horses. I grew up riding them, and I ride now, too. I love being around them – there's nothing like it. When I was young, horses were a way to make myself be brave, because you have to kind of forget that you are sitting on a thousand pound animal, that anything could happen, or else you can't ride. Horses can smell fear; as soon as they sense you're scared, they're scared, too. It remains that way today – riding is the one part of my life where I'm completely mentally and physically engaged, where all my normal worrying just sort of falls away and I'm absolutely in the moment.

You know you can't write southern unless you know how to write heat. Your novel has some seriously steamy love scenes. Do you like writing the love scenes?

I'm blushing! I do like writing love scenes – I guess that's why I write so many! – but it's funny, because the writing of those steamy scenes is pretty mechanical. You have to pay so much attention to the ways bodies are positioned and moved.

What are you most looking forward to as you meet your readers? You should be prepared for their love and enthusiasm – you've written a page turner – it's a spectacular debut.

I am so looking forward to traveling around the country, especially the South, and stopping in all these amazing independent bookstores that I've heard about for years. And also hearing what readers think! This is my first book, so I've never had the experience of talking about my work with readers, and I am so eager to hear their reactions!

Anton DiSclafani discusses books that have stood out for her

CHARLOTTE'S WEB by E.B. White: This is the first book I remember loving. I read it when I was in third grade. I felt so sad at the end, and so astonished that a book could make me feel sad.

ANNE OF GREEN GABLES by L.M. Montgomery: This is the first book I remember loving as a teenager. The world Montgomery creates felt so various and complex; I immediately wanted to lose myself in it. When I think of falling in love with reading, I think of these two books.

THE LITTLE STRANGER by Sarah Waters: Sarah Waters is a genius; I don't think there's any other way to put it. Everything she writes is so different, yet so good. I haven't read anything bad, or even so-so, by her. THE LITTLE STRANGER is equally beautiful and terrifying. I stayed up until the wee hours one night to finish it, and I scared myself silly. It's a ghost story for adults.

THE FOUNTAIN OVERFLOWS by Rebecca West: I discovered Rebecca West in graduate school, and fell in love with her writing. There's nobody that writes families the way she does – the delicate, mercurial bonds that tie us to one another.

THE ORCHARDIST by Amanda Coplin: For historical fiction lovers, THE ORCHARDIST is a masterful, evocative read. It has the most amazing birth scene I've ever read.

THE GARDENS OF KYOTO by Kate Walbert: I'm a sucker for the unreliable first person narrator, and Walbert does this voice so well. It is, I think, the best novel I've read set in wartime; by the end, you understand exactly how war expands lives, even as it complicates them terribly.

MY HOLLYWOOD by Mona Simpson: I just finished this. Simpson is such a deceptively entertaining writer. Her prose is so dense, but delicious – I literally feel greedy when I'm reading her work! This is a beautiful domestic novel, about the intersection of motherhood and work.

© Julie Rutherford

Anton is a skilled horsewoman herself and has competed nationally

Snapper

Brian Kimberling

A woman who won't stay true
A pick-up truck that won't start
A CV like a train wreck . . .

Nathan Lochmueller studies birds for just enough money to scrape a living. He drives a glitter-festooned truck, the Gypsy Moth, and is in love with the free-spirited Lola. He's a small-town boy at heart, but a wider world beckons. Should he stay, or should he go?

'Superb . . . always engaging, sometimes beautiful and often funny' *Daily Telegraph*

'Captivating . . . *Snapper* could do for birdwatchers what Annie Proulx did for small-town newspaper reporters and gay cowboys' *Independent on Sunday*

'Funny and adroit fiction' Margaret Atwood, via Twitter

'Delightfully entertaining' *Esquire*

978 0 7553 9621 4

TINDER
PRESS

Amity & Sorrow

Peggy Riley

GOD. SEX. FARMING.

Two sisters sit, bound together, wrist to wrist. Amity and Sorrow. Their mother is taking them from their father and the only world they have ever known. But Sorrow will move heaven and earth to get back home.

Imagine a novel as emotionally devastating as *Room* or *The Lovely Bones*, but with the pace of a thriller and the setting of *Witness* or *The 19th Wife*; a brand-new debut which reads like a modern classic.

Imagine a novel which makes you want to clutch everyone you meet and say: you *must* read this. That book is *Amity & Sorrow*.

THEY'RE WAITING FOR SALVATION.
PRAY IT NEVER COMES.

'One of the most exciting books to be published this year' *Good Housekeeping*

'An impressive and pretty harrowing debut [of] strength and power' *Daily Mail*

978 0 7553 9438 8

TINDER
PRESS

The Outline of Love

Morgan McCarthy

Persephone Triebold has never felt complete. After a childhood spent in the isolation of the Scottish Highlands with just her father for company, she takes the first opportunity to head for London.

The city is intoxicating, but for Persephone something, still, is lacking. It's only when she meets the celebrated author Leo Ford that she realises he is what's been missing. Persephone works her way into his world, yet he somehow remains just beyond her grasp, and she becomes increasingly curious about hints of a disturbing incident in his past . . .

Praise for Morgan McCarthy

'Dark, addictive and a stunning debut' *Cosmopolitan*

'Bath-time reading sorted with Morgan McCarthy's page turner' *The Sunday Times*

'An accomplished debut . . . McCarthy's exquisite storytelling points to a promising literary career' *Edinburgh Evening News*

978 0 7553 8879 0

TINDER
PRESS

BEHIND THE SCENES
AT TINDER PRESS . . .

For more on the worlds of our books and authors
Visit us on Pinterest
ℙ TINDER PRESS

For the latest news and views from the team
Follow us on Twitter
TINDER PRESS

To meet and talk to other fans of our books
Like us on Facebook
f TINDER PRESS

www.tinderpress.co.uk